Praise for these other novels from *New York Times*
bestselling author
CHEYENNE McCRAY

VAMPIRES NOT INVITED

"Something weird is going on, and it is up to half-human
half-Drow Nyx to figure out what it all means. The versatile
and talented McCray is slowly unveiling a supernatural society fraught with menace and plagued by prejudice and
discord. Her Night Tracker series continues to be fast-paced
and populated with intriguing characters. Hang on, for Mc-
Cray is about to send things into overdrive."

—*RT Book Reviews*

"Set in an intriguing new world, romance, adventure and
non-stop action fill the pages."   —*Romance Reviews Today*

"If you enjoy a kick-ass heroine, a sexy romance and a compelling story that leaves you begging for more, this is the series for you."   —*Nocturne Romance Reviews*

"An excellent continuation of the compelling Night Tracker
series."   —*Fresh Fiction*

NO WEREWOLVES ALLOWED

"Nyx is back and ready to kick more butt in the second
installment of the Night Tracker series . . . McCray intro-
duces some interesting secondary characters that add depth
to this developing world. As always, there is a seductive
sensuality mixed in with the hair-raising adventures."

—*Romantic Times BOOKreviews*

"McCray has written a wonderfully hot story that has characters we will love . . . beautifully fleshed-out, believable,
and intelligent. The storyline is fascinating, intriguing, and
fast-paced. This book is a fantastic page-turner that has

great romance, lots of the paranormal, adventure, thrills, and chills."   —*Night Owl Romance*

"Interesting characters, [a] fast-paced plot, and fascinating world-building make this a must-read."   —*Fresh Fiction*

DEMONS NOT INCLUDED

"The hot new Night Tracker series promises plenty of thrills and chills. McCray does an excellent job establishing this world and its host of intriguing characters. The action is fast and furious, and the danger escalating. Add in some sexy sizzle and you have another patented McCray gem."
—*Romantic Times BOOKreviews*
(Top Pick, 4 ½ stars)

"McCray weaves a supernatural tale of mystery, murder, and blossoming romance. *Demons Not Included* has a well-rounded cast, a captivating storyline, and plenty of suspense to keep readers guessing."   —*Darque Reviews*

DARK MAGIC

Winner, *Romantic Times* Reviewer's Choice Award for Best Paranormal Action Adventure of the Year

"McCray does a stellar job layering the danger, passion and betrayal. Awesome!"   —*Romantic Times BOOKreviews*
(Top Pick, 4 ½ stars)

"Action, romance, suspense, love, betrayal, sacrifice, magic, and sex appeal to the nth degree! [McCray's] heroines kick butt and run the gamut from feminine to tomboy and her heroes . . . well, they're all 200% grade-A male. YUM! Her love scenes left me breathless . . . and I'm surprised I have any nails left after the suspense in this last book."   —*Queue My Review*

"Vivid battles, deceit that digs deep into the coven, and a love that can't be denied."
—*Night Owl Romance*

"A fabulous finish to a great urban fantasy . . . Master magician Cheyenne McCray brings it all together in a superb ending to her stupendous saga."
—Harriet Klausner

SHADOW MAGIC

"Erotic paranormal romance liberally laced with adventure and thrills."
—*Romantic Times BOOKreviews*
(Top Pick, 4 ½ stars)

"A sensual tale full of danger and magic, *Shadow Magic* should not be missed."
—*Romance Reviews Today*

"Cheyenne McCray has created a fabulous new world. You won't be able to get enough!"
—Lori Handeland, *USA Today* bestselling author

WICKED MAGIC

"Blistering sex and riveting battles are plentiful as this series continues building toward its climax."
—*Romantic Times BOOKreviews*
(4 stars)

"Has an even blend of action and romance . . . An exciting paranormal tale, don't miss it."
—*Romance Reviews Today*

"Sure to delight and captivate with each turn of the page."
—*Night Owl Romance*

St. Martin's Paperbacks Titles By
CHEYENNE McCRAY

NIGHT TRACKER NOVELS
Demons Not Included
No Werewolves Allowed
Vampires Not Invited
Zombies Sold Separately

LEXI STEELE NOVELS
The First Sin
The Second Betrayal

THE MAGIC NOVELS
Dark Magic
Shadow Magic
Wicked Magic
Seduced By Magic
Forbidden Magic

ROMANTIC SUSPENSE
Moving Target
Chosen Prey

ANTHOLOGIES
No Rest for the Witches

ZOMBIES
SOLD SEPARATELY

Cheyenne McCray

St. Martin's Paperbacks

This is a work of fiction. All of the characters, organizations, and events portrayed in this novel are either products of the author's imagination or are used fictitiously.

ZOMBIES SOLD SEPARATELY

Copyright © 2011 by Cheyenne McCray.
Excerpt from *Vampires Dead Ahead* copyright © 2011 by Cheyenne McCray.

For information address St. Martin's Press, 175 Fifth Avenue, New York, NY 10010.

EAN: 978-0-312-94643-2

Printed in the United States of America

St. Martin's Paperbacks edition / June 2011

St. Martin's Paperbacks are published by St. Martin's Press, 175 Fifth Avenue, New York, NY 10010.

10 9 8 7 6 5 4 3 2 1

To Pops, with love from your darling dotter.

ACKNOWLEDGMENTS

Thanks to all of my Facebook friends for helping me slay countless Zombies during Nyx's journey.

Thank you to Kerri Waldo for your support of Brenda Novak's sixth annual online Auction for Diabetes Research.

Dead sounds at night come from the inmost hills,
Like footsteps upon wool.
                    —Alfred, Lord Tennyson (1809–92)

WELCOME TO NEW YORK CITY'S UNDERWORLD

Present Day

Dark Elves / Drow: live belowground in Otherworld, never aboveground. Except for me. I'm unique—sometimes I wonder if that's a good thing.

Demons: not a problem. We plan to keep it that way.

Dopplers: these beings can transform into *one* specific animal form, unlike Shifters, who can choose whatever animal form they want.

Dragons: you think fire is hot?

Fae: you asked for it. Don't blame me if you get a headache— *Abatwa, Brownies, Dryads, Dwarves, Faeries, Gnomes, Goblins, Nymphs, Pixies, Sanziene, Sidhe, Sirens, Sprites, Tuatha, and Undines.*

Gargoyles: there's a reason birds poop on statues.

Light Elves: can we say "Divas of the Otherworlds?"

Mages: powerful male wizards.

Magi: young, precious, omniscient female beings whom Trackers are sworn to protect and to keep hidden safely away.

Metamorphs: can shift into human form, mirroring any human they choose to before practicing criminal activities against humans. These jerks have no redeeming qualities. None.

Necromancers: did you have to ask? They talk to and raise the dead.

Ogres: Kermit's not the only one who's green and eats flies.

Seraphim: not your average Angels.

Shadow Shifters: in my opinion their ability to shift into shadow form is pretty cool. But you *do not* want to tick one of them off. Do. Not. Make. Them. Mad.

Shifters: like I said, these guys can choose any animal form they want to.

Sorcerers/Sorceresses: never met one I liked. Come to think of it, never met one. At least I don't think so . . .

Specters: haven't seen one and don't plan to.

Succubae and Incubi: avoid them. Just stay away. That's all I have to say.

Trolls: me, Troll. You, dinner.

Vampires: I think I'm going to throw up.

Werewolves: some of the good guys. Until the full moon.

Witches: flitter, flutter, flighty females who practice only white magic. If you want gray magic, dark magic, or black magic, look elsewhere.

Zombies: <u>I HATE ZOMBIES.</u>

ZOMBIES
SOLD SEPARATELY

ONE

Icy wind and water surged around me as my hair slapped my cheeks. Wind spun so fast, fierce, and cold that a growing storm roared with power.

Hail stung my face and arms. Rain splattered me and rolled down my cheeks and skin. Water blurred my eyesight.

Thumps on hard surfaces. Loud crashes. The sound of smashing.

An object glanced off my forehead as it spun in the storm.

Hurricane. I was trapped in a hurricane.

So hard to breathe. Water in my nose. In my mouth.

No sound came out as I tried to scream.

The storm wasn't natural.

Not natural at all.

It wasn't supposed to be happening.

The storm wasn't natural . . .

Because it was caused by . . . me.

My elemental magic. Air and water.

"Nyx!" I shouted over the shrieking storm. I clenched my fists and dug my nails into my palms. Fought to gain control over my magic. *"Stop!"*

My control over the elements had never been so fragile.

Again I screamed into the wind. Tightened my muscles.

With all I had I grasped the reins of my magic.

The storm ended like a car slamming into a concrete

barrier. Things that had been spinning in the storm crashed to a hard surface, as they hit my wood flooring.

Shock immobilized me. I blinked water out of my eyes, and my surroundings came into focus. I was in my bedroom in my apartment in Manhattan.

For several moments I sat on my sodden mattress and stared at the devastation around me.

How had I lost control in my sleep? I wasn't a child. Only younglings would do something like this without near the destruction I had just caused.

Without realizing I was doing it, I reached up and touched the collar around my neck that signified my Drow station in life. No, I was nowhere near being a youngling. I was of age by Drow standards. By Earth Otherworld standards I was fully an adult.

I looked around me. Almost everything in my room was smashed and broken. Trinkets I had purchased since I had moved from the Drow realm to New York City were cracked, broken, torn, shredded.

As a well-paid Tracker and PI, and thanks to my wealthy Drow heritage, I could replace everything that had been ruined. But I couldn't replace the memories that accompanied a good many of the objects.

I let my hand fall away from my collar and it splashed in the water pooled around me on my mattress. I inhaled and exhaled with long, slow, deliberate breaths.

Even though Dark Elves don't get cold easily, the storm had chilled me enough that goose bumps broke out along my skin. I shivered.

A nightmare.

The same one I'd had countless times since I was young. The worst part of the nightmare was seeing an elder, a man with long, graying red hair in a world with lavender-streaked skies. The vision of the man made me sick.

Unlike every other time I'd had this nightmare, this time my entire being had reacted to the nightmare. It had never happened before. I'd never woken in the middle of a storm I had caused to happen.

My heartbeat slowed while my mind started to clear.

A sick sensation like thick, black sludge weighted my insides. It reminded me of just weeks ago, when I'd been sentenced to death by a Vampire. The thought had bile rising in my throat. I didn't want to think about that. Not at all.

I moved my palms to my belly, over my soaked lingerie. I lowered my head and closed my eyes.

It had been a long time since I'd had such intense nightmares—nightmares that I barely remembered when I woke.

During most of my adolescence I'd woken up screaming, wind whipping around my room from my elemental magic. Sometimes the room would be filled with mist. Sometimes a slow, drizzling rain.

Never a storm.

Mother would come in, rock me until I stopped crying and the rain ceased or mist cleared or wind subsided.

When I got older the nightmares came less frequently. I gained control over my elements and woke with nothing more than a sore throat from screaming.

Even though I never remembered the dreams, somehow I knew they had all been the same.

Once I came of age at twenty-five, they stopped.

I frowned and opened my eyes, blinked more wetness away as I raised my head. The nightmares started again two weeks ago. Over two years since they had stopped.

"Why now?" I said, the sound of my voice loud in my bedroom that was still, save for the sound of water dripping from the doorframes.

The sludge in my insides only worsened.

Winter sunlight slashed through the French doors and into my bedroom. I stared at the fractured pattern reflected in the sheen of water on my hardwood floor.

Light.

Light here, in the Earth Otherworld, often means renewal, rebirth.

In the lives of the Dark Elves, light means death. Death to any Drow who dared to go aboveground during the day.

To all Drow but me.

The mattress made squishing sounds as I shoved the comforter off my legs. I found a place on the floor where nothing was splintered or broken, slid out of bed, and got to my feet. Water ran down my body in rivulets, joining the puddles on my floor.

Had Kali gotten caught in the storm? I hoped not. My blue Persian would never forgive me.

I stepped through the water and felt melting bits of hail beneath my feet. My floor would be ruined if I didn't take care of it. Other than my elemental magic, I knew little Elvin magic, but I did know the word for "clean."

"Avanna," I said and the room dried, including my hair, skin, and the lingerie I wore. My things still lay broken on the floor and I wished I knew an Elvin word for "repair."

I stepped over a broken crystal clock, grabbed a shortie robe, and slipped it on.

A frame with a photograph caught my attention and I stooped to pick it up. The glass had shattered but it didn't look as if the picture of Adam and me in Belize was ruined.

I smiled and traced my human lover's image with my fingertip as my heart skipped. Love for him flowed through my veins warm and sweet as I took in his boyish grin and that dimple I loved. In the sunshine of Belize he looked sexy, adorable, and intensely masculine all at the same time.

I set the picture with its broken frame on my nightstand where my lamp should have been. It, too, was on the floor in shambles.

Avoiding everything sharp and pointy, I walked toward the window next to the French doors leading to the balcony from my bedroom.

Ice-laced sunlight touched my face and body as I peered out the window and the cold made me shiver again.

By day I look a lot like my human mother with my fair skin and sapphire-blue eyes. The exception is that my hair is black with blue highlights and hers a pale shade of blond.

When the sun sets, my skin turns a pale, pale shade of amethyst and my hair a deep cobalt blue. When it's dark I look more like my father with my pointed ears, small fangs, and Drow pigmented skin and hair.

I am not human then and have no choice but to avoid humans who know nothing about the paranormal world. Which is just about everyone.

My mind filled with the fragmented emotions both the nightmare and the storm had left me with. A storm in my house. How had I lost control like that?

I pushed aside the sheer curtain and the glass felt cool against my nose as I stared out at the street from my apartment.

It had snowed last night. From the corner of my apartment at 104th and Central Park West, I had clear views of Central Park from the terrace. No one from Otherworld is used to snow because there is no change of seasons there.

I loved Manhattan. I loved all the seasons. They were each beautiful and unique in their own way.

The Earth Otherworld holiday season had been pleasant so far and Christmas was just days away. The city was locked in winter's grasp and everything was white and beautiful.

Sometimes I tugged on a jacket and boots, and waded through the new powder while throwing snowballs at statues, taunting the Gargoyles hidden inside them.

Today the weight in my belly grew heavier as imprints of the nightmare pressed against my soul. Dread, terror, anger, pain . . . the kind of pain that makes a person's heart hurt as if someone close to them has died.

I tried to swallow but my throat was too dry.

For the first time the image of a face with blurred features shimmered at the edge of my consciousness. Somehow I knew it was the face of someone I cared for.

I brought my hands to my chest. The contours of the image seemed so familiar.

And then the ghostly face was gone, as if it hadn't been there at all.

TWO

The pungent scent of spices rising from the manor's herb garden overpowered even the exotic perfume of the woman kneeling at the Sorcerer's feet.

He had always favored Maia and had always enjoyed her company.

Maia's warm autumn skin and dark eyes made her so exquisite that few could compare to her. Sunlight gleamed on her long black hair that lay perfectly over her shoulders. The air in the garden was so still that not a leaf stirred, much less a strand of her hair.

Unlike most of his people, she had not outwardly started the change—her skin remained unblemished, her eyes clear. When she walked she was a thing of beauty, her movements fluid and graceful.

At this moment in time she was perfect.

Almost.

And that word, *almost*, meant everything.

"Please, Lord Amory," she whispered as she turned her tear-streaked face up to him. She clenched her hands against her belly. "It was an accident. I did not intend for—"

He held his hand up to silence her. She immediately bowed her head and looked at his feet again.

"It is what it is, Maia." His heart ached for what he must do now. "Our people are dying. Your body will begin the change now."

The young woman's sobs were harsh, loud.

Amory let out a sigh. "The baby will take your essence

before it dies. Soon your body will be only a Shell, Maia. You would not be yourself."

"No." Her words came in a frantic burst as she met his eyes. "It will be different here in the Doran Otherworld than it was in Kerra. I know it."

Amory shook his head. "The Doran Otherworld has the same effect on our people as Kerra."

"What about the new Otherworld you have discovered?" The young woman's voice had a hint of hopefulness to it.

The Sorcerer studied Maia, wishing things could be different. "The Earth Otherworld would have allowed you to live and to keep your baby—had you conceived there. In your new body."

He knelt and cupped her face in his palm. With his thumb he brushed a tear from her cheek. "But you became pregnant here. Your body and the baby are now under attack. All is ruined."

"You are a powerful Sorcerer, Lord Amory." Her throat worked as she swallowed, her eyes wide with panic. "You can fix this. You can do anything."

He slowly shook his head. "I cannot."

"Send me there. To the Earth Otherworld." Maia sounded almost hysterical and he knew it was time to end this. "Please send me there."

Pain gripped Amory's heart as if someone squeezed it in his fist. Pain for this young woman and her unborn babe. Pain for all of the suffering of his people that had only grown worse despite his search for a new Otherworld that wouldn't kill them.

"The only way you could have survived was to move your essence to a new Host and only if you were not pregnant," Amory said. "You cannot move your baby to your new Host body. It is impossible. The child would remain in the belly of your Shell. A Shell is a creature with no essence, no mind, no will but to kill, maim, destroy. The baby would die."

"Please let us try, Lord Amory." Maia's tears flowed down her beautiful face and spilled onto her gown. "Maybe it will work for me and my baby."

"I am sorry." He moved his palm from her cheek and now had his hand splayed over her entire face. His skin was so dark that it made her flesh appear even more autumn-kissed. He clenched his fingers in a tight grip and dug his nails into her skin. "I am sorry."

Maia screamed as he did what must be done.

The Sorcerer infused her entire being with his power.

He burned away all of the infection that would have taken her life. As magic glowed around her body in hues of orange and gold, her internal organs started to fail and she began to die.

He was only speeding up what she would have gone through over the next months, ending her and the baby's suffering in minutes instead of days.

Maia's screams echoed throughout the gardens, reverberating off the stone wall behind him.

And then she was silent.

Such a sweet, beautiful woman . . . and now nothing.

Only the pile of clothing lying at his feet and her cremated remains.

"I did what was best." Amory spoke to himself as he stood. "What I had to."

What he'd had to do too many times.

Amory caught the attention of the gardener and pointed to the pile of rags at his feet. "Take care of this."

The gardener gave a slight bow before going to the water pump. He would burn the rags that had once been Maia's dress and then he would wash away her cremated body so that her remains would join others'. It was a place where Amory had been forced to put many out of their misery.

He walked up the path to the back steps of the manor. As he entered the cool interior, he swept his hand over the top of his bald head and felt nothing but smooth, warm skin. It still jarred him a little to not feel his own long, brittle graying red hair, to not see his own reflection staring back at him whenever he looked in the mirror.

But this body was young, strong, powerful. He felt alive

again. With his magic, once he was living in the Earth Otherworld with his people, this body would never die.

The interior of the manor was dark and cool compared to the brightness and warmth of the day. It was as he preferred it to be. He sensed his servants at hand but they kept well out of sight and would only appear the moment he needed one of them. They were well trained.

When Amory reached the Room of Life, he paused at the threshold of the cavern. Thousands upon thousands of egg-shaped stones glittered and sparkled, reflecting the light of dozens of candles that were lit throughout the cavern.

In that place, the life within the stones gave him renewed vigor. It made it easier for him to let go of the pain of extinguishing a single life only moments ago.

Amory took the steps one at a time until he was inside the cavern that was deep below the manor. He strode to a far wall where he kept larger stones that were closer to the size of ducks' eggs than hens'.

Amory picked up one of the larger stones and smiled as he held it to eye level. The front of the stone was flat, like a window.

He called to the magic of the stone, willing it to bring to him what he wished to see.

Manhattan's skyline filled his view.

The Sorcerer smiled.

THREE

Adam would love the red silky panties and bra I slipped into—lingerie that Kali hadn't a chance to shred. Over the lingerie, I pulled on a pair of black jeans and a red cashmere sweater, followed by my black Elvin-made boots. Adam would be here soon and I couldn't wait to see him.

It was a beautiful snowy Tuesday afternoon, two days after the incident, and Adam and I were going out to admire the holiday decorations and enjoy some hot chocolate.

Preparing for Adam improved my mood considerably. This morning I'd woken terrified, shivering, my head filled with more images that were like hollow specters, no substance at all.

I'd felt some relief that I didn't cause another hurricane in my bedroom. It had taken me all day Sunday just to clean up the mess since my maid, a Shifter named Dahlia, was off for the weekend.

New lamps were parked on the nightstands on either side of my bed, the lamps carved wood and painted white to match my blue and white bedroom. Far more sturdy than glass. I'd slipped the photograph of Adam and me into a new white latticed wood frame and put it next to the lamp on the side of the bed where I slept.

Not a lot had had survived the storm so my room was pretty bare. Paintings had to be reframed, the vanity chair leg fixed, and the glass in my vanity mirror replaced.

Could have been worse. My entire apartment could have suffered rather than just my bedroom.

I glanced in the mirror and figured I looked all right. After I pulled my hair back and knotted it, I grabbed one of my red Dolce & Gabbana purses out of the closet and picked out a black leather Burberry jacket.

A familiar knock at my door made me smile and I walked out of my bedroom and went to open it.

When I reached the door, I hesitated only a moment as I thought about the Metamorph who had briefly fooled me into thinking he was Adam and whom I had kissed. The memory made me shudder. I shook off the creepy feeling and opened the door.

Any other thought vanished when I saw Adam standing before me, one hand braced on the doorframe. He wore his brown leather bomber jacket, opened just enough for me to see a forest green T-shirt that hugged his quarterback build and was tucked into a pair of faded blue jeans.

The corner of his mouth turned up in an adorable smile and his brown eyes glittered. His brown hair looked even more tousled than usual and I caught his leather and coffee scent from where I stood.

Adam grasped me around my waist and swung me into the apartment. "Hey, honey."

"Hey, you." I dropped my purse and jacket. I wrapped my arms around his neck and laughed as he whirled me around.

The door shut behind us, leaving us in the total and complete privacy of my apartment.

Adam's mouth was warm on mine and I sighed as he kissed me. Flashes came to me of my big comfy bed and Adam in it with me, but I wanted to spend time outside with him while it was still daylight. Before I shifted.

I slipped my fingers into his silky hair and he groaned as he pressed me flush against him. It was really, really hard not to imagine taking him into my bedroom and having my way with him.

A giggle escaped me just as he raised his head and I bit my lip to stifle another girlie laugh. I had never giggled before dating and falling in love with Detective Adam Boyd.

I was a Drow warrior, a Tracker, a PI.

Drow warriors, Trackers, and PI's don't giggle.

Well, Drow warriors definitely don't.

Except for me when I was with Adam.

I felt young and silly, like I was in my tween years again, having a crush on one of my father's younger warriors. Even then I hadn't giggled, though. A couple of times I'd been a little dopey over a warrior but I couldn't show it.

In a male-dominated society, where females are subservient to males, I had to fight to be respected as a warrior. Unfortunately I never saw that respect because any warrior I'd bested was humiliated at being beaten by a female.

So much for young love. It wasn't until I came to New York City that I'd had my first relationship and I'd fallen for a human. It ended in disaster when I finally let Stan see the Drow half of my heritage.

Stan had broken my heart with all of the horrible things he'd said. The injury was doubled when my mentor, Rodán, had to wipe memories of me from my boyfriend's mind. I would always remember Stan . . . but after Rodán took care of him, it was as if I'd never existed to him and we never had a relationship. All I was left with was the pain.

"Nyx." Adam grasped my shoulder and brought me fully back to him from the flashes of memory I'd just had. "You checked out on me."

I snuggled against him and drew in a deep breath of his masculine scent. "Was just thinking about how much I love you."

"Good." His lips were firm as he kissed the top of my head. " 'Cause that's just what I was thinking, too."

I tipped my head back and smiled before he kissed me again.

He gave me his boyish grin as he glanced at the bedroom, then winked at me as he took my hand. "You ready to go?"

For a moment I wondered if he meant my bedroom, then realized he was teasing me. He released me to scoop up my jacket, then helped me into it before he grabbed my purse and handed it to me.

We held hands as we walked down the stairs. Mrs. Taylor's rat of a Chihuahua, Terror, yapped at us as we passed the open door of the apartment below mine.

Mrs. Taylor stood just inside her doorway. Her face was heavily lined and I was afraid if she ever tried to smile her face would crack.

I gave the grumpy-faced woman a smile. "Hi, Mrs. Taylor."

She slid one hand into a pocket of the apron that she wore over her powder blue granny dress, jerked her head in a short acknowledgment, and then she shut the door of her apartment, blocking out the outside world from her and Terror.

After wading through the seven inches of newly fallen snow, Adam and I reached the street. By then we were laughing and Adam had a firm grip on my hand.

Chill air stung my nose and cheeks. I glanced at Adam. "A little different than Belize."

He grinned. "We can always go back."

"Mmmm." I rested my head against his shoulder. "I'd love to. Next time we get a break, I say let's do it."

He squeezed me to him and I sighed, a feeling of happiness welling up inside me.

I took in the sparkle and glitter of the holidays in the city. "The decorations are beautiful." My words came out in frost-laced puffs of air. "There's nothing like this in Otherworld."

Adam looked down at me. "You don't celebrate holidays where you come from?"

"No." I shook my head. "Some races of Fae in their parts of Otherworld might, but Elves don't. Especially Dark Elves . . . They've got that belowground thing going on."

"Hard to imagine that you come from anywhere other than here," he said and I met his gaze. "You're a city girl through and through."

I grinned. "Even when my hair is blue?"

Adam laughed. "I guess then you belong to the night." He squeezed me tighter. "But no matter what time of day, you belong to me."

I sighed again.

"Ready for some hot chocolate?" he said and I nodded.

When we reached Broadway and neared the closest Starbucks, the strong smell of dark roast hit me even before the door to the coffee shop opened.

As usual, the place was jammed. Some human-looking paranorms, but mostly norms. "Excuse me," we said to at least fifteen people as we made our way to the end of the order line.

Still holding Adam's hand, I dodged one woman in time to slam into a man's chest. The man's body wasn't hard or soft, just in between, about average.

"Sorry," I said as Adam steadied me by my shoulders and I looked at the person I'd almost run down.

In a quick glance I saw that the male was balding, probably late forties, and someone needed to teach him how to dress. Plaid wool pants would get someone killed on the streets of this city.

But the moment I met the man's gaze I froze. He was staring back at me.

A horrible feeling, like worms wiggling across my flesh, caused goose bumps to rise on my arms.

My heart thudded against my ribs. I stumbled back and stepped on someone's foot.

Sounds of coffee cups hitting the table and floor, and liquid splashing. My chest hurt as I tried to breathe. I glanced behind me, unconcerned about the spilled coffee, and focused on finding a path through the crowd.

Immediately I looked back at the man.

He was gone.

As if I had imagined him.

The thump of my heart was strong when I held my free hand to my chest as I looked around to see if the man was still in the coffee shop. I'd had that creeped-out feeling before. And it had been recent.

"Watch where you're stepping," a man was saying behind me but I couldn't move.

"She doesn't even have the courtesy to apologize," a woman said.

I barely heard them over the rush of blood in my ears. When I shook my head it didn't clear away the web of my racing thoughts. Why those eyes had bothered me so much, I didn't know.

"Nyx." Adam's voice, close to my ear. "What's wrong?"

My words stuck in my throat and my insides shuddered. "I think I just saw a Vampire."

FOUR

Trying my best to not think of Vampires, I unlocked the door to my and Olivia's PI office.

I brought my fingers to the collar that circled my neck. It couldn't have been a Vampire that I'd seen in Starbucks last night. I hadn't caught the familiar dirt and must smell that most Vampires have, and as far as I knew, they didn't drink lattes. Blood was their stimulant, not caffeine.

If not a Vampire, then what?

Adam had done his best to reassure me that the Vampire mess that had almost destroyed our city was history. Problem was that I was so sure I'd glimpsed Volod one night during our trip to Belize. That glimpse was enough to keep me unsettled at the mere mention of the V-word.

Not going to think of Vampires, I told myself and gritted my teeth. After what Volod had done to me . . .

Enough.

I shoved the door open. Fae bells tinkled above the glass that had our agency logo and our names in purple and sapphire—courtesy of a chocolate-loving Pixie named Nancy.

NYX CIAR
Olivia DeSantos
PARANORMAL CRIMES
PRIVATE INVESTIGATORS
By appointment only

The office was empty of norms or paranorms when I walked in, save for Kali. She was perched beside the office inbox on the Dryad-wood credenza and her brilliant gold eyes studied me as she licked one paw.

"Good morning, Your Highness," I said to the blue Persian as I set down my purse beside the inbox and removed my black blazer. I wore a cobalt blue silk blouse with a mandarin collar, black slacks, and one of my favorite pairs of designer heels in cobalt blue.

I started to flip through the mail. "Anything interesting come in?"

Kali said nothing. I didn't expect her to. Not that she talked, although sometimes I wondered if she could and I just didn't know. It wouldn't have surprised me if Rodán— my mentor and former lover—had gifted me with a magic cat.

Kali did manage to travel secretly from my upstairs apartment all the way to the ground-level PI office. I still hadn't figured out how in the Otherworlds she managed to do it, but I'd tried.

The cat gave me a haughty look before jumping off of the credenza and onto the tile floor with amazing feline grace. She turned her back on me and her tail twitched back and forth as she started toward the break room.

Uh-oh.

In order to save my panty drawer from her, I did my best to stay on Kali's good side. That cat had one bizarre panty fetish for shredding them. Trying to stay on her good side didn't help much, said my stack of Victoria's Secret receipts.

I'd made a mistake naming her after Shiva's fierce and destructive Hindu wife. Kali lived up to her name and then some.

With a sigh I went back to sorting through the mail. Paranorms, like norms, didn't communicate a whole lot via snail mail. In my office we normally received nothing more than the junk flyers our Werewolf mailman brought us.

Our main modes of communication were email, phone, and video conferencing. Sure, I came from the world of the

Dark Elves, a world that remained in the Dark Ages, but in my office in Manhattan we were a little more high-tech.

Which wasn't much but it was better than parchment and a quill.

Boring. The flyers were specials on Were nail trimming and tooth sharpening, Shifter maid services, Faerie-made warding bells, Witch garden care, Fae grocers, Sorcerer litigation services—Goldbug & Oz . . . The usual.

"Junk, junk, junk." I threw each flyer into the wastebasket that was parked next to the credenza. I stopped when I reached a Nymph lingerie sale flyer, then decided to toss it, too.

Fae bells tinkled and I looked over my shoulder to see Olivia pushing open the door. She looked pissed, her brows angled inward and a scowl on her face, her dark eyes flashing.

"Um, hello?" I dropped the rest of the flyers into the wastebasket and straightened.

Olivia put her hand up in a "stop" motion, as if she was still an NYPD police officer directing traffic, before she was on the SWAT team. "Not in the mood, purple wonder."

It was rare for Olivia to come in looking like she was going to take the Sig Sauer out of her side holster and start shooting first and asking questions later.

I leaned my hip against the credenza and folded my arms across my chest. "What happened?"

Olivia shrugged out of the New York Mets jacket she wore during the cold months and tossed it onto her desk. The neon green sticky notes on her desktop fluttered and a large stack of case folders teetered, threatening to slide onto the floor.

She blew out a breath and faced me. "Got a freaking speeding ticket from that wiener of a cop, Freeman."

I winced. That was enough to ruin Olivia's mood for the day.

Then I noticed her T-shirt.

YOU'RE A REALLY GOOD FRIEND
BUT IF THE ZOMBIES COME
I'M TRIPPING YOU

I didn't laugh. If it had said anything but Zombies—
except maybe Vampires—I would have at least grinned. I
didn't know why, but just the mere mention of Zombies made
my insides feel like someone had gutted me with a Drow-
forged blade and twisted the dagger just to hear me scream.

"That sucks." My words teetered on the verge of trem-
bling as I grabbed my purse off of the credenza and headed
toward my desk, my heels clicking on the ceramic tile. "Traffic school?"

"I already took a class after the last ticket Freeman gave
me. This one will give me points." Olivia made a low sound
in her throat. "Any other cop in this city would let me go—"

"And has," I put in as I rounded my desk, then slid into
my leather office chair.

"—but not that jerk," she finished saying with an even
darker expression. Somehow she still managed to look beautiful, even when ticked off.

If five-foot-two non-Twiggy-esque women with melon-
sized breasts could be supermodels, Olivia would have
knocked the modeling world on its collective butt. With her
Kenyan and Puerto Rican ancestry, her flawless brown silk
skin, rich dark hair, and beautiful dark brown eyes, she was
gorgeous.

But Olivia had to be the most down-to-earth human I
knew. Despite her hefty salary as a PI and Tracker, she stuck
to driving an old GTO and shopped at Target and Wal-Mart
for T-shirts with funny sayings, and blue jeans. She also had
an extensive collection of colorful Keds sneakers.

"Ready to head off to Rita's for Christmas?" I asked as I
placed my purse in a cubby beneath my desk out of Kali's
reach.

"Sure." Olivia's purple Keds squeaked on the tile before
she reached her own chair behind her desk and plopped into

it. "I always look forward to large family events where my parents shout at each other over the dinner table and ultimately one of them ends up wearing the dessert."

Maybe I hadn't chosen the best topic to take her mind off the speeding ticket. Olivia's parents had divorced after the last daughter, Katelyn, had graduated from high school. Frank, Olivia's wealthy plastic surgeon father, hadn't wanted to pay spousal maintenance to Jan, Olivia's successful lawyer mother.

It didn't matter to Frank that Jan had stayed at home to raise their six daughters and that she hadn't been able to start her own career until five years prior to the divorce. Frank had done his best in court to "color" the truth, but Jan had easily and rightfully been awarded a healthy monthly alimony check. Unfortunately the split wrecked their joint family events in a big way.

Time to put a different spin on the upcoming holiday. "You like spending time with your sisters." I turned on the large screen monitor on my desk. "It's not like you get to see all of them at once very often."

"Each time is more than enough to last for months on end." She braced her forearms on the note-laden top of her desk as she looked at me. "You have no idea what it's like to have five sisters, all of whom don't believe in letting the others get a word in edgewise."

I did my best not to smile. I was sure Olivia did more than an adequate job at inserting her opinions. "You're right about the siblings," I said. "I don't have sisters so it'll be quiet as usual when I go see my father and mother for Christmas. Although I do seem to end up in arguments with Father over one thing or another." Like the fact that he hated me being in the Earth Otherworld and not the Drow Realm.

"Arguments?" Olivia blew out a huff of air. "Don't get me started on the last time my sisters and I got together."

No, I didn't want to get started on that topic. I really, really, really didn't, no matter how much I loved my friend and partner.

Bon Jovi's "Wanted Dead or Alive" came from inside

my purse and I gave a silent prayer of thanks for the interruption as I reached in to pull out my XPhone. I had a thing for eighties hair bands, especially Jon Bon Jovi. Be still my heart.

Said heart melted and forgot about Jon when I checked the caller identification screen and saw that it was Adam.

"Hey there," I said, a flush warming my cheeks as Olivia glanced at me. The tone of my voice had undoubtedly told her who was on the other end of the line and she loved to make cracks about my infatuation with the darling detective.

It was almost a relief to see her load up a rubber band with an eraser and aim it at me. Meant she was cooling off if she was going to start shooting me with erasers.

"Hi, Nyx." Adam's voice had a smile to it, but then I straightened in my chair as his tone went serious. "We have a mess here. You'll want to call Rodán and freeze the scene and you and Olivia need to see this."

The way Adam said it sent a chill through me. "Where?"

Olivia frowned and put down the eraser and rubber band as she listened to my tone and watched my expression.

"West Seventy-third and Riverside Park, along Cherry Walk," he said, and I almost groaned.

A Demon had almost murdered me near that location and I would have died if another Demon hadn't saved my life. But that second Demon was another story altogether, one I still hadn't figured out and wasn't sure I wanted to. Torin, or T as I called him, might remain a mystery for the rest of my life.

I'd faced certain death more than I wanted to admit over the past few months. Demons, mad scientists bent on wiping out the Werewolf population, Vampires . . .

"We'll be right there." I stood and snatched up my purse. "Calling Rodán on my way."

"Damn, Nyx." This time the note in Adam's voice was concerned, as if he had bad news to deliver. "I think we have a Vampire problem again."

It felt like my stomach hit my shoes and I almost couldn't stand. "Be there in less than ten," I said, trying not to sound like I wanted to go anywhere than that park and whatever was waiting to greet me there.

"See you," he said and then he was gone.

Olivia was already putting on her jacket as I rounded my desk. I set down my purse long enough to slide into my blazer then press the speed dial number for Rodán. Olivia didn't ask me what was going on as we headed out the office door. She knew that she'd hear it while I told Rodán. Saved me from having to repeat it.

"Nyx." Rodán's voice was smooth, luxurious when he answered.

I told our Proctor what little I knew as Olivia and I tromped through snow and headed to the rear garage where I kept my black Corvette convertible.

When I finished, Rodán said, "Paranorms were murdered last night." Rodán's voice was tight but calm. I wished I knew how he did that—sound calm in the middle of an emergency. "Robert and Tracey think it was a Vampire attack," he said as he named the two Trackers who'd found the dead paranorms.

My stomach sickened more as he disconnected the call. During our last case, Volod, a Master Vampire, had captured me. He injected me with a stolen serum that would have killed me and could have wiped out most of the paranorm world if we hadn't recovered the antiserum in time.

I'd faced death plenty, but to have it injected into my body . . . just the thought made me beyond queasy.

A glimpse of Volod in Belize, the man in Starbucks yesterday, the scene I was headed to now, and Rodán's news . . .

I clamped my jaws tight. I used the remote to unlock the 'Vette and gave a silent prayer that they were wrong. That everyone was wrong.

"Not Vampires," I said beneath my breath as Olivia and I climbed into my 'Vette. "Please, not Vampires."

FIVE

Icy wind stung my cheeks and my hair twisted in the strong gusts of air. Snowflakes touched my face as my stomach churned. I wrapped my arms around myself as I shivered.

I didn't shiver from the snow and biting wind. It was the grisly scene in front of me that had me wishing for a heavier coat.

Scarlet-splattered drifts of snow along Cherry Walk and more red on the walk itself made this scene look like a bloodbath. It wasn't easy, but I made myself study the dismembered humans and look at the places where large bites had been taken out of arms and legs.

I didn't want to breathe in the smells, but I had to scent the crime. All I could smell was blood and death, not what might have caused it.

They crossed over one another, but three sets of bloody shoeprints led away from the body parts. Judging by the number of torsos that remained intact, the dead had been a group of five. Looked like three males and two females.

Even though there had to be fifty norms at the crime scene, it was dead silent thanks to Lulu, one of New York City's Peacekeepers—a Soothsayer. The crime scene was as frozen as the icicles hanging from barren trees and lampposts.

Soothsayers couldn't stop time or the elements. Just the activity of humans within a certain radius. If the area was larger than she could control, we'd bring in a second or third Soothsayer.

Afterward, the Soothsayers spent time wiping key

memories from certain individual's minds. Memories that could compromise the paranorm community.

Snow had been trampled from the activity going on before our arrival, dark footprints stark against the white drifts. I didn't doubt that the perpetrators of this crime had stepped in the blood and left it smeared in some places, not any of the investigators.

I glanced over my shoulder at the Soothsayer. Not counting Lulu, only Olivia, Adam, NYPD captain Alex Wysocki, and I were among the mobile. My companions were studying the scene as intently as I was, only I'd bet that out of our little group I was the closest to heaving my breakfast onto the patch of snow closest to me.

Lulu perched on a park bench behind us in her billowing satin gown. She had her back to us, refusing to look at the blood and gore. Her lovely personality had Olivia itching to pick up a dismembered foot and toss it into Lulu's lap. Olivia had said as much when Lulu made a comment that had something to do with Olivia's voluptuous figure, her petite stature, and Dwarves.

Personally, I thought Lulu would be lucky if Olivia didn't throw a hand or two along with the foot straight at Lulu's perfect golden-blond ringlets.

Lulu was a prima donna snob who acted like a spoiled princess and probably would have turned green if she knew that I am a real princess. I never let her or any of the other Peacekeepers know that I come from royalty and wealth, save for my closest friends.

I might be a princess in title and entitlements, but I refuse to act entitled. I am a warrior at heart.

NYPD officers and other crime scene investigators, paramedics, and one news crew stood stiff and unmoving, their faces and bodies frozen. Snowflakes had already begun to build a layer on their still bodies.

I didn't think Captain Wysocki had really gotten used to frozen crime scenes over the past few weeks after she had a gruesome introduction to the paranorm world.

That unwanted introduction had been thanks to a large number of ruthless Vampires led by Volod, the New York City Master Vampire. It was a group that had decided they were sick of synthetic blood and sick of the control the paranorm world had over them.

But this . . . this had nothing to do with Volod.

"You're wrong," I said after a long moment of studying the scene, and I met the gaze of the tall and slender police captain. My breath fogged in the cold air. "It wasn't a Vampire attack."

Adam and Wysocki looked at me, Adam with a question in his gaze and the captain with a frown on her face.

"How can you say that?" Olivia gestured toward the assortment of arms, legs, torsos, and heads. "Hello? Doesn't this remind you of anything?"

I didn't know whether or not to feel relief or fear. Relief that it couldn't have been Vampires. Fear of what had actually done this.

Because I'm Drow, the Elvin boots I'd changed into didn't sink into the snow-covered grass as I stepped from the walk. The snow remained unbroken where I walked and I avoided a nearly frozen pool of blood. The attack had to have happened recently.

"You've obviously noticed the bites taken out of the victims," I said to the three looking at me for my take on this. "Vampires don't rip out hunks of flesh like that."

The words tasted awful on my tongue and nausea continued to make me feel sick. But I continued talking as I walked from one end of the crime scene to the other.

"If you'll notice, too, the bites were taken by something that's not normally a flesh-eating predator. No fangs. No jagged teeth." I looked at Adam, Olivia, and the police captain. "Those bites look like they could have been made by a human."

"Humans don't have the strength to tear apart bodies like we see here," Wysocki said as she studied me with her assessing gaze.

"I didn't say humans actually did this." I turned my gaze back to the horrific sight. "What I am saying is that Vampires didn't." I glanced at Adam and Olivia. "And no being in Werewolf, Doppler, or Shifter animal form could have been the attackers due to their sharp teeth. Whatever things did this have flat, blunt teeth, like humans."

Wysocki gave me a hard look as I said the words *Werewolf, Doppler, or Shifter animal form*. Adam, Olivia, and I hadn't filled the human NYPD police captain in on the rest of the paranorm world yet. It had seemed enough to clue her in on Vampires when they started attacking groups of humans.

"What if the paranorms stayed in human form?" Olivia asked before Wysocki could say anything.

"Most retain some paranormal strength when in human form," I said. "But I don't think enough to do this." I frowned as I considered it further. "Although anything's possible."

Adam folded his arms across his chest. "What about Demons?"

"Demons?" Wysocki said looking even more incredulous. "And Werewolves and whatever else you mentioned— you've got to be kidding me."

"Also Shifters and Dopplers," I said. "We did mention to you that there's a whole paranorm world out here that humans aren't aware of. Vampires are only a small part of that world."

The fifty-one-year-old captain's short, normally smooth blond hair was ruffling in the wind. She braced her hands on her waist. She didn't look like she believed anything I had told her, but still she said, "Go on."

"All of this blood." I gestured around me. "Vampires make a mess, but not like this. They prefer to ingest, not leave what looks like the majority of their victim's blood covering the ground." I pointed to one head that was still attached to the body. "No neck wounds."

My gaze traveled to the shoeprints. "Vampires would never step in blood, much less leave a footprint of any kind.

It's a sort of sacrilege to them." I added, "Plus I don't scent anything remotely like a Vampire anywhere around here."

"You smell Vampires." Wysocki said it as a statement with a heavy overlay in her tone that meant she had a hard time grasping that concept.

"Yes." I met her gaze. "Their odor is like graveyard dirt. The older the Vampire, the stronger it is."

Her frown deepened. "I never smelled anything like that when I was on cases involving Vampire attacks in the past."

"That's because you're not a paranorm," I said. "Most of us have a keen sense of smell. Some more than others."

Wysocki stared at me for a long moment. No one said anything to break the silence.

With her thumb and forefinger, she rubbed at her temples as she stared at the body parts. Finally she said, "You did a damned good job on the last case. I trusted you on the Vampire slayings and you came through." Her gaze met mine. "What you call paranorms . . . I guess anything is possible in this city."

"You're right," I said. "Anything is possible. Things humans would never believe are a part of the world I come from."

"I take it you're not a Vampire," she said with an assessing look. "If you're not human, what are you?"

"I'm half human . . ." I glanced at Olivia, who shrugged, and Adam, who gave a brief nod. I met Wysocki's gaze again. "I'm also half Drow." The police captain tilted her head to the side, clearly not understanding, so I added, "Drow are Dark Elves. My people live in Otherworld, not here."

Again it was quiet as she studied me. "One of these nights I'll buy you a beer and you can explain everything." She held up one hand as I started to say something. "Not promising I believe every word you're saying, but I'll listen. Enough has happened to convince me there is more out there than I had ever thought."

"Good enough for me." I thought briefly about taking her

to the Pit and decided that might be too much for the captain to absorb.

The change in Wysocki truly was incredible. From the disbelieving police captain who'd wanted to kick us off the first Vampire massacre scene, to her growing if reluctant acceptance of the paranorm world, and her willingness to listen, was a huge difference. Her newfound respect for me had been hard won, but I'd earned it.

I turned to face the horror we had to figure out how to stop from happening again. Snow was already starting to cover the bodies. We needed to hurry and complete our own investigation before Lulu unfroze the scene.

"Were there any witnesses?" I asked.

"No." Wysocki blew out her breath. "However, we did find a couple of cell phones in the snow and a wallet and phone on one of the male victims."

In her rubber-gloved hand, she held up a black Motorola wireless. "Made a few calls from the phone that was on the victim who had a wallet and we got lucky on the fifth call."

She continued, "A family member said that the victim and his girlfriend, along with two other couples, left together to take a stroll down Cherry Walk. They'd been partying just a couple of streets up on Seventy-Fifth. That means the victim was possibly with five other people."

Olivia pointed her finger at each torso. "I only counted five bodies."

Adam's frown deepened. "So we're looking at a possible abduction, too."

"Maybe." Wysocki must have had a killer headache by the look on her face as she rubbed her temples again. "Judging from the brutality of the attack, I have a feeling we'll find her body somewhere else in the park."

I shuddered. I'd seen my fair share of grisly scenes over the past couple of years, but they still made me queasy every time.

The snowfall began to thicken and visibility wasn't as good. "We'd better hurry so that they can get back to their investigation," I said.

We were always conscious of not disturbing the scene or impeding the NYPD's investigation. Minus any paranormal evidence that might require a little cover-up.

Olivia and I did a quick but thorough search and examination of the scene while Adam tracked the bloody footprints leading away from the slaughter. Wysocki was busy making calls.

"Not a damned clue beyond what you've already laid out." Olivia came to stand by me. "Other than those prints Boyd is tracking."

My gaze followed the trail of prints in time to see Adam jogging back. When he reached us, he said, "No more visible prints after the perpetrators leave Riverside Park."

I looked at the captain. "You have my number to update me on whatever you find."

Wysocki looked beyond my shoulder. "We'll finish photographing and processing the prints, along with everyone else, as soon as your princess over there unfreezes the scene."

Adam, Olivia, and I turned to look at Lulu who sat on the park bench with her back stiff and straight.

Olivia glanced at the bodies, then back at Lulu. "Hold on while I borrow a foot."

SIX

After I spoke with Rodán and brought him up to date on the crime scene we'd just come from, I called Tracey, who'd discovered the paranorm murder scene with Robert.

While I talked with Rodán and then Tracey, Olivia started her search on the Internet. Police reports, media articles, blogs, Twitter, Facebook—whatever form of information she could find that mentioned anything close to what we'd seen earlier.

"Hi, Nyx." When she answered, Tracey, a Sânziană—Romanian Fae—sounded sweet on the phone, like she did in person. But like all Sânziene, who were known for their gentle dispositions, Tracey was as deadly as she was sweet. "Rodán said you were going to call on the paranorms we found last night."

"Are you positive it was a Vampire attack?" I asked her as I held the phone tight. I hoped it wasn't Vampires. If it wasn't it had to be something easier to take care of, right? "Was there anything unusual about the scene?" I asked.

Tracey paused for a moment, then spoke. "Robert and I have been talking about it . . . and the more we discuss it, the less likely it seems that it was a Vampire attack."

Like earlier, a rush of relief cruised through me. That rush was followed by a flood of concern over the question of what was actually doing this. The fast shift in emotions made me lightheaded.

"I'm investigating human deaths that were originally attributed to Vampires." I rested my free arm on my glossy

Dryad-wood desktop. "But when I was at the scene I determined they weren't."

"Too much blood," Tracey said. "Not to mention the type of bite marks and no neck wounds."

"Exactly." It was good to hear I was not alone in my conclusion. "Did you smell Vampires?"

I imagined Tracey shaking her head as she said, "No. That's another reason why Robert and I think we were wrong in our initial assessment."

Tracey didn't have much more to offer. What they'd come across was similar to the human deaths that Olivia, Adam, and I had investigated earlier. Mutilated bodies, chunks of flesh torn out, lots of blood.

"Oh," she said just as I was about to disconnect the call. "We think two paranorms that were originally with the group are missing."

"Missing?" I tried to wrap my mind around that one. Now why would some people out of a group be taken? If it was a Vampire attack, that was an easy one. Vampires liked to take select humans and "turn" them. If the turn was successful, then the Vampires had a fledgling to add to their ranks.

After I finished debriefing Tracey, I went into the break room and made myself a cup of hot green tea sweetened with honey. Warmth flowed into my chest as I sipped it.

"Over the past two months there have been unexplained attacks similar to today's, only smaller," Olivia said when I walked out of the break room. She studied her wide screen monitor. "Similar in the way the bodies were dismembered and large amounts of blood. Not to mention huge chunks bitten out of various body parts."

The swallow I'd just taken of my cup of hot tea suddenly felt burning hot. I set my teacup on the credenza beside the mail inbox.

"Let me see." I walked across the tile to lean over her Dryad-wood desk and peer at her screen. Olivia still smelled of a snowy winter's day after being outside for so long.

"Found a police report from Brooklyn that's pretty

interesting." She pointed toward one of the six windows she had open on her huge screen. "Then I dug a little deeper."

"Go on," I said when she paused.

Olivia touched the screen over a coroner's report that she'd managed to hack into. "A college kid was found last week near Dumbo with so many bites taken out of him that he was barely recognizable. Kid was eaten alive." She looked at me. "Missing his heart, liver, kidney, right lung, and most of his heart."

My stomach twisted at the thought of what the guy must have gone through in Dumbo—Down Under the Manhattan Bridge Overpass.

"The police report said he was with his girlfriend, according to a family member," she continued, "but they couldn't find her. She's an heiress from a very wealthy family so it was thought she might have been kidnapped for ransom. She showed up two days later."

"Go on," I said.

Olivia nodded and pointed toward a missing persons report. "She didn't remember a thing. Said she'd been sick, yet no one had seen her or could find her."

I frowned. Strange.

Next to the coroner's and police reports, Olivia showed me another window with a medical report. Olivia had ways of getting into things without actually hacking into them herself. I was pretty computer savvy for someone who had spent the first twenty-five years of her life without technology. But what Olivia did was beyond me.

"The girl took the attack surprisingly well considering what happened to her boyfriend," she said.

I pursed my lips. "Maybe she's in denial."

Olivia rocked back in her chair. "Something like that."

"There was someone missing from the group who was murdered in Riverside Park," I said. "And two paranorms missing from another group hatchet job last night."

She raised her brows, then gestured to the screen next to the coroner's examination, this one a police report. "A month ago in the Bronx, a report came in from someone who said a homeless man tried to chomp on his arm.

"The victim was wearing a heavy leather coat so the attacker's teeth didn't make it through," she continued. "Guy punched his attacker and ran. According to the police report there were tooth marks on the coat. They were deep enough that it showed the attacker's teeth had punctured the thick leather and almost made it through the lining.

"This blog," Olivia said, indicating the third window across, "is written by a teen here on the Upper West Side who swears she saw a homeless man rip off a woman's arm before taking a bite out of it. No other witnesses were around and the police never found a body. The girl says the police didn't take her seriously."

I winced at the images that came to mind from the girl's story. "With no proof it would sound pretty farfetched coming from an adult, much less a teenager."

"On WABC a piece aired ten days ago about a rise in the homeless population." Olivia pointed to another window. "Those who don't go into the shelters even though you'd freeze your ass off in this weather."

"What do the homeless have to do with all of this?" I asked.

"You tell me." She tilted her head. "Two of three reports mention homeless men. Then we have an article about a rise in the homeless population."

I straightened a little and braced my palms on her desktop. "Do we have some kind of homeless paranorms who could do what we're seeing?"

"Maybe it's a coincidence," Olivia said. "And maybe it's not."

"Strange." I rose. "It might be a good idea to interview some of the homeless in areas where the attacks, or alleged attacks, happened."

"My thoughts, too," Olivia said. "But we probably want to do it now while it's still daylight—when you're not purple. Otherwise you might scare off all of those poor guys."

I stuck my tongue out at her. "Amethyst," I said.

"Whatever, grape butt," she said to me and I snatched up an eraser from the pile on her desk and pinged it off her head.

Olivia rubbed her scalp. "You do know this means war."

"What, you and your army of Dwarves?"

She went for the wooden rubber band shooter in her center desk drawer and had it loaded with an eraser almost as fast as she could draw her Sig Sauer.

I raised my hands. "Sorry. Really, I am." But I couldn't hold back a laugh.

She scowled at me. "I'll sorry your ass."

I dodged the first eraser, then threw up an air shield so that the next one almost hit her on the rebound.

"No fair." Olivia narrowed her eyes. "Fight like a woman."

I grinned. "All is fair in love and magic."

After I changed into blue jeans and a simple navy boat-necked T-shirt, I stuffed my ID and a fistful of bills into my pocket and grabbed a black leather jacket out of my closet.

Olivia and I never went anywhere unarmed and I wore my side holster with my Kahr K40 9mm beneath the jacket. I'd also slipped small but wicked daggers with serrated blades into the sheaths on the inside of each of my Elvin boots. I slid my phone into a leather phone holster before clipping it to my belt.

When I was ready, I jogged back downstairs to meet Olivia in the office. The moment I opened the office door, she nailed me with an eraser. Right on the nose.

"Ow." I rubbed my nose and caught the next flying projectile in my hand. "Okay, you got me."

"Not enough." Olivia slid her rubber-band gun into her top drawer. "But it'll do for now." I gave her a pretend glare as she grabbed her Mets jacket and met me at the door. "Let's go, Princess."

"You are so pushing it today," I said as Fae bells jingled and jangled as I opened the door. She also knew I didn't like to be called Princess. "You might want to sleep with one eye open tonight."

"Ha," she said before heading down the sidewalk to where our corner office–slash–apartment building was.

Even with New York City's programs and pledge to get all homeless people into shelters, there were still an estimated four thousand people living on the street, so we didn't anticipate difficulty finding some to interview.

Since the teenage girl who mentioned a homeless man happened to live in my part of the city, the Upper West Side, Olivia and I walked from the office, down 104th to Broadway. There it would be easy finding panhandlers and the obviously homeless.

A bit of sunshine made it through a spot in the gray cloud cover as we walked, but then it was gone, leaving the city looking tired. I shoved my hands into my jacket pockets and we elbowed our way through the crowds once we hit Broadway. Yellow taxis zipped by, weaving through traffic like bumblebees buzzing through a field of sleeping sunflowers.

The first man we met looked tired, haggard, but gave me a smile and an enthusiastic "thank you" when I dropped a tendollar bill into his almost empty collection jar. I had a feeling that any other cash he'd received was tucked away in his coat pocket.

I returned his smile, but it slipped away as I took in his obviously malnourished body and gaunt face. His threadbare but relatively clean clothing hung on him, several sizes too large for his thin frame.

Despite his fatigued and starved appearance, it was easy to see he took pains to clean himself up. I had never become a hardened New Yorker like some, but I was used to panhandlers. I still felt for him as I read his sign that looked like it had been torn from a cereal box, the message written on the side that was blank and gray:

> *lost job lost home*
> *wife and 2 kids*
> *Please help*

I took a deep breath and met his soft brown eyes. "Can I ask you a couple of questions?"

The man said, "Thank you," to a woman who dropped a dollar into his jar before he returned his attention to me. "Sure."

His accent had a distinctive southern twang to it, but I wasn't familiar enough with the South to guess what state he came from.

"Do you and your family sleep in one of the shelters at night?" I asked.

He nodded. "Crowded this winter but as long as it's a place out of the cold, we thank God and count our blessings."

"Have you noticed a rise in the homeless population?" I said, hoping he had something that I could use.

"Not more than a person could expect in a place like this," he said.

"What about at night?" Olivia asked.

"Don't get out much at night." He said, "Thank you," to another passerby who dropped change that rattled in the jar. He addressed Olivia again. "Keep to ourselves. Don't want no trouble."

"I understand," I said, disappointed that our first try hadn't turned up anything. "Thank you for your help," I added before Olivia and I moved on.

The next panhandlers we came across, a woman and a man, were equally unhelpful. One was rude, the other very kind.

We found a guy who was reclined with his back up against a brick wall. In one hand held a sign painted on a broken piece of plywood that had me laughing too hard to talk for a moment.

BOOGIEMAN ATE MY FAMILY
SPARE ANY CHANGE
FOR NEW CLOSET DOOR?

Just for making me laugh I dug in the front pocket of my jeans and handed him a ten. Olivia didn't seem as impressed as I was—but then she'd been an NYPD cop before I met her and had probably seen it all.

I think the man was smiling—his tangled beard was so bushy it was hard to tell for sure. But his "Thank you, ma'am" was loud and clear and he had a spark to his dark eyes. He didn't look as though life had beaten him down. He had the appearance of a man who took it a day at a time and found things to smile about.

My gut told me he wasn't one of the panhandlers who weren't really homeless and took advantage of the city's tourists. And my gut is usually right on.

"What's your name?" I asked after I handed him the cash.

He looked surprised that I'd hung around and was asking his name. "Victor," he said. His voice was deep and lovely. He should probably have been singing for his supper with a voice like that.

"Victor, we'd like to ask you a few questions." Olivia bulldozed right into it with a tough expression to her tone and on her features.

His expression shuttered and if he'd been smiling he probably wasn't anymore. "You're cops."

I held up my hand to Olivia to indicate that I wanted her to shut up so that I could handle the interview. Sometimes she had the grace of a Gargoyle in a ballet with Mikhail Baryshnikov.

"We're private investigators." I kept my voice businesslike and professional but not hard-core like Olivia could be. "Can we talk for a moment?"

The man looked down at the ten in his hand and then back at me. "If you have another one of these."

Olivia gave a disgruntled noise while I pulled another ten out of my pocket. He reached for it but I shook my head.

"I want to talk a little with you first." I stuffed my hands into my jacket which hid the money from his gaze. "Do you sleep in one of the city's shelters, or on the street?"

Victor said, "I hate the shelters."

I studied him, frowning inside. "But it's freezing out here."

With a shrug, he said, "I'm from Alaska. I dig the cold."

"Are there more people than usual hanging around who are not in shelters?"

He tilted his head to the side. "Yeah. I guess. Hadn't really thought about it."

"Have you noticed anything strange at all?" I looked around me as if I might see something weird now. "At night."

"Some of the dudes I've seen hanging around just aren't cool," he said. "Mostly everyone keeps to themselves but these other guys walk around like they're mental."

"Mental?" I said, puzzled.

"Like they belong in a mental institution," Olivia said.

"Oh." I studied Victor's face. "Have you seen any of them attack people?"

Victor's expression changed, his eyes looking almost angry. "Just because we don't have money or a place to live doesn't mean we should be blamed for people getting hurt."

"I know." This was not going easy, but I still felt like I was getting somewhere. "But these strangers—you don't know them."

Tenseness seemed to leave his body. "Hadn't thought about that."

"That's what we're trying to find out." I pushed my hair behind my ear. "Some strange things are happening in this city."

Victor gave a short laugh. "Hell, lady. This is New York City. Strange isn't so strange here."

"Got me there." I slipped the ten out of my jacket pocket. With it I included a business card.

He took both and looked at the card. "I know. Call you if I see any weird shit."

"Please do." I smiled. "Good luck with that closet door."

Six not-so-helpful panhandlers later, Olivia and I spotted a bearded man with a giant sign. He'd taken a black marker and had written in huge capital letters:

**MY FATHER WAS
KILLED BY NINJAS
NEED MONEY FOR
KARATE LESSONS**

Bonus points for making me smile again.

By the smooth skin around his eyes and on the parts of his face his beard didn't cover, I could tell he was only in his early thirties. I wondered what his story was.

The weight of the roll of cash in my pocket was considerably lighter but I still had plenty.

After giving him a ten, Olivia and I questioned the man named Richard. He was a thoughtful man, answering our questions after considering each one with slow deliberation.

"Yes," Richard said when I asked if he'd noticed anything stranger than normal about some of the homeless on the streets at night. "Some of these new guys are creepy. A few that I've seen look like they crawled out of a grave."

I shuddered at that image.

"That went well," Olivia said when we headed back to the office. Her tone held sarcasm, indicating she didn't think it went well at all.

"I don't know about you," I said, "but I think your hunch was a good one and that in part that was affirmed by the two who were most helpful."

"I suppose." Olivia brought her hands out of her jacket pockets when we reached the office door. "I didn't expect much to come out of this anyway. It's a far-fetched idea to begin with."

"I don't think it's so far-fetched." I unlocked the door with my air elemental magic and Olivia stomped the snow from her boots as I opened the door. "And I don't think it's all a coincidence." I shrugged out of my coat and tossed it on the credenza, next to a stack of file folders. "Something is going on and we need to figure out exactly what that is."

"Whatever you say, grape butt," Olivia said with a smirk.

My retribution was swift as I whirled and nailed her in her belly with a jumbo eraser.

Heh.

SEVEN

"Your Highness." I set Kali's Waterford crystal bowl on the hardwood floor in the kitchen as I called to her. "The Fancy Feast is going to get cold."

Kali liked her food a little warm, so I indulged her by heating it for a few seconds in the microwave.

The Persian slipped into the kitchen. Her head was tilted at a regal angle. She gave me the briefest glance with her haughty gold eyes before she began to take dainty bites out of her warm dinner.

I rolled my eyes. Why couldn't Rodán have given me a puppy? Something adorable like Fred was in his Doppler form as a golden retriever. Except a real dog. Not any kind of Shifter dog, of course.

As I started to walk out of the kitchen I looked over my shoulder and saw Kali had paused and was staring at me with those wicked eyes. At that moment I could almost imagine Kali as a Shifter who had infiltrated my home. Maybe she was. How else could she reach a lingerie drawer three feet up and destroy its contents. A cat with a panty destruction fetish . . . Go figure.

A strange feeling tickled my spine and I looked away from her and headed into my living room.

If Rodán had given me a Doppler or Shifter instead of an ordinary housecat I'd have had to kill him. Not that he would do anything like that. Besides, no one could *give* a Doppler or Shifter. That was equivalent to selling one human to another. It was an absolutely absurd thought.

Shifters did make great spies for hire in the human world. It was easy to fool norms.

On the other hand it was very difficult to fool most para-norms. Vampires and Witches, and any other human-born individual with paranormal talents, were the exception. They didn't have the same kind of sixth sense that allows the rest of us to recognize another paranorm the moment we're in the same vicinity. Para-radar. Sort of.

I shook off all of my crazy thoughts. It seemed that since I came so close to death with the Vampires that I'd been pinging all over the place, one thought bouncing against another.

My skin began to tingle. The sun was about to set. Even when the New York City sky is shadowed with winter, I don't shift until the sun actually sinks below the invisible horizon.

The wood flooring was cool beneath my bare feet as I walked toward my bedroom and began to strip off my cloth-ing. The tingling sensations grew stronger and by the time I was in my panties and bra I felt the shift begin.

I tossed my clothing onto the bed, then leaned forward, stretching my body into the change. My body felt strong and lean, and filled with power.

When I shift, my movements are slow and sensual. Like a cat I'm graceful and sinuous as I ease into one stretch after another. Dark Elves and Light Elves are inherently sensual beings and I'm no exception.

As I moved, my black hair rippled into luxurious cobalt blue, black highlights shimmering in the soft glow from my new bedside lamps. My softer and more sensitive skin tone turned the faintest shade of amethyst marble as my body tingled with the change.

I raised my hands over my head and reached high before slowly lowering them as my muscles shifted and my arms and legs became more sculpted, stronger, more powerful.

When my heels touched the floor again, I pushed my hair away from my face and brushed the now pointed tips of my ears. I ran my tongue along the points of my short incisors.

The shift from human to Drow made me feel complete as I left one world and entered another.

Once I was ready, I headed out the door of my apartment into the snowy night. Like I usually did each night, I intended to join the other Trackers at the Pit, the hottest paranorm club in the city. Probably the hottest anywhere.

Most of our team of Trackers met at the Pit to relax before we left to track our assigned territories. Tonight we had a meeting, so all the Trackers would be there.

Snowflakes landed softly on the top of my head, my nose, and my cheeks as I walked the few blocks to the Pit. Not only was it a fantastic nightclub, it was also the location where Peacekeepers met with Rodán, our Proctor. It was rare for Trackers, Soothsayers, Healers, and Gatekeepers to meet all at the same time. We met with him in groups as needed.

The other Peacekeepers generally looked down on Trackers because we were a tough and gritty bunch. Not "refined" like most of the other Peacekeepers thought of themselves. They didn't like to get their hands dirty, and that's what we were all about.

Trackers weren't out to win any awards for social graces. We were too busy saving everyone's butts. Not to mention we really didn't give a damn what the other Peacekeepers thought of us.

Snow swirled around me, but visibility was still good. I loved the winter season but sometimes snow hampered my elemental talents almost as much as mist did.

When I was in my Drow form I had to pull a glamour so that humans wouldn't see an amethyst-skinned, blue-haired woman walking down the street. Not to mention I needed to keep my weapons belt from view, where I'd sheathed my seventeen-inch-long, two-inch-wide Dragon-claw daggers—among other weapons.

At Seventy-second Street, Lawan, a pretty Doppler who shifted into a Siamese cat in her animal form, stood in the dark shadows of the Dakota building. She was a bit away from the magically hidden entrance to the Pit which was snugged up against the Dakota—a famous building that happened to be "haunted" by Brownies.

Lawan crossed her arms beneath her small breasts and her dark eyes had a distant look to them, as if she was seeing something across the street in Central Park.

I looked over at the park, but couldn't find anything interesting enough to keep my attention. The Monday night traffic along Central Park West was pretty low-key and the park itself looked mostly vacant save for naked trees rising from the snowy landscape along with holiday-decorated glowing lanterns and snow-dusted park benches.

Instead of heading to the hidden entrance of the Pit, I walked up to Lawan, who was my friend as well as a fellow Night Tracker.

Lawan gave a little shiver despite her high-necked black fighting suit that covered every part of her but her head. When she left to track, she pulled on a hood, leaving only her long-lashed dark eyes visible. She looked like a slender ninja in a body-hugging leather suit.

Modesty was her motivation for clothing herself in a suit that didn't reveal her flesh, but I could see how males found the way she looked intriguing, enticing.

But she was oh-so-dangerous. The Taiwanese Krabi sheathed at her side and her martial arts skills made her a lethal weapon, a deadly beauty. I knew how to fight. How to kick ass. But Lawan made fighting look like a dance, an art form.

I wasn't surprised that she might be cold when she wasn't in her Siamese cat form. Lawan came from Thailand and had only been in New York City for a couple of years. This was barely her second winter in the city.

"Everything okay?" I asked as I came up beside her.

"Yes." Lawan didn't look at me, just continued staring at the park. "I suppose so."

Her lips parted as if there was something else she wanted to say, so I stayed quiet. She turned her head and looked directly at me. She was petite, very petite, but even though I'm five-eight I didn't feel like she was any smaller than me.

Despite her quiet nature she was a powerful Tracker and had a strong presence.

"It is just . . ." Lawan frowned, her pretty features more serious than I had ever noticed before. "I have had very strange feelings for the past two days. I feel—I feel as though I am being watched."

"Do you think you are?" Despite being Elvin I felt a strong chill and I didn't think it was because my own fighting suit was far more revealing than Lawan's.

"Honestly . . ." She looked back at the park, her dark eyes serious, intent. "Yes."

"Right now?" I asked in a lower tone and she nodded.

For a long moment neither of us said anything as we stared at the snowbound park, the light traffic, the occasional pedestrians who braved the freezing cold, and the small snow flurries softening the night.

"Come on." I touched her arm. "I'll buy you a drink before the meeting."

I waited for her as she continued to stare at the park. Then she turned and we walked side by side to the entrance of the Pit.

Fred, the Doppler bouncer who was a golden retriever in his animal form, greeted us as he always did. He was the kind of being who made a good friend. Devoted, trustworthy, friendly—an all-around good guy. He smiled and gave me a wink before he let us through the doors.

The Pit was rocking and I almost groaned. I'd forgotten tonight was the annual talent competition. The place was packed like Brownies in a bucket of peanut butter.

Brownies love peanut butter.

I tolerate peanut butter and am not crazy about crowds.

Lawan fell a few paces back as we pushed our way through the crush of beings. Laughter and applause had me pausing to raise myself on my toes and look over the heads of two paranorms blocking my view of the stage.

Faerie juggling.

A Sprite was juggling seven tiny Faeries at the same time while the crowd hooted, shouted, and laughed. The Faeries had each tucked themselves into a little ball about the size of an orange. Faeries dress in bright hues which made for a brilliant show of yellow, red, blue, green, pink, orange, and purple. As they spun Faerie dust puffed out and sparkled in the air.

Lawan came up to stand beside me and despite the chaotic noise in the Pit, I heard her sweet laughter.

As a rule, Sprites have always been considered some of the lesser Fae and I had never liked them—until I met Negel, a Sprite who'd died just weeks ago to save my life from the Vampires who had been determined to kill me.

Through Negel I learned that Sprites are good beings, deserving of our respect and concern. The relatively few Sprites who are malicious, destructive, and mean give the whole race an undeserved reputation.

They are ugly, though. Really, really ugly. This adds to the way other paranorms view them and for the most part shun them.

To my surprise, I learned that Sprites are a peaceable race of beings with kind hearts who stay hidden as much as possible from other beings, keeping to themselves. Throughout the centuries they have chosen to ignore the reputation given to them by the few Sprites who wreak havoc.

Negel's bravery and kind spirit changed not only my view of Sprites, but the view of many other paranorms, to the point that they were allowed entry into the Pit. It would take a lot more than that to erase centuries of racism against Sprites, though.

The Sprite on stage was no exception to the ugly rule with his tuft of matted blond hair, floppy ears, and bulbous eyes. He also looked familiar. I wasn't sure, but he could have been one of the Sprites we tracked down when a team of them gave the Statue of Liberty a neon pink pedicure.

From out of nowhere the Sprite juggler produced a large black top hat, held it up and caught all seven Faeries one at a time as they came down. Poofs of Faerie dust floated out of the hat like a sparkling rainbow.

Cheering from the crowd rocked the Pit and the Sprite

took a bow. His jagged teeth flashed as he gave what I think was his attempt at a smile. The seven tiny Faeries peeked out of the top hat and waved at the audience before the Sprite went offstage and disappeared behind the curtains.

When the crowd quieted, Adele, the Pixie vocalist from the band Sweet Cat, came out from behind the curtain. Adele was an amazing singer and she knew she was good, which made her less palatable as far as I was concerned. But she was popular and their band was considered one of the best rock paranorm bands around.

"Straight from Otherworld, Colin of Campton is going to light fire to your world," Adele said in a sexy, sensual voice. "And all of you females . . . I found him first."

A male walked out from behind the curtain and the females in the place went wild with shouts and applause.

I have never been one to act like an idiot over a performer, but for a moment I had to fight to keep from doing just that.

Lawan started crying out, "Colin! Colin!" from beside me, something I would never have thought she'd do.

I wanted to look away from the male taking center stage, but my gaze was riveted to him. I was mesmerized.

With his long glittering gold hair and burnished gold eyes, Colin of Campton had to have been one of the most gorgeous males I'd ever seen. Ever.

Thoughts of Rodán—who I'd always thought of as being the most incredible male specimen ever—kept flashing in my mind.

Those thoughts were pushed aside as my lips parted and I looked at Colin. I stared at his naked chest and imagined running my fingers along his golden skin, his broad shoulders, his well-defined chest and abs. His red leather pants hugged his trim waist and muscular thighs so well that I held my hand to my chest to hold back a sigh.

A part of me knew something wasn't right even as I found myself wanting to go to the stage, climb up on it, and take Colin of Campton down to the floor.

I shook my head to get the images out.

What was wrong with me?

What was wrong with Lawan?

Beside me, Lawan kept screaming and jumping up and down. She was so petite I didn't even know if she could see the stage, but she was going crazy. That was so not her.

The instant Colin raised a burning torch to his lips, then swallowed the fire, I snapped back to reality. I had caught Colin's scent.

I shook my head to get the effects of his intoxicating but unwanted presence out of my mind.

"Lawan." I caught her by her upper arm and tried to keep her from jumping up and down and screaming more. "He's a Dragon."

She ignored me. I shook her as Colin swallowed two burning torches at the same time.

"That damn Dragon cast a spell on this entire room." I shook my friend just enough to get her attention.

She paused and looked at me with a dazed expression. "What?"

"Dragon." When she gave me a confused look, I added, "Dragons can take human form when they choose to." I gestured toward the stage. "They're also good at mesmerizing groups of paranorms or norms, which is exactly what he's doing."

Lawan seemed to come back to herself. "How do you know?"

"Can't you scent him?" I asked. "A little bit of sulfur and sandalwood incense."

"Not all of us have noses like you do," Lawan said as the glazed look went out of her eyes and she appeared almost mortified. "Did I just act like an idiot, Nyx?"

"No more than anyone else." I took her by her arm and tugged her toward the bar, which was close to the corner where the Trackers hung out. "We'll ask Hector for an elderflower Tom Collins. That should counteract the Dragonthrall."

Lawan still looked a little dazed at I took her by her arm and pushed and elbowed our way through the females in the crowd who were still going nuts. He had a pull on females similar to the effect Sirens have on males. Dragons could burn a being to its death, Sirens would sing a male to his demise.

"Damn Dragons, anyway," I muttered as we reached the bar.

"One vodka martini coming up, Nyx," Hector, the Shifter barman, said the moment he saw me. "What would you like, Lawan?"

Hector was going for the Stoli when I held up my hand. "I'm changing things up tonight." His expression shifted to surprise as he stopped in mid movement. "Elderflower Tom Collins," I said and glanced at Lawan before I looked at him again. "Make it two. Heavy on the elderflower liqueur."

He raised his eyebrows and looked at the stage. "Dragon?"

I nodded. "I hope you have a lot of liqueur in the back."

A low rumble came from his chest and I imagined him changing into his lion form. "His kind should not be allowed in the Pit."

"Obviously Rodán thinks otherwise." I glanced over my shoulder to see Colin taking a bow. I caught my breath. Magnificent. He looked absolutely magni—

Stop it.

I shook my head and turned back to Hector. "You'll probably want to bring out a couple of bottles of St. Germaine and give all of the females a shot glass of it."

"Rodán and I will have a chat." Hector growled like the lion he preferred as his Shifter form as he started throwing together two of the elderflower Tom Collins drinks. Lemons, limoncello, vodka, soda water, and of course the liqueur made up the drinks he handed to us.

Hector was stomping into the room behind the bar just as Colin finished his act.

Lawan took a sip of her drink. "It's good. I've never heard of the flower you talked of."

"Elderflower." I felt the intoxicating, mesmerized feeling ease away after my first swallow. "In this Earth Otherworld, for only a few days in late spring, the flower blooms in the Alps. They're gathered very quickly because the blooms lose their potency within a couple of days."

In the time it took me to explain what elderflower liqueur was made from, Lawan had drained her glass. "How do you know all of this?" she asked as she set her glass on the bar.

Hector jogged out of the back room, another growl rising from his throat as he started pouring shots of St. Germaine across the bar to counteract the Dragon-thrall.

"The plants are common in Otherworld," I told her as dazed women started stumbling toward us. I drew Lawan out of the way so we wouldn't be trampled. "When a few Dragons started coming to this Otherworld centuries ago, Gnomes were hired and given the task of planting the flowers here. It took some time before they discovered that the only place the flowers will grow is in the Alps."

"I would prefer not to meet another Dragon," Lawan said as a Mage-mime took the stage. Lawan touched the hilt of her Krabi. "I may have to kill him."

I grinned as we started to make our way to the corner where the Trackers lounged on large overstuffed black leather chairs and couches. It was rare to make Lawan mad, but I thought the Dragon male had just done a good job of it.

As the Mage—dressed in black but with white gloves and his face painted white—performed his act as a mime, the crowd surged, forcing me to come to a stop. I couldn't see Lawan anymore.

Before I could try to make my way through, a hand grasped my upper arm.

EIGHT

I jerked my arm away from the grip and felt nails scratch my skin.

My Tom Collins splashed onto my bare belly. At the same time my free hand automatically shot for the hilt of one of my Dragon-claw daggers. I whirled to see who had grabbed my arm.

"My sincerest apologies." Council Chief Leticia snatched her hand away from me and I saw the long, sculpted nails that had scraped me. "Such a large crowd. A group of Fae bumped into me and I caught your arm to steady myself, only more tightly than I had intended."

I froze in mid-motion and just stared at the Doppler who happened to be one of the most powerful females in the paranorm world. I had no idea what to say. The most respected paranorm representative had just scratched my arm with her nails and she looked upset at having done so.

She easily composed herself, appearing sophisticated and refined as she took a step back with such grace she could have been Doppler royalty. For all I knew, she was.

"Come." She gave a little wave of her hand, indicating I should follow.

It was an order, not an invitation, but I paused and glanced at the Tracker corner before looking back at Leticia. I still had time before the meeting to see what the council chief had to say.

Leticia turned away from me and the lighting gleamed on her silver hair that was smoothed away from her unlined face and pulled back in a chignon. I downed my elderflower Tom Collins, set my glass on a table, and followed.

She headed toward the elevated floor where paranorms played billiards along with games like pinball and air hockey. All of the games had some kind of paranorm twist that norms wouldn't understand. Like the Brownie pinball game where the Brownie inside fought back by knocking the metal pinball away from the bonus points. Made it a lot harder to win.

Billiards is the best game ever invented and we play it like norms do—no magic involved. No one ever beat me at pool, but I was afraid I was going to lose my edge if I didn't start playing more often. I'd rarely had time to indulge since the Demons had almost destroyed New York City not all that long ago.

I rubbed my upper arm where Leticia had scratched it and frowned as I trailed after her. To my right was the stage. The mime was already gone, and now a comedian I'd never seen was performing impersonations of both famous norms and well-known paranorms. I wondered if he'd have the guts to do an impression of the almighty Great Guardian. I would love to have seen it.

Leticia directed us to a dark alcove on the main floor, past the stairs that led to the gaming level. Drow see well in the darkness, and I didn't have to blink to get accustomed to how little light actually penetrated the corner we were headed to.

The council chief sank into an overstuffed chair and looked at me. "That seat will be fine." She gestured to the straight-back chair closest to her and I took it. "There. Perfect," she said.

The whole situation made me feel a little off-kilter. Leticia, a very sophisticated elderly female, was in the Pit of all places. The nightclub, which was a pretty nice place, looked almost primitive compared to her elegant appearance.

I had never seen her outside the Paranorm Council's chambers, not even off the throne she perched on at the center of the crescent-shaped council table. The only thing I'd seen her in before now was a set of brilliant yellow robes.

Tonight she wore an elegant black dress that I thought might be a Dior and it fit her slender frame as if it had been tailored for her. She wore classic low heels that had to have been Burberrys and she held a Fendi clutch in her lap. At least she had good taste.

Around her neck hung a large glittering blue sapphire pendant on a long, delicate chain made from a metal that couldn't be found on the Earth Otherworld. I know because I'm Drow. Dark Elves mine ores and gemstones deep beneath the surface of Otherworld and we're born with an innate sense for anything to do with metals and precious gems. The pendant glittered like that only when worn by the person it rightfully belongs to.

The chain Leticia wore had to have been a gift because the metal is beyond special and Dark Elves hate to part with anything so precious. It was made from the same material as my collar, a metal normally only worn by Drow royalty.

Leticia crossed her legs at her knees and leaned forward, her hands clasped on her lap. "I am so glad to see you, Nyx. I contacted Rodán and he told me when you would be at his nightclub tonight so that I could call on you personally."

I tried to smile but had a hard time. What did the council want with me now?

"It is my desire to express my sincere gratitude and that of the council as well." Leticia's statement caught me off guard. They were thanking me?

I did my best to hide my surprise as she continued. "Why council members understated that kind of horror I'll never understand. It wasn't just a 'situation' but a series of devastating tragedies and near tragedies."

Heat began to burn beneath my skin and I felt a flush rising to my face.

"What you did for all paranormkind almost cost you your life." She placed her hand on my knee as she continued. "All members of the Paranorm Council shall never forget your sacrifices. No one should."

My face felt even hotter now and I wished I was off fighting a Demon instead of receiving praise I didn't deserve.

"I was doing my job." I tried not to squirm in my seat. "I'm a Night Tracker and I was only doing what I've been trained to do."

Leticia gave me what amounted to a patient look, as if I was a child and she was trying to make me understand something. "The council plans to honor your heroics with a special award. We are requesting your presence in one week's time when we have our last meeting before the New Year begins."

"No." I straightened in my seat and there must have been an expression of shock on my face, because that's exactly what I felt.

The council chief looked surprised at my immediate refusal.

"I mean, thank you." I tried my best to sound appreciative. "But I can't accept any kind of award. All of the Trackers deserve recognition, not just me."

Leticia removed her hand from my knee. "You are far too modest, Nyx Ciar."

She stood in such a graceful movement I knew at that moment her Doppler animal form was some kind of large cat.

A lioness. With her regal bearing and commanding presence it became obvious to me. I wasn't sure why I hadn't realized it earlier.

I stood, too. "It's not right that I should be given recognition and not the rest of the team."

"Accept the award on behalf of your brethren, if you wish." The expression in Leticia's eyes was both warm and firm, which I wasn't sure many could pull off. "But accept it you will."

I groaned out loud as the council chief walked away from me, toward the exit. Not that my groan could be heard over the laughter that erupted in the room. I looked at the stage in time to see a ventriloquist's dummy walking across the stage taking bows—while the Doppler ventriloquist remained seated on his stool.

I wondered if the audience even knew that the Doppler's

dummy was actually a Brownie. An exceptionally ugly one at that.

My thoughts turned immediately back to my little meeting with Leticia. How embarrassing. And how very wrong. I almost died because of my own stupidity. My team members were the real heroes. Especially the Sprite named Negel.

Rodán had to get me out of this one.

The crowd seemed even thicker now and I shoved my way through the hoard of paranorms and toward the Tracker corner. I was just in time to see everyone leaving and heading into the meeting room. Good, I wasn't late.

I followed Tracey, the Romanian Sânziană Fae, and Hades, a Shifter, into the conference room. When I entered I did a quick scan and saw that all twenty-two other Trackers were there. I closed behind me one of the two doors leading into the conference room. The place was filled with the hum and buzz of conversation as I walked to the conference room table.

Ice, a Shifter born in Manhattan, was lucky that Mandisa, a very dangerous Abatwa Fae from South Africa, didn't shoot him with a poison-tipped arrow when he made a smart-mouthed comment to her. I grimaced, but she just gave him one of her deadly stares. I so never wanted to be on the receiving end of that look from her.

Kelly and Fere—my two least favorite Trackers—were arguing over something, but I couldn't catch more than a few words that didn't make any sense out of context.

Olivia, the only human Tracker, was talking with Lawan. I was so happy to see Olivia wasn't in the middle of some debate with one of the other beings in our crew.

We were by no means a quiet, peaceable, humble, much less diplomatic bunch. The team was made up of just about every type of personality and paranorm race, but when it came to being Trackers for the most part we were alphas.

We were tough, take charge, and kickass all the way. Even though there were the two Trackers I didn't get along with— putting it mildly—I would still trust them at my back any day.

At the large conference table that could seat as many as twenty-six, I slid into a chair. I was sitting with Joshua, a Shadow Shifter from Australia on one side of me and on the other side was one of my best friends, Nadia, a Siren from the Bermuda Triangle.

Joshua turned his head and gave me a grin and a wink before looking away and continuing his conversation with Nakano, a Japanese Shifter.

It would have been easy to be offended by Joshua's arrogant demeanor and what seemed like a cocky attitude, but I'd learned to appreciate him a lot over the past two cases. That despite his making a few sexist comments that almost had Angel removing his head with the barbed whip she carried at her side.

"Hi, Nyx." Nadia scooted her chair a little to the right so that I could get to my seat more easily.

"Do you know what's up?" I asked her. It was kind of a dumb question because I was so close to Rodán that no one else in our group found out about something relating to our work before I did. Rodán was one of my closest friends.

So it wasn't a surprise when she shook her head. "Do you know?"

I leaned back in my chair that both rocked and swiveled. "I talked with Rodán this morning and I'm assuming this has to do with something that's been attacking norms as well as paranorms."

Nadia looked concerned and her thick red hair fell over her shoulder as she leaned toward me. "What is it?"

"No idea." I kept my voice low. "Hopefully Rodán knows more now than we did when we talked."

"After what everyone went through with the Vampires, we really need a break. Especially you." She frowned. "This doesn't have anything to do with Vampires, does it?"

"We're pretty sure it doesn't," I said. "No doubt Rodán will be filling everyone in."

"Hmmm . . ." Nadia tipped her head to the side and gave a teasing grin. "At least you got to vacation in Belize with Adam Boyd."

A smile crept over my face. "Yes, at least we had that."

"Where are you tracking tonight?" she asked.

I shrugged. "Rodán will no doubt make assignments whenever he gets here."

Not having a set territory anymore felt more freeing and I didn't miss it. Out of the twenty-three Trackers in New York City, fifteen had their own territories that they covered each night. The other eight were either rovers or special teams. We could really use more Trackers, but the Great Guardian apparently didn't think the same.

I glanced at Angel, Joshua, Mandisa, Nakano, and Max, who had all joined us at the beginning of the Werewolf case. The GG had hired them to aid our forces but belatedly as far as I was concerned. Before the new Trackers had been moved to the city, we'd lost too many of our own to Demons. Those losses included one of my closest friends, Caprice.

The pain of Caprice's death was still fresh and it hit me sharp and quick to my gut. I held my hand to my belly. It wasn't that long ago that Demons had killed her, taken her away from us.

A reportedly wise, know it all being, the GG is revered by most. With all of her riddles, she drives me crazy. Nadia always said I was doomed for Underworld if I didn't play nice. I played nice. Didn't mean I had to like it.

"Do you miss tracking the Upper West Side?" Nadia asked.

I looked back at her and shook my head. "I really like special teams."

"Changes things up a bit." She gave a nod.

I'd been selected to lead the Tracker special team when my PI agency took on the Werewolf case. Almost immediately after it was solved, the five of us went on to handle the Sprite fiasco and then the Vampire "situation"—with a little help from our friends.

All went quiet and I looked up to see Rodán near the door that led to the club. When he entered a room I usually felt warmth unfold inside me and today was no exception.

One of the Light Elves, Rodán was breathlessly handsome.

Every movement he made was lithe and graceful like all Elves. His crystal-green eyes were filled with intelligence and an almost ancient wisdom.

And mystery . . . there was always an air of mystery surrounding Rodán. I knew him well in some ways, but that knowledge was only a few leaves in the forest of possibilities that made up the whole of who Rodán of the Light Elves was.

Rodán opened the door and stepped aside. Two beings walked in and both had me catching my breath in surprise.

The first was a Sprite—Penrod, Negel's younger brother.

Next was the Dragon who'd performed onstage.

All of us—even Ice—remained silent as the two newcomers followed Rodán to stand at the head of the conference table.

With his protuberant blue eyes, misshapen and mottled features, and tufts of blond hair, Penrod was still ugly as Sprites go, but carried himself with more confidence than Negel had when he was alive.

Tall for a Sprite at about five feet in height, Penrod had a slow gait and with his knobby joints had a clumsy appearance. Sprites are Fae, though, and a great number of Fae races are anything but clumsy. Including Sprites.

After watching Colin on stage and being a firsthand witness to him intentionally mesmerizing his audience, I expected him to be a showboat.

Right now he had the exact opposite effect on me. He looked calm and self-assured, but not cocky or arrogant like some of our Trackers. His switch was apparently set from "mesmerize" to "off," too.

Instead of being bare-chested and in the red leather pants, Colin wore a pair of Levi's, New Balance jogging shoes, and a sleeveless dark red and black Linkin Park T-shirt. His long golden hair was loose around his shoulders.

A scaled serpent tattoo wound up and around his arm from his wrist to his shoulder. Fire erupted from the serpent's mouth, the flames curling over Colin's shoulder. The tattoo moved with the flex of his muscular arm, almost looking like a living, breathing thing. I hadn't noticed the tattoo before, but I may have been too enthralled by his Dragon magic to have noticed.

"This is Colin and Penrod," Rodán said in his smooth, calm way as he gestured to each male. "Our two newest Trackers."

"What?" Lawan said with a sharp intake of breath and got to her feet. "The *Dragon*?"

We all looked at Lawan, and I think to a one our jaws had dropped. For Lawan to have any kind of outburst was almost a greater surprise to everyone seated at the table than having a Sprite and Dragon thrown into our midst as Trackers.

Lawan's cheeks reddened and she eased back into her seat but she kept her back straight and her head tilted high.

"Yes." Rodán smoothed over the interruption and nodded to the Dragon. "Colin is originally from Campton, a village in Otherworld, but he has lived here in the Earth Otherworld for some time now."

"What, get kicked out of Otherworld for pillaging and burning down the villages?" Ice said.

"Yes." Colin's expression was completely serious. "And for eating the peasants and a king or two."

Ice smirked, obviously holding back a laugh. He might be a real jerk at times, but he knew when he'd been upped one.

Although for all I knew, Colin *had* eaten villagers in Otherworld.

"Colin has been in the metalwork trade," Rodán said. "He is excellent with any weapon imaginable."

I don't know why, but we all looked at Mandisa and her poison-tipped arrows.

"Almost any weapon," Colin said with a smile, as I heard his voice for the first time. Low, vibrant, as smooth and rich as chocolate cream. "Abatwa Fae and Elves are masters like none other when it comes to archery."

Rodán nodded to Colin. The Dragon gave a slight bow of his head then stepped back so that Penrod was in front. Rodán gestured to the Sprite. "Please welcome Penrod to our team."

"A *Sprite*?" Kelly sounded like she was going to choke on something. "The Great Guardian chose a Sprite to be a Tracker?"

Only the tiniest flicker of Penrod's floppy ears told me Kelly's statement had affected him in some way.

Rodán, a master at taking control, being in command, continued in a way that washed right over Kelly's words. "You all should remember Negel," Rodán said, "a Sprite who was instrumental in defeating the Vampires just weeks ago and who gave his life for one of our own."

A low murmur and a few nods around the table, along with glances my way.

"Penrod is Negel's younger brother." Rodán looked at the Sprite before turning back to the Trackers. "Penrod was a professional thief."

Even I dropped my jaw.

"A thief," Fere said with a scowl. "You expect us to work with a thief?"

"Didn't see that one coming," Nadia murmured from beside me. "The GG never ceases to amaze me with her wisdom."

At that moment someone could have told me there were two moons in the sky instead of one and I would have believed it. Lawan acting totally out of character, Rodán introducing a Dragon and a thief into our circle, and Nadia making a disparaging remark about the Great Guardian?

I wondered if the two moons that had to be out there now were both full.

"Yes, Penrod was a thief, but that was many years ago," Rodán said. "He served his time, reformed, and then he served his people using his considerable skills in keeping order. He has proven his character and brings to our table many talents."

Penrod vanished.

Paranorms can often see through glamours, but no one can see through a Sprite glamour.

It was only moments before Penrod reappeared. Only now he was holding a broadsword.

Fere's broadsword.

The stunned look on the big Tuatha warrior's face was truly a joy for me to see.

It was even funnier when seconds later the warrior was holding his sword.

As Penrod reappeared again, Fere growled and surged to his feet, gripping the hilt of his sword. "I will slay you if you touch anything I own again."

A couple of laughs and a few coughs around the table greeted Fere's anger.

The Sprite gave a slight incline of his head but there was a glint in his eyes.

"Penrod is a Tracker now." Rodán's voice was a little rougher than it had been. "You have only to remember that. What he did in the past will serve us well as a team. Keep this in mind—Penrod is no longer a thief. He is a Tracker. You will treat him as one of our own."

Fere growled again but sat while he continued to glare at Penrod.

"My apologies." Penrod smiled which almost looked more like a fierce scowl as he showed his sharp, pointed teeth. "I wished only to demonstrate my abilities."

"Accomplished." Rodán gestured to two of the three seats open at the conference table which could seat a total of twenty-six. Colin and Penrod made it twenty-five. Rodán would be the twenty-sixth when he chose to sit, which wasn't often. "Be seated and we will begin."

The Dragon took the chair between Tracey and Meryl, the Sprite between Nancy and Lawan. Nancy looked at Penrod and grimaced but Lawan was still glaring at Colin.

"We have a serious problem." Rodán said before the two new Trackers had even had a chance to settle into their chairs. "Last night a group of paranorms and a group of norms were attacked, murdered, and mutilated. In a way unlike anything we have seen before."

Most of those sitting at the table looked at Rodán with surprise. Only Robert, Tracey, Olivia, and I already knew some of what had happened.

Rodán gave the team the rundown of the information he had to date, including where the incidents had occurred.

"What connects these attacks is the brutality of them," Rodán said. "Done in such a way that no human could have been responsible.

"In addition," he continued, "in each case there is at least one missing person."

Phyllis, a Were from the Lower East Side, leaned forward in her seat. "Just the two incidents?"

"Nyx and Olivia have the case in their PI agency and have been following up, including research," Rodán said. "They have come across similar incidents on a smaller scale. They include a brutal, fatal attack and a missing person."

"One thing about those cases," Olivia said thoughtfully, "is that in each the missing person turned up again."

"That's odd." Bronwyn looked pensive for a Nymph. Somehow this case must really be bothering her because Nymphs generally have a sensual expression and demeanor when not in battle. In a fight they are fierce, especially Bronwyn.

"We're also looking at a homeless persons angle," I said and explained why. I went on to add, "We interviewed several individuals on the street and they've seen some strange things at night that we're still sorting out."

"What do you think we're looking at?" asked Dave, a native New Yorker Werewolf.

"Vampires?" Meryl, a Shifter Tracker as well as an artist, leaned forward with concern on her attractive features. "Are they back?"

"Vampires have been ruled out." Rodán's gaze moved to each one of us as he explained how the attacks could not have been Vampires. "As of now what we face is an unknown threat."

Lawan was fair-skinned to begin with but seemed much paler, as if she were shaken up over Rodán's statement. That surprised me because she was always so cool under pressure. "What is our next step?" she asked Rodán, seeming to have forgotten her anger at the Dragon.

"I'm assigning one of our special teams to concentrate on chasing down whatever it is that we must contend with." Rodán rarely showed even a glimpse of emotion and he stayed true to that now. "Once we know what we're dealing with, we will determine how we're going to take care of and end this threat.

"We again have Angel, Ice, Joshua, Olivia, and Nyx as members of Special Team One." Rodán gave a quick nod to me. "Nyx is leader of that team. Her expertise as a private investigator and her ability to move fluidly between the norm and paranorm worlds makes her invaluable in this capacity."

Rodán looked at the Dragon and the Sprite. "Colin and Penrod will join the special team."

NINE

When did I become the clearinghouse for new Trackers?

I watched the others heading off to track their territories or handle other assignments then looked back to my seven-man—or rather seven-paranorm—team, which included our newest players, the Dragon and the Sprite.

Angel, who was a squirrel Doppler, and Joshua, a Shadow Shifter, had been new Trackers when they'd been assigned to the Werewolf case with Ice, Olivia, and me. They turned out to be two of the best I'd ever worked with.

I looked from the Dragon to the Sprite. I hoped I could say the same for the two of them.

Fortunately I was good at thinking on my feet. Or on my butt since I was sitting down.

"We'll divide up into three teams." I pointed to Olivia and Joshua—Olivia was less likely to be tempted to kill Joshua than she was likely to shoot Ice. "You two will take section one."

For situations like this op, Peacekeepers had divided the city into three sections or four quadrants, depending on how many teams were being sent out.

"Angel and Ice." I gave them each a nod. "You take section two."

I inhaled and looked from Penrod to Colin. "I'll take the newbies. Section three is our territory for tonight."

"What is the plan you wish us to follow, o empowered one?" Ice said as he leaned back in his chair.

I would have loved to have Olivia's rubber band gun on

me. Rodán would have frowned on me using my daggers or buckler.

Fortunately I was getting good at letting comments like Ice's slide by. "Concentrate on visiting areas where the homeless tend to hang out," I said. "Those homeless who refuse to go to the shelters at night, no matter how blessed cold it is outside."

"Do you have any theories about this case, Nyx?" Colin asked in his smooth, rich tone that nearly made me shiver.

I went on to explain in a little more detail why we were focusing on people forced to live on the street. That included the reports of a "homeless man" in two of the cases and those we interviewed who had said they'd seen a higher number of homeless people at night.

"Let's go see for ourselves and find whatever or whoever is responsible." I pushed my chair away from the conference table and stood. "And no one goes out alone. Stick with your teammate."

Any one of my regular team members could have pointed out that I hadn't listened to my own advice on the last op and that had just about gotten me killed. Thankfully they didn't feel the need to bring it up.

Angel twisted one long blond corkscrew curl around her finger. "And find out what could possibly be weirder than the paranorm world we already live in."

I would have smiled but Colin was walking toward me from the other side of the conference table. A strange flutter went through my belly. At first I thought he'd set his mesmerize switch to "stun" but the reality was he hadn't. I was usually a good judge of character and my gut instinct told me he was actually a down-to-earth guy. For a Dragon, that was.

The belly flutters had to go.

"So," I said when he reached me. "You used to eat people."

"Only the bad ones." Colin had an easygoing smile. "The good peasants I put to work sorting through and polishing all of the treasures and bright and shiny things I stole. The usual things Dragons do."

I almost giggled. I would have been mortified if I had done so in front of a bunch of tough Trackers. In front of anyone but Adam.

The giggle quickly dissolved—for which I was immensely grateful—and I smiled instead.

Penrod had joined us as Colin was talking. I glanced from one to the other. "Well then . . . as former thieves, you two should get along great."

Colin winked at Penrod, which both surprised me and won him a few points on my how-do-I-like-the-new-guy meter. With that conspiratorial wink, it was obvious he was treating the Sprite like a colleague, not a lesser being.

When I started toward the exit, Colin began walking beside me. "Who said I'm a *former* thief?"

"Okay." I looked up at him. He was a good eight inches above my five-eight. "Let's see if you can procure information for us tonight that will help our case, whether you have to beg, borrow, or steal."

"Steal," Penrod said from my other side. I turned my head to look at him and saw his spiky-tooth smile-grimace.

"Allrightythen." I shook my head as we left the relative quiet of the conference room for the pounding blast of music in the nightclub. "Let's do it."

I walked ahead of the pair and pushed my way through the Pit's crowd to the front entrance. There was no sign of Angel, Ice, Joshua, or Olivia when I made it out to the sidewalk. The night was crisp and cold, but in my Drow form the chilly weather and snow really didn't bother me.

The scene Olivia, Adam, and I had been called to this morning was in section three of the city—which was why I had chosen it.

I told Colin and Penrod the location we were headed to first.

"How fast are you?" I asked the pair.

"Fast enough," Colin said with a casual smile.

"I will be waiting for you when you arrive," Penrod said, then vanished.

I didn't wait for Colin. I started running.

When I need to get somewhere in a hurry I use my air element to push me faster. It's like gliding on the wind. A really, really fast wind.

There was always the transference . . . but not really. It was a skill I needed to work on a lot. A whole lot. On the occasion I had tried using the transference during the Vampire op, I'd ended up passing out for thirty minutes, then puking my guts up when I came to. Being unconscious for half an hour kind of ruined the whole point in using that shortcut.

I made it to the park in minutes and figured I'd have to wait for Penrod and Colin.

They were both beneath the bare branches of a tree, waiting.

I put my hands on my hips. "How did you two get here so fast?"

Colin pushed away from the tree he'd been leaning against. "Penrod arrived first."

"Transference." The Sprite kicked the snow with one of his huge feet. "It was a gift from an old Sorceress when I acquired something for her that she wanted very much."

"Acquired equals stealing, I take it," I said.

The Sprite shrugged. "It was a long time ago."

Curiosity had me wanting to find out what it was he stole that would make a Sorceress happy enough to bestow that gift upon him, but decided to save that question for another time.

I looked at Colin. "And you?"

Colin came out from under the shadow of the tree and I saw him more clearly beneath a park light. "Me, I just flew."

My eyes widened. "You *flew*?"

He stepped closer to me and lowered his voice as if he was telling a secret. "That's how I always got away from the villagers carrying the pitchforks and the flaming torches."

I snorted out an unexpected laugh. It wasn't very ladylike. "And I suppose you also flew away from the white knights who came to carve out your heart in order to win the love of some princess."

"Nah." Colin shook his head. "Knights are a waste of time. Ate 'em."

Penrod licked his lips. "Are they good with ketchup?"

Colin nodded. "Crunchy, too."

I couldn't help it. I laughed so hard that my stomach hurt.

"Okay, okay." I recovered and caught my breath as the Sprite and Dragon looked at me with obvious amusement. "I think I'm going to have to separate you two on future missions."

This time Colin winked at me and my belly did that fluttering thing again.

That fluttering thing was not good. Not good at all. I was in love with Adam and he was the only male who should have made me feel like Faeries were having a circus in my belly.

I cleared my throat and looked away from Colin. I pointed in the direction of the crime scene. "Over there is where the pile of human bits and pieces was discovered."

As I spoke I started walking to the location. "The police had it cleaned up, of course, but maybe the two of you can pick up something that Olivia and I, and the police missed."

Penrod and Colin both started working their way around the scene. Neither of them said a word, both males clearly intent on looking for clues. I stood beneath the tree for a few moments and studied them as they worked to see what their methods of investigation were.

Every so often Penrod would crouch, touch the snow, and tilt his head as if he was listening. His large nostrils flared and he closed his eyes as his chest rose and fell with each deep inhalation. He'd open his eyes, dip one knobbly finger into the snow, bring it to his lips, and taste it. He'd murmur something unintelligible, then move on and repeat the process.

Interesting.

Colin paced the circumference of the site. It was hard to read exactly what he was doing, but by the expression on his face and the way he would pause and concentrate, my guess was he was using whatever sixth sense he might have as a paranorm.

He continued pacing, his face an unreadable mask. Then he headed away from the scene down Cherry Walk.

Just as I opened my mouth to ask Colin where he was going, he vanished.

Just vanished.

Colin was the first Dragon I'd ever worked with. As a matter of fact, even in Otherworld I'd never met a Dragon, I'd only known of them. I hadn't known they could disappear.

I looked around the scene to see what the Sprite was up to. Penrod was gone, too. I knew he could be cloaked in a glamour, but why would he do that?

A slow chill rolled through me that was not from the seven inches of snow lying on the grass.

Flashes of memory came to me again of the time I'd been in the park when I'd been tricked then attacked by the Demon. When I'd almost died from the poison in the Demon's claws.

It was dark and eerie in the park and the memories were so much more powerful than they had been that morning.

I concentrated on relaxing so that my heart would stop its growing thunder in my chest. When it slowed, I let out a sigh of relief. Those were just memories. No Demons were here now. Not ever again.

I tilted my head and caught a hint of something riding on the breath of wind that touched my face. It was like dirty water mixed with a little bit of ammonia. Like whatever it was that Dahlia used to clean the ceramic tile floors in the PI office. But something else, too.

My heart started beating a little faster. The small hairs rose on the back of my neck. The smell was familiar in some way that I couldn't identify.

Flashes came to me, hard and fast.

A little girl crouched in bushes, hiding.

A young man slipping away into the woods, crossbow in his hands.

A beast, a creature, a *thing* shuffling the leaves as it passed the hidden girl.

It felt like a hammer blow to my chest as I snapped away from my visions.

I sucked in my breath and inhaled more of that horrible smell.

I knew what it was. *I knew it.* Yet at the same time I couldn't put my finger on it. As if my mind was trying to force me away. Trying to keep me from remembering some horrible thing.

Shrieks and screams came from somewhere north of where I stood. I didn't so much hear them as I felt them. My earth element brought them to me followed by my air magic.

"Colin! Penrod!" I called to them as I started to run in the direction of the invisible, soundless screams that were so far away that likely only I could have heard them.

I had no idea if the Dragon and Sprite heard my yells. I had to get to whoever was being attacked.

At the same time my warrior instincts kicked in, so did fear. A fear so strong that I almost stumbled.

I didn't remember ever feeling so scared. It was as if I was a child again experiencing a terror so great that I was nearly immobilized from it.

I forced myself to master that fear. At least that's what I told myself I'd done as I ran, nearly flying with the wind and my air element.

Within seconds I reached a scene that would have made me want to throw up if I wasn't in warrior mode. Adrenaline throbbed in my veins and my body sang with it.

A quick scan and I saw dead bodies, heads and limbs severed and lying in the snow.

Blood splattered everywhere.

A male that held a terrified female by her throat.

Two females and a male screaming. Trying to get away from males who had tight grips on their arms.

Several strange men wearing ragged clothing.

No, not men.

Some kind of beings.

Milk-white eyes.

Faces and hands in various stages of deterioration.

Confusion clouded my mind. I forced it away.
I drew one of my Dragon-claw daggers.
Grasped my buckler in my other hand.
Took a step forward, about to throw my buckler.
And froze.
A rush of memories assaulted me.
Immobilized me.
Memories I'd repressed from a distant past.
Zombies.
The beings were Zombies.
And six of them were coming straight for me.

TEN

Zombies.

My entire body started to shake as the six Zombies walked, stumbled, and shuffled toward me. What I'd smelled earlier was stronger now. Much stronger.

At that moment I realized the flashes of the little girl, the young man, and the creature weren't random images.

They were memories . . . memories I had repressed as a child.

That little girl had been me.

That young man had been my brother.

That creature had been a Zombie.

My body shook so hard I almost dropped my dagger. Nothing had ever affected me the way these Zombies were now.

I couldn't move. As if the Zombies had me enthralled. Gripped me with some kind of horrible magic.

The shaking grew so bad my teeth chattered. The Zombies were feet away from me now.

Blood rushed in my ears, the sound so loud that I barely heard the Zombies' whimpering moans or the screams of the captured women. My vision blurred so that the Zombies' decaying faces were not more than blobs, like opaque skulls.

A whooshing sound overhead. A roar that caused the ground to tremble. A strange, shrieking battle cry.

The smell of burned flesh.

"Nyx!" My name came to me from somewhere nearby. A powerful roar jarred me. Threw me out of my stupor.

I sucked in my breath and realized I had stopped breathing. My head swam and I struggled to regain myself.

The Zombies were so close I couldn't see beyond them.

A Zombie reached for me.

My reaction was automatic. I brought my dagger down. Bone snapped as my blade severed the Zombie's forearm.

Its moan was a wounded cry.

I didn't pause and I ran the dagger through the chest of the Zombie. It stumbled away as I jerked the blade out.

Other Zombies grabbed for me. They were so close my buckler was useless to me. I dropped it and drew my second Dragon-claw dagger.

I went after my attackers. I felt the heat of the dangerous flash in my eyes. Danger for them.

With one dagger I severed a Zombie's head from its body. Using the other dagger I stabbed another Zombie in the heart.

I planted my boot in the midsection of a third Zombie and thrust it away from me with a side kick.

I twisted the dagger, then jerked it out by the hilt.

The Zombie kept coming.

More hands reached for me.

I dropped to the ground and rolled out of reach.

A blast of heat. Close.

Cries. Shrieks. Tortured moans.

Stronger smell of burned flesh.

I pushed myself to my feet. Came to a stop.

My heart leapt to my throat and I took a step back.

Before me were the smoking remains of the Zombies that had been attacking me.

Towering behind the charred pile of bones was a scaled creature. A burst of fear tore through my gut.

Turn. Run. Get away.

A Dragon.

Huge. Towering above me.

Gold and orange-yellow scales glittered in the light coming from the park's lampposts. The Dragon was the size of a garbage truck. Each of its claws was as long as my arm, the point of each claw appearing as sharp as the blade of a sword.

A long, spiked tail swung back and forth, brushing the snow away in a slow even rhythm. A ridge ran from the back of its head to the end of its tail.

Behind the Dragon and to either side of it, trees had been uprooted and gouged by the creature's tail. And many had probably been knocked down by the scaled wings it held close to its body.

Smoke curled out of its nostrils, and the curved horns on its head and the short horn on the end of its snout were soft gold. Its large burnished gold eyes didn't reflect our surroundings. Instead, flames danced within them.

It spread out its enormous golden wings, tipped its massive head back, and roared. I flinched at the power behind its terrible cry. Gripping my daggers tight, I took another step back.

I knew it was Colin. On some level I knew the Dragon wouldn't hurt me. Rational warred with irrational. What if Colin wasn't conscious of his human side when in Dragon form?

Yet at the same time I knew Rodán and the Great Guardian would never have allowed Colin to be a Tracker if he didn't have control over his inner Dragon. Maybe he had to struggle with it, but he would win that battle within.

I stopped backing away from the Dragon and stared at it before sheathing my daggers. The creature focused on me with its large golden eyes.

The moment the Dragon moved, my breath hitched in my chest. I automatically reached for my daggers again.

But it settled down on its haunches, its tail curled around its side, enormous claws sinking into the ground that was now bare of snow.

Something moved in the corner of my eye. I scooped up my buckler, ready to fling it.

An unconscious woman was draped over Penrod's arms. The Sprite laid her on a park bench that was a little charred but still strong enough to hold her weight.

The Sprite appeared to accept the Dragon's presence as if it was nothing out of the ordinary. Penrod walked past the creature and came to stand beside me.

Penrod looked toward the woman and then at me. "We were only able to save one female."

The sick feeling in my gut made me want to throw up. My inability to perform my job had cost the other woman her life. If I hadn't been frozen with irrational fear, I could have saved both women.

Penrod shook his big head. "It was not your fault."

If mind reading was one of the Sprite's talents I was going to have to go to my father and demand that he teach me how to shield my thoughts. My father taught me talents when he felt it was time to. Well, it might be sooner than he had planned.

Gold sparkled around the Dragon. Light grew bright around the creature until it was a white-hot brilliance that I shaded my eyes from.

When the light faded away and darkness shrouded the park again, I looked back toward the Dragon.

It wasn't there anymore.

In its place was Colin.

The relief I felt at seeing him instead of the Dragon was surprising.

He still wore jeans, T-shirt, and workout shoes, but his face and arms were covered with sweat and his chest rose and fell with his each heavy breath. He pushed his damp hair away from his face and behind his shoulders.

"Better call one of your Soothsayers." Colin walked toward me. "We don't have much time."

I blinked, feeling like I was coming out of a trance. "How long have we been out here?" It seemed like hours.

Colin looked up at the cloud-bleary sky then back at me. "Ten minutes at most."

"That's it?" I unholstered my phone. "From the time I got here until this moment?" Just the time I'd been frozen at the sight of the Zombies seemed longer than that. I don't think I've ever felt so off-balance.

"Yep." Colin looked at the uprooted trees, a downed park fence, a smashed garbage can, and the shattered glass that glittered on snow from a smashed light post. "That's the drawback of being so big without much fighting space." He wiped sweat from his face with his hand. "I hope you have plant Healers."

"Seemed so much longer," I said, repeating my thought as I dialed the phone.

I explained the situation to Rodán.

One Soothsayer and one plant Healer on the way.

In the time it took Lulu and Sara to arrive, Colin, Penrod, and I only had time to take a quick inventory of the place. Assorted body parts, a dead man and a dead woman whose bodies were still intact, and an unconscious woman on a park bench. All of the Zombies had been toasted, leaving only piles of black soot on patches of grass where the snow had been melted away.

A few onlookers gathered and cell phones were in hand the moment they'd spotted the devastation.

"Why me?" Lulu's agitated grumble carried through the park at the same time every onlooker froze in place. "And why you?" she said when she came into view and spotted me.

The Manx cat Doppler, Lulu, and I never had gotten along, not since my very first PI case when she'd had to freeze an entire city block because I hadn't called Rodán fast enough. She'd really been put out over that one.

Every other time I'd seen her on a scene over the past two-plus years, she'd looked perfect. Tonight she looked like a train wreck.

Lulu's tangled hair strung out behind her as she marched toward me, rather than her locks lying over her shoulders in long, glossy blond ringlets. Her lips thinned with anger and looked almost white without her normal bright pink lipstick.

Her face was scrunched into a scowl, her skin Vampire-pale from lack of blusher or foundation. With no eye makeup and no mascara her eyes looked smaller than they usually did when she glared at me.

Instead of wearing one of her lacy frou-frou dresses she was in a pair of gray sweatpants and a stained T-shirt.

"What are you looking at, Sprite?" Lulu scowled at Penrod before she turned her glare back on me. "Another one of your stupid messes that I have to clean up." She was nearly shouting at me as she marched through the snow in rubber boots that did not complement her sweatpants. "No one else creates the kinds of disasters that you do. I don't have time for—"

Then Lulu saw Colin. She came to a stop, her mouth still open. Her cheeks reddened giving her face some color.

She only paused for a moment, staring at Colin, before she turned and fled.

Lulu wasn't Elvin or Fae, so her boots made loud slapping sounds over the ground where the snow had melted. Her steps changed to a muffled crunching sound when she reached a snow drift.

"Did I do something wrong?" Colin looked at me as Lulu ran across the park. "Is that female afraid of Dragons?"

I almost couldn't help it. I wanted to laugh so badly. "Knowing Lulu, she's mortified because she isn't, er, prepared to be seen by a hot guy." I glanced at him and grinned. "No pun intended."

Colin smiled. "Who is she?"

"The Soothsayer who froze this scene and who erases the memories of anyone who witnessed what happened here." I gestured around us. "Lulu's good at what she does . . ."

Colin raised his eyebrows in a questioning look as I trailed off from what would obviously a have been a "but" statement.

It wasn't for me to say anything bad about Lulu. It was one thing to talk about the Soothsayer with Olivia who shared in experiencing Lulu's better-than-thou attitude. The three of us had been in enough personal conflicts that it wasn't gossip if Olivia and I shared a few "insights" on Lulu from time to time.

Colin, on the other hand, didn't know Lulu, and he should be allowed to form his own opinion of the Soothsayer without me coloring his judgment. Even if she was a dolt.

Penrod ambled up to us. "I have never seen such strange beings."

"I have," Colin and I said at the same time.

I looked at him in surprise. "You've seen Zombies before?"

"In Otherworld." The Dragon studied me. "Almost a quarter of a century ago." Leave it to a Dragon to talk in centuries.

Memories started bombarding me again. Memories I'd forced away for so many years hit me, one after another.

Me as a little girl.

My only brother.

A Zombie.

"Twenty-two years ago," I said as I tried to maintain my composure. "When I was five."

"Are you all right?" Genuine concern was in Colin's eyes and in the tone of his voice. "What happened?"

No, I wasn't okay. Something inside me was sick, shaken. The black sludge I'd been feeling after my nightmares filled my belly. I still hadn't pieced everything together and I definitely wasn't ready to talk about it.

I gestured to Paranormal Task Force agents who were coming into the park. "We'd better take a look around before the PTF cleans up."

Rodán folded his hands on his Dryad-wood desk and looked at them. He had long tapered fingers. His skin was smooth, soft, golden.

When he looked at me his crystal green eyes appeared darker than normal. Almost emerald in color.

"I am taking you off the case, Nyx." Rodán's features were set, his tone firm, unyielding.

My jaw dropped and I just stared at him. For a moment there was complete silence in his den as I sat across the desk from him.

I clenched the armrests of my chair. "You did not just say that you're taking me off of the Zombie case." I managed not to flinch at the word "Zombie."

"Yes." Rodán leaned back in his chair. "I'll appoint Angel as team leader in your place."

My skin began to burn and my face grew hot. If the chair

hadn't been made of Dryad wood, the armrests would have broken off as hard as I was gripping them.

"You are too close to this one," Rodán said. "I'd like you to—"

"What do you mean I'm too close?" My voice rose in pitch as I started to rise in my chair.

"You lost a family member." Rodán's features remained calm, neutral. For the first time ever, I wanted to slap him.

"Don't tell me I'm too close to this case to do my job." I stood and clenched my hands into fists at my sides. "I'm damned good at what I do and I'll solve this."

"No." Rodán tilted his head back and studied me. "You compromised yourself tonight when you froze up. You compromised your team."

"Are you saying that I'm unprofessional? That I can't do my job?" So much anger built up inside me that I started to shake with the white heat of it. "If you take me off the team then you might as well consider this my resignation."

Surprise flickered across his features. "Nyx—"

"If you don't respect me, if you think I'm not good enough to lead this team," I said as I jerked my phone out of its holster on my weapons belt, "then I don't belong here anymore." I slammed my phone on his desk. "I won't be needing this to reach you, will I."

My eyesight blurred from the strength of my anger. How dare he?

I whirled and headed away from his desk toward the stairs and nearly ran into Rodán. With Elvin speed he'd gotten up from his chair and was now standing in front of me, grasping my upper arms.

"Nyx." His voice was low now, a soft plea that startled me. "It's not about you being unprofessional. You're the best I have. But there is no perfect Tracker who can do it all. You're simply too emotionally involved with this one, Nyx. I—we almost lost you on the last operation. I don't want to take the chance of losing you again."

All my life I'd had someone make the decisions for me before I left Otherworld. My father wouldn't allow me to participate in actual operations because not only am I a princess and his daughter, but Drow males will never work side by side with Drow females.

Here in the Earth Otherworld I'd never been held back like Rodán was trying to do to me now.

And I wasn't about to let it start.

"What about Angel?" I put my palms on his chest and pushed away from him. He let his hands fall to his sides. "Aren't you concerned about her?"

"Of course—"

"And the next op—are you going to decide it's too dangerous, too?" I had to hold back to keep from shouting at him. "Are you going to decide that I'm *compromised* in some way that will affect my ability to be a Night Tracker?"

"This is different." Rodán took a step toward me, decreasing the distance I'd just put between us. "You saw Zombies devastate your people." His tone was almost fierce with concern. "You lost your brother to them."

"That doesn't mean I can't do my job." My voice was nearly hoarse with anger.

"I told you that you're the best I have," he said. "I just don't think you belong on this op."

"I don't need this." I raised my hands. "You say I'm the best you have, yet you don't respect me enough to keep me as team leader."

"Of course I respect—"

I cut across his words. "When have I ever let you down? When have I ever not come through for you? We lost one of my best friends, Caprice, during the Demon op. Did it compromise my performance? *No.* If anything it crystallized my resolve to defeat the Demons."

"Listen to me," Rodán said in a way meant to calm me down.

"You listen to me." I don't think I'd ever been so angry as I was at that moment. "As I see it, Rodán, you have two choices."

"Nyx—"

I put my palm up, facing him, telling him to shut up with the movement. "First choice is that things stay the way they are and I lead this operation as a Night Tracker."

My hands shook and I clenched them again. "Second choice is I walk away and I'll never track again." My words sounded cold, hard, and that was exactly how I'd meant them. "I'll work on the Zombie case on my own as a PI. Either way I will work on it."

"Wait—"

"I've loved working for you," I said. "I've loved being a Tracker. But I don't need this. I've never been more shocked by one of your decisions. I don't need to work for someone who doesn't have confidence in me." I put my hands on my hips above my weapons belt. "Whatever decision you make right this instant will determine exactly what it is I'm going to do."

I clamped my mouth shut to keep myself from saying anything else while I waited for him to speak. My heart thundered and my skin prickled.

"That is no choice." He looked resigned. "I can't lose you. I won't lose you."

I raised my chin but some of my anger started to slide away, and my tone calmed a bit. "Rodán, you know I'm the best Tracker to lead this case. You know that. But you're removing me for your personal reasons. A fear for my well being."

Before he could say anything, I continued. "This isn't right. None of this. You're replacing me with Angel, who is a good Tracker but doesn't have the record I do. I'm not the one who's compromised by emotions and personal feelings.

"I understand you care and at some level I appreciate that," I continued, "but it's you who must make decisions for the good of all. You can't make a choice to put someone in charge who's not the very best."

"Perhaps my decision is driven in part by my concern for you," Rodán said. "But Nyx, you did lose a family member to the Zombies and it resulted in your freezing up tonight."

Rodán paused. "But I also know that you're right. You have never let me down. You have always come through in the end, have always gotten the job done."

I took a deep breath. "Then what is your answer? Am I a Tracker or not?"

Rodán's eyes met and held mine for a long moment. "Everything will remain as it was," he said, his tone quiet. "You will continue to lead this operation."

I didn't look away or show how his statement affected me. The relief that poured through me.

"As it should be," Rodán said, "it's up to you and your team to solve this case."

ELEVEN

The following morning I was still furious. It didn't matter that Rodán had relented and I was the team leader for the op. What mattered was that he had tried to take me off the case entirely . . . that he actually doubted me.

The fact that we now knew Zombies were in the Earth Otherworld didn't help my mood at all.

Fae bells jingled as Olivia pushed the door open then let it close behind her. At once I wondered if we might need to steer clear of one another—if her scowl and her T-shirt were indicative of her mood today.

I HAVE PMS AND A HANDGUN. ANY QUESTIONS?

Nah. I couldn't let it go. I raised my hand as she tugged off her Mets jacket, then tossed it onto the credenza. "Ma'am," I said. "I have a question."

Olivia saw me glance at her chest. "The shirt speaks for itself."

"But it asks if I have a question," I said in a tone of complete innocence. "And I do."

"Shoot." Olivia touched the grip of the Sig in her side holster. "Or I will." It was obvious to me she was struggling to maintain her irritated facade and not laugh.

"Do you have another one of those shirts I can borrow?" I asked. "Except make it one about a boss and a handgun."

Olivia's expression grew serious as she approached me. "What's up? Something between you and Rodán?"

I tried not to scowl. Didn't work. "After our team met with Rodán and went over the Zombie attack last night, Rodán and I had a little talk."

"Yeah." She nodded. "He said he wanted to speak with you alone in his office. So what happened?"

I ground my teeth before I said, "He wanted to take me off this op."

"What?" Her eyes narrowed. "Why the hell would Rodán do that?"

Without going into complete detail, I told Olivia what Rodán had said and my own threat to quit if he didn't change his mind.

"Stupid." Olivia shook her head. "I can't believe he'd let his emotions get in the way of his job." She paused and cocked her head. "Come to think of it, I didn't realize Rodán even has emotions."

I rolled my eyes at that statement. "It's because of our personal history and because of what happened during the Vampire op."

"I know." She leaned her hip against her desk. "But it's not like him to be so unprofessional."

"Agreed." Just talking about it with Olivia released some of the pressure that had been building inside of me. "This isn't something I'd tell any of the other Trackers."

"Of course not." Olivia folded her arms across her chest. "That's what close friends and partners are for."

I gave a sigh that was still filled with frustration. "Now that I got that off my chest, where are we going to start today?"

Olivia pushed away from the desk. "Zombies, huh?"

Again the word "Zombies" made me shudder. After last night I had fresh images to go along with it. "Unfortunately."

"You've never mentioned having a brother. Why?" Instead of going behind her own desk and sitting in her office chair, she settled in one of the chairs in front of my desk. "Start there, then tell me what happened to you both in Otherworld."

I should have expected that request from her. But thanks to my anger at Rodán, I wasn't prepared for it or the sick feeling in my stomach that I now felt.

With my thumb and forefinger I rubbed my temples. "I don't really want to talk about it." The moment I let that out of my mouth I knew I was in trouble.

Olivia leaned forward and the message on her T-shirt stretched across her generous breasts. "Excuse me?"

"Sorry." I flopped back in my chair and stared at the ceiling before I looked at her again. "I just don't know if I can talk about it."

"No excuses." Her dark eyes had fire in them. "Give me the facts."

"Facts." I sighed and rubbed my temples again. "Facts."

"You're stalling."

I folded my hands on my desk. Took a deep breath. "My brother, Tristan, was twenty-two years older than me. His mother was Drow and she died during childbirth."

Olivia waited for me to continue.

"My father met my mother a year before I was born." I smiled as I remembered what my brother was like when I was a little girl, a youngling.

"Tristan could have been resentful of a human step-mother," I said. "He could have been resentful of me—especially because our father spoiled me so much." I paused. "But he wasn't. Tristan was special."

With a nod from Olivia I went on.

"My brother spoiled me almost as much as my father did." I felt a harsh prickling sensation behind my eyes as I spoke. "He wasn't a warrior like our father, but an artist. He was gentle, thoughtful. But he was also fiercely loyal, which is what ultimately led to his . . . loss."

If I had tear ducts like humans, I would have cried right then, the pain was so great. Memory after memory of all the things Tristan had done for me and with me kept coming to me in waves. Things I hadn't thought of in so long.

"Why haven't you told me anything about this before?" Olivia asked, her voice low, quiet.

"When we lost him I was only five." I swallowed down the huge lump gathered in my throat. "When the Zombies started attacking my people and taking some away."

"I still don't understand why you didn't tell me," she said.

"Everything that happened during that time traumatized me and I repressed all of these memories." I shook my head. "I loved Tristan so much that I didn't want to remember what happened. Thinking about him hurt." I met Olivia's eyes. "It hurt so badly that I didn't want to think about him or what happened anymore."

"So you forgot about him?" Olivia gave me an almost incredulous look. "Forgot you ever had a brother?"

I know she didn't mean it the way it sounded, but her words still had a sting to them. "No, I didn't forget." I was whispering now, my throat hoarse with tears I couldn't shed. "I could never forget Tristan. It just hurt too much to think about him. To talk about him. So I haven't."

"That's no way to honor the dead." Olivia's statement surprised me. "You should celebrate what time you did have with your brother."

I stared at her like she'd grown horns. I could almost swear I saw points peeking out of her dark hair. "Since when did you get philosophical?"

Her expression didn't change. "Tell me about the Zombies in Otherworld."

Emotions wound so tight inside me that my stomach hurt. Pain, anger, even fear.

"Honestly, I don't remember a lot." I pushed my hand through my hair. "I've been trying to connect a few dots, but it's so hard. I'm going to have to talk with my father about it when I go to Otherworld over Christmas."

"What *do* you remember, Nyx?" Olivia's tone was forceful, her expression intense. "You need to separate your emotions long enough for us to try to piece some of this together and figure out how to stop what's happening."

I nodded. "You're right."

"Of course I am." She said it with a straight face. "I'm always right."

With a slight smile, I said, "In some deluded way you probably believe that, too."

She took on an even more serious expression. Her cop

face. "You were five. I get that. But you might remember more than you think you do."

Despite my father trying to shelter me from it, being the daughter of a king meant I'd heard about and had been around things that related to what had happened during that time. No doubt more than most younglings my age.

"Father and his closest advisors were having meetings," I said. "More than normal." My brow wrinkled as I thought about it. "My father wouldn't let me watch the warriors train and I was so upset. He said it was different now. His men were preparing to fight an enemy, not just sharpening their skills."

While she listened, Olivia leaned back in her chair and rested her right ankle on her opposite knee. Today she wore her black Keds that matched her black T-shirt and probably matched both of our moods this morning.

"I didn't understand what was going on and that bothered me." I could remember my five-year-old frustration at being left out. "Father wouldn't talk about it with me but I heard him speak in a low voice to Mother. Sometimes I followed him and overheard him talking to his men. But I still didn't understand."

My father had always allowed me to learn everything he felt I was old enough to learn. Tristan had little interest in anything but art, so I think Father enjoyed teaching me what my brother didn't care for.

"Tell me what you did learn." Olivia's impatience was starting to show.

"Right." I gave a nod. Yes, I was stalling. "At night when our people went out, some would disappear, never come back.

"Father and his men left on hunting parties each night to try and find any males and females had gone missing," I said. "The warriors would come back from these excursions grim, sometimes battle-worn. And sometimes not every warrior would make it home."

"What happened on these outings?" she asked.

"The second time they came back from an outing was when I first heard the word Zombie. The Drow equivalent of the word." My stomach churned. "My father and his advisors had a meeting. They talked about beings that had been stealing both Light and Dark Elves. About Elves being found torn apart."

I caught my breath then let it out. "Then they talked about the Zombies. Described them as beings with rotting flesh, sightless eyes. Beings that had one mission . . . and that mission was to kill. Destroy."

Olivia didn't say anything, so I went on.

"My father and his warriors also talked about beings who looked like Elves but different. Like humans, yet different." I felt the same confusion now that I did then.

"So I guess there was more to it than the Zombies like the ones Colin, Penrod, and I fought last night," I said. "But I'm going to have to ask my father because I really don't remember anything more about that."

"Tell me about your brother," Olivia said. "What happened to him?"

I closed my eyes. Tristan's image was so faint that I could barely remember what he looked like. When I opened my eyes I said, "Tristan's best friend was murdered by the Zombies. My brother was so upset that he took up arms to go out with the next hunting party."

My head was nearly swimming from the memories pressing at me. "I snuck out and followed them. My father didn't know, but Tristan caught me," I said. "He made me hide in a bush, made me promise not to follow him.

"When he left me there—that's when I saw the Zombie." I swallowed and felt so sick inside I wanted to throw up. "It looked hideous. I had a sword made for me and I can remember wanting to run the Zombie through with my small blade. But I remembered what Tristan said and I stayed hidden."

Olivia raised her eyebrows. "Until . . ."

She knew me too well. I never had been good at doing what I was told to do if I thought I could help.

"I saw the Zombie going in the direction my brother was going and I got a really bad feeling." I held my hand to my belly as that same feeling gripped my insides. "So I followed."

Olivia's gaze didn't leave my face as I spoke.

"The Zombie had a lead on me and my legs were short so I fell behind," I said. "I was still a youngling and I didn't have my Drow speed yet.

"I almost stumbled into a clearing, but hid in the bushes the moment I saw light." The memory of the brightness of the light was clear enough to make me feel like flinching now. "There was a doorway in the air. On our side it was night . . . but on the other side it was a sunny day in some place I'd never seen.

"I was so confused, especially when I saw my brother standing at that doorway," I said. "He was a hundred percent Drow with no human in him, unlike me.

"But he was standing in full sunlight and nothing happened to him." I shook my head, still unable to understand. "He didn't burn away like Dark Elves do if they are exposed to sunlight."

Olivia had her head tilted as she listened. "What did you see happen to your brother?"

I pushed my hair out of my face again. "It was all a blur from there. I saw some kind of dancing light between my brother and another male.

"The next thing I knew my brother was kneeling in front of a tall elder, beside the Zombie," I said. "The elder wasn't one of the Elves. I don't know what he was, but he had long red hair that was turning gray." I tried to focus, tried to remember. "I think my brother called the elder 'Amory,' but I'm not certain.

"After the elder touched my brother on his head, my brother stood—then fell." My chest hurt and I clenched my fists to it. "I was ready to jump out of my hiding place when the Zombie scooped my brother's body up and carried him through the doorway of light."

My palms started to sting and I realized I was digging my nails into them. "The elder, and the Zombie carrying my brother's body, vanished." I looked at my friend. "They just vanished, Olivia. The door went away. That was it. He was *gone*."

"How do you know he was dead?" she asked. "Maybe he just fainted."

I put my face into my hands and my words were muffled when I said, "Tristan never came back."

"Hey." Olivia's voice was firm and I drew myself back to the present. "We'll get this figured out, Nyx." She scooted her chair up to my desk. "You need to get your head engaged now. You kicked Zombie ass last night. You'll do it again. And we will figure out what's going on and how to stop it."

"I know we will." I took a deep breath. "Starting now."

"Good." She got up from the seat in front of my desk and headed to her own desk and office chair. "I'd hate to have to kick *your* ass just to snap you out of feeling the way you have been."

I was quiet for a moment. "Do you think Rodán was right? That I'm too close to this?"

"Bullshit." Olivia plopped down in her chair. "He knows that you can separate emotion from your work." She braced her forearms on top of bright green sticky notes covering her desktop. "You're a professional."

"What about this?" I raised my hands. "I practically fell apart talking to you about it."

"We talked it out," she said and I nodded. "You dug out information from your memories." I nodded again. "And now you're ready to take care of business."

"Yes," I said.

"Well then." Olivia moved herself in front of her computer and looked away from me as if the conversation was over. "Get on it."

I smiled.

And started taking care of business.

TWELVE

When I turned to face my large-screen monitor, my current Bon Jovi ringtone came from the cell phone in my purse. I reached into the cubbyhole I kept my purse in and fumbled until I found the phone.

ADAM BOYD. I smiled as I looked at his name on the screen. My body relaxed, some of the anger and pain dissipating as I answered the phone.

"Hey," I said.

"Hey yourself." The warmth in Adam's voice sent heat throughout me. "How's your morning?"

"Right now I'd rather talk about anything but work." I put my elbow on my desk and rested my chin in my palm. "Like when I'm going to see you next."

"I have witnesses to interview and leads to follow up on a case, and a meeting to go to late this afternoon. I don't know when I'll be free," Adam said. "We'll figure something out."

Adam always figured it out. He always made time for me.

"What time are you picking me up to go to your sister's wedding reception tomorrow?" Nervousness and even a little fear made me jittery at the thought of meeting his family. Immediate family members and a few friends had gone to the wedding on a Caribbean cruise liner, so the reception was for friends and family who hadn't been able to make the wedding cruise.

"I'll swing by about one-thirty," Adam said.

"I'm taking the whole day off." Zombies be damned.

"Olivia and I are closing the office for Christmas Eve and Christmas Day. We'll be back to work on Monday."

"Are you looking forward to going to Otherworld to see your parents?" he asked.

Of course he couldn't see me but I caught myself nodding. "Yes. The last time I was in Otherworld was after that Demon attack."

"That was only a night or two," he said.

"It wasn't exactly quality time." I shuddered. "Nearly dying kind of put a damper on things."

"Scared us all, Nyx," Adam said quietly, and I wished I hadn't said anything.

"Didn't help when my father tried to pull the king-laying-down-the-law on me," I said. "I never mentioned it, but my father demanded that I stay in Otherworld because he thought New York City was too dangerous for me."

"You're an adult," Adam said.

"Tell him that." I shook my head and wondered if Adam and I should figure out how to do a video call. "My father is at least two millennia in age, and to him at twenty-seven I might as well be a youngling. I mean a child."

"He is around two thousand years old?" Disbelief was in Adam's voice. "You're kidding me, right?"

"No one, except maybe the Great Guardian, knows how long Light Elves and Dark Elves can live." I switched the phone to my other ear. Should have put on my wireless earpiece, but holding the phone made me feel closer to Adam. "That's because no Elves that we know of have passed to Summerland from old age or illness. The only way Elves have died is if they are murdered or killed in battle." And both were rare.

"Whoa." Adam sounded like he had a hard time believing me. Couldn't blame him. Wasn't like every day you met someone who was two thousand years old. "So will you live that long?"

"I don't know," I said. "My mother is human, so I could take after that half of my makeup and only live as long as a human would." I hadn't really given it a lot of thought. "Or I could take after my father and live for who knows how long. Maybe it'll be a combination—live longer than humans do, but eventually die."

"So your mother . . ."

"Humans live longer in Otherworld," I said. "She could make it a century or two, but eventually she will pass on."

"Tomorrow you'll get to meet a bunch of true mortals." Adam had a smile in his voice. "Can't wait to introduce you to my parents, and my brother and sister."

"I'm looking forward to it." A smile was in my tone, too.

"Need to get going," Adam said. "I'll give you a call later."

"See you," I said.

"See you."

I disconnected and set the phone on my desk. Olivia was looking at me. "Adam doesn't really know a whole lot about you, does he," she stated.

"A little of my life at a time goes a long way," I said.

"Sure does," she said as my phone rang again.

This time the screen showed RODÁN. I frowned, then realized I wasn't really mad anymore. Maybe a little, but a part of me realized where he had been coming from, even if it was wrong.

"Nyx," Rodán said when I answered. "Lawan is missing."

"What?" My heart started pounding and my throat grew dry. "Did anyone see anything?"

"Lawan left to track her territory last night," he said.

"The Financial District," I said.

"She never checked in this morning." Concern was in Rodán's voice. "I sent out several PTF agents to investigate her territory and the surrounding areas, as well as her apartment."

"The Paranormal Task Force isn't as thorough as a Night Tracker." I pushed my chair away from my desk. "I'll go look for her now."

"I didn't finish." Rodán's voice didn't sound so calm this morning. "The PTF did find bodies when they were looking for Lawan. Several paranorms. Dopplers."

Cold washed over my skin. "Where?"

He told me the location and I held my hand to my belly, pressing against the sick feeling I'd had ever since we discovered that Zombies were behind the massacres.

When I told him I'd head there now, Rodán said, "I need you and Olivia to run down all of the angles and leads you can on your end. Pick two Trackers from your team to investigate the scene."

"Are you trying to hold me back, Rodán?" I said as I continued to stand at my desk.

"No," Rodán said. "I need you where you are because only you and Olivia can dig deep enough to find answers and angles that no one else can see."

It didn't appease me, but I didn't argue. What he said was true. We were the only ones who could do what needed to be done.

"Angel, Ice, and Joshua," I said. "I'll call them now."

I didn't know if Dragons needed time to recover so I wasn't going to call Colin. I'd ask him about it later. And Penrod was a Sprite, so him in daylight around norms? Not happening.

My jaws hurt from how hard I clenched my teeth before I spoke. "We've got to find Lawan."

"We will," Rodán said before he disconnected the call.

I stared at my phone and remembered how Lawan had looked last night and that she thought she was being watched. *Had* someone been watching her?

"What happened to Lawan?" Olivia's firm, but concerned voice cut into my thoughts.

I told her everything Rodán had said to me.

"Damn." Olivia shook her head. "We've got to find Lawan. Those sonofabitch Zombies better not have hurt her."

I called Joshua, Angel, and Ice and told them what they needed to do.

When I finished I sat down hard in my chair. "It's happening here. Just like Otherworld."

The clack of Olivia's keyboard was loud as she stared at her monitor. "Not only do we need to look for patterns, but we need to see if there have been a higher number of unexplained disappearances than usual."

"I'll search the Internet for mentions of missing persons via reports, articles, et cetera," I said.

Olivia's gaze flicked from one side of her screen to the other. "I'm accessing police reports now."

It didn't take long before I realized something very strange was going on. I kept up my search, and the more I did, the more I found.

After a good two hours, my eyes were crossing.

"I think I've had it for the day," Olivia said at the same time I came to the same conclusion. "At least as far as staring at a computer screen for hours."

"Agreed." I motioned for her to check out the information on my monitor. "Take a look at this."

She pointed toward a wall where I had mounted swords, daggers, bows with quivers of diamond-tipped arrows, and other weapons forged by the Dark Elves. I looked at the wall and back at her.

"You keep promising you're going to get rid of those dust collectors so that we'll have room for high tech instead of medieval," she said. "Then we'll be able to put all of the information we've gathered in one place to review together." She shook her head. "Dark Ages around here."

"Believe me, I know Dark Ages and this isn't it. You should try living in Otherworld." I leaned back in my chair and rubbed the bridge of my nose. "As far as remodeling, the cases we've taken on over the past couple of months have kept me—us—a little busy."

"Demons, Werewolves, Vampires, Zombies, oh my," Olivia said in a singsong tone.

Instinctively I flinched at the word "Zombie." Had to stop doing that. "Do me a favor and don't say the 'Z' word for a while," I said.

"What? Zombie?" She batted her eyes in a look of innocence. "You don't want me to say Zombie? Because if you don't want me to say Zombie, I'll try really, really hard not to say Zombie."

"You're evil," I said.

She cackled like the witch in *The Wizard of Oz*. "At least I'm not a Zombie."

I narrowed my eyes and glared at her. "I'll find out if it can be arranged."

"Now that we're through talking about Zombies . . ." she said, and I glared more. ". . . Let's talk about that wall. If you don't take care of getting what we need, I will."

"Enjoy." I waved off her complaint and threat and was very happy to have her stop teasing me. "I'll make sure the weapons are moved, you take care of the rest."

Olivia gave me one of her devious smiles. "Just what I've been waiting for."

"Without going overboard," I hurried to add, realizing my mistake and knowing it was too late to go back.

"Don't worry." Her expression was one of someone who'd just been given the key to the Golden City. "I'll take care of everything."

Groan.

She tapped the side of her head. "Starting with headsets. I can't believe you haven't invested in them sooner."

"In the meantime." I gave my screen a half-turn so that Olivia could see it better when she came up beside me. "Take a look at this."

I ignored the smug look on her face in her triumph over bringing the firm's technology up to date and I started pointing to the various windows on my screen.

"All of this is amazing," I said. "Here we have a Navy admiral who couldn't be found for two days and then he was back. He claimed to have been ill."

"Sounds familiar . . ." Olivia said.

"This is Bill Huntington, a Fortune 500 exec who is worth a few billion. Give or take several million or so." I looked at Olivia. "He was missing for two days. No one had any idea what had happened. Family members were prepared to receive a ransom note."

"Then he showed up after a two-day absence," Olivia said. "Said he was ill."

"Right." I nodded. "It gets interesting when government officials start to disappear, then reappear."

"You're kidding me." Olivia's triumph in her victory over getting to do a high-tech makeover on the office seemed to be forgotten for the moment. "Who?"

"Senator Dan Bourne to start with." I rocked back in my chair. "Along with foreign ambassador Deb Ludlum and U.S. Representative Jason Roberts."

Olivia narrowed her brows. "Any others?"

"In our very own nation's capital," I said.

"Washington, D.C." Olivia shook her head, amazement on her features. "This is crazy. Nuts."

"Beyond crazy." I pointed to four more windows on my computer screen. "Each of these windows has information on a high-ranking official or prominent businessman or businesswoman. A judge, a bank executive, an Army general, and a police commissioner. There are also the articles on the same attacks we've been seeing. Not always but often the Zombie attacks are close to where the disappearance occurred."

I continued, "The fact that these attacks started at the same time as the mysterious disappearance and reappearance of these individuals, and the close proximity of the attacks often to the disappearance, tells me something." I frowned as something clenched inside me. "My gut tells me that these cases are related."

"And no one has noticed this pattern of Houdini acts?" Olivia said. "That's unbelievable."

I picked up a pencil and tapped the end on a bright pink sticky notepad. "When I dug deeper, I discovered that each case has been kept very hush-hush. I believe that someone in the government knew of the disappearances but didn't want to panic people. It reminds me the way the government treated the UFOs in this world. Cover up and shut up."

"Found similar information in police reports and other databases." Olivia jerked her thumb toward her computer monitor. "Something bad is going down. I think it goes way beyond a few Zombie attacks."

"All of the cases have been spread so far apart that no one has been connecting the dots," I said.

"Consider the dots connected." Olivia rocked back on her heels and put her hands in her back pockets. "Now to figure out if there are any more dots and what kind of picture we've just made."

"Hold on." I got up from my chair and went to a map of the U.S. and one of New York City that we'd put up on one wall some time ago.

"Hold onto what?" Olivia said in her smartass tone.

I opened a drawer in the map table beneath the maps and rummaged through the drawer until I found one for Washington, D.C. I pinned that map on the wall next to the one for New York City.

"Speaking of dots." I stared at the maps. "I'd like to see what the patterns look like on these."

"That's something else we'll be able to remodel when I take over," Olivia said and I rolled my eyes. "With a wall of monitors, we can bring up several electronic maps at a time. Forget this manual stuff."

"For now we'll just have to do it the old-fashioned way." I reached the wall and picked up a pushpin from a tray on top of the map table. "Start giving me locations."

Olivia did and I pushed pins in each area where we'd found reports of attacks. "New York City and D.C., mostly around financial and government centers." I frowned. "With a few random areas."

"Those aren't random areas," Olivia said. "Those are places where paranorms tend to hang out."

She was right. "So we need to focus our teams on these areas in the city. Rodán can notify the D.C. Trackers."

I returned to my desk, planted my palms to either side of my monitor. I looked at the computer screen then Olivia again. "Could Lawan's disappearance have anything to do with whatever happened to all of these people?"

"If she shows up in two days claiming to have been ill, then we'll see," Olivia said.

I straightened and she moved aside as I walked around my desk and started pacing the length of our office. My heels clicked on the tile floor and Olivia's chair squeaked as she returned to her chair.

"I do need to sit down with my father and have him give me more details about what happened in Otherworld twenty-two years ago," I said. "I don't remember a whole lot about it."

Olivia's tone was dry. "That should be fun, getting King Ciar to tell you that kind of information."

She'd never met my father but she knew enough about him from me that she had a pretty good idea of just how difficult that task might be.

I touched my collar as I paced. "And to get him to talk with me about Tristan will be even harder.

"It started out slow in Otherworld, I think." I continued pacing as I spoke. "But things escalated. Got worse."

"What happened that made the problem go away in Otherworld?" Olivia asked.

"I don't know." I moved my hand away from my collar. "Not long after Tristan . . . was gone . . . it stopped. Just stopped."

"According to our research, I think it's possible we won't be so lucky." Olivia tapped her computer monitor before she went on.

"Humans don't have magic like you do in Otherworld. That might have been why it stopped," she said. "You had ways there of fighting the Zombies and whatever was causing the disappearances. Those skills and abilities your people have in Otherworld could have chased off whatever was responsible for the deaths and missing persons."

"That's one theory." I wiped my palms on my slacks as I slowly crossed the room and then back again. "I agree that something was different in Otherworld than it is in this Earth Otherworld. I need more information to give us a better idea of what happened there and what we're looking at here."

"Regardless of what you learn from your father," she said

as she started tapping a red pencil on her desk, "I really believe we're on the cusp of an epidemic."

"You could be right." I stopped pacing and looked at Olivia. "If you are, we could very well be running out of time."

THIRTEEN

"I don't know if I can do this." I crossed my arms beneath my breasts as I stared at myself in the mirror. "What if Adam's family doesn't like me?"

My reflection didn't answer, of course, and I brushed down the lines of my simple plum Armani jersey dress with my palms and discovered my hands were shaking.

Nerves made me feel like Faeries were being juggled in my belly. A lot like the Sprite juggler had done when he was in the talent competition. Yep. Spinning, colorful Faeries tucked into ball shapes and releasing sparkling Faerie dust as they tumbled.

I thought I was going to be sick.

I tracked down Metamorphs, rogue Werewolves, Vamps, Demons, and any other kind of bad paranorm there was . . . but I was scared to death to meet Adam's family and see a few norms at a wedding reception.

Adam's familiar knock sent another burst of tingling through my abdomen, but this one was caused by excitement at seeing him rather than almost terror at meeting his family.

My four-inch heels clicked on the wood flooring as I went to the door. I'd gone all out when I went shopping for an outfit for the reception. A princess had to dress her very best when meeting her boyfriend's family for the first time.

"So beautiful," Adam said the moment he got a look at

me. He stepped through the doorway, brought me into his arms, and kissed me. "You look unbelievable."

I felt the press of his suit against my body as he held me. When he raised his head he was smiling and I smiled back at him.

As I stepped away, I ran my gaze over him from the shine of his black dress shoes to his tamed brown hair. "I've never seen you dressed up like this." I ran my finger along the lapel. "You look amazing."

Then I gave him an evil grin. "First chance I get, though, I'm going to mess up your hair. It's too perfect." I stopped and reached for his hands. "Do we need to go over my 'story' in case they ask?"

Adam brought my hands to his mouth and kissed my knuckles. "We'll keep it as simple as we can."

"I work as an assistant to a private investigator, which is how we met." I started to recite the story we came up with. "If they ask who, I give them Olivia's name and say she's not in the book, takes referrals only."

"Yes." Adam brought me close to him. "Your parents just moved from New York City to Alaska."

"Anchorage," I said. "And I haven't been there yet to see their new place but plan to soon."

"You grew up right here in the city and went to a private school for girls," Adam said.

I laughed. "Okay. I know just the school. But then you rescue me so that I don't have to answer more questions."

"Get your coat," he said still smiling. "It's cold as hell—I mean it's cold out there."

The cold wouldn't bother me that much, but I grabbed one of my long dress coats from my closet. I had already selected a dressy clutch to carry my ID, credit cards, and cash in before going back into the living room where Adam was waiting.

We closed the door behind us and he took my arm and walked with me down the steps.

Adam had parked on the street in front of the apartment

building. Before I could start to walk down the wet sidewalk, he scooped me up in his arms.

I gave a little cry of surprise and instinctively wrapped my arms around his neck. He carried me to his SUV and I laughed. I didn't argue that I could walk on my own. It was nice being held by him. Strangely it made me feel secure, protected.

Once he had me settled in my seat and he was in his, Adam pulled his SUV on the road and drove it the short distance to West Fifty-eighth Street.

When he neared the Hudson Hotel my stomach pitched. "The wedding reception is at the Hudson?" I asked, hoping it wasn't.

Falling twenty-four floors from the top of the Hudson after being blasted through a window by a Master Vampire didn't bring a whole lot of warm and fuzzy memories.

Adam glanced at me as he started to park the SUV. "You okay, Nyx?"

I did my best to smile. "As long as reception is not in the penthouse."

At first Adam looked confused, but then he said, "Damn, Nyx." He reached out and touched my face with his fingers. "Kasey gave me the invitation weeks ago. I knew it was in the city, but I didn't actually open the invitation until last night," he said. "I didn't make the connection. Are you still okay with going?"

I drew in a deep breath. "I can't let Volod affect my life any more than he already has. I *won't* let him."

Adam cupped the back of my head and leaned forward to kiss me. "We'll make up some new memories. Good memories."

I smiled. "I'm fine with that."

Once Adam had parked and we were walking into the hotel, not-so-good memories came at me anyway. My team had used the stairwell to get to the penthouse where Volod had been living. So the stairwell, penthouse, and the asphalt beneath the window I'd been blasted through were my only experiences at the hotel. I hadn't spent any time in the heart of the Hudson.

The hotel itself was unique, unlike any other I'd been in. It was what the hotel called cheap chic. "Stylish, young at heart, and utterly cool," per the brochure I picked up.

None of those words applied to the Master Vampire who had made the penthouse his lair. An interesting choice for him.

I'd only picked up the brochure to have something to hold onto after we checked our coats. Next thing I knew I'd crumpled it when my thoughts turned to Volod. I stuck it in my clutch and gripped it tight instead.

The hotel's unique use of lighting and colors was nothing but a blur to me as we headed to the banquet room for the reception.

When we walked into the crowded room, I wanted to turn and run all the way back to my apartment. I might have if Adam didn't have such a great hold on my hand.

Adam smiled, greeted, and shook hands with one person after another. Soft background music played as he introduced me as his date then moved on after telling each person, couple, or group that it was great to see them and that he had to find his parents and sister. I did my best to smile and wondered how I was going to get through the reception with all of these humans.

It was an entirely bizarre feeling for me to be around only humans in an intimate environment, with no other paranorms. Now I knew how Olivia and Adam must feel every time they went to the Pit.

"Finally." Adam drew me beside him.

A hot flush from sheer nerves slid under my skin as we walked toward a good-looking man with graying hair and a beautiful blond woman. They both appeared to be in their mid-fifties.

"Mom, Dad," Adam said as he introduced me. "This is Nyx." He turned to me. "Nyx, this is my mom, Laura, and my dad, Ron."

"Adam told us about you," Laura said as she took my

hand in between her palms and squeezed it. "It is so good to meet someone Adam cares so much for."

Heat rose to my face and out of the corner of my eye I noticed that Adam was having the same reaction. But the thought that he'd talked to his parents about me was a great feeling.

Ron shook my hand and smiled and I smiled back at him. I murmured how nice it was to meet them both.

When Laura asked me where I was from and Ron asked the specifics, I had the answers. With Adam at my side this was going to be all right.

"Honey," Laura said to Adam, "will you please go up to the bar and get me a sea breeze?" Maybe it wasn't going to be so all right, I thought when she turned to me and said, "What would you like Adam to get for you?" because it meant that Adam had to leave us.

"Dry martini with three olives." Adam recited my favorite drink and I nodded. He looked a little concerned about leaving me when he said, "I'll be right back."

Wait, I wanted to cry out as he left me with his parents. Instead I made myself smile at Ron and Laura.

Commence the drilling.

Thanks to practicing my answers with Adam, I did all right as they asked me what I did for a living, where I worked, and about my parents. Easy enough.

"They would like that, I'm sure," I replied to Laura when she said they would love to meet my parents the next time they came to the city.

My mom was human, so that wouldn't be a problem— unless someone asked her about Alaska. However, I didn't think anyone could get past my Drow father's long sapphire-blue hair, light blue skin, and silvery-gray eyes. It was such an alien thought, I wasn't sure whether to frown or smile at the image of anyone I knew in the norm world meeting my father. Not that I wasn't proud of my father. It would just be . . . weird.

I wondered what Adam would think when—or if—he met my parents. How strange it would be to take my human lover to the belowground realm of the Dark Elves. Just thinking about it made me feel uncomfortable, which surprised me but shouldn't have. I couldn't picture Adam sitting down and having a mug of ale with a bunch of Drow warriors, including my father.

When Adam returned with our drinks I let my breath out in a rush of relief.

"Adam told me that you grew up here locally. Where did you go to high school?" Laura asked with an animated smile as she took her sea breeze from Adam. "When did you graduate?"

"A private school for girls," I said after I took a sip of my martini. I told her the year Adam said I would have graduated if I had grown up in Earth Otherworld.

"A private all-girls school—was it The Château by chance?" Laura asked.

"Yes." I couldn't think fast enough and the word was out of my mouth before I could stop it.

Laura perked up. "What a small, small world. My close friend Marcy's daughter, Jennifer Dubois, went there. Do you recognize the name?"

"Umm, no. No, I don't think I do." My face started to heat up and I felt an instinctive urge to flee.

"Well, I'm almost certain that she graduated that same year, because I remember not being able to attend the graduation because of my surgery that year. You must know her, the school is not that big."

I almost coughed out my next sip of martini. "Uh—"

"Mom, Nyx and I need to—" Adam sounded almost desperate to leave.

"Jennifer is here somewhere." Adam's mom stood on her toes and peered around the room. "This is wonderful. We can reconnect you."

"Mrs. Boyd." A man with a chef's hat caught Laura's attention. "There is a problem with the canapés."

"Oh!" Laura's eyes widened and she swung her gaze back to me. "I will be right back and we'll find Jennifer."

And then she was gone.

"There's Kasey, my sister." Adam gestured with his beer bottle toward a pretty blonde at the back of the room who looked a lot like Laura. "I want to introduce you to her and her new husband, Jacob," he said to me, "then we'll find my brother, Mike, too."

"Go see your sister." Ron patted Adam on the back and winked at me. "I'll make sure your mother doesn't get too excited over the appetizers," he said before he walked after his wife.

"Adam, that was way too close." I leaned close to him so that no one could hear me. "I can't believe she knows someone who graduated from the same high school I supposedly did. And on top of that, the person just happens to be *here*."

Adam looked a little grim and I wondered if my martini stem would snap if I gripped it any tighter. "I can't keep this going," I said. "There's too much information to track too quickly. It's getting so awkward."

He continued to study me as I talked, looking like the Adam I had known for so long and had fallen in love with— while at the same time like someone I didn't know at all.

"What do I do when she brings Jennifer here?" I set my martini glass on a tray before I could spill the drink on my dress. "Say I hit my head when I landed after being thrown from the penthouse of this hotel . . . and ever since I have been saying stupid things that make no sense?"

"We'll figure it out," Adam said, but he didn't look happy.

"I don't know how this works," I said. "I wish we could just sit and tell them the real story, but of course we can't." I had already spotted the exits to make my escape when Laura came back with some woman in tow. "I'm afraid if I have another conversation with your parents or brother or sister, I won't be able to keep it all straight."

Adam glanced at me and there was a look in his eyes that made me feel like something was off. Maybe even wrong. His smile seemed a little forced as he set his empty beer bottle on a tray.

"Okay, this time I won't leave you alone." Adam clasped my hand. "I'll control this."

I nodded my okay as he led me toward his sister.

Kasey was standing with a man who was my height, a few inches taller than his wife, and a few inches shorter than Adam's six-two. They both looked a little tan, like they'd been in the sun recently. Which of course they had, on their wedding cruise.

Adam looked apprehensive when he introduced me to his sister and her new husband.

My face felt funny from smiling so much as I greeted them. "Congratulations on your marriage."

Kasey's brown eyes were bright, her expression animated, a lot like her mother's. "Adam has never brought someone to a family event before." Kasey's words ran together because she spoke so fast. "You must be special, Nyx."

Red crept into Adam's face and I felt my own cheeks grow hot.

Kasey didn't seem to notice and continued on, full speed ahead. "Nyx is such an unusual name," she said. "Is it N-i-x? Is it short for something like Nicole? Or is it a nickname? What does it mean?"

That was a question I could answer easily enough. Plenty of norms and paranorms had asked me that one. "My mother is into Greek mythology," I said when Kasey paused for breath. "Nyx means goddess of the night. It's spelled N-y-x." When I was young, my mother told me the goddess Nyx was considered a figure of exceptional beauty and power.

"Nyx is also the name of an asteroid and one of Pluto's moons," Jacob said, surprising me. He had been standing so quietly to the side that I'd forgotten he was there. "However," he went on, "the moon is spelled with an 'i' instead of a 'y' to avoid confusion with the asteroid. Both were named after the same Greek goddess you were," he added.

"Oh." I didn't know what else to say.

Adam didn't seem to either.

Kasey laughed, the sound sweet and musical. "Jacob is into astronomy if you can't tell."

"Where's Mike?" Adam asked, probably to keep Kasey from saying anything else that might embarrass him.

She glanced around the crowded room much like Laura had a few moments ago. "I know he's here somewhere."

"We'll find him." Adam kissed his sister on the cheek. "See you later, kiddo." He turned and gave Jacob a light punch in the arm. "I've got a gun and a badge. I'll be watching you."

It was Jacob's turn to look uncomfortable. I think Adam wanted to laugh but he kept a straight face.

Adam couldn't get two feet without someone stopping him to say hello, or to say how long it had been since they'd seen him last. He introduced me each time and moved on to the next person.

An hour and a half later we still hadn't found his brother and had talked with at least twenty different people.

Then Adam did a great duck and roll maneuver.

He pretended not to notice the next person who recognized him, ducked to the side, took me by the waist, and whirled us into the crowd of dancers at the center of the large room.

"This is better," Adam said close to my ear. "Just the two of us."

A shiver ran through me from the warmth of his breath and the sound of his voice. He held me close as we danced and he smiled at me. At the same time he seemed different but I couldn't put my finger on it.

He kept me on the dance floor and had me breathless and laughing. We danced and danced. It shouldn't have surprised me that Adam was such a good dancer considering how athletic he had always appeared to be.

We didn't leave the dance floor, but plenty of couples stopped us to talk with Adam. After he greeted them, he only took enough time to introduce me before he danced me away again.

Then the tingling started.

The feeling jerked me out of my enjoyment of the moment and I backed a step from Adam.

"I've got to go, I've got to go." I said and heard the urgency in my voice as the tingling grew more insistent.

"I totally lost track of time. I can't believe this. I have to leave now."

How could the time have gone by so quickly? It had seemed like more than enough time when we planned today, but the hours had passed faster than I'd expected.

Adam looked confused, then realization hit him.

"Picture time!" Laura's voice sang out from behind us before she grabbed Adam's hand. "Family pictures now."

"I'll meet you at the SUV," I said before I told Laura, "I need to go to the ladies' room."

Tingling sensations pricked at my skin as I fought my way through the crowd and a sense of panic made my throat tight. What if I was already transforming?

I fled the reception and made it into the restroom in time to see blue shimmer down my black hair. I heard the door open behind me and ducked into a stall.

So close. Too close.

The shift is always harder when I'm stationary and can't stretch into the changes in my body. I tilted my head back, closed my eyes, and felt my muscles grow stronger, tighter, more defined. My skin tingled and I knew it was now amethyst. I could feel the change in my hair as it turned completely blue. My small fangs were sharp as my tongue touched them and I even felt my ears shifting so that they were now pointed.

When the transformation was over I opened my eyes and looked down. A strong sense of being out of place came over me. I didn't belong here.

I waited until I heard the flush of a toilet, a stall door opening and closing, and the sounds of water running and paper towels being ripped from the dispenser.

When at last I heard the bathroom door swish open and closed I let out a sigh of relief. I needed to get out of this place. I wrapped myself in an air glamour and slipped out of the stall.

I debated on whether or not to wait until someone opened the door to leave, but I really wanted to get out of there. I left the stall I'd been in and hurried to wash and dry my hands before opening the door to leave. A couple of giggling young women pushed the door from the opposite side at the same time and one of them stumbled into the ladies' room.

"That was weird," one of them said as I slipped past and out into the hotel.

The sense of not belonging was stronger now as I made my way out of the hotel and to where Adam had parked his SUV. Loneliness snuck up on me, tightening my muscles and making my head ache.

It was dark now. And I couldn't be a part of Adam's world.

I used my air element to unlock the door of his SUV before climbing in and shutting the door. I sat there in the cold while I waited for Adam to come and hoped he would get my coat that I'd checked in earlier.

The vehicle was cold inside but that didn't bother me as much as the length of time I sat there alone. I looked down at my dress and felt ridiculous at the way the plum color looked against my amethyst skin. My blue hair clashed with it, too, as I leaned forward and my hair fell over my shoulders.

I had the strong urge to leave. I didn't want Adam to see me like this. It didn't matter that he'd seen me plenty of times in my Drow form. Right now I felt so out of place that I might have cried if I had the ability to do so.

An hour passed before Adam made it to the SUV. He climbed in, leaned over the console, and gave me a quick kiss. "I'm sorry, Nyx." He drew away. "Pictures took longer than I thought they would and a group of old friends grabbed me and I had a hard time getting away."

I'd been forcing smiles all night, so I managed to now. "I'm sorry you had to leave so soon because of me. I should have thought of that when you asked me to come."

"It was nice having you with me." Adam touched the side of my face. "I'm just sorry I didn't get a chance to introduce you to my brother. They all were asking where you were. I told them you didn't feel well."

He started the SUV and drove me back to my apartment before parking and walking me to my door.

Before I could open the door, Adam brought me to a halt,

turned me to face him, and clasped both my hands. "You're going to visit your parents for the next few days?"

I frowned. Lawan was missing. Should I be out looking for her? At the same time I realized that getting answers from my father might be a way to learn how I could find her.

Also, I hadn't spent much time with my parents for the past two years and I'd planned this trip for a long time. They would be disappointed if I changed my plans.

"I'll come back sometime Monday," I said. "Is your family still planning on going to your parents' winter home in Fort Lauderdale?"

Adam nodded. "I'll return on Monday, too. I'll give you a call." He kissed me, a light brush of our lips. "See you when you get back."

I tried not to let my surprise show that he wasn't coming in with me.

"See you," I said quietly before I let myself into my apartment and closed the door behind me.

FOURTEEN

"I can't breathe." The words came out my mouth in a high-pitched squeak as my father hugged me in his tight, muscular grip.

He laughed and set me back on my feet. My father had a deep voice and a laugh that echoed off the stone walls of the transference chamber.

I was still trying to catch my breath as my mother embraced me. "You need to come home more often," she said as we hugged each other.

"Nyx needs to *move* back home, Kathryn," my father said as I stepped back from my mother. He looked and sounded rough, displeased. "It is more and more dangerous for my princess to stay in that Earth Otherworld."

Not this again.

"New York has been my home for over two years now, Father." I looked at the tall, big, and muscular male who looked every bit the king of the Dark Elves. He would be intimidating to most, but I'd had him wrapped around my little finger since I was born. "I love it there."

Mother smiled at my father. "None of this now, you big Troll. We're going to enjoy having our daughter home for the next few days."

"And convince her to stay here where she belongs." His long blue hair fell over his shoulders as he leaned forward and kissed me on the cheek. "It is good to have you home, my princess."

"It's good to be here," I said and added, "To *visit*."

"Humph." My father motioned to one of the guards stationed at the door to the transference room. In the language of the Dark Elves, he said to the guard, "Tell Locke we will be ready for dinner to be served in an hour."

The guard bowed. "Yes, my king," he said before he exited the room.

My father only spoke English with my mother and me. He spoke flawless English with only a hint of an Old World accent.

"Do you ever get tired of people bowing to you and calling you things like 'my king,' or 'my lord,' or 'your highness'?" I looked up at Father. "After all of these years hasn't it grown a little old?"

He looked surprised at my question. "I am king. Of course not."

I'd sure gotten tired of being called "my princess" before I left home. But then my father had been a king for over two thousand years. It was simply how things were with him.

A bare-chested warrior with dark brown skin, silver hair, and silvery-gray eyes came to the transference chamber and bowed to my father. Rhain. He was built much the same as all of the other warriors, muscular and fit. But he was taller than most and to me he'd always been beautiful.

Rhain's refusal to meet my gaze could have been for a number of reasons, including the fact that my father was standing in front of him. Father didn't approve of any warriors giving me attention. The truth is most males didn't approve of me at all because I'd been allowed to train with them and females are supposed to be subservient. My father indulged me—he could never say no to me. And I think that he liked having someone to teach his warrior's skills to.

But I'd had what humans call a "crush" on Rhain since my teen years and at one time he'd been nice to me. So it stung as he pointedly ignored me as he said to my father, "Declan has returned with news."

"Have him meet me in the throne room," Father said, and Rhain gave another quick bow before leaving.

"Yestin," my father said to the guard. "Take the princess's haversack to her chamber."

"Yes, my lord." Yestin came forward and bowed to my father before he took my pack and left.

"I will see you at supper." My father hugged me again and he kissed my mother before striding out of the chamber.

It occurred to me that I was human right now, not Drow, so it would only have made me more different, separating me from all Dark Elves even more than I already was.

I wondered how Adam would like my father and then how my father would like Adam. I frowned. I didn't think he would be intimidated by my father, but I also didn't think they'd be best buddies right off. I wasn't sure my dad would approve to begin with just because Adam was human.

"Is something wrong, Nyx?" Mother put her arm around my waist and I put mine around hers as we started out of the transference chamber. She was wearing a beautiful long gown in royal purple, a gown befitting a queen, and the material was soft beneath my arm as we walked together. She added, "You look like you're thinking about something you're not happy about."

Trust Mother to know when things weren't right with me. I suppose that's what mothers are for.

When we reached the hall outside the chamber, I looked at Mother and gave a half smile. "Just thinking about things."

"Guy things?" she asked while we headed arm and arm toward my personal chamber.

"Yeah." I shrugged.

Mother had always been my best friend and confidante growing up in the Drow Realm. I was more or less an outcast with females for the same reasons I was an outcast with males.

It had taken time, but the Dark Elves had eventually fallen in love with my mother even though she was human. She didn't practice the submissive lifestyle, but was beautiful, feminine, kind, caring, and obviously loved my father deeply.

She'd proven herself to those who became her people, time and time again with her acts of kindness and generosity.

"Tell me." My mother said it in a way that only best friends could. "You've fallen for someone, haven't you?"

I looked at her. She was a couple of inches shorter and her skin fairer than mine from living underground for so many years, but she looked to be about my age. Once she had come to live belowground, she had stopped aging.

"His name is Adam." Usually his name sent pleasure through me, but right now I felt confusion. "He's an NYPD detective. We've been dating for a few months but we've known each other longer than that."

"Ah." Mother had grown up in New York City so she was familiar with the NYPD. "A human, yes?"

I nodded.

"Tell me about this Adam." She gave me one of her brilliant smiles. "Are you in love with him?"

"Very much so." I wish I could have smiled, too, but after last night and the way it had left me feeling . . .

"You're having doubts," she said as her expression grew more serious.

We reached the heavy wood and iron door to my chamber and stopped. "Yes," I said as I waited for the male guarding my door to open it.

He bowed to Mother and me before we walked into my room and he shut the door behind us. My bag was waiting in the room. Burning wood crackled in the small fireplace, the smoke carried up through air vents that were released somewhere aboveground. Fat candles had been lit throughout my room and both the candles and the fireplace cast shadows on the walls.

Mother had made sure my old room felt warm and welcoming, not cold and dreary. It didn't have the musty odor shut off places normally did. Instead, I smelled the potpourri she had simmering in the fireplace along with burning wood and the tallow candles.

The realm of the Dark Elves had been stuck in the Middle Ages like the rest of Otherworld, but my mother had made sure I had many comforts from the Earth Otherworld she'd grown up in. Like a huge mega-comfortable bed that I loved.

I flopped down on the end of the bed, lay back on it, and stared up at the stone ceiling. The bed dipped as my mother sat beside me and then I felt the warmth of her palm on my knee.

All of the nooks and crannies on my ceiling were so familiar. I'd stared up at this ceiling for the first twenty-five years of my life. The ceiling I looked at when I woke up in my apartment in the city had become normal, but this one made me feel like home. I wasn't sure I liked that because New York was my home now, not Otherworld.

"Tell me about this young man." Then I heard the smile in Mother's voice. "Around here anything under a century is young."

I pushed myself up so that I was sitting on the edge of the bed and smiled at my mother. "He does fit that bill. Adam is in his thirties, so Father would just consider him a babe."

"Adam," my mother said. "I always liked that name when was I was growing up in the Earth Otherworld."

"Do you miss it, Mother?" My tone became more serious. "New York?"

"Sometimes." She braced her palms on the bed to either side of her and met my eyes. "But it's been a very long time since I lived there. Over thirty years."

"You were young." I swung my legs back and forth as I talked. I was wearing a pair of Dior slacks and a cashmere sweater. Not being in a dress set me apart from other Drow women, too. "I'm surprised Father didn't think eighteen was too young."

"Your father thinks that 'too young' applies to you because you are his little princess." She smiled. "When we met it was magical. And I had always been mature for my age."

"Strange how you ended up in Otherworld," I said. "One moment you were in Manhattan, and then *poof*, you were here."

"Down the rabbit hole, I always thought." She started

swinging her legs, too, her purple-slippered feet peeking out from beneath her dress. "I found out much later, after we were married, that your father had seen me in a vision. He had the Seer locate me and then your father used the transference to bring me here.

"One day I was walking to my first class my freshman year at NYU," she said, "and the next I found myself aboveground in Otherworld where it was night. I met him in the forest with only moonlight to see him by."

"I've never heard the whole story," I said. "Didn't you feel manipulated?"

"It was romantic, exciting, new." She smiled. "He was so handsome and strong. Intelligent, powerful. I fell for him the first night I met him."

"The blue hair and blue skin thing didn't freak you out?" I said.

Mother tilted her head to the side. "It was dark, so the first few nights I thought it was just a trick of the shadows in the forest. Each night he sent me home and then brought me to him again the next night. Night here, not in the Earth Otherworld. So it was like being in the night all of the time."

"And you just went with it?" I said.

"I was young and rebellious." She looked at me. "I'd spent my entire life as an orphan in foster care and I wasn't your average eighteen-year-old."

"You must not have been average," I said, "to have left behind everything you had and knew for a life here."

"It took some getting used to, but I was so in love with your father . . ." She sighed, a happy sigh. "I still am."

"What about all you left behind?" I said. "You didn't have family, but what about friends?"

"Because I was moved around so much, I never had a chance to develop many close relationships," she said. "And your father was worth everything that I did give up."

"You are amazing, Mother." I looked at her. "You came from a world where you were an independent young woman to the medieval male-dominated world of the Dark Elves."

"Nothing amazing about that," she said. "I was in love

with your father." She raised her hand, only her pinky finger lifted up. "And I had him wrapped around here long before you had him wrapped around your little finger." It was almost as if she had read my thoughts earlier.

"You sure did." I shook my head. "Although I can picture the kind of reception you got as a new human queen who refused to be submissive."

"I submitted to your father, Nyx," she said, suddenly looking serious. "But it's not about doing things against my will. He honors and loves me. It's easy to want to please him. He has always treated me like a queen. And I treat him like a king. It's why we still love each other and why we are still happily married after all these years."

I thought about her and my father for a few moments. "I went to a reception with Adam and met his family yesterday," I said. "His family was nice, but it was so hard evading their questions and not being able to tell them the truth about me."

"I understand." Mother squeezed my knee with her hand. I'd forgotten it was there. "Don't let that hold you back in your relationship. Don't shy away from it and don't fight your feelings. There are no rights and no wrongs in love if it is love. It is what it is."

"No rights and no wrongs?" I said. "What about abusive males and females?"

She stared at the fireplace. "Not every man is meant to be a lover, a husband, a father. Just like not every woman is meant to be a lover, a wife, a mother." She turned her gaze to me. "I believe they have some need they want fulfilled and they can't figure out what that is. The people they harm . . ."

This time when she looked away I thought there might be a tear in her eye. "That child or adult doesn't fill the need of their abuser so the abuser's internal pain is taken out on the one they supposedly love." She still didn't look at me as she added, "A person like that doesn't know what real love is."

I felt a deep sadness for the girl my mother had been as I placed my hand over hers. "You've never talked with me about your life growing up in foster care."

"Like most abused children, it's not something we like to talk about," she said.

"I'm sorry. I leaned my head on her shoulder. "I had it so good growing up and I know that." I gripped her hand. "I love you and Father so much. Even though I don't come home often, I miss you."

"I know." Mother kissed the top of my head. "I don't have to tell you, though, to keep standing up to your father and live your life. Not the life he wants you to lead."

I raised my head and smiled at my mother. "Maybe one of these days he'll 'get it.' "

Mother laughed. "Not likely."

FIFTEEN

Supper was held in the huge banquet hall with my mother, father, and about twenty of his closest advisors, the highest ranking warriors, my uncle, and my step-uncle—the brother of my father's previous wife. My father sat at the head of the table with me on his left, Mother on his right.

"You look lovely, my princess," Father said as he smiled at me. "You and your mother have always been the most beautiful females in the realm."

I smiled back. "Thank you, Father."

Because I knew it would make my father happy, I wore a velvety soft gown in royal blue as well as a circlet on my head. The circlet was simple, made of the same metal as my collar, but it had Drow-mined sapphires and diamonds on it that sparkled in the torchlight. I was still human, but I had a couple of hours before I'd have to excuse myself to transform to Drow.

Father squeezed Mother's hand on top of the table and she gave him a radiant look. She had changed into a crimson gown, her blond hair pulled back beneath her delicate crown. She looked beautiful and regal, every bit the queen she was.

My father was a powerful male with a commanding presence and few would dare to question or argue with him. Rodán had been one of those few, for which I'd always be grateful. Rodán was the reason I had ended up in New York City as a Night Tracker.

"You look quite handsome, Father," I said.

Tonight he wore jewel-encrusted chest straps over his

muscular chest and he had on leather wrist bands. The jewel-makers had studded his crown with precious gems. The crown rested on his long, wavy blue hair that was almost the same shade of sapphire as my eyes.

"To my daughter's homecoming." Father spoke in Drow as he raised his tankard of ale and everyone around the table did, too.

"To the princess," they responded in unison before taking huge swallows of the ale. Most of them said it without looking at me.

After the toast, for the most part I was ignored by everyone at the table—all males with the exception of my mother. I'd been used to it before I left for Otherworld, but now it had a sting to it, like Rhain's intentional dismissal of me had earlier.

The only males who paid any attention to me were my uncle, Simon, and my step-uncle, Garf. I'd always liked Simon, but Garf was nothing but a lecher who'd love to take my father's crown. He despised my mother even though he kissed up to her in front of my father.

Because my brother was gone, Simon was next in line for the throne. Garf was in line after Simon—but only if Garf married me.

As if.

The thought made me ill.

Garf and I weren't blood-related, but it still creeped me out. Truth was that everything about Garf made my stomach churn. If Father had known the lecherous way Garf looked at me, starting when I was eighteen, he probably would have had my step-uncle's head cut off. That really would have been for the best.

"Have you enjoyed your time in the Earth Otherworld?" Simon asked me as he broke of a hunk of bread.

After he handed me a too-large piece, I said, "Yes, Uncle." I reached for the freshly churned butter—it was so good on hot, homemade bread. "I love it there. But it is nice to be home. For a visit."

My uncle Simon and I made some conversation, but most

of the meal I talked with my mother and father, asking them about what they'd been doing, and they asked me questions in return. My father was gruff, but he managed to not bellow out anything about me staying in the Drow Realm and never returning to New York City.

Dinner was a traditional celebratory three-course meal of roast chicken and a whole roasted pig, nuts, cheeses, fruits, and crisp vegetables. Dark Elves bartered with Light Elves for most of our food because it grew, was made, or was raised aboveground.

"Yum," I said in English as my favorite dessert was brought out by servers. Egg custard tart. "Thank you," I said in Drow as I looked from my father to my mother. "This is all wonderful."

For my parents, the celebration was having me at home. For everyone else it was an excuse to drink my father's best ale and to eat until they couldn't stuff themselves anymore.

After I finished my tart, I said, "I have important questions for you, Father." I kept my voice low and spoke in English, a language few at the table would understand. I had intentionally waited until now to ask the questions that I needed to.

"Ask." He bit into his third tart.

"It might be better somewhere else," I said. "I want to talk with you about Tristan and what happened to him." Even as quietly as I had spoken, several of the males at the table looked at me when I said my brother's name.

My father stopped in mid-chew. Without looking at me, he set his unfinished tart on his plate, picked up a wet piece of cloth and began wiping his fingers. "That topic is not open for discussion."

The way he said it made my stomach twist. A combination of anger and pain, and matter-of-factness.

I place my fingers on his arm. They looked so pale against the blue of his skin. "It's not only about my brother." Pain flashed in my father's eyes. "I need to speak with you about them, the Zom—"

"Enough." I don't think my father had intended to speak

so loudly or harshly, but he captured everyone's attention at the table.

I felt warmth in my face and met my mother's eyes. She looked apologetic.

He cleared his throat and in Drow said, "I am finished here. I have work to attend to." He looked to Simon and Garf. "Come, we have business to discuss."

We all stood as my father did. My stomach hurt as I set my napkin in my plate and my father left with Simon and Garf. Mother came to me and we walked out of the chamber together. I had to think of a way to get my father to listen to me.

"Talking about Tristan brings great pain to your father," Mother said as we reached the archway leading from the banquet chamber.

"Why won't he talk about it?" I asked, then suddenly knew the reason before she gave it. For much the same reason my five-year-old mind blocked the memories away.

My mother and I entered the great hall. It was circular with several archways leading from it. "Your father blamed himself for the loss of his son." She looked toward the throne room which also served as a high-level conference room for my father. "He has never forgiven himself."

"That's why I couldn't talk about Tristan, too." I met my mother's gaze. "I felt so helpless when I saw it happen. If only I'd been older, stronger."

"You couldn't have done anything to save your brother." My mother had the kind of concern on her face that a parent has for a child she almost lost. She came to a stop and hugged me. "You could have died or vanished too, Nyx. That is more pain than any parent should have to bear."

I returned her hug and felt her warm tears on my shoulder, through the material of my gown.

She touched my face and her tears glistened in her eyes that were the same sapphire blue as my own. "It is what your father faced and probably why he is so protective over you. If he lost you . . . If I lost you . . ."

"You won't." I kissed her cheek. "Don't worry. Please."

She tried to guide us diagonally from the banquet room to the hallway that led to our chambers, but I wouldn't let her.

"Whatever we need to do to get Father's attention," I said, "we have to do it."

"What's wrong?" She brushed away a tear from her cheek with the back of her hand.

I took a deep breath. "What happened here . . . what happened to Tristan . . . it's happening in the Earth Otherworld now."

Mother grasped me by my upper arms. Her eyes were wide. "Are you serious?"

I nodded. "The same as here, at least what I can remember since I was so young." I started to pull away to go find my father.

"Ciar needs to know this at once." She looked toward the throne room. She brought her gaze back to me. "But I need to get his attention. I'm the only one who can get away with interrupting him without him losing face in front of his men."

I stared toward the throne room. "You're right, of course."

She released my upper arms, patted her eyes dry, and straightened her spine. "Go to our chambers and wait for us in the sitting room."

"Okay." I kissed her on the cheek. "Thank you."

Mother kissed me back. "Go on now. Your father and I will be there in a few moments."

I had no doubt that my mother would succeed in getting my father's attention. I should have gone through her to begin with.

While I waited our conversation haunted me. I'd thought I couldn't talk about my brother because of the pain of his disappearance and probable death. But it had been more than that. I had blamed myself from the beginning.

Not more than three minutes had passed when my father came charging into the sitting room where I waited for him. I stood at the center of the room and he nearly knocked me over, he came in so fast.

"I will not lose my daughter to those beasts." His cheeks were dark blue, his silvery-gray eyes flashing dangerous white like mine did when I was angry.

"Then help me," I said. "Tell me everything you know. Tell me how you got rid of them."

"You cannot go back." Father spoke in Drow, his voice a huge bellow. I was thankful the stone walls were too thick for him to be heard by anyone outside the room. "I will not lose my daughter."

"I *am* going back." I spoke in Drow as I put my hands on my hips, but I kept my tone even. It wouldn't do me any good to lose my temper. "Norms and paranorms are being slaughtered and some are disappearing. One of my friends, a Tracker, is missing."

He shoved his large hand through his hair, knocking his crown to the stone floor. It clanged, then rolled around in a big circle before it came to a stop with a rattle.

"I need to know, Father." I returned to English again. "There seems to be so many similarities to what I remember happened here. We can't let the same thing continue to happen in the Earth Otherworld."

"You must explain everything to me." Father began pacing the floor. "From the beginning."

I told him all I could think of from what had occurred so far. I explained the research Olivia and I had done that made us believe it actually started weeks before, just in smaller attacks.

My father said some very scary Drow curse words. No one in any language can curse like the Dark Elves, and my father had an exceptional knack for using them.

"That is how it began here, with Light and Dark Elves." He continued pacing, much like I had done the other day in my office. "Small attacks, with one or more of our people vanishing here and there.

"We did not understand what was happening," he went on. "Then Light and Dark Elves counseled together. We drew on our separate experiences and came to the conclusion that not only were Elves under attack, but so was our entire Otherworld.

"Fighting parties were sent out," he said. "The attacks only worsened and more of our people died or disappeared."

As my father spoke my skin prickled. If Elves had had difficulty fighting this threat, then did we even have a chance?

"They were a ruthless people," Father said. "Our Seer visioned their leader. A Sorcerer of great power whose intent was to invade Otherworld, destroy our people, and take it for his own. We tried to find this Sorcerer, but we could never locate him."

Father's voice sounded hoarse. "Others were disappearing. Then when your brother vanished—" he met my gaze "—when you saw him taken, I went after the beasts with every warrior I had."

He looked away from me. "We were too late. They never came back."

"Why?" I had to remind myself to breathe. "How did you defeat them?"

"We did not." Father shook his head. "They simply stopped coming. We never saw them again."

"There must have been some reason." I looked from my father to my mother. "Why would they just stop?"

Father shook his head, then pushed his long hair from his face. No matter he was over two thousand years old, he continued to look like he was in his thirties.

"That remains a mystery," he said. "They never came back and all we could do was prepare for the chance that they might return, and to pray that they never would."

"So no clues, nothing?" I asked.

Father gave a frown. "When we killed some of their people we found stones. The stones are odd. They have a smooth face on them that make it appear that one is looking into another world. But nothing is there."

My father spoke in the present tense and a little bit of excitement curled in my belly. What if they were a clue? "Where do you keep the stones?"

Father looked surprised at my question. "The Seer has them."

"May I have a look?" I asked. "Maybe it will offer up a hint of some sort that could help us in the Earth Otherworld."

He looked as if he wanted to argue again that I was to stay here in the Drow Realm, but instead he turned and said, "Come."

Mother and I followed him across the round great hall to an archway I hadn't been allowed through as a child. It always held a hint of mystery for me and little Faeries bounced in my stomach at the realization I was actually going to be permitted to go there.

The hallway was dark with only one torch at the entrance. Open geodes with dark purple and black crystal glittered from the walls as we made our way further down. Three doors fashioned of a dark Dryad wood were along the hallway, one on the right, one on the left, and one dead ahead. We went to the one at the end of the tunnel.

"Oren." My father's voice boomed as he knocked on the door.

I had never met the Seer before—my father had always said when I was old enough, he would allow me to. Once I became of age I'd left the realm, so I'd never had a chance to meet Oren.

Earth Otherworld television and movies must have influenced me because for some reason I expected to see a male who looked old and wise. Which was a dumb thought considering Elves don't show age beyond twenty or thirty human years.

When the Seer opened the door I blinked. Oren was not a male, Oren was a female. She was truly what one could call mousy. Elves tend to be tall, but Oren was petite. She wore plain gray robes and she had dishwater-gray hair, light gray skin, and pale pink lips.

Her eyes were amazing, though. A strange greenish-yellow, like the color of the antifreeze that Olivia put into her GTO.

Oren bowed to my father, then to my mother and me before she gestured for us to come inside.

The chamber was neat and orderly. Obsessively so. I'd never seen any of the Dark Elves with such a tidy streak. Niches were carved into all four walls, and in each cubby were books or objects. Books were not common in Otherworld, and I wondered if she had spent time writing some of them herself.

"A stone," my father said in his commanding voice.

He didn't have to specify what stones he was talking about. The Seer went to one niche in one of the huge walls, picked up a stone, and brought it to him. He inclined his head toward me and the Seer bowed as she handed it to me. She was careful not to let her fingers brush mine.

An odd sensation prickled through me. At first I thought I might be ready to shift into Drow, but then I realized it was the stone.

I looked it over, examining it while I felt the prickles, primarily where I touched the stone. It was egg-shaped and like a geode the way one side appeared sliced off. Smooth gray stone everywhere but on the side, which was like shiny, flat black glass.

When I looked at that side, I could tell what my father meant at once. But rather than looking into an empty painting, I thought it was more like looking into a TV, but nothing was there. It felt like something should be there, but wasn't. Of course my father wouldn't think to reference it as looking into a TV.

"Can I take this with me back to the Earth Otherworld?" I asked my father. "I want to see if Rodán has seen anything like it."

Father narrowed his brows and frowned at the mention of Rodán's name. Dark Elves aren't crazy about Light Elves to begin with and he'd never gotten past the fact that Rodán had recruited me as a Tracker.

It was a really good thing my father never knew Rodán and I had been lovers for a time. I'm not sure which one of them would have made it out alive if he had found out.

Father looked at the Seer. "Is it safe for my daughter to take?"

The Seer gave a low bow of her head in acknowledgment.

My father turned to me. "You may take it."

I held the stone tight in my hand and wondered why it suddenly felt so wrong.

SIXTEEN

Amory's dress tunic scratched his skin as he pulled it over his head and tugged it down. He would need his seamstress to make him something more comfortable than what she had put together to fit his new form.

The Sorcerer's old body had been thin and frail, his joints aching with pain. His clothing had hung on him like sails without wind drooping from their riggings. His once long, vibrant red hair had turned mostly gray and brittle many, many years ago.

Now what he dressed in fit him well and showed the physical power of his new form. Magic remained in his gaze, even though his eyes were now the color of ironwood. The eyes of his old body had been the shade of the early morning sky, somewhere between gray and blue.

A low murmur of countless voices was like an oncoming storm. Amory strode from his bedroom suite in the manor and up the sweeping staircase. The sound of a mass number of voices grew louder.

He and his people had left Kerra behind over twenty years ago to take over this Doran Otherworld. No matter its beauty, Doran had turned out to be as cruel to them as their homeworld.

As he took the steps at a jog, Amory felt a confidence and power within him that he had not felt since the old days when Kerra was still home and his rule encompassed millions.

When Kerra started to die, so did his people. He had

been forced to search for options. Ways to save and preserve his people while at the same time looking for a new home-world.

He'd started with the original Otherworld. The one that fathered all of the others.

It did not take Amory and his advisors long to discover that it was not the place for him or his people. Doran had seemed the better choice at the time so they'd abandoned their assault.

He'd been wrong though. Doran ultimately was not com-patible for them.

Amory gritted his teeth as he took the third flight of stairs. Twenty-two years—*twenty-two years*—and he had finally found the right place for himself and his people. The perfect environment, the perfect Hosts.

Earth Otherworld.

The bodies from the Earth Otherworld were strong, healthy, the world hospitable to his people.

Amory reached the highest floor of the manor. Thou-sands and thousands of voices were louder now. A low roar of people gathered together.

To see him. To hear his voice. To know that they were saved.

Amory cloaked himself with magic as he strode from the stairs. He crossed the open room toward the glass-paned, arched double doors that were between him and the balcony, and his people.

He didn't pause. He gave a slight flick of his fingers and the doors swung open, thumping hard against the walls to either side of the archway. Loud, expectant gasps came from those who waited.

The gloriously almost clear sky was blue with a hint of lavender. It was the element that created the lavender in the atmosphere that was so deadly to his people. Faint clouds streaked the sky like a brush had painted a few opaque strokes of white.

He looked from the sky endlessly stretched out above to the thousands of his people below.

The Sorcerer dropped his cloak of magic.

More gasps and murmurs. Most had not seen him since he had traded his old body for this one. But even with this different face, they would know it was him.

The Sorcerer raised his hands and shouted out great words of magic, strong words, powerful words, words that no one but he and other Sorcerers could understand.

Once-clear lavender-streaked skies turned dark and black thunderheads rolled in, forming from what had been misty threads of white. The smell of rain and sulfur rode the winds that now pressed his tunic against his body, outlining every muscle from his broad chest to his tapered waist and strong thighs and legs.

His people gave cries of shock and fear as lightning crashed to the ground from the clouds. Thunder pounded the air, the sound as loud as if the shafts of lightning were living stakes being driven by great hammers into the ground.

Men and women, their bodies in different stages of deterioration, cowed as he lowered his hands.

"It is I, the Sorcerer Amory, Lord of the Kerra and Doran Otherworlds." The roar of his voice carried over the sound of thunder. "You do not recognize this body as it is new, but you recognize *me*."

When he felt he had adequately proven himself to be the Sorcerer Amory, he let the clouds drift away, allowing the sky to lighten to its deadly lavender tint as it had been.

Every person in the crowd was quiet and he nodded his approval. "Good. You have come as expected. Those who continue to follow my rule will be rewarded well."

Silence continued to reign when he was not speaking. "As I told you the last time we gathered, we have discovered an Otherworld that suits our needs and more.

"We sent in our reconnaissance teams, then began our experiments." His gaze roved over the throng of people. "It is working." He let his words ring out so that they could be heard by every male and female standing before him.

Hope lit their features at his statement, but still they made no sound.

"I alone know what must be done," Amory continued. "I have perfected it.

"Each of you must now begin your preparation as you did when we left Kerra for Doran." The Sorcerer let urgency fill his command. "We must speed up the exchange, must step up more quickly."

Men and women looked from one to another and a slow murmur began to travel throughout the crowd. A murmur of excitement filled with hope for better days to come.

"Our plan is coming together." The Sorcerer leaned forward and gripped the rough stone surface of the balcony. "The people of the Earth Otherworld will not understand until it is too late for them. It will no longer be their world . . . it will be ours."

SEVENTEEN

Monday, December 27

Cold sunlight and crisp air felt good on my face as I arrived via the transference to Central Park. The chill helped keep my mind off the queasiness that I always felt when I traveled that way.

My head swam a little and my eyes unfocused and focused again. Even when my father handled the transference, I wasn't crazy about it. As I traveled, my head had felt like the pressure would make it pop and my stomach curdled and cramped. But when he did it, I didn't throw up or pass out.

I rubbed my face with my chilled palm. Once my head stopped whirling, the first thing I planned to do was call Rodán and ask if there were any new developments in the Zombie case and to find out if Lawan had returned or been tracked down—and I prayed that she would be safe and well.

Christmas Eve night and Christmas Day in Otherworld with my parents was enjoyable. We had exchanged presents Christmas night. My father had always tried to keep some Earth Otherworld traditions for my mother and for me.

I gave my mother a digital camera and my father a digital frame with a few pictures of New York City and of me. I knew Mother would have fun with the camera and the laptop I'd given her for her birthday. The frame was a wonder to my father, king of a medieval world.

My father gave me a heavy ring with a very large diamond that he'd had specially crafted for me. I'd get mugged for wearing it in the streets of the city, but I could take care of myself. It was a little on the big side, but it was from my father so I loved it.

From my mother I received a leather-bound journal with blank parchment pages. The pages were made by hand and real flowers were infused in the parchment. It was almost too beautiful to use. The ring and the journal were both in my bag until I got home.

I waited until Monday, two days after Christmas, to leave, and the day here was beautiful. It was nice to be above-ground again, nice to be in the place I now considered home.

A combination of reasons sent me back this morning rather than waiting until the evening. I was too worried about Lawan and there was also my concern over what was happening here in the Earth Otherworld. I missed Adam too, and hoped that he would make it back to the city today.

Then there was the fact that the longer I stayed in Other-world, the more my father thought he could control me, the more he demanded I should stay. Especially now that he knew what was happening with the Zombies.

I hitched my pack up on my shoulder and glanced at the Alice in Wonderland unbirthday party a few feet away from me. Snow topped Alice and her friends like helmets of icing.

Father hadn't believed it was possible for me to do the transference accurately since I was "only twenty-seven" and I should have been at least a century old before I could even start learning it, much less perform it.

Before I left, I told him, to his dismay, that I'd done the transference twice on my own—recently. He shouted that I could have killed myself, but I'd insisted that I'd done just fine.

Puking and then blacking out afterward didn't count—of course I didn't mention that part of my experience.

I had never done it on my own from Otherworld to Other-world. I also didn't want to end up in the middle of a snow-drift or in a dumpster somewhere in the city. So I let my father do the transference for me with no complaints.

While I drew out my cell phone, I absently kicked the snow so that it fanned out in a white spray. I leaned up against Alice's backside and the mushroom she was sitting on.

As usual, Father had sent me from the transference chamber in Otherworld to Alice's party. It was built over the Paranorm Center and the magically hidden entrance to the PC was beneath the largest mushroom, close to my feet.

My cell phone felt cool in my palm as I pressed the speed dial number for Rodán.

He answered on the first ring. "Welcome back."

"Hi, Rodán." I clenched the phone in my hand. "Did anyone find Lawan? Is she okay?"

"Lawan appears to be fine." Rodán's voice was neutral, which seemed odd. "She showed up to track Thursday night."

Thank you, I prayed and tension in my muscles relaxed. "Where was she?"

"Lawan's twin sister, Malee, was ill," Rodán said. "Apparently Malee recently arrived from Thailand and was sick upon arrival."

I hadn't known Lawan had a twin sister. I suddenly felt like I hadn't spent nearly enough time with my friend if I didn't know an important detail like that. A twin, no less.

It was strange for Lawan to just take a couple of days off without telling anyone. "Why didn't she let you know?"

"Lawan said she left a voice mail for me," Rodán said. "I suppose it could be a case of technology not cooperating with the paranorm world."

I nodded. Many times that was the case. Paranorms and technology don't always mix.

"It's an understatement to say I'm glad she's back and that she's okay." But tension came back into my muscles and my voice when I asked the next question. "What about Zombies? Anything new?"

"A couple of attacks," Rodán said. "No clues. We have much to do to solve this case."

"Are you available?" I thought about what was in my pocket. "I have something I need to show you."

"Yes," Rodán said. "I'll be here."

"Great, I'll be by in a bit," I said before I pushed the OFF button.

Next I pressed the speed dial number for Adam and smiled, looking forward to hearing his voice. It was easy to imagine being in his arms, feeling his hugs all the way to the core of my being.

Memories from his sister's wedding reception came to me in a rush as his number began to ring. I had the urge to hang up, although I wasn't sure why.

Maybe because I felt embarrassed over how things had gone. What if Laura had talked to Jennifer who had attended the Château and she had said she'd never heard of me? What if his family hadn't liked me?

The fact that I'd had to run outside and hide in the SUV in my Drow form made my stomach clench. I don't know if I'd ever felt so out of place in my life as I had that night.

Stop it, Nyx.

"Hi." Adam's voice came over smooth and warm and it gave me a thrill low in my belly, relaxing the tension I'd just been feeling. "I don't suppose you're still in Otherworld since you're calling."

"Father was driving me crazy so I decided not to wait until tonight." I hugged myself with my free arm and looked out at the snowy park and the kids playing. A pretty intense snowball fight was in the works. "I love being with my parents but three days are more than enough when it comes to my father."

"I'll be back late night." Adam sounded a little distracted and I heard voices in the background. "I have to be in a meeting with Wysocki first thing and a couple of cases to work on, so I probably won't be around tomorrow until later in the day."

"I was hoping you'd stop by after you got home tonight," I said. I tried to keep the disappointment out of my voice.

"It'll be late when I get in," he said. "Some cousins are dropping in this afternoon so I won't be able to leave until I get a chance to spend a little time with them."

"Have fun." I wanted to say *I love you*, but something held me back. "Can't wait."

"Same here," Adam said. "See you."

"Bye," I said and brought the phone away from my ear. The conversation left me a little empty rather than with the bubbly excited feeling I usually got when I talked with him.

When I started to walk away from the sculpture, something hit the back of my head. I caught my breath in surprise as snow covered my hair and slid inside my sweater and down my spine. I whirled to face my attacker.

The devious face of a well-bundled kid, who couldn't have been more than twelve, peered out from the other side of Alice and her friends. I wondered if he'd seen me arrive then decided it wasn't important.

What was important was a little playful revenge.

For fun I used my water elemental to form a snowball at my feet. Without touching the snowball with my hands, I used my air elemental and shot a snowball straight at the boy. It smacked his hooded face.

Heh.

The kid wiped off the caked snow with his gloves and his eyes were wide as he looked at me. I smiled. He turned and ran. For a moment I wondered if I'd shifted and my hair was blue. But no, it was daylight, my skin wasn't amethyst, and I was perfectly human.

Smiling, I tromped in the direction of the Pit, my bag over my shoulder. The snow was up to my calves and I was glad I was wearing my jeans tucked into my Elvin boots.

When I shoved my hands into my jacket pockets, I felt cold stone against the fingers of my right hand. My heart started to beat a little faster as the chill from the stone traveled through my arm straight to my chest. I swallowed and wrapped my hand around the stone and felt an even greater chill.

After checking to make sure no one was close enough to see, I stopped beneath a leafless maple and drew the stone out of my pocket. The flat side rested on my palm and tingled where it touched my skin. Holding it in both hands, I eased it over so that I could look at it again.

The stone's flat side looked different. It was still like looking into another world as my father said . . . but there was a glimmer of lavender inside it. I looked at the sky above me which was gray dusted with darker gray clouds.

It wasn't a reflection. What was it? The pounding of my heart increased as the lavender grew brighter, like a pinpoint of light at the center of the stone. A terrible feeling of wrongness overcame me.

For a moment I was five again, hidden in the bushes as a Zombie followed my brother, feeling that same sense of horrible wrongness.

My breath came in short gasps. My body jerked and trembled. I wanted to throw the stone to the ground. To run away.

What was happening to me?

I swung my pack off my shoulder. Still holding the stone, I unzipped a pocket of the pack and flung the stone into the opening.

Relief made me weak and I dropped to my knees in the snow. My breath came hard and fast and my sight blurred again, as if I had just gone through the transference.

Rodán. I got to my feet I had to see him now.

I ran.

My breathing would never have been so fast if I wasn't so spooked. The way the stone had made me feel had been so creepy.

The Pit was dead. It was the middle of the day and the only beings in the open area of the nightclub were part of a Shifter cleaning crew.

I ran past them, through the mist curtain in one wall, down a long hallway, straight for Rodán's chambers. The huge dungeon-like door opened the moment the identity monitor recognized me.

"What's wrong, Nyx?" Rodán came toward me, concern on his features.

I held out my arm, barely holding the strap of my bag with my fingers. "It's inside."

"What's inside?" He took the bag from me, then frowned.

"Do you feel it?" I asked

Rodán paused, then nodded. He set the bag on the floor. "Tell me what it is."

"You're not going to look at it?" I asked.

"No." He glanced at the bag and back at me. "Something is very wrong with whatever is in there. Very wrong."

If Rodán wouldn't even touch it—that thought alone was enough to magnify the chills that had been causing me to shiver ever since I touched the thing.

"It's some kind of stone." I explained to him everything my father had told me. "They got them from the bodies of Zombies during the same kind of attacks in Otherworld, when I was a small girl. I thought it might help us fight whatever it is we're facing here. A clue."

Rodán studied me, obviously taking in how affected I was by everything that had just happened.

"This *stone*," Rodán finally said as he looked at my bag, "needs to be examined by those who can tell us more about it. I sense the strength of its magic, magic that should not be explored by either you or me."

"Really?" I could feel the lines on my forehead furrow when I frowned. "You're not even going to look at it?"

He switched to the formal language of the Elves. "I cannot. This stone would harm me as it would harm you should you touch it again. It is not of our worlds. It is not meant for our hands."

The way Rodán spoke the words and the language, with such formality, chilled me.

"Whose hands then?" I responded in the same language. While I spoke, I felt the magic of the language and I understood why he had used Elvin. A barrier seemed grow around me like a cushion between me and the bag with the stone. "Where should I take it?"

"To the Magi."

The word "stunned" did not define how I felt the moment he said "the Magi." Not even close.

"No one sees them." Perhaps incredulous described my emotion. "Only the Magi-Keepers and they report solely to the Paranorm Council," I said. "And no one asks the Magi anything. They come forward if they have something to say."

"Rare circumstances arise where they will take audience, Nyx." Rodán's voice was calm. "This is one of those circumstances."

If they didn't help with Demons or Vampires, I sure didn't know why he expected them to help with Zombies. But I hoped he was right.

Rodán went to a wall with a huge framed oil painting of a Faerie, titled "Take the Fair Face of Woman," painted by French artist Sophie Anderson in the 1800s. Rodán mentioned knowing the artist personally and had introduced her to the Fae, thus encouraging her amazing pieces of art relating to our Otherworld.

The painting's entire name was "Take the Fair Face of Woman, and Gently Suspending, With Butterflies, Flowers, and Jewels Attending, Thus Your Fairy is Made of Most Beautiful Things."

Right then I wasn't thinking of beautiful things or paintings and I wondered why Rodán was taking a moment to look at it. Then without his touching it, the painting swung away from the wall, as if hinged on the left side. Behind the door was a rectangle shape with a seamless surface. He said a word I couldn't hear and then a portion of that rectangle swung open like the painting had. A safe.

He reached inside, rummaged through whatever was inside the safe and drew out a plastic card. It was about the size of a credit card and I wondered what he would need with a credit card.

The safe door and the painting each swung back into place and Rodán returned to me and handed me the plastic card. I saw that it was actually a hotel room key. "I'll let the Magi-Keepers know you're on your way," Rodán said, switching back from the Elvin tongue. "Use the card rather than knocking. Loud sounds are difficult for the Magi."

I gripped the card before sliding it into the front pocket of my jeans. I started to lean over to grab the strap of the bag, strangely feeling let down by Rodán. I'm not sure why . . .

maybe because he had never pushed away something so important as he had the stone. He had refused to look at it.

"Nyx." Rodán's voice was soft as he called to me.

When I faced him, his features seemed different than I'd ever seen before. He looked almost . . . vulnerable.

The thought shocked me more than his refusal to look at the stone.

"The stone is dangerous." He came within inches of me and cupped my face with his palm. "Very, very dangerous. I wouldn't have you carry it at all if you hadn't already been in contact with it."

"I understand." Prickles erupted up and down my spine at the thought of picking up my bag again. "And because you are a male, you can't go to the Magi yourself. I'm the only one who can carry it."

"The only drawback to being male that I've come across," he said with a slight smile. His smile faded. "I'm certain you'll be safe with it in your bag. Keep it in there and don't allow it even to brush against your skin, understand?"

"Don't worry," I said. "I have no intention of ever touching that thing again."

Rodán clasped my head in his hands and kissed my forehead. "Go now," he said when he stepped back. "Don't stop for any reason. You must get that stone to the Magi."

I tried to smile. It didn't work.

What felt like an electrical charge ran up my arm, causing me to jerk my hand away.

"Are you all right?" Rodán rested his hand on my shoulder. "Perhaps we can find another way to transport it."

"No. I've got it." I grabbed the bag's strap, and gritted my teeth against the buzzing feeling running up and down my arm.

"I'll have Angel meet you there." He caught my hand before I could leave. "Be very, very careful," he said as his gaze held mine.

I turned and left his chambers, and headed out of the Pit toward the Mandarin Hotel.

EIGHTEEN

Fifteen minutes after I left Rodán's office, Angel met me at Sixtieth Street and Columbus Circle. The Mandarin Oriental, a fabulous five-star hotel, was where we hid our most precious paranorms. And we hid them in luxury.

What was inside my bag had such a strong feeling of wrongness that it made my head ache. I don't know why it bothered me now. It was like something had been triggered in the stone when I returned to the city.

"Wow." Angel put her hands on her hips and tipped her head back to look up at the hotel. "So this is where the Magi are kept."

"The Magi-Keepers and Magi have the Presidential Suite on the fifty-third floor and the Oriental Suite on the fifty-second." I wished I'd had time to change. In my jeans and sweater I felt underdressed, but I had to take the stone to the Magi as soon as possible. "Magi . . . Magi are extraordinarily special," I said.

"I'm new to a lot of this." Angel pushed her long corkscrew curls away from her face. She was dressed much the same as me except she wore black jeans and a short blue coat, and she wasn't carrying any kind of bag or purse. "All of this Peacekeeper and Paranorm Council secrecy."

"You do know that all Magi are females and they are Dopplers, like you are, right?" I asked. Angel was a squirrel Doppler with human pinup girl looks and body, and a mind like Einstein. We started toward the front entrance of the

Mandarin. "But you also know that they can't change into an animal form like all other Dopplers?"

"Yes. They're very, very rare and born with a special birthmark that lets the midwife know that the baby is a Magi," Angel said as we walked. "I have no idea what that birthmark might be and I don't know much else about them."

"Magi-Keepers are notified right away by the midwife when they see that mark," I said as we neared the Mandarin entrance. "The babies are whisked away from the family before the world overwhelms them."

"Overwhelms them?" Angel looked at me with curiosity. "How?"

"They literally would never survive the real world because their senses are so much more heightened than any other being we know of." I spoke a little quieter as we came up to a bellman. "They'd be bombarded by the six senses and gradually go insane, beyond the help of even the Magi-Keepers."

"That's incredible." Angel and I walked through the entrance of the Mandarin as the bellman held the door open for us.

"Magi need to live somewhere quiet where they can learn to use their senses and abilities," I said. "Especially their sixth sense."

The interior of the Mandarin was beautiful but neither Angel nor I paid much attention to it as we went toward the elevators.

"There's real danger for those poor girls." I pushed the UP button.

Angel looked at me as we waited for an elevator. "How's that?"

"Magi can foresee the future," I said. "Far, far into the future. They could tell you every winning lottery number you desire." I lowered my voice even more as a couple with three children approached the elevator from behind us. "They can look into the past and even know where a ship sank hundreds of years ago that contains incredible treasures," I said.

"They can locate almost any object or person the asking individual wants them to."

"I can see how that talent could be exploited big time." Amazement was on Angel's features.

"Right." The bell dinged for an elevator stopping at the lobby level and I glanced to see that it was going up. "Against their will," I continued, "the Magi can easily be put under control or the influence of other beings."

"Their abilities would definitely be very dangerous in the wrong hands." Angel and I stepped back and waited for people to exit the elevator.

"Yes." I nodded. "Elections could be rigged, lotteries won, the finest gemstones and paintings stolen."

We got into the elevator and stood to one side as the family of five came on behind us. I pressed the button for the fifty-third floor. One of the children, a boy with freckles and a devious gap-toothed grin, started pressing all of the buttons until his mother slapped his hand. He'd had time to press at least fifteen floors.

"Anything a person wanted," I said, "they could have if they had control of a Magi."

The man and woman who got into the elevator with us were arguing. I didn't think we could be overheard considering how loud their conversation was and the chattering of their children. Still we kept our voices low.

Angel shook her head. "I don't think there's a power out there that can match a Magi's."

"I'm sure you're right." I looked up at the digital numbers flashing by as the elevator went up. "It wouldn't take long to break a Magi, though," I said. "To overwhelm them entirely."

"How does that work?" Angel asked.

"Ask too much in too short an amount of time, and it's like they short-circuit."

Angel was a Harvard graduate and former NASA intern and could easily relate to technological examples.

"If the Magi are pressed beyond where they short-circuit, it can mean death to her because she can't handle all of the data that would bombard her," I said. "For a Magi that includes all six senses." I thought about the cruel part of the gift. I wasn't sure that what they had was a gift at all. "What would happen to them is beyond a norm's version of a nervous breakdown."

"That would be unbelievable in the real world." Angel and I scrunched a little back as the elevator came to a stop and the doors opened for other passengers. "Of course you and I don't live in the real world, at least as far as norms are concerned."

Two businessmen in tailored suits, both of whom were carrying briefcases, stepped through the sliding doors and crowded the elevator even more.

As I thought of how delicate the Magi are, I glanced at my own hands and turned them. Such physical strength that was a part of me had always been there. I thought about the power in my body and my ability to battle, to kill, and to save lives. The fact that I could live a normal life—for a half-Drow, half-human warrior slash Private Investigator.

"They're like prisoners," Angel said. "And the Magi-Keepers their jailers."

"I like to think of the Magi-Keepers as their protectors." The elevator stopped again and the family got off. Suddenly it was a lot quieter in the elevator. The two men stood side-by-side without speaking. "The Magi are completely unable to protect themselves," I whispered.

"They can't even be trained?" Angel's forehead wrinkled as she frowned. "Have someone come in and teach them basic fighting skills?"

"The Magi are delicate and frail." I glanced at the businessmen then back at Angel. "In no way are they fighters or ever could be."

Angel looked thoughtful. "So they can't even meet someone and raise a family."

The elevator stopped again and the businessmen got off. It was just Angel and me now. "All Magi must remain chaste." It was an old-fashioned word but seemed to suit the Magi. "If they have sexual relations, they'll die."

Angel shuddered. "None of that is any way to live."

"I agree," I said. "But it's all they know." I paused as I met her gaze. "Few know the details I am giving you. Rodán trusts you, Angel, or you wouldn't be here."

"It's a privilege to be told this information and to actually meet them." Her expression was contemplative, serious. "I'm honored."

"Rodán believes it is essential to visit the Magi in twos," I said, "so that there is a witness who hears every detail. When he and the Great Guardian called you to be a Tracker, you took an oath of confidentiality."

Angel nodded. "Of course."

"According to Rodán, the Magi can immediately sense any plot against them." I glanced at the flashing digital numbers. Almost there. "If someone attempts a plan to take them down or exploit them, there is a whole series of emergency steps that are taken and that threat would be immediately terminated."

After several stops, thanks to the boy who had pushed several buttons, the elevator finally stopped at the fifty-third floor. We left the elevator to go to the door of the Presidential Suite and I hesitated a moment, then slid the card in. A soft chime accompanied us as I entered the room and Angel followed me. We let the door close quietly behind us.

The sophisticated interior had an Asian theme. Four cans of Pepsi, a bowl of tortilla chips and salsa, and four small green plates seemed out of place on the dark wood table in the center of three couches that were arranged in a U shape. Embroidered cream throw pillows were tossed on the green couches and the room had dark red, green, and cream accents. All of the rich wood furnishings were hand carved, the lighting soft. The Asian pieces of art and the huge chandelier over the dining room table gave the room a graceful, elegant appearance.

It wasn't the furnishings or décor that captured my attention, though.

One of the most ethereal beings I had ever seen reclined on a couch. Looking at her was like studying Rodán's painting of the fairy, but seeing it through a shroud of misty gold.

Brown hair highlighted in shades of autumn leaves, eyes that reminded me of polished Dryad wood and features that looked almost Elvin. She was petite and dainty, as fragile-looking as a tea rose. But a rose with no thorns.

"Hello, Nyx." The girl, who couldn't have been more than sixteen, had a sweet, lovely voice with an Irish lilt. The sound was what I'd truly call musical. She looked fascinated as she studied me. "You are quite pretty as a human. I would so like to see you after sunset as Drow. What I vision of you is very beautiful."

Surprise made me speechless. For this girl to know things about me so quickly—had someone told her?

"I am Magi, and I visioned of you and of your coming to me, Nyx." The Magi made my name sound like a word in a song, not as brief and hard as it could have been said. Like it had been said many times.

Lighting played on her airy purple robe as she adjusted herself to clasp her hands in her lap. "I only know what I have visioned of you," she continued, "and what I see of you now. You have a good soul and a kind heart despite the path you have chosen."

I recognized at once that what she said wasn't a slam or meant to be a condemnation. It was said as though she was simply recognizing what it meant to be a Night Tracker.

"And you are intelligent enough to know that you chose that dangerous path," she said with a note of simple fact in her voice. "The path did not choose you."

More surprise made me weak. I sat down on the couch opposite her and failed to come up with anything to say. My bag hit the floor with a *thump* when I set it down beside my feet. She had seen through what was in my heart, what I never expected anyone to know about me. It was something I hadn't even admitted to myself.

The Magi tilted her head as she smiled at Angel. "You look like what you are named for, one of the Seraphim. May I see you as a squirrel?"

Angel sat beside me and smiled back at the Magi. "If you'd like me to, sure."

"Yes, please, Angel." The young Magi sat straighter in her seat. "I do not get to see Dopplers often and I, myself, have no animal form. I would so love to see you as such."

Angel nodded and stood. Dopplers, Shifters, and Weres are gifted with little magic but the ability to shift, and to do so without taking their clothes off. The clothing melts away into the fur that covers their bodies and then returns as clothing when they shift back.

I'd watched Angel transform into a squirrel plenty of times, but it was different seeing her do it in a casual setting like we were in with the Magi. Angel was a little over five feet tall before she shifted to her squirrel form, shrinking like Alice did in Wonderland after downing some of the magic that was in the "drink me" bottle.

The blond squirrel paused before she scampered closer to the Magi but she kept about two feet in distance between them. Angel rested on her hind legs with her bushy tail curving over her head, raised her front paws in the air, and sniffed as if looking for food. Maybe she was hungry and caught the scent of nuts.

The young Magi clapped her hands together and gave a brilliant smile. "Thank you, Angel."

Angel shifted back to her human form and took her seat again. "It was my pleasure," she replied.

The Magi looked from Angel to me. "Would you like a drink and a snack?" She gestured to the Pepsi cans on the coffee table. "They are quite cold and the chips and salsa are very good."

"Thank you." I reached for a can and popped the tab. Angel did the same. "May I ask your name?" I asked so that I didn't have to keep referring to her as the Magi.

"Of course." She inclined her head in a naturally regal manner. "I am Kerri Waldo."

"From your accent you're obviously from Ireland," Angel said. "And Kerri is an Irish name." Angel tilted her head. "But Waldo is Germanic, like my last name which is Pfarr."

Kerri smiled. "A year ago when I emigrated from Ireland, I was told I would have to take on a last name."

"That's right," I said before I took a drink from the can. I decided not to have chips. "Magi don't take the last name of their birth parents."

"You are correct." Kerri picked up her drink from the coffee table. "We usually do not have last names." The young Magi sipped from the can. "When I reached New York City with Mrs. Andersen, I met a woman and her daughter Brooke." Kerri said. "They were so very kind to me. I decided to take on their last name, which is Waldo."

Kerri looked thoughtful. "Brooke, the daughter, was adorable. She must be ten and a half now. A year ago she wanted to make sure I knew she was nine and a half."

"That's enough, Kerri." A woman spoke and I startled. I turned my head and saw a Doppler female whose voice and face were as harsh as the Magi was beautiful. I'd been so caught up in the loveliness of the Magi, and what she had to say, that I hadn't even noticed the older woman enter the room. "These guests are here for business, not to listen to your stories."

"Yes, Mrs. Andersen." Kerri spoke to the woman in her soft, sweet voice and said it with a gentle smile.

The woman turned to look at Angel and me. "I am this ward's Magi-Keeper." Mrs. Andersen had the kind of face that I thought would always look hard to please. A sophisticated but tight face with sharp blue eyes and lips pursed in permanent reproach. She wore a simple yet elegant blue dress with plain heels and her pure white hair was drawn away from her face in a knot. "Kerri is one of three Magi in this suite. She knew of your coming before Rodán called."

She said "Rodán" in such a sharp way that it was clear she disapproved of him. I wondered why.

Mrs. Andersen looked at me, ignoring Angel, her eyes narrowing. "You must be Nyx of the Drow," she said to me, sounding almost as disapproving of me as she had of Rodán.

Her eyes then rested on Angel. "And the blond Doppler is Angel, who I expect to remain silent," she said, and Angel and I glanced at each other. "Discuss your business with Kerri and be quick about it."

"Yes, ma'am." Calling the Magi-Keeper ma'am came out without me even thinking about it. Anything else would not have fit and wouldn't have been considered acceptable, I was certain.

"May I see it?" Kerri glanced at the bag resting at my feet. "The stone that you carry."

I hesitated. It felt wrong to have this lovely creature of the light touch the thing which resonated with such darkness.

"Set it on the coffee table." The Magi tucked her feet beside her on the couch and her purple robes covered her toes. "I do not intend to touch it."

I nodded, relieved in that respect, but dreading having to get it out myself. I grabbed my bag off the floor and unzipped the pouch where I had put the stone when I left the park. My hand shook a little as I wrapped my fingers around the object.

As soon as the stone was in my grasp the bag fell to the floor and bright flashes came from the flat side of the stone. At least it felt like flashes. Within that TV-like surface, I saw New York City, then a world of incredible beauty, and a man. A male with a featureless face and colorless skin, as if the stone couldn't decide what either should be.

At the same time I was seeing the flashes, electrical energy charged up and down my arm. My teeth clinked together. My head pounded. Prickles ran along my scalp.

"Set it on the coffee table," came Kerri's calm but firm voice. "Now, Nyx." When I hesitated she said in a much firmer tone, "Do it *now*."

Angel grasped my arm as if to help me move closer to the table. She jerked her hand back at once and gave a soft sound of surprise and maybe even pain.

"I can do it." I closed my eyes to block the images and leaned forward so that I could set it on the clean surface of the coffee table. I yanked my hand back and opened my eyes.

I had set the stone down with the flat side facing Kerri. She was looking at it and she appeared paler, but her features were placid, not telling me what she was thinking. The Magi stared at the stone for so long without talking that

I worried that somehow she had become enthralled by the stone's magic.

Kerri raised her head and looked at me with her beautiful brown eyes. "It is as I had visioned." She had such a mysterious look and air to her that I couldn't tell if she'd been affected or not by the power contained within the thing on the coffee table. "What you have brought back with you from Otherworld is a keystone." And then more softly. "A keystone to yet another Otherworld, one called Doran."

"Doran?" I cocked my head as I mentally ran through all of the Otherworlds that I grew up knowing. "I've never heard of it." There were a lot more Otherworlds than any of us were aware of, I was certain. Except for the Great Guardian, who seemed to know everything.

The Magi closed her eyes for a long time. I heard Angel's soft breathing and the scrubbing sound of Mrs. Andersen's skirt rubbing against her chair as she shifted her position. The room's scent of chai was strong enough that I could identify each warm spice—cinnamon, cardamom, and ginger.

When the Magi opened her eyes, she focused her pretty brown gaze on me. "Doran is not the concern. The leader of that world is."

I stared at her, knowing that she had more to say.

"You must seek out a Sorcerer here named Desmond. He will not be easy to convince to speak with you and he will be angry at having been found," Kerri said. "It is a task you are well up to, Nyx of the Drow."

Something dark passed across the Magi's features, a darkness that did not belong with such ethereal beauty and mystery. It came in a flash, then was gone.

"You must take Olivia DeSantos with you when you go to the Sorcerer," Kerri said more quietly. I would have wondered how she knew about Olivia, but she was a Magi after all. "I cannot see why taking your partner is important, but it is. Do not visit the Sorcerer Desmond until she can be with you."

"Olivia wouldn't have it any other way, I'm sure." I was surprised I finally found my voice as I imagined me trying to keep Olivia from going. The reaction I pictured wasn't pretty.

"I see both darkness and light." Kerri showed no emotion as she continued. "The knowledge of what will transpire is being withheld from me. That is because what you will do when you are with the Sorcerer will determine what happens in the future. The future is not set."

"Is the future normally set?" I asked.

"If knowledge and free will are not a part of the equation, then at times yes," she said. "You have both knowledge and free will, so no, I believe that your future is not set. I can see light and darkness. You must make the right choices to see which you will live in."

I grasped the drink can in my hands more firmly. "I don't understand."

The Magi smiled. "There are times when I can see the future clearly. At some times I see two outcomes. This is one of those times. Two great powers will be in opposition, vying for very different outcomes. Which power prevails is dependent in part on what you can do."

For a moment I didn't say anything. I was the one who could impact the future in this situation because I had knowledge and free will according to the Magi. I had never thought a future to be set to begin with. I had always believed we each made choices which would affect the outcome. Always.

"How do I find the Sorcerer?" I asked.

"He is an artist." Kerri met my gaze. "Like your brother."

Shock jolted me. "How do you know about my brother?" I realized it was a dumb question once I said it.

"Look for Desmond where many workers of the arts reside," Kerri said. "His art is displayed in a small gallery." She tilted her head as if listening to something. "You will find him in the sun."

"I will find him where?" I asked, puzzled.

"Simply do as I instructed," Kerri said.

I didn't understand why she didn't just come out and say it, then remembered that Magi are not all-knowing even though it might seem like it.

"What do I do once I find the Sorcerer?" I asked. "How do I convince him to help?"

The Magi gave a slight nod toward the stone on the coffee table. "Show him the keystone."

I looked at the stone. I could only see the backside of it, and right now I was grateful for that.

"Handle the stone as little as possible." The Magi glanced at it before returning her gaze to me. "Every time you touch the stone it becomes a beacon and will draw the enemy."

Heat burned beneath the skin along my arms. What had I done by bringing the stone to this Earth Otherworld? It had seemed so benign. But now . . . what was it? What was happening?

Kerri drew two silky white handkerchiefs from a pocket in her robe. She set the handkerchiefs on the coffee table. "Wrap the keystone in one of these. The material is warded. It will protect you when you must hold it. Take the other. You will need it."

"Thank you." I leaned forward and picked up the cloud-soft handkerchiefs. I put one in my bag and laid the other across the stone. Making sure to not let the stone brush my fingers, I wrapped it in the cloth before tucking the stone back into the zippered pocket of my bag.

I'd stuff it someplace safe in my apartment—

"Keep the stone with you at all times," the Magi said, negating my thought. "You must protect it."

"Okay," I said, even though I abhorred the idea of keeping it with me.

"Show it only to those you trust and only as absolutely necessary to accomplish what you need to do." Kerri seemed to grow suddenly weary before my eyes. "I suggest you not even show it to your partner unless you have to."

"Why not?" I asked. "Not even Olivia?" Kerri seemed not to hear.

"You must do whatever the Sorcerer Desmond asks of you," Kerri said, her voice a monotone now. "It is vital."

"What—" I started to say but stopped when she continued talking.

"Zombies you can eliminate, but do not kill the Sentients or the Hosts." The Magi's eyelids drooped and her features slackened a little. "Friends will die."

"What do you mean 'Friends will die'?" My stomach grew queasy at the thought of any of my friends dying. "What are Sentients? And Hosts?"

"Do not let a stone-bearing Sentient touch you with his hands," Kerri whispered. "Lock . . . away."

"That is enough." Mrs. Andersen's voice cut across my desire to ask the Magi more questions. Many more questions. "Kerri must rest now."

"The New Year will bring destruction and ruin if they are not stopped." The Magi's voice rose, but she sounded sleepy and almost as if she wasn't actually there, with us. More like a Seraphim ready to fade and vanish. "Stop them . . ."

I jumped to my feet. "What—"

"I said that's enough." Mrs. Andersen stood beside the Magi's couch now and grasped her hands to help her stand. "Quiet your mind, Kerri."

The Magi turned her head to face Angel. "I am sorry. So very sorry." Kerri said it simply, as if she was offering up her sorrow for something that had happened or would be happening in Angel's life.

Angel's eyes widened and she opened her mouth to speak, but the Magi walked away, allowing Mrs. Andersen to lead her.

Then Kerri drew the Magi-Keeper to a halt and turned just enough to see me and Angel. The Magi looked deathly pale now. "A storm is brewing," she said. "You must stop it, Nyx of the Dark Elves and Night Trackers. Only you can do it."

I wanted to run after Kerri and ask more questions. But Mrs. Andersen took Kerri's arm and led her through the archway before disappearing down a dark hall.

"By all of the worlds and Sorcerers, what did she mean?" Angel looked both concerned and puzzled. "She spoke in bits and pieces and none of it sounded good at all."

"No, it didn't." I slung the pack onto my shoulder as I did my best to ignore the creepy feeling I got just from the stone being in my bag. "For now what we need to worry about is finding a Sorcerer in SoHo."

NINETEEN

Tuesday, December 27

"Where are you, girl?" I said on Olivia's voicemail Tuesday morning. "Thought you were going to be back today." I glanced at the time on the computer monitor. Eleven-thirty and Olivia was usually in no later than nine. "I have some big leads on the Zombie case that we need to follow up on right away. Call me."

I wanted to tell her about the stone which still gave me the creeps even though the Magi had wrapped it in a protective cloth. I had it tucked away in my purse, which I figured was considered close enough to protect it. Then I remembered that for some reason I wasn't supposed to share anything about the stone with her.

Apparently Olivia was spending an extra day with her large family although I would have bet money that she'd be home early like I was. Sometimes a little family time can go a long, long way.

Olivia had more than earned the time away. I couldn't remember the last time she'd taken a vacation. If she missed the Tracker meeting tonight I'd fill her in tomorrow. I smiled at the thought of Olivia and her sisters and wondered what it would have been like to grow up with sisters myself.

The moment after I punched the OFF button, the phone started to ring and Adam's name and number came up.

Warmth flowed through me and I answered, "Hey there."

"Hey, Nyx." Adam's voice sounded so good. I wanted to

kiss him so badly I could have crawled right through the phone to get to him.

"Did you make it back all right?" I asked, already picturing us making dinner tonight before I went tracking.

Adam said, "I'm still at my parents' home and not sure when I'll make it back."

Disappointment flowed through me. "I miss you."

"Why don't we plan on a late lunch tomorrow?" I was taken back for a moment because he hadn't said he missed me. I hadn't realized I was so needy for attention like that.

"Okay." I picked up a pen and started doodling on a sticky note with "Her Royal Highness" written on it to remind me to get Kali a supply of Fancy Feast and to get myself some bottles of green tea as well as a few groceries. Maybe some crackers, cheese, dried salami, and a bottle of Ghost Block cabernet sauvignon for the next time Adam came over. The pantry and fridge were looking bare.

"Let's go to Little Italy," he said.

"Il Cortile on Mulberry Street?" I loved their special capellini dish. "How's one o'clock sound?" We had always preferred to avoid as much of the lunch crowd as we could.

"Sure," he said. "See you tomorrow."

And then he was gone. I didn't even get a chance to say goodbye.

Thoughts of the Zombies we had fought remained at the forefront of my mind despite all that I was doing. Actually fighting them, along with all of the odd coincidences that were happening . . . I hoped that this Sorcerer Desmond could help and that we could fix whatever it was that was going so terribly wrong.

Kali startled me when she jumped up onto my desk as I set my phone aside and turned back to my monitor. She walked across the keyboard and letters started randomly appearing in my open case-notes document before another Internet browser window popped up.

"Kali!" I picked her up and she gave an indignant *meow* as she twitched her tail in my face. I set her back on the floor and. "Stay off my keyboard."

She jumped back onto my desk, only this time across my sticky notes all over its surface. She plopped her big furry butt in the middle of them and looked at me with an expression of disdain.

Kali continued to stare at me with her freaky golden eyes. I glared at her in return.

She won the staring contest. No one could beat Kali in a staring contest.

Under my breath I muttered something about finding a foster home for a cat who shredded new lingerie and walked across computer keyboards.

Thoughts of Adam kept pinging at me but I turned back to my monitor and reviewed the lists of galleries in both SoHo and Chelsea.

I wasn't sure why, but my gut had told me from the beginning that we'd find the Sorcerer in the former but the latter was a possibility, too. I'd already skimmed the names of galleries in both areas. No Desmond anything as far as a business name. Likely a gallery simply showed his work.

Thinking of a Sorcerer as an artist who showed his work in galleries in an artistic community was an adjustment. Didn't they stay in dark caves of rooms with bottles of potions, casting spells?

What else had the Magi said?

"You will find him in the sun."

"Sun . . . sun . . ." I looked at both lists again.

And shook my head when I came to Sun Lee Gallery in SoHo. "I guess maybe Kerri did tell me exactly where to find him," I said to Kali who decided to jump onto a stack of file folders before pouncing back onto my desk and landing on a fluttering bright pink sticky note.

I decided to ignore Kali and called the gallery. A recorded message by a woman with an Asian accent said they were on winter hours and opened daily at noon. Might as well head there and see if I could at least track down the location of the Sorcerer. If I happened to see him, I just wouldn't make contact.

The Magi had said that Olivia had to go with me when I

talked with the Sorcerer. When a Magi tells someone to do something, if at all possible that someone does it. Kerri had her reasons and I had the strong sense I needed to go with what she instructed me to do.

From my purse in the cubbyhole in my desk, I drew out my wallet that had my undercover ID and some cash. I pocketed it and also slid daggers into my Elvin boots and holstered my Kahr 9mm in a sheathe that I attached to the belt I threaded through the loops on my jeans. The weapon wouldn't show beneath the jacket I'd be wearing.

Lastly I took the stone wrapped in cloth out of my purse and put it into an inside zippered pocket of my jacket. Despite the cloth, my arm still tingled when I touched the wrapped stone.

I prefer to drive when the weather is good, not when there's snow on the ground. Snowflakes drifted from fair clouds as I headed out of the office. I decided to walk the four and a half miles to the gallery as opposed to catching a cab. Most norms would think it unusual to walk that far. For me it was like walking around the block.

By the time I reached the gallery on Wooster Street, my cheeks felt flush, my nose cold, and my mood vastly improved. I stood on the sidewalk and studied the two framed paintings and art glass pieces in the large windows to either side of the door. Did the Sorcerer do either one of the paintings?

One was an oil painting of a waterfall spilling into a glittering pool of water beside a patch of wildflowers. Shadows of leaves from surrounding trees reflected in the pond. It had a magical look to it, almost as if it wasn't of this world.

The other was beautiful too. It was a painting of a geisha sitting beneath a tree, her small hand holding a delicate painted wood fan that covered the smile I knew was on her lips. Cherry blossoms swirled around her like confetti in Times Square on New Year's Day.

I couldn't read either artist's signature—the one with the pond was just squiggles, starting with what could have been a "D."

The signature on the Japanese piece of art was done in Kanji script.

I was betting on the waterfall and the squiggles for Desmond. It really wasn't much of a stretch.

Bells tinkled as I pushed open the door and immediately by scent, sound, and senses, I knew I was in a shop at least inhabited by one of the Fae.

The Fae wardings were exceptionally strong. The wardings wouldn't notice the Drow daggers in each boot because the boots were Elvin-made, but the Kahr sheathed at my belt was another story.

My thoughts strayed to the stone in my pocket and I hoped that the wardings couldn't detect it through the cloth the Magi had wrapped it in.

A petite, elegant woman swept into the room, wearing a frown. I wasn't surprised by her expression. I was disheveled from walking in the wind, hadn't dressed like a potential client, and I was carrying a gun.

"What business have you here?" The woman was Asian and had delicate yet hard features. She wore her hair cropped close to her head in a fashionable style, and she was dressed in an Armani suit that was to die for.

And she was Fae. Definitely Fae. I just had no idea what—I couldn't gauge her by scent or appearance. The fact that I failed to recognize what she was made my muscles tense. I wondered if perhaps she was an Undine or Siren because of the numerous paintings of lakes, waterfalls, rivers, and the ocean lining the gallery walls.

I hoped for the business's sake, though, that she didn't treat every customer like this.

"I'm Nicole." I gave her my undercover name that wouldn't make it easy for her to follow up on me. "Are you the owner?"

"Yes." She continued to eye me with suspicion. "I am Sun Lee."

"I noticed you have a piece by Desmond in the window." I made sure my smile was pleasant and natural. I was very much hoping the oil in the window was by Desmond.

The woman continued to look wary of me. "If you are familiar with his work then I am sure you will have no problem locating the pieces he has on show at this time."

I took that as a yes.

Sun Lee walked away from me, looking beautiful in her perfectly tailored suit and three-hundred-dollar heels.

The only thing I had to go on was gut instinct, so I went for the grouping of paintings done in the same style as the waterfall painting in the window. I walked up to a whole series clearly painted by the same artist.

The largest was gorgeous and grabbed my attention immediately. It was love at first sight. The painting was of a fair, dark-haired human woman staring at her reflection in the surface of a shimmering pond. Looking back at her from the water was an Elvin female with delicate pointed ears. The water was dark enough that the female in the reflection could have been Drow. It couldn't have been more perfect for me.

The brass plate under the painting had:

WORLDS INTERTWINE
Artist: DESMOND

Gotcha.

I smiled but then frowned. How was I going to get Sun Lee to give me the Sorcerer's address? I glanced at the warding bells, then sent out my air elemental magic to explore.

The entire gallery was protected. I couldn't just slip into glamour and start searching the place. First, the wardings wouldn't allow me to cloak myself in a glamour if I wanted to. And second, the woman was Fae so she would be able to see straight through my glamour anyway.

I was either going to have to coerce the information out of her or try to break in tonight. Considering the strength of her wardings, I didn't think I had a prayer at being able to break in.

With the power of the protection, I also didn't think any

of my friends could get in easily. Joshua was a Shadow Shifter who could slip into any crack or opening, but could he get past the wardings? Could Ice find his way inside as a mouse? No, they'd be detected the moment they took human form. I was on my own.

Coercion wasn't likely an option, so I'd try another tactic.

I walked up to the elegant desk Sun Lee was sitting behind. She raised her head the moment she realized I was coming toward her. Tension radiated off her along with a good dose of irritation. Guess she didn't like the fact that I was armed and right then I probably didn't look like someone who could afford anything in the gallery.

"I'd like to purchase that large painting by Desmond," I said as I approached her. *"Worlds Intertwine."*

"Oh, really." Her tone was one of amusement, as if she found something about my request for that painting funny. She looked over my appearance then met my gaze again. "It's ten thousand dollars. Will you be paying by cash or credit?"

A Sorcerer who commanded that kind of price—amazing as well as surprising. Although in the paranorm world, I shouldn't have been surprised at all.

"If you can arrange a meeting with the artist, I'll pay you now and use a card." I dug the wallet out of my pocket, opened it, and chose my American Express. "I'm a huge fan of Desmond's work and I would love the opportunity to see the man behind the art."

She stared at me in total surprise and I smiled in return.

I'm a Drow princess. There isn't much that I can't afford considering the size of diamonds and other precious gemstones that Dark Elves mine, not to mention all of the different metals. I was also paid very well as a Tracker and as a PI.

"I can bring you cash in the morning if you prefer." She was Fae—you never knew what the Fae would like. I held out my card to her. "I just don't happen to carry that many hundred-dollar bills in my pocket."

"No, of course not." Sun Lee had regained her composure and reached for my AmEx. "I'll put it on your card now."

"As long as I get to meet the artist," I said, holding her gaze.

"This is a favored painting of his, so I believe I can arrange it." Sun Lee looked at the card, which was under the name Nicole Carter. I handed her my ID with my picture and the same name as well.

The moment the charge went through, she asked if I would like it delivered. I told her I would schedule my own pickup tomorrow. I wasn't about to give out my real address. I'd call my friend James. He and Derek would be glad to help me out. They were awesome that way.

"Did you drive or may I call you a cab?" she asked as I signed her copy of the receipt that her credit card machine had spit out. She certainly was anxious to please now.

I gave my most sincere smile. "That would be so kind of you." Not a hint of sarcasm in my voice. Really.

She picked up a cell phone from on top of her desk and hit a speed dial number. I'd bet that Desmond's number was on her phone. If anything happened to interfere with her arranging a meeting with him, I'd track her down and take her phone one way or another.

"It's so lovely." I looked up at the painting. It truly was and it had a way of making me feel at peace. Every time I studied it, I swore it looked a little different. Like a new ripple in the pond, a strand of her dark hair let loose in the wind, eyes blinking slowly.

"Desmond's work is quite incredible," Sun Lee said.

"I'm very excited to bring it into my home," I said as she walked me to the gallery's entrance. "I know exactly where I'll put it."

"I thought perhaps because of the gun you carry that you are a police officer," she said as we stopped at the door. "I am . . . uncomfortable with weapons."

"How did you know?" I feigned ignorance. She was testing me and likely knew I wasn't human and she had just as much of an idea of what I am as I did her. Which meant she probably didn't have a clue that I'm Drow. "I carry one for protection. One never knows in this city."

"So true," she said with a bow of her head as she let me out the door. A cab had already pulled up. "Thank you, Ms. Carter. I will be calling you."

"I appreciate it, Sun Lee." I walked down the front steps and to the waiting taxi.

My belly twisted a little at the thought of meeting the Sorcerer.

I drew my phone out of my pocket and called my friend James to ask him to pick up the painting for me tomorrow. I had a feeling I was going to be too busy to worry about it for a while.

TWENTY

Colin and I left the Pit after the Tracker meeting and headed for the Bronx, the area he and I were covering tonight.

Thoughts of Zombies wouldn't leave my mind.

I wore black leather like most Trackers did when we went out at night. The leather was enough to chase away what little chill would bother me. I'd tucked the stone into a pouch on my weapons belt next to one of my Dragon-claw daggers.

"How long have you been in New York City?" I asked him as we headed up the street in the direction we needed to go to eventually make it to the Bronx.

"Not long." Colin had an Otherworldly hint of an accent to his voice.

We came to a stop at the light. "Two years ago for me."

At the Tracker meeting tonight I'd doled out all kinds of information about the attacks in Otherworld, but I didn't mention the stone my father had given me.

The other Trackers were ordered to avoid touching any "Sentients" that might be carrying "stones" or the stones themselves. I described them as best I could without actually saying I'd seen one, and though I mentioned having met a Seer I avoided saying that she was a Magi.

I'd explained that we had been told by the "Seer" to not kill Sentients or Hosts, yet it was okay to kill Zombies, but we weren't clear about what the Seer had meant. How could we tell the difference?

Of course I hadn't shown the stone I hid in the pouch on my weapons belt. For one, I didn't want to touch it, and two, the Magi said not to let anyone know I carried it with me. No matter that they were all fellow Trackers, every one of them someone I'd trust at my back, times were a little strange right now. And the Magi. I needed to heed the Magi.

When Colin changed the conversation it caught me off guard. "I was in another part of Otherworld when the Elvin people were being murdered and taken," he said. "I heard of what was happening and that other races of beings intended to rally together to help the Light and Dark Elves. But the threat was gone before they were organized enough to aid them."

"I didn't know that other beings had been planning on helping," I said. "I've always thought that we'd been left to our own fate while Fae and Other alike went on with their lives."

"How old were you?" Colin asked as he met my gaze. "It surprises me that you weren't aware of that."

"Five." I brushed a strand of hair from my face. "Too young for my father to have shared that kind of information with me," I said. "But it's good to know that there were those who'd planned to help." Unfortunately it had been too late.

"You were just a babe." Colin gave me a smile that was drop-dead spectacular. I wondered if his Dragon charm was on auto, but realized the flip in my belly was purely a reaction to his natural male magnetism.

I knew better than to ask, but I still said, "Oh, and how old are you?"

"If your father wasn't King of the Drow and as old as Elves are young, I'd say I'm old enough to be your father." Colin laughed. "As it is, I'm only a youngling in comparison to him."

I raised an eyebrow. "And that is . . . ?"

"Tell you what." His grin turned devious. "I'll make a bet with you. We'll have a little race."

"Oh?" I managed to keep a straight face even though his naughty little boy expression made me want to laugh.

"If you win, I'll tell you how old I am," he said. "If I win, you'll buy me a beer when we're done with tracking for the night."

"You've got it." I shook hands with him. With my air element to help me, I'm faster than a cheetah. However, I have endurance where a cheetah is only good at his maximum speed for short sprints.

"We just need to go somewhere not in the zones with the high number of attacks and disappearances," I said. I had my team focusing on areas with the most instances. "I need to be able to do a little exploration with my elements and it'll be much safer in a place with no people."

"I have a great idea." His smile was like a man who knew he had it in the bag, which made me want to win even more. "Beat me to the Bronx Zoo entrance. I'll even give you a head—"

I was gone before he finished the end of the sentence.

He was waiting for me when I got there.

I put my hands on my hips and walked to where he was standing, beneath the Bronx Zoo sign. "How did you beat me?"

"You owe me a beer," he said.

The zoo animals sounded a little agitated. I wondered if they could scent a Dragon.

"How about best two out of three?" I wasn't ready to give up that easily.

He shrugged. "I'll just win again."

That remark made me want to beat him even more.

"Which Seer did you go to?" Colin asked as a monkey shrieked from inside the zoo.

"Guess we all have our secrets," I said, teasing him back.

During the Tracker meeting, I hadn't mentioned that the Seer Angel and I had visited was a Magi because paranorm leadership wanted to keep the Magi as safe as possible. That included not mentioning them in combination with anything they might have assisted with.

"Fair is fair." He acknowledged me with a nod. Then he said, "What you talked about in the meeting tonight. Do you have any other theories as to what the Seer meant when she warned that we can only kill Zombies, not Sentients and Hosts?"

"Honestly, I have no idea." During the meeting there'd been some speculation based on what other Trackers had seen during attacks they'd fought off, but it was all only speculation.

I'd mentioned that the Seer told us to find a certain Sorcerer in the city and I'd explained that I was attempting to locate him now. I managed to avoid naming him.

There were a few other things I'd kept to Rodán, Angel, and myself because the information seemed too important to release on a broad basis.

That included the fact that I'd located the Sorcerer and hopefully would have a meeting with him tomorrow. For ten thousand dollars I certainly hoped so.

I really did love the painting.

"You didn't mention the Sorcerer Desmond's name to all of the Trackers," Colin said. "Just to the team members."

"It was an executive decision." I tilted my head back and felt the soft fall of snow on my face. "The fewer who know that detail, the better. Once we have more information, we'll share it with all of our Trackers."

A big cat, possibly a lion, gave a low rumble from inside the zoo.

Colin's amazing burnished gold eyes studied me. "What do you think about Lawan having been missing for a couple of days? Is that why you held back on the Sorcerer's name?"

"She's one reason why we didn't share everything tonight. We need to be careful." We started to walk away from the zoo entrance. "Although she sure seemed like herself tonight." I frowned. "But the day before she went missing she thought someone was watching her."

"Has Rodán considered taking her off duty?" he asked.

"Yes." I thought about the conversation I'd had with him earlier. "But there's no proof, and no reason to. Lawan's twin sister, Malee, did arrive from Thailand like Lawan said. We're just being cautious for now."

Colin nodded. "Cautious is good."

"Let's see what we can locate." I took a deep breath. "We need to see if there's any Zombie activity going on around here." I looked at him. "You've got my back?"

Colin gave a nod but didn't say anything. He watched as I stood with my feet shoulder-width apart, my hands at my sides. I took another deep breath and closed my eyes.

I sent out my elemental magic. I couldn't use too much at one time without weakening myself, so I used what would take the least amount of energy. When there was snow, it was one time of the year when I could use my water magic easily to explore.

At the same time I let my water elemental cover the ground through the snow, I released my air magic and sent it searching.

I searched for any imprints of beings that did not belong and for activity that might be wrong. Behind my eyelids, I saw flashes of people and streets and cars and businesses closed for the night. Nothing wrong or out of the ordinary.

No Zombies.

The magic I used to search such a large area put a strain on my body and I knew I needed to reel myself back in.

I gasped as I came fully back to myself as if I hadn't been breathing the entire time my essence was traveling with my elemental magic.

"Nothing right now," I said when my gaze met Colin's. "All's quiet for the time being."

Snow had started to fall thicker and I noticed Colin shiver. Unlike other Trackers, Colin wasn't wearing leather. He wore jeans and a T-shirt beneath a dark blue jacket that looked warm and comfortable. He'd pushed his long blond hair over his shoulders away from his face, and his nose and cheeks appeared a little ruddy from the chill.

"Dragons can't handle the cold?" I said as I shook off the remnants of the out-of-body experience I always felt when I used my elements to search large areas like I just had.

"Not too crazy about it." Colin smiled. "Since we don't have snow in Otherworld, it's going to take some getting used to. Rodán thinks I should wear black leather that has been spelled for the weather and durability like the rest of the Trackers, but I've never been good at falling in with the crowd."

I leaned down, grabbed a handful of snow, and formed a ball. "Ever been in a snowball fight?" I said right before I nailed him in the face.

Colin sputtered and I scooped up another handful and hit him again.

Then I found out Colin wasn't only fast when it came to racing, but he threw snowballs with the best of them.

We were both covered in snow and laughing by the time he held his hands up and said, "I give up. No more."

"Are you up for something hot to drink? It's got to be better than a cold beer for a shivering Dragon," I said with a grin.

Colin grinned back. "Is there a place nearby where Dragons and Drow can go this time of night?"

"There's a coffee shop owned by a paranorm here in the Bronx." I inclined my head in the direction we needed to go. "On Arthur Avenue." I gave him the address and said, "Best two out of three."

And I was gone.

When I got there I looked around and didn't see Colin. Ha. I'd made it before him.

Then he stepped out of the coffee shop.

Damn. "How—?"

"Come on in," he said. "It's cold out here."

"Sheesh." I followed him inside. "How do you do that?"

"I ordered hot chocolate for both of us." He went up to the Witch at the cash register who only glanced at me with mild curiosity. I was unique in being the only Drow in New York City, but paranorms got used to seeing different types of beings and many seemed almost immune to the surprise of something new. Like a female with amethyst skin and blue hair.

Colin pulled out a wallet and paid while another Witch handed me two large ceramic mugs topped with whipped cream and marshmallows. The mugs were hot to the touch and the contents smelled of rich chocolate.

The café was empty save for the Witches, Colin, and me. We went to a round table in the corner and the mugs made a clunking sound as I set them on its surface. I positioned us in a way so that our backs were to the corner we were in, and we could both see the front entrance.

As I sat, I took a sip of hot chocolate and whipped cream. "Yum."

Colin settled in his chair and I asked, "What made you decide to become a Tracker?"

His long blond hair had fallen over his shoulders as he leaned forward to take his mug. After he took a sip he said, "The Great Guardian asked for me. She thought my skills would come in handy."

"The GG herself asked you?" My jaw dropped. "Or did she do it through Rodán or someone else?"

"The GG?" Colin tilted his head. "Are you talking about the Guardian?"

"Yes." I wiped off whipped cream from the end of my nose. "She came to you?"

"She sent Rodán." He gave a wry grin. "When one is requested by the Guardian, one listens."

I shook my head while at the same time saying, "I suppose you're right."

"No supposing about it," he said.

I nodded. "She's something else."

Colin looked at me as if wondering about my remarks and my obvious attitude. "What part of the city do you live in?" he asked instead.

"Upper West Side," I said. "At 104th Street and Central Park West."

"I'm around Sixty-sixth Road in *Queens*," he said. "I cannot seem to get away from royalty no matter how hard I try." I laughed and he added, "Although I don't mind being around princesses. I don't suppose you have a knight waiting in the wings to rescue you from a Dragon?"

Heat crept over my cheeks and I nodded. "His name is Adam."

Colin shook his head, his expression pretend-grim. "I haven't eaten human in a long time," he said. "This Adam had best stay out of my way."

Before I could even think of a response or have a reaction of any kind to what Colin had said, I felt a strange sensation creep down my spine. Tingling erupted near my waist where the stone was in the pouch.

A shuffling sound caught my attention and I looked toward the entrance. I frowned as a couple came through the door, neither of them wearing cold weather clothing. Both the male and female met my gaze.

I knew then what the Magi meant about Sentients versus Zombies. The pair I was staring at were not Zombies, but I could sense they were not of any paranorm race that I'd ever come across. I caught their faint unusual odor which was slightly different than Zombies.

They gave me the creeps, that horrible feeling, like grubs wiggling on my skin. Just like the male had in the coffee shop that night with Adam—the male that at the time I'd thought might have been a Vampire.

My fingers brushed the hilt of the dagger by my right hand. I sensed Colin's attention on the beings too, and felt his tension mount.

The male and female came toward us—

And then the café started to fill with Zombies.

TWENTY-ONE

Both Witches screamed as Zombies poured into the coffee shop.

Colin and I surged to our feet so fast we knocked our table over. It hit the floor with a crash. Our mugs slammed to the floor. Ceramic shattered. Hot chocolate sprayed in an arc, reaching the legs of the beings coming toward us.

My heart thudded. The keystone burned hot through the pouch of my belt and I felt its heat against my hip.

Colin was suddenly holding a sword. I didn't know where it came from. I had a second to be relieved that a garbage-truck-sized Dragon wasn't filling the place. Would have made it difficult to maneuver well enough to fight.

"I think the first two are Sentients," I said over the moans and groans of the Zombies. There was something different about the smell of the Sentients. Not as bad as the dirty dishwater smell of the Zombies, but not human, either. "I'll take them down first. For now the Zombies are yours."

"I've got them." Colin dodged the two Sentients as I rushed them.

The move confused both of the Sentients for a moment and I used that to my advantage. Since I couldn't kill them, I'd have to find other ways to take care of them.

I felt the dangerous white flash in my eyes right before I slammed my fist into the male's nose and used a knife hand strike against the female's neck at the same time. I used only enough force to stop, not kill.

It wasn't enough.

The female didn't go down and the male leapt for me. I had a fraction of a second to remember the Magi's warning.

"Do not let a stone-bearing Sentient touch you with his hands," she had said as she left. *"Lock . . . away."*

I didn't know what that last part meant, and I didn't know if these Sentients carried stones, but I didn't want to find out right now.

As the male grabbed at me, I ducked between the pair, hitting my knees. I flung my arms out, striking them behind their knees and caused them both to drop to the floor.

The female shouted and the male cursed. They each rolled away with surprising speed.

As they moved out of the way, three Zombies lunged for me.

I somersaulted backward and was on my feet with the corner behind me. Trapped if I didn't get out of here.

Over their shoulders I saw Colin using his sword and his strength to battle Zombies.

More Zombies were behind the three in front of me and that didn't count the Sentients who were now to the sides.

I drew both Dragon-claw daggers and charged the three Zombies. The one on my left went down as my dagger made a clean slice across his neck and beheaded him.

The middle Zombie stumbled back when I rammed my right dagger into her chest where her heart should be—but when I yanked back, blood didn't cover the dagger.

As I kicked his jaw at just the right angle, the third Zombie's neck snapped, its head twisted at a freakish angle.

The headless Zombie was down, but the one I'd impaled came right back at me again. I heard a crack and a snap and my stomach clenched as the third Zombie's eyes popped open and I saw it had wrenched its broken neck back into place.

And the two Sentients were coming for me, too.

Adrenaline pumped through me and blood rushed in my ears. I had to get out of the corner. I was almost pinned with no place to move to.

Then I saw a stone. A Sentient was holding it. The female. My heart thudded. I didn't know what it meant for a Sentient to have a stone, but I sure remembered the Magi's warning.

Two remaining Zombies and the two Sentients closed in on me. The female holding the stone said something that sounded like it was spoken in French, but it wasn't French. The other three backed off a little as she came toward me.

I dove to the side, close to the wall, propelling myself beyond the four of them. I slid along the floor, skidding on my shoulder with enough force that I slammed into two more Zombies beyond them.

The Zombies I hit toppled onto their backsides. I leapt to my feet and grabbed my oval double-sided buckler from my weapons belt and flung it at the two Zombies that had attacked me. It beheaded them both. The bodies collapsed to the café floor as the buckler returned to my hand.

More words in the French-sounding language and the Sentients were charging me again. The two Zombies that I'd knocked down when I slid across the floor were now on their feet.

Back to four against one.

I went after the Sentients.

Avoiding the female's hand, I balanced on one leg while I kicked her head then her arm. She cried out as she fell and the stone spun across the room. It hit the far wall with a *clunk*.

The male Sentient went after the stone.

The two Zombies came after me.

In the background I heard Colin's shouts and the sounds of other Zombies, their cries, moans, and groans.

I turned away from the male and faced the Zombies. Like the others, these two were in various stages of decomposition. The Sentients, on the other hand, looked whole and healthy.

I drew my second Dragon-claw dagger and beheaded one Zombie while lopping off the arm of the other that was reaching for me.

The male Sentient rushed toward me with the stone. The female was right behind him.

With one stroke I finished off the armless Zombie, ridding it of its head.

I faced the Sentients. They were almost on me.

A roar shook the café and my gaze cut to the side just enough to see that a Dragon the size of a horse now stood where Colin had been.

Fire blasted from its snout at the remaining Zombies in the room. Moans and cries filled the area as they were roasted.

The Sentients ran through the front entrance.

I bolted after them.

Zombie bodies littered the café. I leapt over them as I went after the Sentients. They were faster than I'd have given them credit for.

I caught up to the male and lunged for his legs. I wrapped my arms around them and brought him down.

His face hit the concrete. The stone flew out of his hand and into the street. A Toyota zipped over it, barely missing hitting the stone with its tires.

From out of nowhere, a woman I hadn't seen before cried out and dove for the stone—right into the path of an oncoming truck.

Brakes squealed as the truck slammed into the woman.

She lay still in front of its bumper as it came to a hard stop.

The male and female Sentients fled. For one second I debated about whether to go after them or grabbing the stone. I went for the stone.

Sirens in the distance. Sounds of people talking. Sights of some looking at the apparently dead woman. Others looking at me.

We were going to have to call the PTF and a Soothsayer in a hurry.

I wrapped myself in an air glamour and vanished from human sight.

More gasps and cries echoed in the street.

"Did you see that?" came one voice. "A purple woman?" said another. "She just disappeared," and "I got her on camera with my cell phone."

Great.

The woman continued to lie still in front of the truck as the driver came out and started patting her shoulder and asking her what her name was.

Was she alive? My senses told me she wasn't a Sentient, she was human. Yet she'd gone for the stone.

Right now the stone was mine. Just in time I remembered not to touch it with my fingers.

I'd tucked the second handkerchief into the weapons belt in the pouch next to the first stone. I pulled it out, tossed it over the stone lying in the street. I grabbed it up and ducked out of the way before I was almost hit by a car that came to a screeching halt behind the truck that hit the woman.

When I glanced at her body, my stomach churned. Something was very wrong about the woman and however she was involved with the Zombies and Sentients.

"She's alive," I heard the truck driver say. "Breathing but unconscious."

Relief that she hadn't died made my blood move again. I went to where she was lying face down on the asphalt. I looked over the shoulder of the man who'd hit her and two other men who'd gathered close. I couldn't see the woman's face, but noticed that she had short dark hair and a crescent-shaped wound behind her left ear.

Still in glamour, I turned and rushed into the café. The floor was covered in Zombie bodies. The Witches were nowhere in sight.

Colin stood in the center of the café, the horse-sized Dragon gone. Gold sparkles still glittered around him. He must have shifted back moments ago. His jacket was lying on the ground, shredded, and his T-shirt was torn.

He gripped his sword in one hand. In the other hand he held a cell phone and was talking on it. The scaled serpent tattoo winding up his arm seemed to glimmer.

Sirens in the distance. Obviously able to see through my glamour, Colin gave me a quick nod as he was explaining the situation and requesting cleanup.

After he snapped his cell shut and stuffed it in his pocket he looked at me. "Well, the chill is gone. Ready for that beer?"

"In the worst way." A sigh rushed out of me in a whoosh. "I could use a six-pack right now."

Colin lightly kicked one of the headless bodies. "I'm willing to bet that these will be just like the others. No ID, nothing telling us what or who these things are."

"Or were." I put my hands on my hips as I around us. "Are the Witches okay?"

"I think so." Colin pointed toward the doorway behind the counter. "I saw them run through there as soon as the Zombies rushed in, and someone called the PTF before I did."

I recognized the sirens as they drew near. Not NYPD but PTF. "They must have called the agency while we were fighting off the bad guys."

"Good girls." Colin gave a nod of approval. "That will save some headache."

We found the Witches and calmed them down as we consulted with the PTF.

The second stone weighed heavy at my hip as I went outside. I waved to Karen Tanner, who'd been called in as Soothsayer for this incident. The Soothsayers had been kept busy lately with all of the Zombie attacks.

I walked to the ambulance, where the PTF emergency techs were bent over a gurney. The unconscious woman was strapped down on the gurney, and Sara, a Healer, stood to the side of the ambulance.

"Hey, Sara," I said to the Healer as I went to the woman who'd been hit by the truck.

Sara shoved her gloved hands into her pockets. The Healer was shivering and her teeth chattered as she said, "Hi there, Nyx."

I wanted to take a look at the human now that she was on her back and I could see her features. One side of her face was scraped from skidding on the asphalt.

The woman looked Hispanic, about thirty, and a couple of inches shorter than me. She had long lashes that were black crescents beneath her closed eyes. She had a naturally olive complexion yet her face was pale.

That strong sense that she was *Other* came to me along with the sense that she was human. Not like me, half human and half Other, but something was different. Impossible, of course. But what was she?

"Is the woman going to be all right?" I asked Sara as the techs put the gurney into the ambulance.

"She has multiple lacerations and a few broken bones." Sara watched the ambulance doors shut behind the woman. "She's in a coma."

"A coma?" I rubbed my arms. "Do you think she'll come out of it soon?"

Sara shook her head. "I saw into her mind and it is still. Very still."

My skin prickled even as I rubbed my arms. "Is she human?"

The Healer frowned, looking perplexed. A little confused. "She's human, but I sensed something *different* about her when I reached into her mind. Yet she's definitely human."

I frowned, too, but I didn't mention I'd had the same feeling.

After talking with the Healer, I spoke to one of the PTF agents who said they'd found a wallet on her. According to her New York driver's license, her name was Candace Moreno. Her wallet held pictures and she had a laminated badge with the name of a stock brokerage company on it.

Stock brokerage and not really human. Very weird.

When Colin and I had talked through things until we had exhausted every angle we could think of, we were ready to get out of there.

The only thing I hadn't told him about was the stone, and this wasn't the place to do it.

TWENTY-TWO

The Sorcerer Amory's heart pounded and his chest ached as he stood on the balcony and looked down at Tieve and Una. They had just returned from the Earth Otherworld and now knelt at his feet, both with their heads bowed.

The lavender-streaked skies crackled, lightning passing from one cloud to another as rage shook him.

"What do you mean, Bryna might be dead?" Amory's voice shook with both fury and fear for his niece who was also one of his trusted advisors. "Why was she with you if you say she had found her Host?"

Una looked up and licked her dry lips. Amory could smell the beginnings of decay from the sickness on her breath.

"Yes, Bryna found her Host and had taken the body," Una said. "She was prepared to go to you with her Host's stone but she asked Tieve to hold it for her."

"Why would she do something so idiotic?" Amory looked at Tieve. "Bryna is not stupid. As soon as she exchanged essences with her Host she should have returned in the new body with her stone."

"The Host body wasn't taking well to her essence, Lord Amory." Tieve's voice trembled. "She felt ill and weakened, so she asked me to carry her Host's stone until she could get to the portal."

"Why did you not bring her straight to the portal?" A slow burn began to warm the Sorcerer's chest and he clenched his fists at his sides. He would have taken care of her. He could have cured the sickness his people sometimes felt when they took a new Host's body.

Una said, "The Shells of those left behind—what Earth Otherworlders call Zombies—were hunting. The Shells found two paranorms. They seemed drawn to them. As if they held a vacated stone."

Amory frowned. "That is not possible," he said and dismissed that thought.

Tieve looked at Una. "The paranorms appeared strong, magical. We were certain they were some of the Trackers whom we have studied and just what we were looking for. Una and I stopped with the Shells to capture the paranorms and trade our essences."

"What happened?" The growl in the Sorcerer's words made both Una and Tieve flinch.

Lightning flared across the sky. Thunder rumbled and the balcony shook. Wind blasted them, pressing his tunic and breeches against his body, sending cool air over his bald head.

"The Trackers were much stronger than we anticipated," Tieve said. "They fought off thirteen Shells as well as both of us."

Una nodded. "One was a Dragon."

Shock filtered through the heat of Amory's anger. "A Dragon? In the Earth Otherworld?" And the possibility of a stone. Had he been wrong to dismiss that idea?

"We saw him change," Tieve said. "And the other Tracker must be Drow. She looks much like the Dark Elves we fought and the one we captured in Otherworld. This one had blue hair and purple skin."

"A Dragon and Drow in the Earth Otherworld," Amory said aloud, unable to believe his fortune. "That would explain both paranorms' strengths."

The Sorcerer felt more than heard Una's and Tieve's sighs of relief because he hadn't killed them for the news they had returned with. Nor had he eliminated them for leaving his niece behind.

No, he wasn't going to kill Una and Tieve. He had better plans for both.

For a long moment he stared off the balcony and at the rich lands and let Una and Tieve shiver with the knowledge that he still might hurt them. Cloud to cloud lightning continued to crackle overhead and hair rose on his arms.

What lay before him and around him had served as their homeland for over twenty years and he would be sorry to leave it. The world they had taken control of when they fled Kerra had been a good home.

With the exception that Doran had eventually rejected the current bodies they were in even as the Kerrans' home world had rejected their original bodies.

Amory turned back to the two, who had their heads bowed. "Stand."

Una and Tieve hurried to their feet. They cowed when he put a hand on each of their heads, but they did not move.

The Sorcerer delved into their memories and the image of Bryna finding a new Host filled his mind. It was with some sadness that he watched her Shell join the others. A Shell was a being neither alive nor dead that would help his people find new Hosts while ridding them of those who were unwanted.

Candace Moreno was the name of the Host Bryna had taken. She had been what humans called a "CEO" of a "brokerage house." Amory wasn't clear on what that position entailed, but his research team and advisors believed it to be a good thing for him to have control of in their takeover of the Earth Otherworld.

Amory moved on from that memory and images of the Drow female and the male Dragon rushed through his mind. He brought the memories to the forefront, making them strong in the minds of Una and Tieve.

They would now be able to remember every single detail about the Trackers. Details they hadn't consciously noticed would now be firmly set within them.

When he removed his hands from their heads they slowly looked up at him. Both had expressions of surprise on their features.

"Where they live," Una said. "They were talking about it when we entered the café."

"Yes . . . the female will be easiest to watch for." Tieve glanced at Una as he spoke. He looked at Amory again. "The Dragon will be far more difficult to find because he did not give as accurate of an address as the Drow did."

"Locate the female and she will likely lead you to the male," Amory said, then continued, "You will find my niece and recover Bryna. You will recover her stone and if there is a vacated stone, you will recover that as well. You will take the Drow female and the Dragon male as your Hosts."

He had seen more in their minds than the memories Una and Tieve had of the pair and it bothered him enough that the snap and sizzle of the lightning grew louder and thunder shook the valley.

"This Nyx and Colin will be trouble for us if they are not taken." Amory considered the situation. "However, they will be great assets once they are taken. They can aid in our plan to infiltrate the Paranorm Council." He nodded to himself. "Yes. That is what we will do."

He scowled at Una and Tieve. "Get the Drow and the Dragon and get Bryna. If you do not, you will suffer for what you have done and have not done."

The pair bowed and fled.

Amory took a deep breath and drew his magic within himself. He let his body relax, tension leaving him.

The skies cleared until they were a lavender-streaked whitewashed blue and nothing more than a soft breeze stirred the leaves of the trees that shaded part of the balcony.

He turned and strode to the manor, entering the large hall and walking toward the Inner Circle chamber where his advisors should have convened by now. The polished marble floor was smooth and cool beneath his bare feet.

The Sorcerer entered the room and in one glance he saw that eleven of his advisors were there, standing around the large circular table. Only Bryna was missing. That thought alone made his belly boil as though hot oil had been poured into it.

Several of his advisors had already taken over Host forms that controlled important positions in the Earth Otherworld. Amory had arranged this meeting so that he might tell them he was prepared for the next step.

Each one of his advisors remained standing as he entered the room and with a gesture he bade them to sit. The circular table had been in the manor when the Sorcerer Desmond had ruled. When he had exiled Desmond, Amory had found it amusing to refer to his advisors as his "Inner Circle" and began using this as a strategy room.

"We have chosen a venue for our trial takeover en masse." Amory raised his hands and the glow of his magic traveled like mist to the wall behind him.

A picture formed of what humans called a "concert" with hundreds of people gathered around the stage of musicians. Not that Amory considered them true musicians with their version of "music." It was nothing like what the people of Kerra embraced and had brought with them when they fled their dying, murderous world.

"This is a theater known as Town Hall," Amory said and the floor plan of the building floated into existence onto the wall. "It seats eight hundred, and we arranged the purchase of four hundred tickets. Four hundred humans will be in attendance and four hundred of our own people will go to the theater with stones. We will have our first mass exchange of essences."

"What about sealing their Hosts?" Jalen asked. He was dressed as, and in the body of, the Host he had taken over. A U.S. Army general. "That many people leaving the Earth Otherworld at one time would cast suspicion."

"Suspicion upon whom?" Amory waved the statement away. "They have no way of knowing, no way of even suspecting our infiltration."

"These humans are intelligent." LeeLa, now an Earth Otherworld surgeon, looked thoughtful. "They will be searching for answers."

"Let them search." Amory continued, "As to the Hosts returning for sealing . . . I believe I have perfected a way that the Hosts will not need to return. I will go myself and seal them all at one time. Thus no one in the Earth Other-world will know anything has happened at all."

"What about the Shells?" Roan asked. "Will they not wreak havoc? Four hundred is a large number to turn loose on the city."

"I will program the stones to stay with the Shells, and the Shells will bring them back to Doran while their new Hosts stay in the Earth Otherworld," Amory said.

"The Earth Otherworlder paranorms call the Shells 'Zombies,'" Xella said with a smirk.

Amory ignored Xella. "For now the Shell attacks in the Earth Otherworld will be kept to a minimum," Amory said. "Once we have taken this world and control it with all of my people transferred, they will be released to terrorize and destroy those not taken."

His advisors nodded their approval.

Amory turned to his image on the wall and pointed out sections of the theater and explained how the plan would work. "I have our teams working with those of our people who will be making the journey and taking the essences. They will know what must be done."

"What if this test fails?" Jalen asked.

Amory scowled at being questioned in any way. "Then I shall work to perfect it. Once I have perfected it, we will then be ready for the humans' 'New Year's Eve' celebration in their Times Square."

Amory's scowl slipped into a harsh smile. "And thus it begins."

TWENTY-THREE

We started out the exit, past the frozen crime scene. "Too bad the Pit doesn't have any Belgian beers," Colin said as we walked down Arthur Avenue. "I have two six-packs of Hoegaarden in my fridge."

"Never had Belgian beer." I frowned at the thought of going to the Pit. It still bothered me that Rodán had refused to look at the first stone and sent me straight to the Magi instead. And now I was carrying a second stone. What would he do? Send me to the Magi again?

I still hadn't quite gotten over him trying to kick me off the case, either. I looked at Colin. "Since you have it and I'd like to try it, why don't we go have one of your, whatever they're called, Belgian beers at your place? If that's okay with you."

"Sure." Colin scooped up his shredded jacket. "I'm not much in the mood for socializing and the Pit is still going strong this time of night."

I smiled. "Maybe you should turn down that Dragon charm of yours."

"I only use it on stage." He gave a wicked grin. "It's part of the fun of the act."

"What do you call it when you're off the stage?" I asked.

Colin winked at me. "Natural-born sex appeal."

I laughed. "And you have it in spades."

He shrugged, suddenly looking a little embarrassed, which completely surprised me.

"Hey." I squeezed his arm and he glanced at me. His skin was warm beneath my palm. "Best three out of five."

"You are persistent," he said. "I like that."

"You have no idea," I said. "Where do you live?"

He gave me the address of a coop on Sixty-sixth Road in Queens. As soon as he finished giving me his address, I was gone.

The door was open when I arrived. Colin already had two bottles of chilled beer out and sitting on the counter.

"I give up." I raised my hands. "For tonight, anyway."

Colin handed me my bottle and grinned. "You can never beat a Dragon, Nyx."

"Ha." I took a drink of the pale beer. "Not bad," I said. "Although an elderflower Tom Collins has it beat."

I grinned at the Dragon's sheepish expression at the bar-keeper having to give all of the women shots of elderflower to counteract the Dragon-thrall.

"I don't think Hector is going to forgive me for a long time," Colin said.

"He does tend to hold a grudge," I said.

"I need to get cleaned up." Colin looked down at his torn T-shirt and smears of something on his arms. Zombie blood and soot, I thought.

"Allow me." I gave a little bow and almost laughed as Colin cocked an eyebrow.

"*Avanna*." I spoke the Elvin word for "clean." The tears in his T-shirt vanished and his skin and hair were cleansed of soot and Zombie goo and sweat. I did the same for my-self, feeling refreshed at once.

I smiled as I took a look around. "Nice. Did you do the decorating?"

"A little. Haven't been here long enough to do much." Still holding his beer, he indicated I should follow him with a crook of his finger of his free hand. "I'll show you the place."

It had one bedroom, but all of the rooms were exception-ally large, which included the kitchen and dining room, and the bathroom.

"That has to be the biggest bed I have ever seen," I said when he showed me the bedroom. "And I'm the daughter of a king."

Colin took a swig of his beer. "They call this the emperor-sized bed."

"I guess Dragons need plenty of room to lie around," I said. "Does it wear you out? Shifting, that is."

"That's where the beer comes in," he said as we walked back into the kitchen. "Great for recovery time." Colin tossed his empty beer bottle into a wastebasket and grabbed four more Hoegaarden from the huge fridge.

I downed the rest of mine and threw away the bottle, and he handed me two of the ones he was holding. I took them but said, "I don't know if I should drink that much."

I thought about the stones in the pouch on my belt, then decided I might have three beers tonight after all. I still needed to talk with Colin about the second stone.

Colin set his bottles on the spacious counter and ducked down so that he was looking into his fridge again. "Are you hungry? I'm ready to eat a cow. Whole."

I grimaced. "Don't tell me you really do . . ."

He brought out what looked like an entire roast. "Never ask questions you don't want to hear the answers to."

"You're right." I set one of the two full bottles down, opened the other, and started drinking.

Colin grabbed mustard, mayo, thick slices of wheat bread, and three kinds of cheese.

He made us sandwiches and carried the plate to the living room. Instead of sitting on the couch, we sat side-by-side on the floor at the coffee table where we placed our food and beers, and we ate. And talked.

Even though it seemed we had exhausted going over the details of the Zombie attack tonight, we still found ourselves talking about it until my head ached.

One thing about Colin was that he could mix humor in with the bad, and he did it in a way that didn't negate the horror or severity of what had happened.

After we finished talking about the attack, again, we started in on other subjects.

I had to admit Colin was a lot of fun to be around. He made me laugh as he told me about some of his experiences living in New York so far, and how he'd set his first bed on fire and chewed up his pillow when he'd dreamed he was burning down a village and eating peasants.

He was teasing, of course.

I think.

Colin's sense of humor and the easy camaraderie we had together made me feel warm inside. Instinctively I knew he'd make a great friend, someone who'd have my back. Always.

He winked at me and I felt a flutter in my belly that caught me off guard. The time I'd spent with him had just been as friendship with a fellow Tracker, even with the teasing in the café.

But that wink, and the feeling in my abdomen had me looking at him differently.

It shouldn't have. I had Adam and I wasn't interested in a relationship with anyone but him. Adam was my knight in shining armor.

Thoughts sped through my head, though. Like the fact that Colin was from my world, Otherworld. Despite the fact they'd be Dragons, if I met his parents—if they were still alive—I knew I wouldn't feel as out of place as I had with Adam's family. Colin was a paranorm. We understood each other on an entirely different level than Adam could.

I could imagine Colin sitting around with my father and his men, drinking ale and telling stories of battle and women. Adam just didn't fit the picture in the same way.

Guilt ended the tingling in my belly. I shouldn't be having thoughts or feelings like this.

Colin pushed his plate away. He'd eaten most of the entire beef roast. I'd put away my share. It had been delicious.

"Thank you." I shifted on the floor, stretched my legs out under the coffee table, and relaxed my back against the couch, my hand on my stomach. "That was awesome."

"Something's bothering you, Nyx." Colin caught me off guard like he had earlier in the night. "Want to tell me about it?"

The tingling I'd been feeling at my hip where the two stones were seemed stronger now. Kerri's warning about not showing the stone weighed heavy on my mind.

But she'd been talking about the stone I brought back from Otherworld, not the one I found tonight. I'd been waiting for the right time to tell Colin. Now seemed to be it.

"One of the Sentients was carrying a stone." I reached for my pouch and grasped the stone on the left which was where I'd put the one I'd found tonight. "He lost it and then that woman dove after it before she was hit by the truck." My arm prickled as I drew the cloth-wrapped item out and set it on the coffee table. "I picked up the stone."

I met Colin's gaze which held a hint of surprise as I spoke. "I think Olivia and I need to take it, along with the other stone, to that Sorcerer whenever we meet with him."

"May I look at it?" Colin didn't reach for the stone, simply waited for my permission.

"Whatever you do, don't touch it." I leaned forward as he left the stone on the coffee table and pulled an edge of the cloth aside. "When I showed her the other one, the Seer said, 'Every time you touch the stone it becomes a beacon and will draw the enemy.'" I tapped my chin with my forefinger. "As far as I know, even just having the stone might draw the enemy. I think that's what happened at the café."

Colin paused and looked at me. "You didn't visit a Seer, did you," he stated. "You had an audience with a Magi."

Shock made me catch my breath. "How did you know?" Had I given it away somehow?

Colin drew away another edge of the cloth very slowly. "I know Seers, Nyx," he said. "I also know of Magi." He paused in moving the cloth. "One of my gifts is being able to read beings and situations and see through what is being said."

My eyes narrowed. I wasn't too sure I liked the sound of this. "You can read minds?"

"No." He pulled aside another section of the cloth. "I can

just tell the difference between truths, untruths, and skirting the subject."

"Okay." I supposed I could live with that. Our gazes met. "Now for this."

He nodded and finished unwrapping the stone.

My heart thudded. The dryness in my mouth made me feel like I wouldn't be able to speak if I had to. Goose bumps prickled my skin and I rubbed my arms to try to chase them away.

The stone looked gray, plain, and unmarked when he unwrapped it. "It seems like a regular rock," he said as he glanced at me.

I tried to swallow but my throat was too dry now, too. "Move the cloth so that we can see the opposite side of the stone."

Colin eased it around so that a flat, shiny side faced it. For a moment the glare from his track lighting made it look like a blank TV screen, like the other one had.

A woman's face appeared and I reeled backward. It was the woman who was hit by the truck tonight.

Colin dropped the cloth and moved his hand away. "What the—"

I held my hand to my chest. It was a stone. Just a stone that was like a mini TV.

So I studied it as if it just hadn't shocked me senseless.

Looking at the image of the woman on the flat, black side of the stone was like seeing someone on the other side of a TV screen.

"That's the woman from tonight—the one who was hit by the truck." I could barely breathe. "This is so lifelike— it's as if she's in there. Really in there."

Colin was quiet and I glanced at him. He was focused so intently on the stone that it was almost like he wasn't there. Like he was in another world.

"This can't be right." Colin shook his head, the movement slight, barely perceptible. He said his next words slow and precise as if trying to make sense of each one. "The woman *is* in the stone."

"How can she be inside the stone?" Confusion knocked on the inside of my skull. "Not only is that unbelievable, but we saw the ambulance take her away."

"Is it unbelievable, Nyx?" Colin moved his gaze from the stone to me. "We live in a paranormal world. Anything and everything is possible."

"How?" A chill rolled through me as I focused on the stone again. "If what you say is true, how did it happen? And what makes you believe it did?"

"The same senses I was just talking with you about earlier," he said. "I can sense a lie from truth and the difference between the unbelievable and the believable."

"Whatever it is," I said, "I don't understand."

"Neither do I." He reached out as if he was going to pick up the stone. "We need to figure it out."

I grabbed his hand and kept it from getting any closer to the stone. "Remember what the Magi told Angel and me. We can't touch it or it will draw the Zombies and the Sentients to us, wherever we are."

"She was talking about the other stone," Colin said, but he lightly squeezed my fingers and allowed me to bring his hand away. He didn't let go of me, though, and he rested both of our hands on his thigh.

I met his burnished gold eyes. "Just the same, Colin, I don't want to take chances."

"We won't." He held my hand a little tighter. I wasn't sure why, and I wasn't sure why I let him. "I think you need to take this to your Sorcerer along with the other one whenever you meet with him."

"My thoughts, too." I finally tugged my hand away from Colin's and he released me.

It had been far too intimate allowing him to hold my hand, even though I was certain he had only been attempting to calm me down in some way.

Had it worked? Was I any calmer?

I didn't think so.

"The PTF agent said her name is Candace Moreno," I said as I studied the woman.

"She prefers to be called Candy," Colin said quietly.

I cut my gaze to him. "You never did meet her, plus she was in a coma. So how could you possibly know that?"

"Sometimes words form in my mind if a being is strong enough to project them." He let out his breath and leaned his back against the couch again. "She's human but she has a powerful presence of self that I can sense."

"I need to call Rodán." I reached for my phone on my belt. While I did, I couldn't take my eyes off the woman. Same short dark hair, olive complexion. But she didn't have a single scrape or cut on her face.

"Nyx." Rodán answered on the first ring. "I just spoke with Karen and Sara about a fairly large Zombie massacre they assisted with. Apparently both you and Colin were involved?"

"I'm sorry, Rodán." My heart pounded a little faster. I'd never failed to call in before. "I just—just—"

"Just what?" he said. "Did something happen after you left?"

"No." I glanced at Colin and my skin burned hot. This wouldn't sound good, but it was the truth. "I came with Colin to his place to wind down after the battle."

He spoke in a soft voice. "Why didn't you come in?" I had no idea what he was thinking from his tone.

I clenched my phone. I didn't want to get into it right now, especially in front of Colin. "I'll explain when I see you."

Rodán sounded more like an employer than a friend. "You have something to tell me," he stated.

I took a deep breath, then let it out. "I found a second stone at the scene."

Dead silence.

"I think I should take it to the Sorcerer when Olivia and I meet with him," I hurried to say. I looked at the stone and the woman. "This one is different, Rodán. Very different."

"You are correct in that you should take it to the Sorcerer." Every one of Rodán's words was short, clipped. I'd never heard him talk this way and it made me feel strange, as if I didn't know him. "But you were wrong in not coming directly to me."

"I'm sorry." I closed my eyes. "You didn't want to touch the other one and instead sent me to the Magi—"

"Being immediately apprised of a significant situation is mandatory, Nyx," he said and my face grew hotter. "Regardless of how you believe a problem or situation should be dealt with, if it is something like this, it is for me to be consulted with, and it is for me to judge. I am your Proctor."

I didn't want to look at Colin. My amethyst skin did look purple when I flushed.

"Yes, Rodán." I took a deep breath and opened my eyes. "I understand."

"Good." The word was said with such brevity it felt like a slap. "Tell me about this second stone."

I stared at it and told Rodán about everything that had happened that night. The image of Candace or Candy looked tired.

When I finished telling Rodán everything I could think of regarding the night's activities, he said, "I want to see you at eight, before you meet with your team tomorrow night."

"Yes, sir." I don't know why I tacked on the "sir." I'd never called him that before. Ever. But then he'd never been angry with me like this.

"I will see you in my office then," he said before he clicked off.

"That went well," I muttered as I tucked the phone in my belt. "I really screwed up by not going immediately to Rodán. I should have gotten that over with—debriefing with him about tonight and about the new stone, regardless of whether or not he'd have wanted to look at it."

I hadn't wanted to see Rodán, but the choice that I'd made hadn't been professional at all.

Colin placed his hand on mine and squeezed before releasing it. "How about another beer—on the house."

"I think I'm all beered out." I gave him a little smile. "I'll just be collecting my woman-rock and get home to bed."

I had told Colin about the other stone rather than bringing it out to show him. I hadn't thought I could handle any more than I already had tonight. I let out a breath when both stones were secured in my pocket.

Colin walked me to the door as I left. I paused in the doorway and he reached out to me and brushed my hair over my shoulder. "See you tomorrow night."

I nodded.

Then turned and ran.

TWENTY-FOUR

Wednesday, December 29

"About time you got your ass in to work," Olivia said as I dragged said ass in through the door of the PI office at ten the next morning.

"You decided to make it." I smiled then winced. My head ached thanks to the four beers I'd ended up having last night. I was usually only good for two. "Stay an extra day with the family unit?"

Olivia rolled her eyes and stood from behind her desk so that I could see her shirt.

SILENCE IS GOLDEN
DUCT TAPE IS SILVER

"Took sixteen rolls to shut all of them up," Olivia said and I laughed.

"Lots of interesting things to tell you." I plopped my purse onto my desktop, then pulled my hair back from my face and knotted it.

"Get going then." Olivia leaned back in her chair and put her orange Keds up on her desk and crossed her legs at her ankles. "I'm ready."

For a moment I hesitated. How was I going to do this without telling her I had not only one, but two of the stones. But the memory of the Magi's words was clear.

"I suggest you not even show it to your partner unless you have to."

I paced back and forth in front of our desks as I started with the trip to visit my parents and the discussion about what had happened twenty-two years ago; my visit to Rodán and then to the Magi; my search for the Sorcerer Desmond; the Zombie and Sentient attack last night. I told her that we were supposed to watch out for stones and mentioned the Sentients had at least one, but I managed not to tell her that I had two of them with me.

"You were a little busy while I was gone." Olivia looked thoughtful as she made the understatement. "Tell me more about the Sorcerer."

I went around my desk and drew my cell phone out of my purse before setting it on the desktop. "I don't know anything about the Sorcerer except that he's an artist who shows his work in a gallery."

"Desmond, right?" Olivia scooted her feet off her desk. "Does he have a last name?"

"Yes on Desmond, and for all I know that is his last name." I pulled out my chair and sank into it. "That's how he signs his work."

She straightened in her seat and turned to her computer monitor. "Gallery name?"

"Sun Lee," I said.

The click-clack of Olivia's keys on her computer keyboard was loud as she typed. "In SoHo," she said, apparently finding the gallery.

"You've got it." I rubbed my forehead as I wished shifting from Drow to human could get rid of mild hangovers. "Hopefully Ms. Sun Lee will call soon with some good news."

"If she doesn't call you soon, maybe you should give her a little reminder," Olivia said. "But for now, tell me more about the stones."

I stared at my purse and thought about the Magi's instructions again.

Why couldn't I show the stones to Olivia?

The phone rang and I looked away from Olivia to glance at the identification screen. I didn't recognize the number.

"This is Sun Lee." The woman's voice was quick and efficient when I answered. "Desmond will meet you at his studio at two-thirty this afternoon."

"Can he meet earlier?" I asked. That wouldn't give me much time to talk with him and then get back home to shift before sunset, which was close to four-thirty this time of year.

"It is the only time he has available, Ms. Carter," Sun Lee said. "Desmond is a difficult individual to pin down for any kind of meeting."

I'd just have to have the speediest conversation possible on Zombies, Sentients, Hosts, keystones, and women in stones, and hope he wasn't late. I sure wasn't going to be.

"Okay," I said. "Two-thirty it is." I grabbed a blank pink sticky note from a dispenser on my desk. "What's his address?"

"Just one second while I look it up . . ." Sun Lee's voice trailed off. "My apologies, Ms. Carter, I neglected to update my files with the address of his new studio," she said. "I'll let you know in time for your appointment."

She hung up before I had a chance to respond. I scowled at the phone then rolled my shoulders.

"Where is he?" Olivia asked.

"Sun Lee is going to call me back with the information." I looked at the time on the computer. "We have a little while before our meeting. I just hope that it'll be enough time to get what we want and leave."

Olivia frowned. My cell phone rang and I glanced at it. I smiled.

"Adam," I said when I answered the phone. "Did you make it back?"

"Late last night," he said. "Are we still on for lunch at one P.M.?"

"Can't wait to see you." My smile broadened. "Feels like it's been forever."

"I'm working up a few leads on a new case for Captain Wysocki," he said, "so I'll meet you there."

"Okay." Something suddenly felt a little strange. Off. Or maybe it had been there all along and I had just missed it. "Is everything okay, Adam?"

"Yeah," he said. "See you then."

An odd feeling made my stomach twist in the strangest way as he disconnected the call.

In Il Cortile, an Italian restaurant, I sat alone at a table for two, facing a tall alabaster sculpture of a woman with her leg bared, her skirt flaring away from her knee up to her thigh. It was a pretty sculpture, I thought. Sultry.

It was after one. Adam was almost fifteen minutes late, which was unusual for him.

"Nyx." Adam touched the back of my shoulder as he came up from behind me. The warmth of his hand burned through my blouse to my skin. I tilted my head and smiled at him, and he gave me a light kiss on my lips. "Sorry I'm late. Accident on Canal Street."

My eyes, head, heart, and soul were so hungry for him that I wanted him to wrap his arms around me and hold on tight.

Everything about Adam drew me to him. His smile, his touch, every intimate conversation we'd ever had. The way he cared for me. Accepted me. I didn't realize how much I'd missed Adam until he took his seat across from me and I met his gaze.

I didn't realize how much I needed him until then. Something I hadn't recognized or acknowledged before. A need to be with someone I loved, and to be needed.

Then an odd sensation tightened my belly at the look in his eyes. The feeling I was getting from him wasn't the excited thrill I usually felt when I was with him.

Like I had when we were talking on the phone, it felt off. Wrong. I wanted to ask him if something was bothering him, but it didn't feel right to do so.

When the waiter took our order, I went with the capellini

like I'd planned, even though I'd lost my appetite. Adam ordered bruschetta as our antipasti as well as gnocchi for his meal. I let him choose the wine and he went with a Barbera.

Adam asked me how my holiday was with my family, and I found myself avoiding anything that made it different. Like saying "Otherworld" or "Drow Realm" or anything magical. I talked about my trip as if they lived in another part of New York.

In turn I asked Adam about his visit to his family and I felt distanced from him when he talked about all of his relatives—his cousins, aunts, uncles, sister, her husband, and his brother.

It's so different with Elves in Otherworld. It's more like a large extended family, not broken down into smaller groups as humans do.

When we finished eating we both declined dessert and I didn't order the limoncello I would normally have gone with.

The plates were cleared away and the silence between us wasn't a comfortable one. I knew he had something to say, and my senses told me I wasn't going to like it.

"Nyx." He looked uncomfortable as he cleared his throat. "I've been thinking a lot about us."

My face washed hot. I knew what was coming and I didn't want to believe it.

"Last week, at the reception, it put a lot of things into perspective for me. It was a dose of reality." Adam clasped his hands on the table and focused on me as he spoke. "We are literally from two different worlds."

For the first time ever I was glad I couldn't cry. At least not tears. The need to cry was strong, the pressure backing up behind my eyes. But the Drow part of me had no tears to shed.

It felt like it was coming from a long distance when my phone rang inside my purse. I just ignored it as I stared at Adam.

No words would come to me. I just listened to him, feeling an almost out of body sensation, as if he was talking with someone else.

"We would constantly be making up stories, living a lie when around my family and friends." He looked down at his fingers and then back at me. "We could never go out together anywhere close to sundown. That means no night out on the town with friends. No dinners with family." He paused. "I can't even take you out to dinner and a Broadway show if we wanted to go to one."

My back felt stiff and straight, my body frozen. This was happening and I barely comprehended it. Adam was breaking up with me.

"My parents could never meet yours." Adam sighed. "You couldn't join my family for anything that involves an overnight stay. Like going to the family's Adirondack cabin with my parents and other family members, or whatever else involved the sunset or sunrise."

Everything I'd thought before, everything I'd felt, started to crack then shatter.

"You would be a secret I couldn't share," he continued. "That's not fair to either one of us."

The desire to scream at Adam rose up within me so swift and strong that I could barely hold it back. How could he do this? From the beginning he knew what I am. *He knew.* But he continued seeing me and now he was breaking my heart.

"It's not your fault," he said. "It's mine. I led you to believe it could work because I thought it could work."

His words nearly made me split in half.

The air around us crackled. Water whirled inside our glasses like mini whirlpools. Our table shook, silverware rattling on the table. Wine sloshed over the lip of my wineglass and splashed onto the white tablecloth, staining it deep red. The whole room was shaking.

Adam looked around us then back at me with a stunned expression. He seemed to recognize that I was causing everything that was happening.

Embarrassed that I'd lost control like I had, I dragged my elemental magic back to me. When everything was calm again, I picked up my purse and stood.

"Thank you for lunch," I said, managing to keep my voice from shaking like the room had been.

"Nyx, wait," he said as he stood, too. "I don't want it to end like this."

"Maybe you should have thought about that when you first found out what I am," I said and held up my hand before he could say anything else. "There's nothing more to talk about."

I turned and walked out of the restaurant, my heart breaking with every step I took.

"Nyx!" Adam called after me but he hadn't gotten the bill yet from the waiter and was trying to pay it while calling after me.

A taxi was coming up the street and I ran to the curb and flagged it down. The cabby pulled into traffic just as Adam made it out of the restaurant.

TWENTY-FIVE

"Just drive," I said to the driver as I told myself to breathe.

Breathe, Nyx.

I sucked in a lungful of air and let it out. I had to get myself together. For the life of me I couldn't remember what I was supposed to be doing right now. And it was important, whatever it was.

Oh. The Sorcerer.

I glanced at my cell phone and saw that Adam and I had spent about an hour at lunch. The call I'd missed was from Olivia. I'd forgotten that the phone rang while Adam was . . . while Adam was breaking up with me.

I took another deep breath, trying to shift focus. The light blinked telling me I had a message and I saw that it was a text from Olivia:

Do you have the address for the meeting with the Sorcerer?

I'd forgotten. I couldn't believe I'd forgotten.

It was a quarter after two and Sun Lee hadn't called with directions yet.

Just as I was about to dial her number, a call came through. I recognized it this time as the gallery.

When I answered, Sun Lee said, "My apologies, I only now received the address. Desmond was unavailable," she said. "His loft is in the Gunther Building." The southwest corner of Broome and Greene Streets in SoHo.

She gave me the apartment number and I thanked her before I told the cab driver where to go.

I clutched my purse to my chest, over my breaking heart.

I tried to relax against the seat of the taxi but my muscles remained tense. I had a job to do and I needed to focus on that.

Not Adam.

We were almost there when I remembered I needed to tell Olivia. My brain just wasn't cooperating with me right now.

Instead of sending her a text, I called and gave her the information. "Sorry," I said. "Just got the address a few minutes ago."

Olivia said she was on her way and would meet me there.

When the cab driver pulled up to the Gunther Building I tossed him a twenty, not caring that I'd just way overpaid him for the short drive.

It was a beautiful cast iron building, and I might have enjoyed looking at the architecture if I wasn't so heartbroken.

I felt sick inside, a weighted awful feeling. I couldn't stop seeing Adam's face. Hearing his words.

When I stood in front of the elevators I straightened my spine, lifted my chin, and focused on the meeting. This was too important to screw up. Lives counted on me gaining the assistance of the Sorcerer Desmond.

Now that it was time to meet him, I felt the weight of the stones in my purse. Not the physical weight, but a weight on a different level. As if just having them with me put pressure on my head and shoulders, pushing me down to the floor. When I got on the elevator and the doors closed behind me the pressure seemed to increase with every level we passed until we reached the top floor.

I found the apartment number of the loft and knocked on the door. It occurred to me then that I'd forgotten about waiting for Olivia, that I was supposed to go to the Sorcerer with her. Maybe as long as she showed up, it didn't matter if we arrived at the same time or not.

A sound came from inside the loft, like someone was brushing up against the door to look out the peephole. I realized I was holding my breath, hoping the Sorcerer wouldn't realize he had a paranorm on his doorstep and that something could be up, before I had a chance to talk with him.

The Magi had said he wouldn't be happy about being found. Her exact words were that he'd be angry.

Not promising.

The rattle of a chain lock, the sound of a bolt lock, and the twist of a lock on the door handle were loud in the still-ness of the corridor as I waited. The door squeaked as it opened and Fae bells jangled.

Terrific. The door was warded and he'd know I wasn't totally human the moment I stepped over the threshold.

I barely had time to think that over when I registered the Sorcerer himself. I'd been expecting someone older, maybe even someone with a few wrinkles and gray hair.

What I didn't expect was a man who looked to be in his early forties with shoulder-length wavy brown hair and a day's growth of stubble on his cheeks. He was startlingly good-looking and in incredibly good shape with a swim-mer's build. His naked chest had a slight sheen of sweat and his Levis fit him a little loose around the hips and thighs.

I'd never expected to find a hot Sorcerer.

His blue-gray eyes had a wild, excited, impatient look to them and he had a smudge of green paint on his cheek as well as on his bare chest.

"Desmond?" I said. "I'm Nicole Carter."

"Hurry on then." He gestured with his hand for me to come into the loft.

His fingers were stained brown and green and he held a paintbrush in his left hand. Behind him I saw a tall painting of a Siren in song. The Siren had a slight greenish tint to her skin like my friend Nadia had when she was in full song. The painting was so lifelike and looked so much like Nadia, gorgeous thick red hair and all.

Behind it were at least a dozen paintings lining the plain white walls, leaning up against the red couches, and any other available space in the somewhat sterile room. Mostly outdoor scenes with meadows, lakes, mountains, forests.

"I'm in the middle of a thought and I need to get back to my painting until the thought is on canvas." His accent sounded Scottish yet not.

He turned away. "Allow me a few—"

The moment I followed him through the doorway the warding bells jangled like crazy. The door slammed behind me and I heard all three locks click or bolt into place.

Desmond whirled to face me, his hands raised. Green electrical currents sizzled and snapped from paint-stained fingertip to fingertip. His paintbrush hit the wood floor and rattled as it rolled away.

My heart pounded and I got ready to throw an air shield around me. I should have expected this.

His eyes looked wild and it passed through my mind that I might be facing a crazed being.

"What are you?" His words came out like he was gritting his teeth, as if holding onto his magic like trying to rein in a horse with a piece of ribbon.

"I'm Drow." I kept very still as I spoke and clenched the strap of my purse. "My real name is Nyx Ciar."

"Dark Elves cannot come out in the light. Yet my magic tells me you are speaking the truth." Desmond looked incredulous. "What are you doing here? How did you find me?"

Rather than go into details immediately, I just said, "The Magi sent me to find a Sorcerer named Desmond. So here I am."

"The Magi?" The look of disbelief on his features was even stronger now. "Why would the Magi send Elves to me, much less one of the Dark Elves?"

A spark of anger stirred in me. Bigot.

I held back from gritting my own teeth. "I don't know why the Magi think you can help us but that's why I'm here."

He narrowed his gaze. "What do you mean *us*?"

"My partner should be here any moment now." I should have waited for Olivia. Although maybe not. She didn't take well to being threatened, by magic or by any other means. "She's human and her name is Olivia. We're private investigators."

The Sorcerer had backed up so that there was about five feet between us now. He hadn't lowered his hands. "A human?"

"Yes." I still hadn't moved, afraid he'd shoot me with a little green bolt if I did. Maybe a big green bolt.

The electrical sizzle between his fingers went away. "Why not?" he said, gesturing with his hands while he spoke. "Why not send the whole damned city here?"

I relaxed a little. "I—"

A loud knock at the door cut me off and the Sorcerer raised his hands. Electricity crackled again. "Get out of my way."

"Yes, sir," I mumbled and moved aside from the door.

The Sorcerer flicked his fingers in the air and the locks undid themselves one at a time. He used his magic to open the door, staying a good ten feet away. His hands were in a ready position, but the electrical charge seemed to be in the "off" position.

The door swung open and Olivia stood in the hallway. A startled expression crossed her features, which surprised me. Very little caught Olivia off guard. The look vanished.

"You didn't wait for me," she said and took a step forward.

The warding bells went totally nuts. I would have chocked it up to the handgun holstered at her side underneath her Mets jacket, but there was something about the ferocity in the way the bells rang.

"No!" Desmond shouted.

The door slammed in Olivia's face. Every one of the locks slid into place.

"What the hell?" Olivia pounded on the door. "Let me in," came her muffled voice, "or I swear I'll take this door down."

Desmond whirled to face me. "You brought one of them here. To my sanctuary. What have you done?"

Stunned, I looked from the Sorcerer to the door and back. "What's going on? That's my partner, Olivia. She was an NYPD cop. She's one of the good guys."

"She's evil." Desmond said in a growl. "They got to your partner."

"What?" I repeated, dumfounded.

"Twenty years I've been safe, then *you* show up at my door." Desmond turned away and rushed to a closet, jerked the doors open. He yanked a Yankees sweatshirt over his head and slid on a pair of hiking boots, no socks. "We must get out of here before they come." He pulled on a jacket but didn't bother to zip it.

The Sorcerer grabbed a worn leather messenger bag from the closet floor and slung it across his body. "This place has been compromised." He paused just long enough to glare at me and say, "Thanks to you and the Magi."

I followed him as he jogged to a window. "I don't understand."

The lock flicked open on the windowsill and the window rose without him touching it. Cold air flooded the formerly warm room, making goose bumps pebble my skin.

Desmond paused to look at me as he stuck one leg through the window so that he was straddling the windowsill. "If you want to live, you'd better come with me."

"Are you nuts?" I pointed back to the door. "That's my partner and one of my best friends. She's not some evil being sent here to destroy you, or whatever it is you think she'll do."

"They got to her." Desmond's gaze flicked to the door. I glanced at it, too, and I saw it shake from the force of the pounding against it. The Sorcerer looked back to me. "Her body is a Host now. It may appear it is her, but who she is no longer exists in this Otherworld."

My head was nearly spinning with confusion.

A Sorcerer who I'd been sent to by the Magi was acting like a madman and he was trying to get me to climb out onto a fire escape several stories above concrete and asphalt.

My best friend was pounding on the door and yelling that she was going to break it down. She was only five-two but I wouldn't put it past her level of abilities.

The Sorcerer had said Olivia's body was a Host now. That person outside the door wasn't really her. The warding bells had gone nuts the moment she tried to cross the threshold.

The Magi had said to bring her with me.

Was this why? To find out the truth about Olivia? She'd been late getting back from Christmas vacation and I hadn't pushed her on the reason.

But she'd seemed so normal.

"Come on, now." Desmond held out his hand, looking frantic and concerned all at one time. "This might be your and the Magi's fault, but I can't just leave you. Get out here. Hurry!"

The door exploded inward.

Wood scattered across the room.

A huge piece, the part with the doorknob and locks, flew at me.

I threw up an air shield just in time and the wood rebounded off the shield, straight back at Olivia who'd just bolted into the room.

The warding bells started jangling again, rising in the air instead of lying flat against the wall.

"Nyx!" Olivia ducked under the flying debris and ran toward me.

Desmond grabbed me by the back of my coat and yanked me hard, away from Olivia. He'd come back through the window to get me.

"What's going on, Nyx?" Olivia looked genuinely confused, hurt even, as I stumbled back.

That wasn't the way Olivia would normally act. No, she'd get pissed before she'd act hurt or confused.

He was right. This wasn't really Olivia and we needed to get out of here.

I let Desmond grab my hand and draw me back. Before I could get to the window, Olivia lunged for my purse. Jerked me toward her when she tried to yank it out of my hand.

The stones. She wanted the stones.

Two males and one female ran into the loft, dodging jagged pieces of shattered wood jutting out from the doorframe. The warding bells jangled with such ferocity that I could barely hear.

"Sentients." Desmond snarled from behind me and I heard the sizzle and crackle of his magic.

I tried to yank my purse away from Olivia but she was strong. As strong as the Sentients had been that Colin and I had fought off just last night.

I gathered my air magic and blasted it at her. Olivia gasped and tried to take a breath but my magic hit her too hard. She lost her grip and stumbled backward into the easel with the painting of the Siren.

The easel collapsed. Olivia's feet tangled with the easel's legs. She landed on top of the painting, her well-rounded rear end going right through the canvas.

My chest ached. Instinct to help my friend warred with the realization that it wasn't really her.

And the Sentients—the Magi had said we couldn't kill them or the Hosts.

I knew what I needed to do. Capture Olivia and the other Sentients, take them to the PTF detention center until we could figure out what was going on.

Olivia got to her feet.

The Sentients rushed toward me and Desmond.

I gathered my elements. Prepared to throw up a shield of protection until I figured out how to contain the Sentients and Olivia.

The room crackled with magic. Electricity snapped through the air, green currents bouncing from object to object.

My scalp prickled and hair rose on my arms. It was like being in the middle of a lightning storm, tension in the air gathering and gathering until I felt squeezed by it.

Desmond was going to fry the Sentients and Olivia with his magic.

My eyes widened as I shouted, "No—"

The power of the explosion of magic threw me back. My head hit the wall. My purse landed on the wood floor with a loud *thump*. Stars sparked behind my eyes.

I scrambled to my feet and came to a sudden stop. A cry of horror and disbelief rose up inside of me.

The three Sentients and Olivia were sprawled on the floor. Dead.

TWENTY-SIX

Eyes wide open and sightless.

Chests not moving to draw in breaths.

Limbs at odd angles.

The Sentients and Olivia's Host body were dead.

"No!" I screamed.

I whirled to face the Sorcerer, drew my arm back, and punched him. He brought his hand to his jaw as I shouted, "You killed them. You're not supposed to kill them!"

Desmond raised his hands to ward me off. "They're not dead."

I held my arm up, ready to punch him again. "They sure look dead to me."

"It's a spell." Desmond grasped my arm. "More Sentients may come. We need to leave."

"Oh." I looked at them again. "Are you sure? Will they recover completely?"

"Yes, they will be fine." Desmond tugged me toward the window again. "I swear by all that is magic that I will leave you here to face them alone if you do not come with me now."

I had to talk with the Sorcerer. He seemed to know a lot about about these Sentients and Hosts. And then there was the fact that the Magi had sent me to him. No, I couldn't let Desmond leave without me.

"I need to call Rodán and the PTF to clean this up and take the Sentients and—" I scooped up my purse and glanced at Olivia's body, a lump rising in my throat. "—take my partner to the infirmary."

"Make it fast," Desmond said as I drew out my phone. "The spell will not last over an hour."

The phone was ringing for Rodán as I said, "More than enough."

Rodán answered and I told him, "I don't have time to talk. I'm with the Sorcerer and we have three Sentients captured who need to be taken in to custody."

"Where?" Rodán asked.

"The Sorcerer's loft." I told him the location then said, "I don't understand it, but they got to Olivia. Desmond said her body is a Host now. I have to find out what is going on and he seems to have some answers. He's leaving and I'm going with him. He's concerned more Sentients will get here soon. Olivia will appear and act like Olivia, but it's not really her."

"Call me when you have additional information," Rodán said. "The PTF, Lulu, and a team of Trackers are on their way."

I didn't ask how he'd managed to contact them all with the information while talking with me, and how he could know that they were coming.

"Thanks," I said.

"Call me as soon as you know more," Rodán said.

"I will." I hung up, slipped my phone into my belt, and took one last look at Olivia. Her neck was twisted and I was afraid it was broken. I could see a crescent-shaped burn mark behind her left ear. Had Desmond's magic done that?

"Are you sure they're okay?" I asked the Sorcerer. "What if more Sentients get here before our people?"

"They're fine, you have my word." Desmond jerked me harder toward the window and this time I ran with him. "I'm sure your Tracker team can handle anything they come across."

How had he known that they were even coming? Maybe Sorcerers had exceptional hearing. Or it was a good guess.

The icy wind stung my cheeks and the iron railings were cold beneath my palms as we rushed down the fire escape. I kept my purse with the stones pressed close to my side. Metal clanged beneath his boots and his messenger bag bounced at his side as he rushed down.

When we reached the final rung, the Sorcerer grasped it, swung, and landed with surprising litheness and grace. After all of the noise he'd made getting down I thought he might fall on his butt.

I landed in a crouch next to him on the side of the building.

Thoughts of Olivia kept bombarding me. How could that have not been Olivia? I'd talked with her. She knew details about things that no one could fake. She acted and looked like Olivia. How had some being taken her over like that without me even knowing?

I ached. Had I lost my friend forever? Was she really gone?

Desmond let out a shrieking whistle as a taxi zipped by. The cab came to a screech and a halt and backed up in reverse so quickly that it was as if a pulley was drawing it to us.

The Sorcerer grabbed my hand again and we ran toward the cab. I got in and slid onto the bench seat on the passenger side and Desmond ran around to the other side.

We both slammed our doors shut and Desmond said, "JFK."

"What?" I seemed to be saying that a lot today. "We're not going to the airport."

"Trust me," he said.

"Should I trust you?" I asked.

"If you want to know what's going on and have a chance to stop it then yes," he said. "And just maybe you'll be able to restore your friend."

My stomach clenched. "Restore Olivia?" I grasped his arm. "Is that possible? Restore her from what?"

"I'll explain," Desmond said. "Once we get to my safe house."

The cab driver maneuvered the taxi through heavy traffic. I turned enough that Desmond and I could face each other.

"Who *are* you?" I said. "What do you know about Sentients and Hosts and how did you know they would come after us? How do you know we can save Olivia?"

Desmond glanced at the blond cab driver who had a

goatee along with dreadlocks beneath a skull cap that had red, green, yellow, and black stripes around it.

The Sorcerer raised his fingers and I saw a shimmer in the air as if a window had been raised between us and the driver. Desmond had put up a shield. A green spark snapped in the air where the shield was.

He met my gaze. "I know everything. That is why the Magi sent you."

"Well, good." I settled my purse in my lap. "Now you can tell me."

Desmond pushed his wavy shoulder-length, wild hair away from his face. Wild looked good on him. His gray eyes had calmed considerably, and I had no idea why except that perhaps he had accepted the situation for whatever he thought it might be.

"Like I said, once we get to the safe house it will be easier to explain to you," he said.

"Safe house?" I glanced out the car and saw that we were well on our way to the airport. "We're not flying anywhere," I said again. "We're staying right here in New York."

"Of course." He looked out the back window. "But we're going to make sure we're not being followed."

I blinked. "Okay."

Desmond didn't seem inclined to talk so the trip was mostly silent. I kept thinking about Olivia and all that had been happening. It was getting beyond crazy. Out of control.

We changed taxis at JFK, then headed for downtown Manhattan. Desmond gave a Greenwich Village address.

"That's practically around the corner from your loft," I said.

He nodded. "That's why we needed to make sure we weren't followed."

Made sense in a convoluted way, I supposed. There would have been easier, faster ways to do the same thing.

It was so close to sunset that I was afraid I was going to have to stop the cab in the middle of the street and run for some place safe to shift.

The taxi stopped on MacDougal Street in Greenwich Village. The cabbie parked beneath a big restaurant sign with neon green lettering, directly across the street from a tavern with a red awning.

Because I didn't have time to wait for Desmond to root around in one of his pockets again for cash, I threw a couple of bills in the direction of the driver and scrambled out of the cab.

I grabbed Desmond's arm, dragged him after me, and rushed toward a nearby building. "We need to make a stop," I said as I pulled him down an empty stairwell of a closed business that might have been a restaurant at one time.

It was impossible to tell by sight because of the gray skies, but the tingling beneath my skin told me the sun was about to set.

Desmond resisted. "My safe house—"

I used my Drow strength, catching him off guard, and jerked him into the darkness. He almost tumbled down the stairs.

"Turn your back and stand right there." I ground my teeth as the change started. "I have to shift and I'm not doing it with an audience."

"Shift?" He looked puzzled but I put my hand on his shoulder and pushed him so that he turned away from me. "Oh," he said as he turned. My hair had already turned blue.

The shift was a little painful if I didn't stretch into it, but I wasn't taking my eyes off the Sorcerer. I clenched my jaws together as my body took on its changes from my stronger muscles, my small fangs, to my amethyst skin. My arms were a little bigger causing my blouse to feel tight around my biceps and my slacks were more snug.

When I finished the change, I held onto my purse and walked up behind Desmond. "Let's go," I said.

The Sorcerer faced me and looked me up and down. "Definitely Drow."

"And your first clue was . . . ?" I said as I walked past him. "How far away is your safe house?"

"I'm going to draw a glamour so that I can't be seen now," I said.

"A glamour?" He frowned as he glanced behind him. I almost ran into his back. "Where are you?"

"Here," I gave a light push to his shoulder.

"Why didn't you just do that when you shifted?" he asked.

"If I could pull a glamour while shifting, it would be great," I said. "However, I don't have that particular talent."

Desmond looked around us as he stopped at the top of the stairs. "By any chance can you cloak me, too?"

"Sure." I took his hand and called on more of my air elemental magic to cloak us both.

"Interesting," he said. "I can see you now."

"Yeah, but no one can see us." I gestured for him to go. "Lead the way."

"With your ability, I suppose we could have avoided the long cab ride, couldn't we?" he said.

"It would have saved a bit of time and the fare," I said. "But you were sketchy on details, except to say that we were going to JFK, or I would have suggested it."

"Well, I will know next time," the Sorcerer replied with a slight crack of a smile.

I certainly hoped there wouldn't be a next time.

We slipped into an apartment building above an ale house restaurant with a Scottish name and thought that it was probably a place where the Sorcerer might hang out. With a few tweaks of his accent, he'd fit right in.

We jogged up the stairs to the top floor. "Do you have a thing for heights?" I asked him.

He shrugged. "I like to have a few options available and the rooftop gives me another one."

"Options for what?" I asked but he only shrugged.

When we reached the last apartment down the hallway, Desmond held his hand up to the door and paused. He closed his eyes and a green glow radiated from his hand until the surface of the door was entirely covered with the glow.

"It's safe," he said as he opened his eyes. He held his

hand above the doorknob. It clicked and creaked as the lock turned and the door opened.

I dropped the glamour when the door closed behind us. "This is more like I thought a Sorcerer's place might be." I studied the front room as we walked in. "Not the stark look your loft in SoHo has."

"Stark?" He raised his eyebrows. "You call that stark?"

"Compared to this, yes," I said

Paintings hung on the walls, so many that every available space seemed to have an oil, an acrylic, a watercolor, or a multimedia piece of art.

I swept my gaze over the work. "None of these are yours."

"Not only do I enjoy painting," he said, "but I enjoy collecting, too."

"I see that." And I saw a whole lot more that told me about the Sorcerer. "You've been here a while." The collections of books in the built-in bookcases looked worn and well-read, but there was a certain feel to them, as if this had been their home for a very long time. That everything here had been a part of his life for countless years.

"How long have you lived here?" I asked as my gaze returned to meet his.

"Since I left my home," he said. "The Doran Otherworld."

I frowned. "I've never heard of Doran before the Magi mentioned it."

"As we preferred it." Desmond set his messenger bag on top of a black piano next to a bookcase on my left. "Unfortunately my world was discovered by a ruthless race of beings, the Kerrans."

My forehead wrinkled as I concentrated. I let him continue.

"They came from Kerra which is a relatively small Otherworld and you have even less of a chance of knowing what it is." He shook his head. "Or was."

"What do you mean?" I asked.

"One moment." Desmond went to the center of the room. The room was filled with an eclectic selection of chairs, lamps, end tables, and a coffee table, along with two book-cases and the piano. It managed to look comfortable and roomy at the same time. Maybe it was magic. "I'm better with pictures," he said.

Made sense. He was an artist, after all.

Desmond held his palms close together and formed a ball of green light that sizzled and crackled. His fingers were still stained green and brown but the streak that had been on his cheek was gone.

He released the ball of light. It floated upward and ex-panded into a sort of magical hologram of a planet.

"This is Doran." The Sorcerer gave a wistful smile that faded away. "It is beautiful and it was my home."

When I started to say something he held up one hand. "This will move on quite a bit faster if you stop asking so many questions."

"Fair enough," I said as I gripped my purse, feeling the weight of the stones in it and wondering when I'd get a chance to show him.

He held his palms close again and this time formed a blue ball of light. He released it and it floated a good dis-tance away and formed a much larger hologram.

"Otherworld," I said, somehow knowing at once that it was my home world.

He nodded as he formed an orange ball and it expanded and the easily recognizable Earth Otherworld came to be. It was smaller than the other two holograms, considerably smaller than my Otherworld.

Then the Sorcerer released a red ball of light that grew almost as large as the one for my Otherworld. "Kerra," Des-mond said with a scowl.

I studied it and the amazing detail of the Sorcerer's magic floored me. I could see desert wastelands, volcanoes spewing lava, great rivers and oceans, all in a holographic outline.

"Kerra is almost dead." He touched the magic hologram and it turned around, blackness eating the world in a slow flood of black sludge.

It gave me such a creepy feeling that I shivered.

"When the world started to kill its people, their leader began to look for a new world to take over." Desmond flicked his fingers and a figure appeared, an older man in about his seventies, wearing a blue robe. The man's graying red hair was long enough to reach the middle of his back. He looked so . . . familiar.

"The Sorcerer Amory," Desmond said with clear disgust in his voice. "With him is where it all begins."

"Amory . . ." The name turned over in my mind and a shudder rippled through me. "I've heard that name . . . I've *seen* him."

Desmond glanced at me. "That body was failing when I last saw him. He should have taken a new Host."

I shook my head. "I saw him. I know it."

He moved to the larger blue hologram of Otherworld. "You must have been very young," he said.

A slow chill rolled over me. "I saw that male when the Zombies came to Otherworld." My gaze snapped to his. "I was five."

Desmond gave a slow nod. "Otherworld was the second world he chose, but the atmosphere proved incompatible in the long term for them, so they moved on." He held up his hand again when I started to talk so I closed my mouth and listened.

When I was quiet again, Desmond formed another ball of light in his hands, this one purple. He released it and it floated near Kerra. "This is Yorath, a magical Otherworld. Twenty-five years ago when Amory's world started to die, the atmosphere was changing and becoming uninhabitable. Amory began searching for ways to save his people."

Desmond frowned at the image of the Sorcerer Amory. "Without finding another world, his people would all die eventually. He had to find a new world where his people could thrive. Not to share, but to take over," Desmond said. "When they found another world, Amory wanted to own that Otherworld. So with few weapons and no presence of strength in a new world, Amory had to develop a way to quietly take control of the selected Otherworld."

I listened to Desmond talk, trying to imagine a being caring for his people but ultimately evil in his intentions to people of any other world.

"Amory had an idea, but he had to develop and perfect the method. He began to travel back and forth between Yorath and Kerra," Desmond said, "stealing Yorathians and experimenting on them. He killed many Yorathians in his search."

Desmond's expression turned sad as he studied the purple hologram. "It took Amory much trial and error but he found a way to harness a person's essence, their brain if you will. Some might call it their personhood, or even their soul." Desmond drew something in the air next to the image of the Sorcerer Amory. "He discovered a way in that first magical world to retain essences which are taken over in stones found there, and allowed them to maintain life while held in a suspended type of existence."

I started to tell Amory about the stones in my purse but he gave me a look that had me shutting my mouth.

Desmond showed an image of a male standing next to the Sorcerer. "Step one . . . Amory gave an 'empty' stone to one of his people, a Sentient." The Sorcerer in the image gave the stone to the male in front of him. It was like watching a movie in 3-D.

"Step two . . . the Sentient traveled through a portal to the Yorath Otherworld and went to a preselected Host body."

The image of the Sentient with the stone floated over to the purple planet. An image of another male appeared, coming from Yorath.

"Step three . . . the Sentient with the stone needed only to touch the individual from Yorath." The Sentient from Kerra reached out and touched the image of the male from the other world.

"Their essences were exchanged." Light traveled from the Sentient to the Yorathian's head and another burst of light went to the stone. "Now the essence of the Yorathian is trapped in the stone. The essence of the Kerran is now in the Yorathian's Host body."

My forehead wrinkled in concentration. "So the Sorcerer gives a stone to one of his people, a Sentient. That Sentient travels and touches a person in the other world and their essences are traded."

"Yes, in a way," Desmond said. "The essence of the person whose body becomes a Host is trapped in the stone while the Kerran's essence takes over the Host's body. Those in the stone exist in a suspended world. They are there, but it is as if no time moves. They are conscious, yet they are not."

My head hurt from trying to make sense of what he was telling me. "So now that person is in the stone, the other person is in the body of the first."

"Yes." Desmond smiled. "You are a quick study."

Sure I was. It still had my brain twisted. "Then what happens to the Sentient's body?"

"Once the essence is gone from the Sentient," Desmond said, "the body becomes a Shell. What you call a Zombie."

"Step one give the stone to a Sentient, step two find a Host, step three exchange essences from the Sentient to the Host and the Host to the stone." I was determined to figure this out. "The former Sentient's body becomes a Zombie."

"Yes." Desmond nodded.

A chill crept over me at the thought of the beings. "Why are the Zombies so . . . so murderous if they no longer have an essence?"

"Amory programs them with an appetite to hunt, to kill, to eat." An angry expression crossed Desmond's features. "They assist him in taking over the Otherworld he wants to conquer. He can turn that program on or off to fit his purpose."

I swallowed. This so did not sound good. The more Desmond talked, the worse everything sounded.

"Let's get back to my explanation," he said with a nod to his holograms. "Step four . . . the Host returns to Kerra with the stone now containing the Host's essence."

The 3-D image of the Host went to the image of the Sorcerer Amory that was still standing beside the red hologram.

"The Sorcerer takes the stone and keeps it in a special room, after he performs a spell to seal the Sentient in the Host's body. If it isn't sealed the exchange can go awry."

My brows furrowed in concentration. "What do you mean it can go awry?"

"It means that if the stone is touched by another being, an exchange of essences can happen instantaneously."

My head was spinning, trying to comprehend it all. "So does this mean that if a Host is sealed it can't be reversed?"

Desmond frowned. "No . . . there is a spell which will allow the exchange of essences from a stone into the original Host's body. The Sentient's essence would then go into the stone."

It was too much to absorb all at one time. "Okay, skip the hosting part and move on to the next step, if there is one."

"Step five." Desmond took a deep breath. "After a 'normal' exchange of essences, and a 'normal' sealing, Amory then puts the stone into a collection he keeps and sends the Host back to the Otherworld he's trying to take over. The stone must not be lost or damaged or its Host body will die, so great care is taken to preserve and protect these stones."

"So the Host's essence is still around," I said. "It's just trapped in a stone now."

"Yes," Desmond said, "that is exactly what happens."

I said, "That means all of these Zombies running around were once Sentients."

Desmond nodded.

"So you said the purpose of this was to take over this new world?" I asked.

"Correct. No cause was known, but Kerra was a dying planet and killing its people with no remedy to change that," Desmond said. "Amory had to find someplace to take his people. A world to take over and make his own."

"What happened with Yorath?" I asked.

"The world turned out to not be hospitable to the essences the Hosts now carried so he had to abandon his takeover," Desmond said.

I glanced to the blue sphere. "What about when he came to Otherworld?"

Desmond moved so that he was now beside the hologram of my Otherworld. "The environment wasn't as hospitable as they had hoped."

I tried not to think about those dark days. "They weren't there for long."

"Amory found Doran." Desmond rubbed his temples. "The Sorcerer's magic worked in my world and his people thrived. He was ruthless. He and his Sentients took over my world and my people.

"The entire world." Desmond turned his pain-filled gaze to me. "Amory took or murdered everyone."

TWENTY-SEVEN

Slow chills rolled down my spine. "Everyone?"

"Yes," was all he said. An incredible sense of sadness filled the room.

I had the urge to touch his hand to comfort him, but I didn't. "How did you end up here?"

"This Earth Otherworld was Amory's second choice for his people, so I knew of it," Desmond said.

"How exactly did he overcome you?" I asked.

"He tricked me." Desmond shook his head. "I gave up my power for my people in my world so that he would let them live and not use their bodies for Hosts." Desmond scowled. "He lied and took my people or murdered them, and I ended up powerless in my home world."

The black sludge I'd felt in my belly after my nightmares returned. This was a living nightmare.

"By the time I discovered the plan, his people had infiltrated everything." Raw pain and anger made Desmond's jaw tighten. "I was too powerful for his magic to work on me directly. My power was as great as his."

It wasn't boasting when Desmond spoke about his magic, that much was easy to see. It was simple fact in his reality.

"But when it came down to it, my power meant nothing." Desmond looked away from me, toward a window covered with a dark curtain. "Amory had numbers, and his numbers won out. By the time he had infiltrated our ranks, we as a people could not defend against so many."

Desmond sounded as if words stuck in his throat and he had a hard time getting them out. Pain like I'd never seen was on his face. The pain of loss so deep it could never be overcome. "And then they were gone. My people. The people of my world. Gone."

The genocide that had happened in the Doran Otherworld because of the Sorcerer Amory and the Kerrans was incomprehensible. How could anyone, *anyone* be so evil?

Even the Vampires, as evil as they are, could not come close to doing what had happened to Desmond and his people. An entire race. An entire world.

Desmond paused, as if he was trying to collect himself. He turned away from the window. "Amory had an ability to detect wherever I was in Doran. He had a mission initially to capture and kill me after his double cross, but he realized it was far worse for me to know that I had no power to recapture Doran and I posed no threat to him."

Desmond gave a heavy sigh filled with what must have been the hopelessness he had eventually felt in those days. "And then it was too late. My world's fate was sealed and there was no chance to reverse it. I chose to flee that world and come to the Earth Otherworld."

The Sorcerer went to the hologram of the Earth Otherworld and lightly caressed it. The glow of the hologram rippled. "I chose to come here and I have lived a quiet life."

He moved his finger and all of the Otherworlds started bouncing against one another like balls in a game of billiards. "I knew he would attempt to destroy me. Now that Amory's Sentients were led to me, he may know that I am in this Earth Otherworld. I don't believe he would consider that I have my powers here. If he did he would do whatever he could to kill me. He doesn't know that that I may be the only one with the power to threaten his plan."

For a long time I was quiet, not knowing what to say to a man who had lived through so much. But I had to work to save this world now and I had to ask him questions. "Why is he here if your world worked for him and his people?"

"I can only guess." Desmond shook his head. "It's either for power, or my world must have turned against him, too. It just took a while for it to happen."

"When I first came to your loft," I said, "you were afraid. Like you expected this."

"I was concerned it might happen one day here," Desmond said. "The Earth Otherworld was his second choice."

I had so many questions spinning through my mind, so much I didn't understand.

Desmond walked between the holograms of Otherworld and Yorath, a sparkling wave of light rippling away from his path. He picked up a thick, heavy book that had to be at least a thousand pages off an end table. He rubbed his thumb on the cover. *Neurology* was written in large letters across the top of the book.

I raised my eyebrows. "Sorcerers use textbooks on the brain?"

Desmond gave a slight smile. "I've had twenty years to study the human species and how a norm's brain functions." He set the book down with a loud *thump* on the coffee table. "I have an entire section of my library devoted to it."

"Science and magic," I said with wonder.

From a bookcase he selected another thick book, this one with a red cover but no spine. Hand scribed in gold on the cover were runes I didn't recognize. He opened the book and I smelled old parchment and dust.

The Sorcerer carefully turned a few pages of the book. "I've also researched as much as I can on nearly every paranorm race." The parchment pages were covered with illustrations drawn by hand as well as elegant script I couldn't read from where I was standing. I wasn't sure I could read it if I was looking right over his shoulder. "Paranorms have not been brain-mapped in the same manner as norms, but I understand much of how each species' minds work."

"Has Sorcerer Amory studied humans and other races of beings in the same way you have," I asked, "in order to perform such heinous acts against other beings?"

"I do not know." Desmond carefully closed the book and

I heard the soft brush of the parchment pages. "But it is a wise thing to do if the resources are available."

"How different are paranorms and norms when it comes to the brain?" I asked.

"Even though paranorms and norms appear entirely different," Desmond answered, "in many ways we're not so. Our brains function in very similar ways."

"How exactly does it work," I asked, "when the Host body is taken over?"

Desmond eased the tall book back into its place on the bookshelf. "The Sentient who takes over the Host body now has access to every part of that person."

I thought about what the Sorcerer was saying. "So even though the Host's essence is removed and put into a stone, a part of the being the Sentient possesses is still there?"

"Yes." He turned away from the bookcase, this time holding a textbook with *Memory: Imprints on the Brain* in block print on the cover. "The Sentient brings his own knowledge and his personhood to the Host, but he combines that with all of the physical and mental capacities of the person now in the stone. Therefore, the Sentient has total access to their brain, their speech, their physical abilities. They can transition between their own mind and the Host mind at will, conscious of both."

All I could do was listen to Desmond and try to grasp what he was saying.

"Someone like you, a Tracker with powers of the Dark Elves, would be particularly appealing." Desmond pushed the book back into its slot. "If your friend Olivia is a Tracker as well, Amory would use someone like her to infiltrate and take over your group. By now he knows what Olivia knows about your structure, your approach to the case. What you are aware of and what you are not. What your leadership structure is. All of it."

I sucked in my breath. "The Sorcerer taking over the entire team of Trackers would be devastating."

"Yes," Desmond said. "Trackers are powerful and could threaten his effort, so you all would be prime targets. By now, if he has been here any length of time, there are government officials that have been taken as well and he knows everything they know."

"I need to make sure I understand this all correctly," I said. "As an example, Amory targets someone with intimate knowledge of nuclear weapons, perhaps a scientist. He then has a Sentient take over his target. . . . To everyone that scientist knew, he would appear to be the same person, someone completely trusted by others in the sense that he was before."

"Yes," Desmond said.

"That scientist would actually have the mind of the Sentient," I said, "but all of the knowledge and access of the scientist. But the scientist himself would be in the stone."

"Yes, and no one would ever know," Desmond said. "Your friend Olivia . . . You could not tell she no longer inhabited her body."

A slow chill rolled over me. "No, I couldn't."

"After his technique is perfected in his targeted world, Amory goes after people of power first. Those in government, law enforcement, military leaders and business leaders. He infiltrates every area of the world." Amory looked at the floating magical hologram of the Earth Otherworld. "When Amory has his numbers in place, he will enact his plan . . . from finding Hosts for his Sentients, to genocide of the rest of the human race.

"How he will do that in this world, I don't know," Desmond said. "In my world, he wiped them all out. Every one of my people." Desmond's voice sounded hoarse. "Once he had tricked me out of my powers, I think he only left me alive so that I would forever be tortured by the memories of the people I love."

For a long time silence hung between us. "I'm so sorry," I finally said.

Desmond looked away from me and stared at a painting of a dark forest that hung over the piano. "So am I."

I took a deep breath. I needed to find out as much as I could even though I hated the pain it obviously caused Desmond. "I have something to show you."

The Sorcerer turned and studied me as I set my purse on an end table and opened it. I brought out the two cloth-covered stones and started to unwrap one.

Desmond's face went ashen.

"No." He stepped back, his hands held up to ward me off. "Put them away. *Put them away!*"

All of the holographic Otherworlds in the middle of the room sparked and exploded into showers of blue, green, red, and purple as Desmond backed away. The images of the Sorcerer Amory and the two other beings disappeared as well, and then there was nothing. All of the holograms were gone.

Desmond's eyes looked wild again, like they had back at the loft. "Keep those forsaken stones away from me."

I stared at him. "This is part of the reason I'm here. The Magi said—"

"Magi." The Sorcerer started pacing. "Magi, Magi, Magi." He continued to pace for several moments and scrubbed his hand over his stubbled jaws. "Of course. Of course I'll help." He seemed to be having a conversation with himself and his sort-of-Scottish brogue sounded stronger. "There was never a question."

Desmond came to a full stop. "Fine," he said. "I'll take a look at those stones now." He pointed to the coffee table. "Set them there but do not unwrap them yet."

I picked up my purse on the end table and held the wrapped stones in my other palm. In addition to the pricking feeling I always got when I touched them, they seemed to weigh me down and my arm felt tired, aching, until I set the stones on the coffee table. They'd felt so heavy that I could imagine them breaking through the wood and landing on the floor with hard thumps.

Desmond closed his eyes for just a moment, then seated himself on the edge of the couch. He gestured for me to sit and I took the closest chair and set my purse on the floor. I leaned forward, my forearms on my thighs and my hands clasped.

The Sorcerer looked at me with a sad expression. "I am

sorry, but I never expected to see one of these again and here you have brought two to me. Just knowing they are here made the memories somehow fresher than before."

I waited for him to gather himself and tried not to let the feeling of sadness take away from my concentration on what was happening now, in this world.

When I finally spoke, I said, "One is from Otherworld." I gestured toward the larger of the two still-wrapped stones, then to the smaller one. "The other we got a hold of last night."

"Have you touched either of them?" Desmond asked.

"The larger one, when I brought it back from Otherworld," I said. "I haven't touched it since the Magi gave me the cloths and told me to keep it wrapped."

"Damn." The Sorcerer pushed his hand through his wavy hair. "You touched one." He stood and pointed at me. "I have no choice but to do this."

Desmond's finger sizzled green right before he zapped me with a powerful dose of magic. An electrical sensation rolled over my skin. I tried to move but I was frozen in place. It was a helpless feeling and my chest constricted with fear.

My heart pounded. I couldn't move my lips, much less speak, as he strode over to me. I wanted to pull away, but I couldn't as he pushed my hair from the left side of my face and looked behind my ear.

He gave what sounded like a sigh of relief. "It must be benign if there was no instant transfer."

A moment later I could move again.

As he went back to his seat on the couch I straightened in my chair, narrowed my eyes and glared. "Don't ever do that again, unless you want to be eating one of your own paintings."

"I needed to make sure you were not a Host since you have touched a stone," he said.

I was still glaring at him. "Why did you look behind my ear?"

"When a Sentient takes a Host body and removes its essence," Desmond said, "the entry and exit point are always behind the left ear. Neurologically this is because it is the analytical part of the brain that processes the information it receives and allows the Sentient to take control of the Host."

Science and Sorcerers. It still took me aback as he explained.

"The fact that you touched a stone can draw the Sentients and Zombies in," Desmond continued.

"That must have be how the coffee shop attack happened to me and Colin, another Tracker," I said.

Desmond nodded in agreement. "That is how it happens."

I tried to process the information he was giving me even as I asked, "So what does this have to do with why you were looking behind my ear?"

"There is always a burn mark behind the left ear where the entry and exit point is," he said. "When it heals, which is very fast, a scar remains."

"In the shape of a crescent?" I pictured both Olivia and Candace Moreno. He nodded and I said, "When we were leaving I saw a mark like that behind my partner's ear."

He nodded. "That is correct."

I gestured toward the second stone. "And I noticed one on Candace after she was hit by the truck."

"Explain." He looked with a wary gaze at the stone. "Although I have a good idea of what you have here."

I told him what had happened and about what looked like a real woman in the stone.

Desmond pulled the chain on a Tiffany lamp on an end table. Muted patterns of green, blue, purple, and orange scattered on the coffee table as the light made its way through the lampshade's colored glass. "Go ahead and unwrap the stones," he said.

I started with the smaller one and turned it so that the glossy side was facing us. The woman was in the stone just like she had been last night.

Desmond was studying the stone but not touching it. Almost like a doctor examining a patient.

I leaned forward so that my forearms were resting on my

thighs again. My eyes met Desmond's. "She's in there, isn't she? The woman's essence was stolen and put in that stone."

"Yes." The Sorcerer's voice was quiet. "And a Sentient took control of her body." He moved his gaze from the stone to me. "Where is the Host now?"

"Probably in the infirmary," I said. "She was hit by a truck and went into a coma. At least I hope she's still alive."

"She is," Desmond said. "Or the stone would be empty. If the Host body dies then the essence dies in the stone as well."

I thought about Olivia. "What about my partner? Where is the stone that contains her essence? Is it possible to return her to her normal self?"

"Yes, it is possible," he said. "If you can get the stone back from the Sorcerer in the Doran Otherworld."

"She's not here anymore?" My skin went cold. "How do I get to her and bring her home?"

"I have to think on it." Desmond stood and started pacing again. "I didn't expect this to happen here so I am unprepared." He stopped and his expression was serious. "It won't be easy, but I will do whatever I can to aid you and the people of my adopted world."

"Thank you." Thoughts of Olivia made it hard to concentrate on anything else. "How is it that you didn't hear about the disappearances and the attacks on all the media reports," I asked.

"When I came here, I chose a lonely life," he said "I do what I love and I love to paint. It is how I make a living. I visit with very few people and choose not to get involved in this world in any other way. I watch no television nor read any newspapers. So that is why I have missed any reports."

I drew out my cell phone. "I need to call my boss again."

When I reached Rodán I explained that I was in Greenwich Village with the Sorcerer, and then I told him about the crescent-shaped burn mark. "Hold on a second," I said to Rodán.

To Desmond I said, "Wouldn't the mark heal or go away when a being shifts?" I asked. "Like a Doppler, Shifter, or other being that can transform?"

Desmond shook his head. "It is a permanent mark magically received so it cannot be removed by any means."

I relayed that information to Rodán. "Check Lawan," I added. "She was missing for that time period and didn't call in."

I told Rodán that I'd be getting back with him again to explain what I was learning about everything that was happening. "The enemy knows all that Olivia would know," I added. "We have to be on high alert from this point on."

When I ended the call, I looked at the essence of Candace Moreno. "What's going on in there with her?"

"Time means nothing to a being when his or her essence is transferred to a stone." Desmond glanced at Candace. "What will be years to us will be but moments to them. At least they have that." He picked up the cloth and dropped it over the stone and I couldn't see Candace anymore. "Like the Magi told you, cover it and keep it safe."

"If the Sorcerer takes all of the stones," I asked as I took the cloth and wrapped the stone, "why is this one here?" I slipped the stone into my purse.

"It is likely she had just taken over the Host and had not returned to Amory yet," Desmond said. "Which would mean she is not sealed by the Sorcerer."

"You mentioned sealing earlier," I said, "but I'm not clear on it."

"Because the Candace Host is probably not sealed, another being could take the place of the Sentient who made Candace her Host," Desmond said.

"Which probably makes it still dangerous to touch," I said.

"Yes." Desmond gestured to the other stone on the table. "Let's see that one."

When it was sitting on the table, Desmond was staring at it with shock on his features. "You have a keystone." He looked at me. "A *keystone*."

"That's what the Magi called it." My stomach did a little flip from either excitement or concern, I wasn't sure.

"Incredible." He leaned forward from his seat on the couch but didn't touch it. "You obtained this in Otherworld?"

I nodded. "I'm not sure how it was found but a Drow Seer kept it all of these years."

"This stone will help you find a portal to Doran." Desmond flicked his gaze to me. "It will help you get to the world where your friend's essence is being kept in a stone."

"How?" I asked.

"When we're ready," he said, "it will show us."

I thought about that for a moment. "Are you sure?"

Desmond rubbed his jaw again. What hours ago had been a day's growth of stubble now looked like two days' worth. "I will show you how it works once you are prepared."

I told him what happened with the Magi with the keystone. That I'd seen New York City, then a world of incredible beauty with lavender skies, and a man. I described the male I'd seen, one with a featureless face and colorless skin.

Desmond didn't say anything so I asked, "Where do we go from here?"

"First," he said, "tell me what's been happening."

I started from where I came in—the massacre at Riverside Park, our research on other instances, and even what seemed like ties to the homeless.

"What people are seeing are not homeless people," Desmond said when I paused. "Zombies and Sentients have been sent here on a mission."

I gave a frustrated shake of my head. "What is this mission and what is happening?"

"The Sorcerer isn't just taking Host bodies." Desmond sighed. "He's infiltrating this world and he intends to conquer it."

"That's impossible," I said.

He cocked an eyebrow and I was reminded of the conversation with Colin when Desmond said, "Is it?"

"Please continue," I said.

"Amory and his people are ruthless, aggressive conquerors." As Desmond told me that Amory's people had probably been here for months, more and more horror twisted my gut.

According to Desmond, Amory and his people were likely busy transforming Hosts and testing the atmosphere.

His expression was grim. "They will and probably have been infiltrating major financial hubs, military, law enforcement, municipal and national governments, and those in control of natural and synthetic resources. As I said earlier, they will take people of influence and power as Hosts first."

"But why was he going after the homeless people first? That was where the attacks began." I explained how reports said that people claimed they were attacked by homeless individuals.

"I don't think he would go after the homeless at all," Desmond said. "My guess is that perhaps the portal is near a homeless shelter. The high numbers being reported of homeless people are actually Sentients who have crossed over and have not yet found their Hosts. That, and it could be their Shells, or Zombies, left behind that were not well programmed by Amory.

"As far as Zombies go," Desmond went on, "the desire to destroy is difficult to contain in a Zombie, even for Amory. They have an instinct to feed. That instinct actually originates in the Sentient who now lives in the new Host. There is some connection there."

Desmond frowned. "The Sentient in the new Host draws power and energy from those beings which the Zombies kills. Eventually when all of the Sentients have found Hosts, Amory will release the Zombies on those he does not want spared in order to strengthen his people with the power and energy of others."

I sat there overwhelmed. It all had a surreal feel to it.

"Once they have control, those beings who Amory does want spared from the Zombies will be enslaved." Desmond stared a long time at the keystone. "The Sentients would have lists," he said. "Lists of norms and paranorms who they want as Hosts and those they will enslave. Likely all paranorms and then those norms who are in positions of power as I mentioned."

Unreal. All of it. "How are these lists prepared," I asked.

"Amory likely had his trusted people visit this world. They would have carried stones. Those stones would draw in the profiles of every person. They would categorize and prioritize who he wants to take as Hosts, who he wants as slaves, and who's left would be for his Zombies to devour. The stones do the work for him and gather all the information he needs."

Desmond explained more about how Amory and his people took over Doran and its people, and how Desmond no longer had magic in that world.

"What he hasn't known," Desmond said, "is that I've been here and that I have power in this Otherworld. He may now know I am here, but he couldn't possibly know I have my powers. He will not view me as a threat. If he sent your friend's Host and the Sentients after me it could be that he does know or they could have been after you. Whatever the case in the end, he will view me as a mere inconvenience."

"Why is the Sorcerer bent on infiltrating and ruling this Earth Otherworld?" I said.

"Like we spoke about earlier, my world must have turned on him and his people, too." Desmond started tapping his fingers on the edge of the couch. Green sparks of light trickled from his fingertips and bounced on the floor until they rolled away and disappeared.

"There is only one way we'll be able to defeat the Sorcerer." Desmond was staring in the direction of a painting of a forest in moonlight and he seemed to be speaking to himself. "What must be done, must be done. We have a lot of work to do."

I was grateful that he'd said *we*.

I wasn't so grateful when he said, "You will need to switch bodies with a Sentient so that you can find the portal and infiltrate the Sorcerer's world."

My jaw dropped. "You want me to go into a stone?"

"No." The Sorcerer stopped tapping his fingers on the couch and scooted down the length so that he was closer to me. "The Sentient will go into the stone, and you will take over the Sentient's body."

"I don't think so." I drew back from him. "If I understand everything correctly, my body would become a Zombie. No way. *No way.*"

"I will make sure your body is safe," he said. "I will keep it under control here."

"That's nuts." I got up from the chair and folded my arms across my chest. "Crazy."

"It's the only way, Nyx." It was the first time he'd said my name. Like the Magi saying it in her Irish accent, Desmond made it sound unique. I would have loved to hear him say it again if I wasn't so worried about leaving my body and it becoming a Zombie.

A Zombie.

"You, along with a team of your Trackers, must to go to Doran." Desmond's gray eyes looked like dark clouds heavy with snow. "Only one of you needs to take over a Sentient's body."

So I could either shove that responsibility onto someone else, or I could do it myself. Then I remembered the Magi's words, too, when she said to do whatever the Sorcerer Desmond asked of me.

Looked like I was going to be a Zombie.

TWENTY-EIGHT

I leaned back against the cushioned chair in the Sorcerer's apartment and rubbed my temples with my thumb and forefinger.

It was unbelievable . . . allowing my body to become the one thing I hated more than anything else . . . a Zombie. *A Zombie.*

I blew out my breath and drew it back in again and imagined breathing through someone else's lungs. Would things look the same? Feel the same? Taste the same? Smell the same?

"My magic—will it work when I'm in the norm's Host body?" I asked.

"No." Desmond shook his head. "You'll have whatever powers the Host body has and if she's a norm that means you'll have none."

My magic was such an integral part of me that I couldn't imagine not having it. Not being able to command the elements or use what other magic I knew. Not even the few powerful Elvin words I used on occasion.

"Where do we start?" I asked Desmond even as thick blackness twisted in my belly.

"The better question is *who* do we start with?" Desmond sat on the couch, close to the chair I was seated in. "The female in the stone. Candace, did you say?"

I nodded, feeling wary as I watched him. He'd gone from a wild, freaked-out look in his eyes to what appeared to be a gleam of wild enthusiasm.

"You're scaring me," I said with narrowed eyes. "You're a little too excited about this."

He brushed the comment aside with a wave of his hand. "The female never made it back to the Sorcerer to give him the stone and to be sealed. That means she is still open to the transfer of another essence much more easily than if she had been sealed. We could do it regardless, though."

"She was in a coma last I saw her." I rubbed my palms on my thighs, a restless, jittery feeling beneath my skin. "Is it smart to be inside the head of someone with possible brain damage—providing she actually wakes up?"

"The female is fine." Desmond nodded toward my purse. "In the stone she looked healthy. If she was seriously ill we would have seen a fainter image of her in the stone. As it was, the image of her was strong."

I lightly ran my fingers over the runes on my collar. "If it's successful, if somehow my 'essence' transfers into Candace's body . . . what happens to the Sentient in there now?"

"The Sentient's essence will join Candace's in the stone." Desmond looked positively lively now with interest, like a scientist on the trail of a new discovery. "I believe that not only will the imprint of Candace's essence remain in the stone, but an imprint of the Sentient's will as well."

I pictured three of me in one body. "In other words I'll be a schizophrenic."

"First the infirmary." Desmond bounced up from the couch and started pacing the moment he was on his feet. "I'll need to go with you to help wake 'Candace' if needed and to interview her."

I raised my brows. "Aren't you worried about the Sorcerer's people finding you?"

"Yes." Desmond didn't seem upset like he'd been when I met him, even as he continued talking. "But we will find ways to avoid being found in case the information did get to him."

Desmond picked up my jacket from the back of the chair where I'd left it, then handed it to me. "We need to get to Candace before the Sorcerer's people do. It's likely they infiltrated the paranorm world enough to know where the infirmary is."

"It's almost time for me to meet with the other Trackers." I glanced toward the window where a faint green neon glow could be seen from the huge restaurant sign across the street. "Looks like as of tonight we'll have a big change of plans."

"The sooner we get to the infirmary, the better," Desmond said. "We need to make sure we get to the Host before Amory's people do."

I stood, took my jacket from Desmond, and slipped it on. Just as I was about to zip it up, my phone rang from inside my purse. I abandoned the zipper in favor of the phone.

"Angel" came up on the identification screen.

She started talking as soon as I said "hello."

"I'm positive something's about to happen at Town Hall, the theater." Angel sounded beyond concerned as she spoke in a rush. "I tried to reach Rodán but there's something wrong with my phone. I'm surprised I got through to you."

I held my own phone tight to my ear, my senses going on full alert. "What's going on?"

"I got here late for a concert," she said. "They're about to pass out stones, Nyx, during intermission."

I glanced at Desmond. "Stones?" Immediately I pictured the one Candace Moreno's essence was in. "They're going to give away *stones* at Town Hall?"

"Similar to the one you took to the Magi," Angel said. "Probably anywhere from three to four hundred stones in boxes in the lobby. Several males are starting to take the stones into the theater."

I headed for the door. "I'll be there in a few minutes," I said before I disconnected the call.

Desmond had slipped into his jacket. "This is not a good sign." He met me at door. "If Amory is attempting to do a mass exchange of essences that could not only bring hundreds of his people here—it might leave hundreds of Zombies to ravage the streets of New York if Amory chooses to release them."

"That's what I'm afraid of." I slipped past Desmond as he

opened the door. I glanced back at him. "For a guy so freaked out about being found, I'm surprised you want in on this."

"I have to admit that all of this took me by surprise." Desmond's expression became grim. "I didn't know then what he was doing to this world. I cannot let Amory succeed here as he did in Doran. I must make an attempt to stop him."

"Unless you can keep up, you'd better call a cab," I said as he closed the door behind us.

"What—" he started.

I was gone before he could finish his sentence.

The run to the Theater District took me two minutes and that was because I had to run down four flights of stairs on my way. It would have been seven minutes by cab.

I rushed through the double doors and into the lobby.

The moment I stepped inside, everything went black. Completely dark within the theater and outside as well.

Blackout.

I caught my breath. Only the exit signs glowed in the darkness.

Screams came from the theater.

I sensed waves of panic coming from the people inside.

The doors rattled like someone was trying to get out. Pounding on the door, but then the pounding stopped.

I ran for the doors and opened them

Being Drow, I had no problem seeing the mass of people jumping out of their chairs and scrambling to get out.

Brilliant colored lights flashed, traveling between people.

Then everything began to calm despite the darkness, despite the strange things going on in the theater.

The stones? Did the lights have to do with the stones?

A male I didn't recognize approached me. A Sentient—the same creeped-out feeling I'd experienced before flooded me and I stepped away, back into the main lobby. I glanced over my shoulder. Another male was coming up from behind me. I looked from one to the other and dove out of the way before they could touch me.

I rolled to a stand keeping the males in sight while looking around me.

Other Trackers came in through the theater's main doors.

"Trackers!" I shouted. "Don't let anyone touch you, not even each other. If you can't see in the dark then get out."

Light flooded the lobby, flaring from the front doors. Brilliant and green-tinged. It took no time for my eyes to adjust and see that it was Desmond holding a large ball of light.

The Sorcerer released the ball and it floated to the ceiling, remaining bright enough to light the entire lobby.

Three Sentient males rushed Desmond.

Green sparks sizzled and snapped all around us, bouncing from one object to the next. Like it had in his loft—when he'd taken down the Sentients and Olivia's Host body.

"Don't," I shouted as a rush of static made hair rise on my arms. "You might knock out Trackers."

"Only if they are Sentients or Hosts," he shouted back before electricity zigzagged through the lobby.

A sound like the crack of thunder deafened my ears and the floor bucked and trembled. Males and females in the lobby dropped like the eight ball on the final shot of a billiard match.

The only ones in the lobby still standing were several Trackers, a couple dozen norms, and Desmond.

"Nadia, Hades," I shouted. "Get the norms out of here." I motioned with my arm toward the closed doors of the theater. "The rest of you, let's go."

I turned my attention on the theater. Silence. No more screams.

Desmond was on one side of me, Colin the other. I didn't bother to get close enough to open the doors by hand. I gathered my air element, let it whip through the air, and blasted the theater doors open.

We came to a stop at the threshold.

The theater was empty.

A gaping hole, a dark archway, was cut—or burned—into the wall beside the stage. Sparks sizzled along the inside edges of the archway. Even the glow of the exit signs didn't permeate the darkness within the hole.

I looked at Desmond. "What is that?"

"A portal." Desmond looked stunned. "Only Amory has the power to make a portal wherever he chooses," he said. "It's a power that I never had." Desmond's eyes met mine. "He was here. Amory was *here*."

"A portal?" I glanced around the empty theater. "Did he take everyone here with him? I saw them. There were hundreds of people."

"I am not certain any being in Otherworld has that power," Desmond said. "Except the Great Guardian. A rare 'talent,' if you will." Desmond said the words as if he tasted something bitter and nasty on his tongue.

The darkness was deep inside the theater. Desmond's light from the lobby didn't penetrate the darkness through the doorway. Most Trackers could see well in the dark, although not as keenly as I could. None of them grew up underground.

Desmond released several large balls of light that floated and lit up the theater in an eerie greenness.

It occurred to me I hadn't seen Angel and I started looking around me. "Angel!" My voice carried throughout the theater with an answering echo. "Angel, are you here?"

No response.

"It is most likely your friend was taken." Desmond touched my arm. "I am sorry."

I heard the Magi's voice in my head.

"I am sorry," the Magi had said to Angel. *"So very sorry."*

Was this it? Was this the reason the Magi had looked so sad when she'd said those words to Angel?

"Damn." I clenched and unclenched my fists. "Damn."

I'd lost another friend.

I would get them back.

I would get them back.

Not only was I worried about my friend and fellow Tracker, but the knowledge Angel had would not be good in the Sorcerer's hands.

"Angel went with me to the Magi," I said in a low voice to Desmond and Colin who had remained at my side. "She knows everything I do from that visit."

I met Desmond's gaze as I continued. "The Magi told us

to find you and gave clues on how. She gave us your name. Why wouldn't the Magi have given us more information on Angel? Instead she detailed much, knowing she would be taken with that information."

Desmond shook his head. "Magi are not given to interpret the facts. Their information can be almost a puzzle. The Magi might have only understood harm was going to come to your Tracker friend." He looked around the theater as if searching for something. "The fact that Amory can obtain that knowledge from the Tracker gives us even less time to find the Sorcerer."

"Angel was also a lead Tracker on our team." I looked up and saw the other Trackers gathering around us.

I heard sirens coming in the direction of the theater— PTF sirens. A cleanup detail was on its way.

"Let's divide our team and search for any being who might still be here." I directed Trackers to various sections then each headed for his or her assigned area.

I kept Colin and Desmond with me. "Is the portal still open?" I started jogging toward the huge archway. "Is it possible to go through it?"

At ten feet away, Colin grabbed my arm and held me back.

I swung my gaze to his. "What are you doing?"

"Wait." His expression was tight, grim. "Listen to the Sorcerer before you get any closer."

"It is probably benign." Desmond stepped past me and moved toward the hole. "But as your friend says, safer to stay away until I check it out."

"Okay," I said and Colin released my arm.

When Desmond was a few feet away from the hole, he raised his hands. The area around the archway flared green. By the light his magic gave off, all I could see was a solid wall where blackness had once been.

"Closed." Desmond's jaw tightened, then relaxed. "Probably better for now. We're not ready to follow him."

"Even though hundreds of people are missing?" I said.

"We don't know what would have been on the other side of that portal." Desmond gestured toward it. "Ultimately salvation for your people, or a trap. It could have been either one."

"Of course." I rubbed my hand over my head. "It is hard to give up on that many people."

Desmond glanced around us at the Trackers who were searching the theater. "We need to check every Tracker for a mark."

"Colin," I said. "You first."

"What mark?" he asked looking confused.

I made a motion with my hand. "Bend over a little so that I can see behind your left ear."

He leaned down and I pushed away the soft gold of his hair. His skin was warm as my fingers brushed the soft flesh.

Colin straightened as I stepped away. "No marks at all," I said to Desmond.

"Fill me in then," Colin said.

I explained the mark to him, only found on Hosts that a Sentient has taken over.

"We should work as a team, examining one Tracker at a time," I said. "The three of us together in case one of our bunch does happen to be a Host and controls that Tracker's abilities."

"Let's do it," Colin said and we headed toward Joshua.

TWENTY-NINE

Amory kept his emotions contained as he stood in front of ten of his twelve advisors on his balcony and looked out over the nearly four hundred unsealed Hosts and an equal number of Shells—what the paranorms called Zombies.

He would have found the term "Zombies" amusing if it hadn't been for the fact he didn't know what to do with the Zombies. It was not supposed to have turned out this way.

"It did not work," Jalen said from behind him. "What now, my lord?"

Amory's jaw tensed and his fingers twitched. He ached to turn and blast Jalen to cinders. The advisor questioned him at every turn. If not for the others, Amory would have done away with him long ago.

But he needed the trust and allegiance of all of his other advisors and he could not afford to eliminate one of them simply because that advisor continued to question his actions.

Although it would be extremely satisfying.

"Do not trouble yourself as to what is next, Jalen," Amory said after letting moments pass. "I will deal with this problem and the issue will be solved in time."

Amory continued to let his gaze pass over those assembled in front of him, including members of his military who were ensuring none of those assembled could leave.

Were there any significant acquisitions?

"In days you plan to take the bodies of a million new Hosts," Jalen said and Amory ground his teeth. "You cannot bring such an incredible number of beings through the portal in order to seal the Hosts."

Amory kept his back to his advisors. "This was a test."

"A test that failed," Jalen said.

"Enough." Amory whirled and faced Jalen. Lightning flashed just yards from the balcony and the immediate crack of thunder was deafening. A rush of wind spun dead leaves and dust across the floor of the balcony, around the feet of the ten advisors in attendance.

None of the advisors flinched, and Amory had not expected them to. But if he wasn't mistaken, the corner of Jalen's mouth twitched as if amused that he had affected Amory. Advisor or not, Jalen might soon die.

"I will seal these Hosts today." Amory's Host had a much deeper voice than his own had been. It sounded more deadly and more powerful in this body than the one he had grown old in, then discarded. "As I seal them I will be able to perfect the process."

"I would hope so, Lord Amory," Jalen said. "You have little time or our move to our new world could be endangered."

"Endanger. What will endanger my plan? What can stop this?" Amory bared his teeth and narrowed his eyes. "Nothing can or will."

LeeLa, the Earth Otherworld surgeon, cleared her throat. "I understand you have excellent news regarding your niece."

Amory calmed his expression and let the storm of his emotions subside a little. "Una and Tieve brought back word that Bryna has been found in a paranorm infirmary. She is in her target Host, the female named Candace Moreno." Amory released an inward sigh of relief that his favorite niece would soon be recovered. "Tonight they will ensure she is freed and returned here to Doran for sealing."

"It will be good to have her back amongst us," LeeLa said.

"Bryna is too valuable of an asset to have been lost as she had," Jalen said with a scowl. "As an advisor she has information that would be unfortunate in the hands of those in the Earth Otherworld. I am surprised she has not been recovered yet."

Amory studied the male who looked the part—just as arrogant and pompous as the Army general whose body he had taken. Information on the general had been well researched before Jalen had been sent to replace him. Perhaps it hadn't been such a good idea to give Jalen that Host body.

Unfortunately it was too late.

Amory ground his teeth. But he had other ways to deal with problems. "You may be excused," he said to his advisors.

They began to bow and turn away but Amory said, "Jalen, I wish for you to stay and oversee today's sealing."

"I must return to the Earth Otherworld," Jalen said.

"And I must insist you stay." The chill in Amory's voice made Jalen's eyes flicker. Almost imperceptible, but it was that slight moment in time when Amory knew Jalen was afraid of him. It was one of the few instances he had seen weakness from the advisor.

A smile threatened to turn up the corner of Amory's mouth. But he maintained his scowl. "Join me. We have much to do."

Jalen hesitated only a fraction before he walked forward to stand beside Amory.

The Sorcerer turned his attention from Jalen to the crowd and let his voice ring out as he said, "Do any of you have information from your Host that may be of significance to our takeover of the Earth Otherworld?"

Out of the four hundred Hosts standing before him only half a dozen approached the balcony and looked up at him. One by one they gave him information they considered significant.

The first five would be very useful. A well-known news reporter for *The New York Times* who had been researching instances of slayings and disappearances; the daughter of the owner of a major television network; a scientist who studied biochemical warfare; even a paranorm who was a Metamorph, able to take on the persona of any human she wished to . . .

And the best prize of all . . . a Tracker.

Amory looked over the sea of Hosts and Shells. "All

Hosts, please sign in for your scheduled time. You may not know what knowledge you possess that may be valuable. You will fill out the questionnaire and will be called as needed."

He pointed to each of five of the six Hosts standing in front of him. "You five, go to the Knowledge Center now for your full debriefing.

"Tracker." He looked at the sixth Host. "You will remain with me for now." This Host looked far from one of the elite paranorm fighting force known as the Night Trackers. Instead she looked more like a silly young female with her pert features, small frame, and long blond curls that tumbled over her shoulders and down her back.

But when she spoke it was with intelligence and authority. In just a few words and with the power he commanded, he determined she was decisive, independent, loyal, and could not only protect herself but others as well.

"What is your name?" Amory asked.

"My Kerran name is Aela." She tossed curls over her shoulder. "My Host's name is Angel."

"Angel." He repeated the name aloud because he liked the sound of it. It had been a long time since Amory had felt the stirrings of desire and his new Host's body felt it with a power he hadn't experienced before. "I'm sure you have much to tell me." His voice lowered to a deeper rumble. "I would like to discuss it with you in private."

The Host's self-assured expression cracked and Amory saw the underlying Kerran's fear to be alone with him. He remembered the female she had been before. A plain, forgettable female with no backbone.

No longer would that be true. Her plain, forgettable Shell was out there somewhere and would one day be destroyed or fail.

Amory just smiled. "Join me on the balcony, Angel."

"Aela." There was a stubborn set to her jaw. "I am Aela."

"Not anymore." Amory gave the young female a look that made her cringe. "Now, Angel."

The female moved through the crowd until she was at the foot of the balcony. He flicked his finger and heard the raw scrape of metal against metal as he unlocked the gate. Its hinges squeaked as it swung open.

Her footsteps were almost silent as she ascended the steps. He barely heard the breath of sound as she climbed higher on the staircase.

Amory turned his focus on Jalen. "You will organize the Hosts and Shells and arrange for their care."

Jalen opened his mouth but Amory made a slight turning motion with his fingers and the advisor's mouth snapped shut. His eyes widened and his jaws worked as he tried to open his mouth.

"Much better." He wasn't killing the bastard, was he? So there was no conflict with his advisors as far as he was concerned. "You will organize the Hosts by age and separate males from females." It wasn't necessary, but it would keep the advisor busy. "Have the wranglers take the Shells to the corrals. We'll deal with the *Zombies* later."

Jalen put his hands to his mouth, begging with his eyes for Amory to release the spell.

Amory flicked his fingers at Jalen, and an exhalation of relief and fear came out the moment the advisor's mouth opened.

The Host named Angel approached them. Amory smiled at her and she looked terrified in response.

For some reason he'd always had that effect on females. With the exception of those paid to please him.

"Go." Amory turned to Jalen and waved his fingers in the direction of the stairs that Angel had just walked up. "Bring word to me yourself when you have completed your task."

Jalen nodded, but before he could turn away, Amory said, "Send the five Hosts I spoke with earlier to my garden, after they are debriefed, so they can be sealed. Assign two escorts. The others can be sealed tomorrow after their tests are examined."

Jalen rushed down the flight of steps leading from the balcony to where eight hundred Hosts and Shells waited for instruction.

Amory held back a smile as he watched as Jalen approach the heads of his military. The advisor would gather them together to perform the exercise he had been requested to do.

"Come." Amory looked at Angel and gave a slight inclination of his head toward the open archway leading back into the manor.

Normally he would have taken her to the garden like the others. It was where he preferred to seal individual Hosts or small groups. He wasn't sure what he would do yet with the four hundred Hosts he needed to seal.

Instead of taking her to the garden, he would bring her to his personal chambers and debrief her. The she would serve him in ways that made his own new Host body stir.

He sensed fear coming from the female, yet at the same time the strong impression of the female Host's will to fight. For some reason both emotions coming from her pleased him.

When they reached his bedchambers, Amory released the two servants from the quarters, sending them away. He escorted Angel to the largest sitting room that had airy open windows, comfortable couches, and soft floor cushions.

The air was still but cool and smelled of the flowers from the garden as well as the female Host's soft perfume.

"Sit." Amory pointed toward the smallest reclining couch with its soft cushions in silks and velvets that matched the rest of the sitting room. Everything surrounding them was in shades ranging from sugar-snap green to deep-water blue and sunrise purple.

Angel kept her eyes on him and perched on the edge of the reclining couch, her hands clenched at her sides. She looked like she would either run or fight him at any moment.

Ah. He nodded to himself in understanding. Because she wasn't yet sealed she didn't have complete and singular devotion to him.

Amory found her rather entertaining in this state. He would wait until he was through with her—through with her in all ways—before he sealed her Host.

"What news do you have for me, Tracker?" He sat near her on the couch and she scooted a little farther from him. "Tell me all that you know."

"Desmond." The name came out of her mouth like a slap. "The Sorcerer Desmond is alive."

"What?" The name caused Amory to recoil. "In the Earth Otherworld?"

Was that satisfaction on her face as she told him something she had to know would upset him? He had the sudden desire to backhand her. He ground his teeth to get his emotions under control.

"Explain," he said.

Angel told him about the visit to the Magi, how they had heard about Desmond, and what the Trackers were doing to try and stop Amory. This Tracker, Angel, knew far more than anything the Host named Lawan had been able to give him.

When she was finished, the Sorcerer let his anger rise up and manifest in one way he hadn't expressed for longer than he could remember.

"Remove your clothing," Amory said, and Angel's eyes widened.

"No." She stood and glared at him. "I will not."

Amory scowled, not sure if this would be good sport or not.

"Take them off." He rose to his feet, his voice a deep growl.

She took a step back. "No."

He started to make a gesture that would take total control of her.

She dissolved . . .

Melted away . . .

Shifted into a squirrel.

Amory was so shocked that for a moment he didn't know what to do. There were no shapeshifters in his world and he hadn't expected her to shift without his permission.

Before he had a chance to recover, the squirrel named Angel scampered under the couch, up the window seat, through an open window, and out into his gardens.

Rage shook Amory to his core.

He went to the window and looked out. "Angel!" he bellowed.

She was nowhere to be seen.

A bell jingled behind him and Amory whirled.

"My Lord." A messenger stood at the entrance to the chambers, his head bowed.

"What is it?" Amory said, trying to restrain the fury he felt within.

"I have a message from Fala," the messenger said, naming Amory's twelfth advisor, who had not been present today.

Amory gestured to the young male. "Speak."

"The Earth Otherworld Council is taken," the messenger said. "Fala and her team have secured them all."

THIRTY

"NYPD has been flooded with calls." I frowned at my computer monitor while Desmond ate his bagel.

It was only a few hours after finally leaving the mess at the theater and heading to my office.

"Almost four hundred people were reported missing from the concert at Town Hall last night," I added before I frowned. "Including Angel." My stomach twisted. "Did the Sorcerer get her?"

"I hope for her sake that he did not," Desmond said. He sat in one of the chairs in front of my desk, eating a bagel with lox and cream cheese with chives. He looked even more rumpled than he had last night. A sexy sort of rumpled in a good-looking, mad-scientist kind of way.

Desmond nodded, but his eyes had the look of a man mulling things over in his mind and barely registering the comments of those around him.

"Town Hall's box office reported ticket sales of over eight hundred for that concert." I looked at my cinnamon raisin bagel, but with Angel missing, I didn't feel like eating anything. I hadn't eaten since lunch yesterday and Desmond had gone out and bought us fresh bagels for breakfast from a place on Amsterdam Avenue.

I turned my thoughts to the larger part of the problem. "What happened to the other four hundred not reported missing?"

"Amory." Desmond wiped his fingers clean with a paper napkin and rubbed a spot of cream cheese off his mouth. "I believe this was a botched attempt at something done on a greater scale than he's done before. Whatever it is that he's done, Amory hadn't planned to take four hundred Hosts and four hundred Shells back to Doran."

"You think that the Sorcerer had that many Sentients there at the concert to trade essences?" I asked.

He rested his elbow on the chair's arm and rubbed his stubbly chin with his fingers "On Doran I never saw or heard of Amory doing such a large exchange of essences at one time." He moved his hand away from his face and rested his elbows on the chair's arms. "If he is able to perfect it, he could exchange essences with thousands. Millions even. Theoretically it is entirely possible."

I pushed at my bagel on its napkin before I rubbed my arms with my palms trying to suppress a chill. "If he can do this with a mass number of people . . ." I trailed off while shaking my head. "I can't begin to imagine what that would mean to this world."

"Quick, complete, and total takeover," Desmond said. "This world would eventually no longer be your own. And there is nothing the humans can do about it."

"It's up to us." I looked at Olivia's empty desk and swallowed down an ache that developed in my throat. Not only was my friend missing, but her body was Host to a Kerran now and I was going to have to interview her.

I blew out a sharp breath. "Where do we start?"

Desmond got to his feet. "First we need to get to the infirmary and interrogate the Host Candace Moreno."

I was relieved he didn't pick interviewing Olivia's Host first. It was not going to be easy.

Rather than driving, we decided to take the C train because it would take us to the 168th Street station. The paranorm infirmary was deep below Columbia University Medical Center.

On our way out of the office to the subway station at 103rd Street, I called Rodán to tell him what Desmond and I had just discussed, and what we were doing now.

I'd already filled Rodán in on everything that had happened yesterday and so far today, with the exception of my lunch with Adam. That, I left out.

When I told Rodán about Desmond transferring me into a Host body he was concerned, but I reminded him that the Magi had said I must do whatever the Sorcerer Desmond asked of me. There really wasn't a choice anyway.

After everything that had happened since then, it was hard to believe my lunch with Adam was only yesterday.

There were six secret paranorm entrances into the infirmary. The C train sped us to the 168th Street station where we clambered off in a crowd of people. From there we slipped away to the glamour-hidden elevator in the subway's darkness. The elevator carried us down below the medical center to the paranorm infirmary.

In the Earth Otherworld, I'd been in norm hospitals as well as medical and scientific facilities that I really wanted to forget, and one thing had held true in all of those cases. Sterile white prisons.

After my last two cases involving a mad scientist, Werewolves, and Vampires, I'd had more than enough of anything to do with medical or scientific research. And despite being Drow, after a horrific chain of events, in this Earth Otherworld I didn't like being deep below the ground.

Yet here I was.

Of course in a paranorm infirmary there were a lot of differences, including the fact that magic replaced any other form of healthcare. Our Healers used their gifts for all paranorm needs. It didn't mean the paranorm would be instantly well, it just meant that they would heal without the use of knives, lasers, medication, or whatever else they were using in the medical center above our heads.

"Let me go," came a shout from the room we had been directed to. "I swear you'll all be killed if you don't let me out of here. I'll make sure of it myself."

Desmond and I looked at each other then picked up our pace to reach the room. After I showed my PI and Tracker credentials to the guards, Desmond and I went through the door.

The moment we entered the room I almost dropped my purse from the sudden heaviness of the stones within. At least one of the stones recognized the being within the Host body. I had no doubt it was the stone whose essence the real Candace was in.

We approached the female who was manacled to a hospital bed and strapped down tightly from ankles to chest. A cloth strap harness held her head secured tight. She had a snarl on her face and she was yanking against her restraints.

The Healer Sara stood at the foot of the bed and smiled at us as we walked in.

"What the hell are you smiling about?" Candace shouted at the Healer. Then she caught sight of me and her eyes narrowed. "*You*. Tracker." She made a sound like a growl. "That idiotic Una should have taken your Host."

I smiled. "But she didn't."

Candace narrowed her eyes. "You have *it*. I can feel it. *Give it to me*."

"Give you what?" I said, even though I knew perfectly well what she wanted.

The draw of the stone from my purse made me light-headed. The feeling crept up my arm and slowly made its way throughout my body like a virus. I shuddered. The sensation wasn't a pleasant one.

Desmond stepped beside me. "What's your Kerran name?"

The female looked from me to Desmond. "You're supposed to be dead." Her lips parted in obvious shock. "He killed you. I *saw* my uncle kill you."

"Bryna." Desmond gripped the handrail of her hospital bed and studied her, his jaws tight. "Worthless bitch."

"You're the one who ended up without a world, Sorcerer." Bryna laughed, a mirthless laugh.

The muscles in Desmond's arms and forearms were well-defined as he strained to gain control of himself. At least that's what it looked like.

"Perfect." He fixed his gaze on me. "We have Amory's niece. She's an advisor in his Inner Circle and he'll be happy to see her."

"You're letting me go?" Bryna stopped straining against her manacles. "Give me my stone."

Desmond's smile was cold, ruthless. "You will never see your uncle again as an independent being."

"What are you talking about?" Bryna jerked against her restraints. "Lord Amory will never stop searching for me."

"Let him." Desmond shrugged then looked at me. "I obtained the information I need out of this one. We can go."

"That's it?" I asked as Bryna started thrashing her head and arms in the hospital bed, her attempts futile.

"Just knowing she's Amory's niece is good enough for me." Desmond patted the bars of Bryna's bed. "You be a good little bitch. We'll be back for you later."

"Bastard!" Bryna shrieked. "This time I'll make sure you're dead."

Desmond smiled. "No, honey. This time you'll be helping me bring down your uncle."

As Bryna screamed, I looked at the Healer and gave a single nod.

"Delighted." Sara closed her eyes as she placed her hands on Bryna's strapped-down ankles.

Bryna's screams ended abruptly and her Host body went limp.

"Sweet, blessed silence," the Healer said, and I agreed.

When Desmond and I walked out of the room I frowned at him. "All we learned is that Candace is the Host body for Amory's niece. Why didn't you question her more?"

"No point in it." Desmond shoved his hands into his front jeans pockets while we headed down the hallway toward the exit at the subway. "Anything else we need to know from her you'll absorb once you're in her body. This just gave us an excellent heads-up." He grinned as he turned and walked backward in front of me. "Amory's niece. Perfect. She is a confidant of Amory's and in his elite Inner Circle. She is a treacherous woman and very loyal to Amory."

"So I'll know exactly what to do when I'm in that Doran Otherworld?" I said as he turned and started walking at my side again.

"Everything." Desmond and I stepped into the elevator that would take us way up, back to the subway. "And in theory, you should know everything the Host Candace knows, too."

"In theory." I raised one eyebrow. "Have you ever done this before? Put two essences into one stone and then another essence into a Host with two imprints?"

But the time I finished saying it, I'd just confused myself. The whole of it wasn't easy to follow.

Desmond shrugged as the elevator shot up. "Never had the chance to do it, but I don't think it will be a problem."

"You don't *think*?" I shook my head. "What about my body? What if it starts acting Zombie-ish? Attacking people and eating them?" That last part made me shudder.

The elevator paused for a moment, waiting to open its doors until certain there were no norms close enough to see us exit.

"We'll strap your body down in place of Candace's," he said. "Your body won't be able to hurt anyone, or get hurt for that matter."

"Guards aren't good enough." The doors opened and we exited the elevator. "I'd like a couple of Trackers on watch, too."

"You might want to settle for some PTF agents," Desmond said. "We're going to need all of the Tracker help we can get, sooner rather than later."

I groaned. This was not going to be my all-time favorite assignment, I knew that right now. "So I won't be able to use any of my abilities when I'm in Candace's body . . . What about fighting skills?"

"Magic, no." Desmond looked apologetic. "But fighting skills, yes you'll still have those. The body might not be yours, but your will replaces the experience and will of the Host. It's rare for the Host body's remaining essence to have any ability to act on its own."

"Rare . . . meaning it has happened." The nervousness in my belly threatened to climb up my throat, making me want to puke.

"Rare." Desmond repeated in a tone meant to reassure me, although I wondered if he really believed what he was telling me. "Very rare. Your will is much too strong to be overridden anyway."

"I sure hope so." I glanced over my shoulder in the direction of the elevator doors to the hospital. "I'd say that one has a pretty strong will of her own."

The A train arrived and we stepped into the almost empty car before it took off again. Desmond and I sat near the doors, side by side.

I studied him. "I get the impression you're a lot older than you look."

He shrugged one shoulder. "I am."

"How old?" I asked as the train came to a stop to let on more passengers.

Desmond ran his hand over his stubbled cheeks. "Doran time versus Earth time. Two very different things."

I shifted in the uncomfortable orange plastic seat. "How about a guess?"

"Hmmm . . ." Desmond tipped his head. "Somewhere over a century, I think."

"Eh, still a baby, as my father would say." I grinned and flopped back in my seat. "Although no matter how old I get, I'll always be a baby as far as my father is concerned."

"My father died during Amory's first wave of attacks." Desmond turned his gaze for a moment, looking outside the train at the concrete and metal and lights that went flashing by.

"Your father was a Sorcerer, too?" I asked.

Desmond looked back at me. "He was a blacksmith."

"We'll take care of Amory." I laid my hand on Desmond's. "I promise."

"As do I," Desmond said. "He won't take over this world. I won't allow it."

"So big Sorcerers don't have baby Sorcerers?" I said with a teasing smile.

He gave a little smile in return. "Those of us showing talents of any kind are put into apprenticeship as soon as the gift is recognized."

I rested my arms on my purse in my lap. "What did you do that gave them a clue you were Sorcerer material?"

"I blew up the stables when I was quite young, just a few years old." Desmond shook his head. "Fortunately all of the livestock was out when I did it."

The train jerked and I saw that we had reached our stop at Seventy-Second Street and Central Park West. It was the station closest to the Paranorm Center beneath the Alice in Wonderland unbirthday party sculpture.

"How did you blow up the stables?" I stood and Desmond followed me out of the subway car.

He held up his hands as he walked beside me. Currents of green ran up and down and between his fingers. "One day I was angry with the owner of the stables. I wanted to play there and the owner told me to get out.

"My anger simply manifested itself," he continued, "and I was too young to control it. To even know what was happening. I had no intention of doing damage to him or his possessions. I had to learn to control and contain my emotions and my newfound power."

We jogged up the subway steps and made our way to the snowy wonderland of Central Park.

"So you were whisked away to live with a Sorcerer who taught you all you know?" I said.

"Something like that." Snow crunched beneath his shoes. Being Elvin I couldn't have made a sound when I walked if I tried. "Sorceress, and she was already ancient when she took me in. I was the first Sorcerer to be born in decades."

I pushed the strap of my purse up on my shoulder. "It's not a hereditary thing?"

"No." He shook his head. "Completely random."

"Interesting." I looked ahead of us and saw the unbirthday party sculpture as we walked on the northern end of Conservatory Water. "So when the Sorceress passed away, Doran rule was turned over to you."

Desmond seemed a little more subdued and I wondered if the subject bothered him. I really couldn't tell, though. "I was trained to rule from the moment I was taken in as the Sorceress's apprentice."

Of course, Desmond had never been in the Paranorm Center. Very few were allowed there, so it took me a bit to convince the Dryads to let Desmond go to the detention center with me.

When they finally let us pass, Desmond seemed impressed by the Dryad and Shadow Shifter security as well as the immensity of the place. We walked past the closed doors of the Paranorm Council where Leticia and the other council members were likely making rulings on things that really didn't matter. I wondered if Rodán had filled them in on anything regarding the Sorcerer Amory yet.

The Sentients locked up in the paranorm detention center gave me the creeps, just like the first Sentient I had seen in Starbucks just a little over a week ago. It seemed so much longer.

Thinking about that day made me think about Adam again. I didn't want to think about him and the pain it caused in my chest.

"Nine Sentients captured and arrested," I said as I looked down at a sheet of paper. "And one Host." I felt like I'd been punched in the belly. "Olivia."

Desmond took the sheet from my hands and there was understanding in his tone when he said, "Let's start with the Sentients."

The PTF was used to magical things that caused all kinds of good and bad to happen. Per Rodán's instructions, the PTF had used warded leather pouches to save the stones and had them put into a vault.

The first Sentient was a female. The Kerrans looked human but they had a few differences, all subtle enough that it didn't really seem to matter. All of the Kerrans had small ears, small noses, and long, delicate fingers.

But their bodies were also starting to rot.

"It's why they're looking for Host bodies," Desmond said

close to my ear while we waited in front of the cages. "The Doran Otherworld is rejecting them just as Kerran did. They need to put their essences into new Hosts or they will die."

"So that's why most of the Zombies are so disgusting?" I asked. "They're discarded, rotting bodies?"

"More or less. When the essence leaves the body, the deterioration of the body is then accelerated," Desmond said, then followed the PTF agent through the gate into the first cell.

A female Kerran sat passively on the low cot in the cell. She was almost bald, barely a few long wisps of hair remaining, and her eyes were almost milky white.

No matter what we asked her or how we asked her, she refused to talk. She didn't even give a sign that she'd heard us speaking. Short of being aggressive, I didn't know how to get information out of the female.

"Your stone." Desmond knelt in front of her. "If you don't tell us what we need to know, then your stone will be destroyed."

The female startled and looked at Desmond. "No. You can't."

He gave a slow nod. "I can, and I will if you don't start cooperating."

"He will kill me." She reduced her voice to a whisper. "Lord Amory will kill me if I tell you anything."

I folded my arms across my chest and leaned back against the bars of her cell. "Lord Amory isn't here right now."

"It doesn't matter." The female looked from me to Desmond. The wisps of her hair floated over her head. "He will question me because he knows I have been captured. He will know the truth of it because I cannot lie to him."

"So you're in a pretty bad place, aren't you?" I said. "We destroy the stone and you have no way of getting into a Host. You tell us what we need to know and you go back to Amory and he'll discover what you did."

A sad look was on her once pretty face that was now pocked with whatever disease was eating these people alive. I would have felt sorry for the Kerrans if they didn't steal bodies and murder beings just so that they could live.

"What's your name?" I asked her for the tenth time.

"It doesn't matter." She looked away from us. "Do whatever you will. I'm already dead."

Desmond and I moved away from the female, cattycorner from her. "She's right," I said in a low voice. "She's a female with nothing to live for if she can't have a Host body, and we won't let her have one. So why should she talk? She has no incentive."

"Let me try," Desmond said.

I extended my arm, my palm up in a "do whatever you want with her" gesture.

Desmond squatted in front of her again. This time he took her head between his palms. She looked surprised yet didn't move as green sparks moved from Desmond's fingers, across her forehead and over the top of her head.

He closed his eyes and she did the same. His eyes moved beneath his eyelids as if he were watching a movie.

When he finished he removed his hands from her head. She sucked in a breath and gasped as they both opened their eyes.

"Thank you," he said to the female.

"What?" She looked confused. "I didn't tell you anything."

Desmond just smiled and rose to his feet. We left the cell and it closed with a hard clang behind us.

"I saw bits and pieces of what might be Amory's plan," Desmond said. "And a lot about Doran and how it's changed that is good information to have."

"Why didn't you just do that sooner?" I asked.

"I wanted to see how they react to questioning," he said.

"Okay," I said. "Think we can skip all of the other steps and go straight to the one where you're doing the mind-thing and getting answers that way?"

"Yes." Desmond smiled. "I'll do the same with the other Kerran prisoners. I can put together more pieces that will help us get you safely to Doran and back."

"Do it," I said as I looked in the direction of Olivia's cell, at the far end of the corridor. *And no rush*, I thought, dreading seeing Olivia—seeing her body that was now a Host for a Sentient, a Kerran.

After about five minutes alone with each remaining Sentient, I asked Desmond what he had learned.

He looked up at the low stone ceiling of the corridor between cells. "A lot."

I rolled my eyes. "That tells me so much."

His expression was distracted. "I need to work it all out and then I'll be able to tell you more."

"Let's see her then." My voice was low and rough with emotion as we went to the cell.

"What the hell is going on, Nyx?" Her tone and the expression on her face were so classic Olivia that it just wouldn't register that it wasn't my friend in that cell.

She came up to the bars and gripped them with her hands. Hands that were still lethal weapons if what Desmond said was true about keeping one's skills as long as it wasn't magic.

"Where's Olivia?" I asked. "Her stone, wherever you put her."

"What are you talking about?" Olivia—her Host body—was looking seriously pissed. "I'm right here, and I am so damn tired of this. Someone is going to get hurt when I break out of here."

"We're not going to get anywhere with her," I said to Desmond who was standing beside me, observing the Olivia/Host in front of us. "Let's just get out of here."

"I can go in with her," Desmond said and a fire sparked in the dark eyes of the Host in front of us.

Because that's what I needed to think of her as right now. A Host. Not Olivia, but a Host.

We'd find Olivia's stone and make things right. That's all we could do.

"No." I shook my head. "I'm making the call on this one and I think we have enough."

Desmond looked like he was going to say something but stopped himself and nodded.

"Get me out of here, Nyx," the Host was saying. *"Get me out of here."*

I felt sick as we walked away and I heard Olivia's voice screaming at me. That was the body of my best friend and partner, but it wasn't her.

Where was Olivia's essence now? The stone she was locked inside of?

We didn't speak until we were out of the Paranorm Center and walking back toward the subway so that he could take the train back to Greenwich Village.

"At my place I can get to work preparing for tomorrow." He looked at me.

I held my hand to my belly as I said, "When I become Bryna and go to Doran to meet the Sorcerer Amory himself."

THIRTY-ONE

After seeing the Host, I didn't want to go back home. I didn't want to think about Olivia like that. I needed some time and space and fresh air.

A mindless break from thinking about Olivia, Adam, Angel, Lawan, Sorcerers, Sentients, Hosts, and Zombies. And the fact that my body was going to become a Zombie in just a few short hours.

I told Desmond I needed some time and I would take a cab back. I had it drop me on Fifth Avenue. I had to be by myself for a little while and process it all, and shopping seemed a pretty mindless thing to do before I went to the Pit. I got out of the cab. Victoria's Secret just across the street. "Why not?" I thought out loud. A drawer full of lingerie needed to be replaced.

Nothing better than the feel and scent of new lingerie.

Through a gap in the dark clouds, cold sunlight came through the huge storefront window. I held up a pair of zebra-striped panties. Cute.

"Those are perfect for you."

The sensual male voice had me whirling around, clutching the panties to my chest.

My cheeks felt hot when I came face-to-face with Colin. He had his arms folded across his broad chest, his head tilted slightly so that his long gold hair fell to one side.

Damn his Dragon magnetism. He was entirely too hot for words. "What are you doing here?" I asked, not knowing what else to say.

Colin gave a slow, sexy smile. "What male doesn't look into a Victoria's Secret store window when he's walking by? Saw you and decided I had to do some shopping myself."

I choked out a laugh. "Why, do you need panties?"

"Maybe." He rested one of his arms on a sale rack as his gaze drifted over me, his burnished gold eyes dark with sensuality.

Now not only was my face burning but my whole body was. "Stop that," I said, pretending to be indignant.

He looked directly at my chest and I realized I was still clutching the zebra-striped panties. "Why don't you try those on? I'll tell you how good they look."

"Funny." I relaxed and let myself enjoy his teasing and flirting.

"You can model these, too." Colin held up a pair of satiny soft panties in a fiery red color.

I snatched them out of his hand. "Maybe I will." I glanced at the tag. "At least you got the size right."

Colin grinned and I put the zebra and red panties into the mesh shopping bag that already held six other pairs, two bras, and a chemise.

He walked with me around the store, making me smile and laugh and for a little while I was able to forget all of the terrible things happening. Not really forget, but a few moments to set aside and take a deep breath in the brief calm before the storm that we were on a collision path with. What we were rushing into. Dead center.

I paid for the lingerie and Colin and I headed to the entrance to the store. He insisted on carrying the bags and I humored him and let him.

As I stepped out of the store, someone bumped into me and I stumbled back against Colin. I looked up to see Adam's surprised face just as Colin caught me from behind.

"Nyx." He stared at me a moment before he realized a man's hands were on my shoulder from when Colin had steadied me. Then he stared at Colin before looking at me. "That was fast," he said in an almost bewildered way.

"No, it's not what it looks like." My face was so hot I

could barely talk. "This is Colin. He's a Tracker. Just came on the team when the Zom—when the attacks started."

Adam's mouth tightened. "I'll see you around, Nyx."

He turned and walked away.

I wanted to call to him, but what was the point? He'd dumped me yesterday. But at the same time I wanted to run after him. To explain that this was nothing. Colin was just a friend that I'd bumped into.

"Your boyfriend?" Colin's voice had gone from playful to something like cautious.

"Yes." I shook my head. "I mean no. Not anymore."

Colin held my gaze with his. "You love him."

"He broke up with me." I looked away. "Because I'm who I am and he's who he is."

"Because he's a norm and you're a paranorm," Colin stated.

I sighed and looked back at Colin. "On Christmas Eve we went to his sister's wedding reception. I had to rush out of there. Time got away from me and I had to shift."

Colin nodded with perfect understanding in his gaze. "Brought it home to him that you two would have a few issues if you made it more serious."

"It was a mess from the moment I got there," I said. Colin and I started walking down Fifth Avenue with him still holding my bags. "We had a story set up as to where I went to school, where my parents were—whatever might come up, we'd be prepared." I sighed again. "It definitely didn't go as planned."

Colin pushed a strand of hair away from my face. "I'm sorry."

"I'll get over it." I looked over my shoulder as if Adam might have come back for me. "One of these days," I said beneath my breath.

I turned back and took my pink striped shopping bags from Colin. "It was fun panty shopping with you." I managed a genuine smile. I really had enjoyed spending time with him. "I'll see you tonight."

Colin surprised me by grasping me by my shoulders and

kissing the top of my head. The warmth of his lips traveled straight from my scalp to my toes.

"It'll be all right, Nyx," he said before he drew away and stepped back a few feet.

I backed up, too. The conflicting emotions inside me caught me off guard. I'd enjoyed all of the time I'd been spending with Colin, but my love for Adam was too strong to even consider looking at anyone else in a romantic fashion.

Adam and I had just broken up yesterday. *Yesterday.*

My phone rang, breaking the strange current running between Colin and me. I dug into my purse and pulled out my cell phone. "Rodán" was on the ID screen.

I swung my hair over my shoulder and pressed the phone to my ear.

"Hi, Rodán," I said as I avoided looking at Colin.

"The Paranorm Council has requested both your and my presence at tonight's council meeting," Rodán said. "Thirty minutes after sunset."

"That's around five." My brow wrinkled in thought. "What's the meeting about?"

"I don't know." Rodán's voice didn't betray anything as he spoke. "But I want you to change the location of tonight's Tracker meeting and make sure everyone is notified."

It occurred to me that it was exactly a week since Leticia told me that they were giving me the award. I frowned, confused. "Isn't it just the end-of-the-year meeting that Leticia told me about?"

"My senses tell me something is wrong." As Rodán said the words, a chill rolled through me. "I never second-guess my instincts."

"Where should we have the Tracker meeting?" My gaze met Colin's. "My place?"

"No," Rodán said. "Something tells me that you shouldn't return to your apartment without another Tracker accompanying you. And you need to get out of there as soon as the sun sets."

A sick feeling started to weigh heavy in my belly. "Why?"

"Right now all I have are my instincts to guide me and

something is not right," he said. "We must be cautious, guarded, and trust no one. I need you to listen to my instructions."

"Of course," I said. "Before anyone enters, however, we should check behind his or her left ear to look for a burn mark. If there is a burn mark, then we know they are a Host. Any suggestions on where we should hold the Tracker meeting?"

"We can use my apartment," Colin said.

"Yes on the apartment and good idea to look for the mark." Rodán had apparently heard Colin speaking to me. "Colin's place will be fine. Tell everyone to be there at eight instead of nine."

"All right." Something cold and dark began sliding around inside of me. "I'll meet you at the unbirthday party just after sundown, after I shift."

Rodán added, "And, Nyx, everything is on a need-to-know-basis from this point on. Do not give out any information to any Tracker or other individual without consulting with me."

"I understand," I said.

"Be prepared for anything," he added, then ended the call.

"Wow." I didn't know what else to say as I stared at my phone. I met Colin's gaze. "I wonder what's going on. Rodán never acts like this and we've never had the meeting anywhere but the Pit."

Colin studied me as I pressed the speed dial number for Nadia. "I need to make a couple of phone calls."

"It'll be sunset soon." Colin looked up at the sky then back to me. "You can make your calls while I go home with you." He held up his hand as I opened my mouth in surprise. "Rodán doesn't think you should be alone with these new developments, and I agree." Dragons apparently had super hearing along with their many other talents.

Colin whistled for one of the cabs zipping down Fifth Avenue. Three cabs stopped, tires screeching, the odor of burned rubber joining the smells of hot dogs from the vendor a few feet from us. People honked their car horns and leaned out the windows to yell at the cabbies for stopping in the middle of the street.

The way Colin got those cabs to stop—Dragon magnetism must work on more than just females.

Tracey answered as Colin waved two of the cabs on and we slid into the remaining cab. I gave the driver my address then told Tracey about the meeting place and time being changed. I asked her to call several of the Trackers, then disconnected to call Nadia.

Within five minutes we were climbing out of the cab in front of my apartment building and I was still on the phone. Nadia would take care of calling everyone on the team handling the Zombies, including Penrod. I explained that I'd already informed Colin.

Colin insisted on holding on to my shopping bags as we headed upstairs to my place. I got ahold of Tracey and she said she'd call the rest of the Trackers that Meryl and Nadia didn't have on their lists.

"Okay, that's done," I said and slid my phone into my purse as Colin and I reached my front door.

My stomach flipped as the door opened and I went into my apartment with Colin right behind me.

After running into Adam while I was with Colin, I had a funny feeling about having Colin in my apartment. Like it wasn't right because I was in love with Adam.

But Adam and I weren't together anymore.

My skin started to tingle the moment Colin shut the door behind us. The sun was going down.

I turned and looked at Colin, and swallowed. With his tall, muscular build, and the power of his presence, he seemed to fill my living room. As if he was in full Dragon form.

The tingling along my skin grew more insistent. "I need to get ready." With a nod toward the kitchen, I backed up and said, "Help yourself to anything in the fridge if you're hungry."

"Sounds good." He handed me my shopping bags. "Don't you know that Dragons are always hungry?" he said with a teasing grin before heading into the kitchen.

Dragons. Mmmmm.

I mentally shook my head as I hurried into my bedroom and closed the door. I tossed the bags onto my bed and stripped out of my clothing as fast as possible.

A sigh of pleasure seemed to flow through my entire body as I stretched and moved into the shift.

When I was finished I paused in front of my mirror and traced the point of one of my ears. I wondered what Colin thought of me like this. My long cobalt blue hair framing my pale amethyst skin, my small incisors.

Adam had accepted it. Adam had loved it.

Then why was he gone?

The ache in my heart had me clenching my arm to my bare belly.

After slipping on the new zebra-striped panties, I went to my closet and dressed in one of my many choices of leather fighting suits. A girl could never have too much leather when it came to fighting Demons, Vampires, Zombies, or anything else that crawled out and into the night.

When I was finished dressing, after I had put on my weapons belt, I left my bedroom. Colin wasn't in the living room and I heard some sort of faint rumble. I went to the kitchen.

And came to a complete halt.

Kali was rubbing up against Colin's legs and purring. Purring so loudly that I'd heard the rumble of it all the way into the living room.

"What did you do to her?" I asked as I gestured to the cat. Kali delicately rose on her hind legs and balanced herself with one paw on Colin's knee, clearly asking to be picked up. "She hates everyone," I said.

"This beautiful girl?" Colin leaned down and carefully scooped Kali into his big arms. The way the Persian rumbled and kept butting her head against his hand to be petted had me shaking my head. "I can't imagine her being anything but a little sweetheart."

"Well, try," I grumbled as I looked at the sandwiches Colin had set out on the kitchen island. "Traitor," I said to Kali who just ignored me.

"Club sandwiches," Colin said as he stroked the cat. "A little bit of everything from your fridge. I already ate three."

"Yum." My stomach growled. "I forgot all about lunch." I went to the fridge and grabbed a bottle of chilled green tea. "I need to hurry, though, and get to the Paranorm Center."

I wolfed down my dinner and finished the iced tea. After Colin said goodbye to Kali with a kiss on her nose—a kiss on her nose!—we headed out of my apartment, down the stairs, and out into the night.

As soon as we reached the sidewalk I came to an abrupt halt. Colin paused beside me. "What's wrong, Nyx?"

"Something feels . . . off." I slowly turned my head and looked across the street into the near darkness of Central Park. It reminded me of the night Lawan and I had stood outside of the Dakota Building, near the Pit, and she'd told me how she felt like she was being watched.

That was how I felt right now. Watched. Hunted.

"We need to get out of here." I kept my voice low. "Rodán said that we can't come back to this apartment until daylight. But even then I'm not sure."

"I sense something's out there, too." Colin radiated tension as he stood beside me. "Let's get you to the Paranorm Center, Nyx. Now."

THIRTY-TWO

Colin and I ran.

This time he kept right beside me as I sped to the Paranorm Center, rather than beating me there. If I wasn't so concerned about being watched, hunted even, I would have felt more wonder over his speed and grace. I knew then that it was going to take a lot to actually beat him in another contest.

As soon as Colin and I reached the unbirthday party sculpture, Rodán stepped from the shadows. He wore a sleeveless brown tunic and breeches. His white-blond hair shone beneath a park light and his crystal-green eyes had a dark, solemn look to them.

"Stay here and wait for Nyx, but be wary," he said to Colin.

"Of course." Colin gave a brief nod.

I walked counterclockwise around the sculpture and recited the line engraved in the granite circle, from the nonsensical poem, "The Jabberwocky," also by Lewis Carroll. "'Twas brillig,'" I recited, "'and the slithy toves did gyre and gimble in the wabe.'"

As I spoke the last word, the hidden entrance opened behind the sculpture at the base of the largest mushroom. I gave Colin one last look before I followed Rodán down the stone steps to the Paranorm Center. The door closed behind me with a rumble while torches glittered and came to life on either side of us, lighting the way down.

The council guard was waiting for Rodán and me, a large

pair of Doppler males. I frowned as they met us at the archway leading from the circular hall. The Dryads were in their wooden columns, their faces unusually still, as if simply carved from the wood and not a living part of it.

None of the guards were Shadow Shifters, who usually guarded the hall. I glanced at the shadows that seemed thicker and heavier than normal. Shadow Shifters, likely told to stay out of the way because the council's guards were going to take care of us.

The thought came to me out of the blue. Why would the guards need to "take care of us"? A crawling sensation crept up my spine and goose bumps rose on my skin. Something wasn't right.

The smell of crushed rose petals was thick and cloying as we entered the chamber where the five council members were seated around a crescent-shaped table at the back of the room.

At the center of the table was Council Chief Leticia, a Doppler who also represented all Dopplers. She was wearing the Drow-made chain and pendant over her bright yellow robe, but it didn't glitter like it should have. Like it had when I saw her at the Pit.

I held back a frown when I saw the almost disdainful expression on her face. What had happened since the days before Christmas, when she was so kind and complimentary? I felt her anger, strong, palpable, and that anger was directed toward both Rodán and me.

Bethany, a striking blond Siren, represented all fifteen or so Fae races. Haughtiness in her sea blue eyes was normal, but today they looked almost . . . vindictive.

The envoy for all Weres was a Werewolf named Eric. Like all of the older Werewolves, he came from the Czech Republic. I didn't know him well, but Eric had always seemed like a pretty nice guy—for a council member. Now, though . . . he looked scary. About-to-shift-at-the-full-moon scary.

That saying—about a person being so uptight it looked like he had a stick up his butt—that's what I'd always thought of when I'd looked at Reginald. He represented all Shifters, including Shadow Shifters. The elderly male's face looked so tight right now that I swore I saw cracks where his wrinkles should be.

Caolan, the delegate for Light and Dark Elves, looked . . . unpleasant. Light Elves are beautiful beings as a rule. Unlike Dark Elves, they tended to keep their emotions hidden behind smooth exteriors. Perhaps his expression shocked me the most because he had a nearly hateful glint in his eyes.

I looked from one council member to the next, trying to comprehend the fierceness I saw in them as a whole. Rodán and I had stood before this council just weeks ago during the nightmare we'd all been through with the Vampires.

The council and their idiotic decisions, like choosing to not destroy a deadly serum, or at least not having it guarded appropriately, which resulted in the Vampires holding the paranorm and norm world hostage. Those were the kinds of things this council would do. Idiotic.

At this moment I saw something akin to death in each council member's eyes. I glanced at Rodán.

As always he was beautiful in every single detail from the crystal green of his eyes, his shining white-blond hair, and the strength in his build. The power within him seemed to expand to encompass me, somehow giving me comfort at a time when I didn't think I should be feeling any kind of comfort.

"Rodán, Proctor of New York City's Peacekeepers," Leticia said in a cold voice to him before turning to me. "Nyx Ciar, of the Night Trackers."

My heart started thumping as my gaze went from one council member to the next. Their expressions remained the same, from cold to angry to hateful.

"What's going on?" I half whispered the words to myself and half to Rodán. He didn't respond, just kept his gaze fixed on Leticia.

"You both have been called to us to answer for your crimes." Leticia's voice was like a slap that I jerked away from. "Your complete disregard for our laws, your defiance in following the rules of our kind, your violations of all we hold sacred—every offense has led this council to the conclusion that we must put an end to your many transgressions."

I caught my breath, protests rising to my lips but I couldn't get anything out. What was she talking about?

Rodán said nothing but clasped my elbow with his fingers.

"Furthermore," she said, her voice echoing in the chamber, "the Night Trackers continue to act outside the law whenever they choose to. All of you are a disgrace. As of this moment, we are eliminating Trackers as a paranorm organization altogether."

My mind spun as I looked at Rodán. What was happening? Why wasn't he saying anything?

Leticia nodded to the guards who'd escorted us into the chamber. "Take Rodán and Nyx to the detention center where they will await their sentencing."

My jaw dropped. "What?" Her words didn't make sense. Just a week ago she told me the council wanted to give me some kind of award and now they were arresting me?

A Doppler guard reached for me.

Rodán's grip on my elbow tightened. I heard him whisper a word. Everything went black.

We shot through the transference so quickly I didn't have time to be sick. Rodán's power was unlike anything I'd ever felt before. One instant we were in the council chambers, about to be arrested, the next we were standing beside the unbirthday party sculpture in front of Colin.

"Come," Rodán said to Colin as he still gripped my elbow with one hand. He reached out and clasped Colin's forearm. "Take us to your place, Colin. Now."

Darkness again. And again we traveled so quickly that I didn't feel the usual clamping sensation on my head or pressure on my body.

Central Park vanished and then we were inside Colin's apartment. We had arrived in the darkened living room and the only light on was in the kitchen.

Rodán released us both and stepped away. Shadows darkened his already hard expression. "It was a setup to take us over as Hosts. I believe the Sorcerer Amory is coming after the Trackers."

Realization dawned on me. Why hadn't I thought of that? Even the fact that Leticia's pendant didn't glitter should have been a big clue. "Amory's Sentients got to them," I said slowly. "And it appears to the entire council."

"I had my suspicions that something wasn't right when I received the order to appear before the council," Rodán said. "It was worded in a way that caused me some concern."

"I'm glad you figured it out." I shook my head. "I'm not sure I would have until it was too late."

"From this point on," Rodán said, "Night Trackers must meet away from the Pit until everything is righted as it should be."

"We can't let anyone through the door without checking them for the burn mark," I said.

Rodán gave a short nod. "Agreed."

A knock on the door caused my heart to leap. I looked at Colin and we went to the door. "I'll check, you cover me."

He was suddenly holding a very wicked-looking dagger. "I've got your back."

Rodán took one side of the door, Colin the other.

At the threshold stood the Sorcerer Desmond, wearing faded jeans and a Grateful Dead t-shirt. "Hi, Desmond." I made a gesture toward his ear. "Just to be safe we're checking everyone."

Desmond drew his long hair away from the left side of his head and turned so that I could see there was no burn mark.

"You're sure we don't need to check the right side?" I asked as he raised his head.

"Positive," he said.

When Desmond came through the doorway, Colin greeted him with an Old World hand-to-elbow grip as I made the introductions.

"Pleased to meet you, brother," Desmond said to Colin in his almost-Scottish accent.

I introduced Desmond to Rodán who gave a slight inclination of his head. Desmond responded in kind.

We checked each Tracker as they arrived and I told each
of them that I would explain later the reason we were doing
that.

When they walked in, most of them gave Desmond a curious look. Fere, a Tuatha from Otherworld, was late arriv-
ing. He always tended to run late.

Almost all of the Trackers looked either concerned or
curious. Ice just had his usual cocky expression and Joshua
seemed like it wasn't anything out of the ordinary.

Colin had a generous-sized living room, but with all of
the Trackers present, half of the group being large males, it
was a little crowded.

The three not present were Olivia, Angel, and Lawan, and
I missed them desperately. Were they okay? Would we be able
to save their essences and return them to their bodies?

"Where's Angel?" Nadia asked as she looked around the
room. "For that matter, where are Olivia and Lawan?"

Nadia was one of my best friends and I felt bad for not
letting her know what had happened. There just hadn't been
time.

"We will discuss this shortly," Rodán said to her.

When we'd all taken a place whether sitting or standing,
Rodán positioned himself at one end of the room and explained what had just happened at the Paranorm Center and
with the Paranorm Council.

"I don't understand," Tracey said. "Why would they do
this?"

Rodán gestured to me. "Nyx will explain further."

"With a little help from a Sorcerer," I said to the group of
surprised Trackers.

I went to the head of the room where Rodán was standing.
He stepped back and I motioned for Desmond to join me.

"Desmond is a Sorcerer from the world the Zombies and
Sentients are traveling from." I continued before anyone of
the surprised-looking Trackers could interrupt. "I'm going
to let Desmond explain that part. It's complicated."

The distracted artist-Sorcerer I'd caught off guard just one day ago was gone. In his place was a confident male who'd made the decision to help this Earth Otherworld and do whatever it took to stop Amory.

Desmond used the same holographic magic now as he had with me in his apartment, to demonstrate the facts to the Trackers. He told the story starting from Amory's search for a new home for his people and why. Hearing it another time made everything even more clear to me.

It didn't, however, make it any easier to know that I'd soon be out of my body and in someone else's and my own body would become the thing I hated the most. A *Zombie*.

Several of the Trackers asked questions as Desmond spoke, clarifying different aspects of the situation until everyone seemed satisfied.

"Got it." Meryl, who preferred the form of an oriole when she shifted, perched on an arm of the couch. "Sentient's essence goes into a Host, Host's essence goes into a stone, stone goes back to Sorcerer for safekeeping, and Sentient's body becomes murderous Zombie."

Nadia shook her head. "Not to mention that said Sentients and Hosts, along with a badass Sorcerer, are planning to take over the world."

"That's the sum of it." I stepped aside so that Rodán could take the floor again. Desmond retreated to where he'd been standing with his shoulder hitched up against the wall, and I sat on the couch between Nancy and Colin.

"Sounds like a C movie," Kelly said. "Too bad to even make a B."

"It's worse than you realize," I said. "You've all been wondering where Lawan and Olivia are." I cleared my throat. "The Sentients took over their bodies and the Sorcerer has their essences in stones in the Doran Otherworld."

Dead silence before Ice said, "Shit."

"We have Lawan's and Olivia's Host bodies," I went on. "I've interrogated the one who took over Olivia, but didn't learn anything of value."

"Are they gone forever?" Tracey asked, looking horrified.

I glanced at Desmond. "There should be a way to recover the stones with their essences and Desmond can handle the exchange. It's part of what we'll be working on."

"Wow." Nadia shook her head. "Can't believe it happened to Lawan and Olivia."

"Don't worry." I heard the conviction in my voice. "We *will* get them back."

Nadia frowned. "What about Angel?"

I glanced at Rodán before looking at the rest of the room. "We don't know. She vanished after the attack at the theater."

"Shit," Ice said again.

I agreed wholeheartedly.

"Captain Wysocki has disappeared," Rodán said to me. "I fear she has been taken."

My breath caught in my throat. The captain, too?

"I would like to address the issue of you as Trackers." Rodán took control of the meeting. "Even though it is not the real council that has made the ruling to disband the Night Trackers," Rodán said, "we must now operate covertly. No one outside of this room is aware of what has happened to the council members."

Nancy finished the last piece of a Godiva chocolate bar before she said, "How do you know for sure that the council members are all now Hosts?"

"If you'd been there, you'd be certain." I twisted in my seat to look at her. "I didn't realize it until Rodán told me after we'd escaped. It's the only thing that makes sense."

"What now?" Nadia shoved back a lock of her thick red hair, her expression earnest as she spoke. "If we've been disbanded, what happens to our territories?"

"We still do our jobs." Ice wore an expression of anger rather than the smart-assed one he usually had on. "This bullshit won't stop us."

"Ice is not correct." Rodán brought everyone's attention back to him. "This is not bullshit. Worrying about our normal concerns as Peacekeepers won't matter if we as a world are taken over."

Rodán continued, "This matter commands our full focus and attention. Nothing matters except solving this and stopping the Sorcerer Amory." Rodán looked calmly at each of us. "It is like tracking a Metamorph who is mugging a norm while at the same time someone is trying to wipe out the world with a nuclear bomb."

We were all quiet as we absorbed his words. Even Ice was silent, which was saying something.

"As Trackers," Rodán added, "you'll need to avoid the PTF because they will now be on the lookout to arrest each of you."

"The big question," Nadia said, "is how do we solve this?"

"It's complicated," I said from my seat on the couch. "I'll go over it in more detail with my team."

"Only your team?" Kelly said. "Why not the rest of us?"

"The fewer who know the details, the better," Rodán said. "In the case that one of you is captured and taken as a Host."

Rodán looked at Mandisa. "You will take Olivia's place on Nyx's team."

Mandisa gave a slight bow of her head. She would be an asset—as long as she didn't shoot any of us with one of her poisoned arrows. The tall Abatwa Fae had a look about her that said, "Cross me and die."

Next Rodán caught Meryl's gaze. "You will go in place of Angel."

Rodán met the eyes of every Tracker as his gaze slowly swept the room. "We must isolate this group. We cannot have one more of you taken with information we possess and have that go to the enemy."

Max, a scarred, auburn-haired Werewolf who grew up in the Bronx, got to his feet. "You've got it, boss."

"Check in by phone?" Tracey asked as she stood.

Rodán shook his head. "I have a place for all of us to stay, where you will be safe. I've already made reservations at the Mandarin Oriental."

"Nice," Kelly said.

Rodán didn't mention that was the same location we

housed the Magi, but that wasn't something he likely wanted in the minds of anyone who could potentially be caught.

"You will all be called upon," Rodán said. "For the time being, until we are ready, I need you all to lie low."

The room gradually emptied as Trackers headed to the Mandarin. Then only my team assigned to the Zombie case was left, along with Desmond and Rodán. Mandisa, Penrod, Colin, Meryl, Ice, and Joshua stayed.

Once the room was cleared of everyone not on my special team, I started outlining our plan. Our team would go to the Doran Otherworld and find out whatever we could before returning to the Earth Otherworld and making our stand. Each member of the team interrupted whenever they had a question. We had to know Amory's plan and anticipate his next move in order to have a chance to stop him.

But when I told my team that I would take over Candace Moreno's body, it caused a small uproar.

"Not acceptable," Joshua said with a scowl.

Ice snarled. "Are you out of your damned mind, Nyx?"

"We can't take the chance of you never being able to return to your own body, Nyx," Meryl said with a stubborn tilt of her chin.

"We need to do what it takes to beat Amory." I got to my feet from the couch and started pacing then stopped and looked at Desmond. "And I trust Desmond."

"I will keep Nyx's body safe," Desmond said. "This task must be done. I believe that I can put Nyx back in her own body once you've completed your mission."

"You *believe*," Meryl said with a skeptical look. "But you don't know for sure, right?"

Desmond met my gaze. "It is a chance you must take."

Colin studied me with concern as did the others. Ice's face was unreadable, but he didn't look pleased.

I swallowed, trying not to picture my body as a Zombie. "Listen to what Desmond has to say so that we can get started."

"One of the recovered stones is a keystone," Desmond said. "We will be able to use it to locate the portal to Doran."

"Are you coming with us?" Meryl asked.

Desmond shook his head. "I would go with you but my powers have been rendered useless there. I would be more of a hindrance than a help. I can do a much better job here where I still have my powers."

"How will you be able to help us here?" Colin asked.

"Amory needs to come here, on what is now my territory, my soil. Once he does, then I will have the power to defeat him."

"You all have talents that will help you on Doran," I said. "Joshua will be able to go as shadow and Ice as any form of animal he chooses, such as a mouse when we're in the mansion. Meryl goes as an oriole, and Mandisa and Penrod can use glamours."

"Will our powers work there?" Meryl asked.

"Yes," Desmond said, then looked at me. "Except for Nyx. She will only have the power of her Host body."

"Which means none since the Host body is human," Colin said dryly.

"The advantage I do have," I said, "Is that the Host I'll be taking over is that of a Sentient who happens to be Amory's niece and a key member of his Inner Circle."

"At least you've got that going for you," Meryl said, still not looking pleased.

"At least," I agreed with a nod. "Now to put our plans into action."

THIRTY-THREE

Friday, December 31
Morning

"Is it going to hurt?" I asked as I moved away from Colin and Desmond. I seated myself in a hardback chair, directly across from the chair Candace Moreno's Host body was strapped to.

The gagged Host fought against the bonds, looking wild-eyed as the Sentient Bryna struggled from within.

It was morning and the four of us were in Desmond's apartment, after I'd used my glamour to help us steal Candace's Host body from the infirmary. Lucky us that we managed to get away without getting caught.

I wondered if we counted as five persons instead of four with Candace in the stone and Bryna in Candace's body.

To be ready for anything when we returned, I was in my leather fighting outfit, but had handed my weapons belt to Desmond for safekeeping when I'd arrived. Wouldn't do to have an armed Zombie-body left behind.

"I don't think it will hurt." Desmond answered my question with a casual shrug. "Although I have never asked anyone if it does."

"Great." I swallowed and tried to relax. "How can you do the same thing Amory can do in the transference of essences?" I asked.

"The magic is in the stones," Desmond said. "My powers are similar to Amory's and I understand the mind and the process like he does. It is a matter of tapping into the power of the stones. We both can do this."

"What are you doing?" I said as Desmond and Colin began to strap my own body down.

"We need to make sure your body remains safe when you exchange essences," Desmond said.

I tested the restraints. "These aren't strong enough to hold me."

"They will be." Desmond rose and stepped back and Colin did the same.

Desmond raised his hands and a yellow glow radiated from his palms. The glow felt warm against my skin and I suddenly felt relaxed, languid. The bonds tightened around me and I pulled against them. The magic he used was so strong that the bonds had no give to them at all.

The Sorcerer picked up the cloth-wrapped stone that had Candace Moreno's essence locked inside. He pulled the cloth aside and I saw the tiny image of Candace staring out the flat side, as if she was trying to look through a TV screen.

Desmond placed the cloth and stone on the end table closest to me. "As long as no one else is touching the stone at the same time, you are safe and you will have control." He crouched beside my chair. "Because you have control of the stone, your essence will go into Candace's body, and Bryna's essence will join Candace's in the stone."

I swallowed and looked up at Colin who gave me an encouraging nod. I knew he wanted to argue against my doing this, but he also was aware that this was a way to get in with the Sorcerer Amory, something we really needed right now.

"It's just temporary," I said to Colin and he gave me a grim smile.

Desmond stood beside me, looking deceptively calm. Colin was on my opposite side.

When I picked up the stone an electrical sensation shot through my arm, straight for my head. It was like my brain was suddenly connected in some way to the stone.

My heart beat faster and I looked up at Desmond. "Go on," he said. "Touch her."

"Okay." Maybe I said it to shore up my courage as I took a deep breath. Then I repeated the word. "Okay."

I can do this.

My heart pounded, my breathing become tight and painful in my chest.

Bryna struggled, her eyes growing wider as I reached for her hand. It all seemed to happen in slow motion, as if I had to force myself to do it.

She screamed behind her gag as my fingers met hers.

Brilliant white light flashed in my head. My whole body prickled when I felt myself grasp the stone.

At the same time I realized that it wasn't my fingers wrapped around it anymore. Yet I was holding it.

The thoughts didn't make sense as I felt myself rush forward, straight for Candace's body. At the same time I wanted to scream for it to stop. To change my mind. Not to do this.

Too late. I felt myself flow into the other body.

Colors exploded in my mind. If felt like I was surrounded with brilliant flashes of light in green, blue, purple, orange, red.

Pictures flashed around me. It was like I was standing in a circular room filled with screens. On each screen were images I didn't recognize. They swirled around me, and then began bombarding me with so much information I thought I might pass out from it.

A mixture of Candace's memories, Bryna's memories, and mine, too. Information came to me with each image, as if they were my own memories.

Christmas with Candace's large family in Mexico; Bryna talking with a tall dark-skinned man she referred to as Amory and the knowledge that he was in a new body; Adam and I in the Italian restaurant when he broke up with me; Candace at work in her position as the CEO in a brokerage house; Bryna stalking Candace, holding the stone, ready to trade essences with her; Bryna watching her own body walk away, now a Zombie, after she made Candace her Host; Colin and I fighting Sentients in the coffee shop.

One image after another after another . . . a

hundred different thoughts all at one time . . . everything flying around in my brain until I thought my head would explode from it all.

"Nyx!" I heard Colin's shout somewhere outside my head and the bombardment of thoughts and memories.

Someone was shaking me—but not me.

I grasped onto the thread that was me. A thread that felt drawn so tight that it might snap.

"Nyx." Desmond's voice. "Open your eyes."

My eyes. Not my eyes.

Warm hands on my own. Not my own. But grounding me. Bringing me forth out of the swirling haze that surrounded me.

"Open your eyes," Desmond repeated.

I gripped the strong male hands holding my own and clenched my teeth, and willed everything to slow and come into focus.

Gradually it all fell into place, memories slotted but ready for me to draw on when I needed them.

I opened my eyes. Colin was crouched in front of me, his hands grasping mine tight. "Nyx?" He looked concerned. "Are you all right?"

He looked different, the outline of him not so sharp, the colors of his clothing not as brilliant. His light blue shirt looked grayish-blue, his hair a darker gold than I was used to.

I was seeing him as Candace would, through her eyes. The scents of Desmond, Colin, and even the smells in Desmond's apartment were dull, muted. My hearing didn't seem as acute as it always had.

When I looked down at my and Colin's hands, I saw small hands with smooth light brown skin and long, manicured nails. I wondered vaguely how one would fight with such long nails.

All of the aches and pains that Candace's body had, I now felt, including the bruise from the IV that had been in her hand while she was at the infirmary.

I felt everything—the scrapes along one side of her face from the asphalt as well as other cuts and bruises, along with her injured backside from being hit by a truck. She really needed a chiropractor.

Other than that, Candace's body was toned and fit. She obviously worked out, but I felt nothing near the power of my own body.

My own body . . .

I raised my head—Candace's head—and saw myself in the seat across from me. My heart thumped harder.

Seeing myself through another person's eyes sent a shock through my core. The fair-skinned woman across from me with black hair would have been pretty, but her face was slack, her expression blank, her eyes vacant.

My body looked so . . . Zombie-ish, and a sick feeling churned in my belly. Despite the blank appearance, the shell of a body was pulling against the bonds that held her to the chair. Held me to the chair.

I turned my gaze toward Desmond. "You do know," I said, startling at the sound of the unfamiliar, sultry voice, "that I'll have to kill you if you don't get me back into my own body."

Desmond and Colin studied me.

"Are you sure it's Nyx in the driver's seat now?" Colin asked.

Desmond gestured to the floor and Colin and I looked down to see the stone by my foot where I'd dropped it. On the smooth side two women now shared the stone. Candace, of course, was one of the women. The other I recognized as Bryna when I drew from the memory of her looking at herself in a mirror in Amory's manor. Words actually came to me in that odd French-sounding language the Sentients had been using the night Candace-Bryna was hit by the truck.

"It's me in here." My throat felt different as I spoke, the body I was in strange, feeling somehow fragile compared to my own body.

Desmond moved around me and looked behind my ear. "Two burn marks." He frowned as he came back around so that I could see him. "I'd thought the first mark would be the one used to transfer Bryna's essence to the stone, and yours into Candace's body. Let us hope that Amory doesn't notice. With your Host body's short hair, it's a possibility."

"Great." I tried to move but then realized I was strapped to the chair. "Think you can let me up?"

Desmond and Colin unstrapped my loaner body and I rubbed my wrists and arms where the bonds had been the tightest. I did my best to avoid looking at my real body because this whole thing was creeping me out.

I wobbled as I got to my feet, as if the muscles in "my" body were confused as to which memory they should be working from.

Colin caught me by my upper arm and steadied me. His palm felt warm against my skin. The sensations of being touched in this body felt alien.

Candace was gorgeous, her body more rounded than mine. The heaviness of her breasts and the stretch of her slacks around the hips felt so different. I'd never had short hair and hers tickled at the neck and the lack of any length and weight felt naked.

Worst of all was the feeling of impotence. My powers, my magic had all been left behind in my own body. The absence of the elements made me feel alone, as if I'd been abandoned by family and friends.

The remnants of Candace's essence told me she'd worked out at a gym regularly, including weight training, and that she was strong for a human female. But without my Drow strength I was weak and vulnerable in a paranormal world.

I glanced at my real body again even though I'd told myself I wasn't going to. It was a mistake. The Zombie-like expression and the drool rolling from one corner of the mouth made me shudder.

"I don't know if this is going to work." I brushed my palms along my hips, a nervous movement. "I don't have any of my magic or paranormal strength. What if something happens when I'm in the Doran Otherworld?"

"That's why I'll be with you, along with the rest of the team." Colin tried to give me a reassuring smile. It didn't work. I wasn't reassured.

Then I realized that it was my team he was talking about, and I had every confidence in them that they'd get me in and out safely.

"Most of all, pay close attention to Bryna's essence." Desmond took one of the cloths from the Magi, went down on one knee, and wrapped the stone before picking it up and setting it on the coffee table. "You will be fine."

I took a deep breath and nodded. "What now?"

"Step two." Desmond remained on one knee as he met my gaze. "What more can you learn from Bryna's essence?"

With a nod I closed my eyes. *Relax, Nyx.*

I let the images start to roll through my mind again. This time I focused on Bryna. Her thoughts, her feelings, her knowledge. I allowed it all to flow through me until I felt as if I was walking side-by-side with her, only I was the one in control.

"Bryna is Amory's favorite niece," I said. "She is also his confidante."

"We couldn't have been more fortunate than to have found his niece." Desmond gave a grim smile. "What does he have planned?"

The words came easily to me, as if they were my own thoughts and memories that I was speaking from. "Amory's planning a lot for this world, but he's only revealed it on a limited basis."

"What do you see in regards to Amory sending his people here?" Desmond asked.

"It's what we suspected," I said. "Amory is having his people take over positions of power and they did take the entire Paranorm Council, exactly as we thought.

"And they have been taking norms in positions of political power," I continued. "Bryna doesn't know the list."

"What about the theory that he's working on converting mass numbers of norms and paranorms at one time?" Colin asked.

"Yes." I gave a slow nod. "Amory has been experimenting and wants to accelerate the process and take this world over sooner. She believes Amory was prepared to reveal a lot more as the next stages of his process gets closer," I said. "One problem is that because she's been in this world for a few days, Bryna has limited new information."

I went on, "She knows he's probably very worried about her disappearance and she's sure he won't stop searching for her."

"That's another reason why the sooner the better that we get you to Doran," Desmond said. "We need to make sure you're clear on your capture and subsequent escape."

"Yes." I nodded.

"Anything else?" Colin asked.

"Amory has a new body," I said. "He'd stayed in that old body—frail and wrinkled with graying red hair—until recently."

"Even twenty years ago he looked like he might wither and blow away," Desmond said. "But his magic was so strong that his presence was powerful in a magical way."

As I continued to read Bryna's essence, I tilted my head. "Amory's new Host is a very large, very intelligent human. He's built like a body builder and was one of the named partners in one of Manhattan's most prestigious law firms. So not only is he powerful magically, but also physically and mentally."

I frowned as I turned my focus on Desmond. "How can he keep his magic yet I couldn't bring mine along with me?"

"It is different for some," Desmond said. "For Amory it is because of the strong magic he wields as an extremely powerful Sorcerer."

"Normally whatever power the Host body has, the Sentient will have," I said. "So if he was a normal Sentient he wouldn't have kept any of his magic."

"Yes," Desmond said. "On the other hand, your friend Angel's body likely can turn into her Doppler form even with a Sentient having taken it over as a Host. She is a Doppler, is she not?"

"A squirrel." I bit the inside of my lip as I thought about her and prayed we'd find her essence along with Lawan's and Olivia's.

"So . . ." I said, "The Sentient who took over Angel's body would have powers because Angel did. But I have none because I'm in a body that has no powers."

"You've got it," Desmond said.

I sighed. "Bummer."

"You might need these," Desmond pulled a few pieces of material from one of his pockets. "I spelled the cloths in case you need to carry any other stones."

I took them and stuffed them into my own pocket. "Thank you."

"Nyx, do you have a grasp on what it will take to 'be' Bryna?" Desmond asked.

I paused for a moment, then nodded with confidence. "I already feel like I know her inside and out. I can turn that switch on at will."

"Good." Desmond brought the other stone to me that rested on its own cloth. "Now you can use the keystone," he said. "Go ahead, pick it up. As one of Amory's key people it is yours to command."

The moment I took the stone from the cloth and wrapped my fingers around it, I felt warmth travel through me. Warmth and confidence and knowledge.

"Where is the portal to the Doran Otherworld?" Desmond asked.

Mentally I asked the question as I stared at the stone. In the shiny, flat side of the stone appeared a local homeless shelter.

"Thirty-second Street between Park and Lexington avenues," I said as I recognized the area. "It's right by the location where a higher number than normal of homeless people have been cited."

"You were right." I looked up at Desmond. "That's the connection we've been looking for. The number of homeless people in the city is at a tragic high. But the inflated number in that area must have to do with Sentients and Zombies coming through the portal."

"Let's get the team together." Colin drew his cell phone out of his pocket and started pressed a number. "It's time to go."

* * *

My entire body shook rather than just shivered in the freezing outside air. Despite the muffler wrapped around my face and neck, my cheeks were so cold they felt almost hot and I thought my nose might freeze off. I'd never been so cold in my entire life. How did humans live like this?

Slush on the sidewalk made wet squishing sounds beneath Colin's and Desmond's boots and my shoes as they walked to either side of me. I wasn't used to making sounds when I walked and I felt like the whole world could hear all the noise my human body made.

We'd had a taxi drop us off at Lexington and Thirty-second Street, and I drew the heavy coat I was wearing tighter around me with my gloved hands.

Before we'd left Desmond's apartment Colin had gone out to buy the coat. Within fifteen minutes of the time he'd left, he'd returned with a Macy's bag containing a heavy, lined coat, a muffler, a pair of leather gloves, and a wool cap.

At the same time I was cursing the cold, I was thanking Colin for helping put some barrier between me and the icy chill. I was almost too cold to feel all of Candace's injuries.

"Doing all right, Popsicle?" Colin asked and I gave him a pretend glare.

"Let's just say in some ways I am very glad my Drow half is dominant when I'm in my own body." As I spoke the muffler did a very good job of doing just that—muffling me—making it so that it was a wonder the Dragon could hear me.

Colin's cold-weather clothing was practically summer wear compared to what I was wearing. That despite him shivering in the cold before we'd gone to his apartment that night for Belgian beer.

I looked at the Sorcerer Desmond, who wore a jacket and gloves, along with a muffler, too. But his clothing was light in comparison to mine and he didn't look cold at all.

"I sure hope it's not this cold in Doran." I shivered even more.

"Weather in my home world is pleasant year-round." Desmond had an almost wistful expression on his face. "We just need to get you to that portal reasonably unfrozen."

"This is reasonably unfrozen?" I said, my teeth chattering with every word.

The stones were in the pocket of my slacks, beneath the coat, and I felt their weight against my leg as we approached the homeless shelter on Thirty-second Street. We were on the opposite side of the street and I saw that most of the rest of our team was already there, waiting for us.

Meryl perched on a newspaper stand in her preferred oriole form while Ice sat beneath her as a pure white cat. His tail twitched from side to side as he looked up at her like he was ready to pounce on her and eat her whole.

Joshua was in his shadow form on the ground near the cat, and I saw Mandisa through her glamour close by.

"Can you tell if Penrod is there?" I asked Colin, not sure if he could see through Sprite glamours. I wished I could. Of course Penrod wouldn't be able to walk among norms unless he was in glamour.

"Can't see him, but I can sense him," Colin said. "And smell him."

There were some benefits to having a human nose and not being able to smell as well as I could as Drow, I supposed. Penrod might be an all-right male and an asset to the team, but he smelled like overcooked broccoli, the same as most other Sprites.

"It's on the other side of that barricade," I said to my team as I gestured toward the blocked-off space between two huge buildings.

The street was busy, vehicles driving up and down its length and pedestrians crossing at the intersections and striding down the sidewalk.

"Let's go." I started across the street with Colin and Desmond to either side of me.

The Zombies and Sentients traveled when it was dark here in the Earth Otherworld. Bryna had made that clear to me, so I wasn't worried about being seen by any of Amory's people. All I had to worry about were norms seeing me go through that barricade since I couldn't go in glamour.

We crossed the street and Meryl flew over the barricade

while Ice found a place to slip through. Joshua simply slid beneath the fence in shadow form. And Mandisa . . . while still in her glamour, the Abatwa Fae walked right through the barricade.

"Some trick," Colin said.

"Sure is." The first time I'd seen her do that was just a few weeks ago at the Vampire compound and it had been a little unnerving.

"I'll see you when you get back," Desmond said as Colin easily pulled apart a section of the barricade, large enough for us to walk through.

I nodded to Desmond, feeling too frozen to say anything else. As he walked away, I glanced around to make sure no norms saw us. It was clear. Then Colin and I squeezed through the opening he'd made.

When I made it through, something bumped against me and I stumbled to the side. Penrod said, "Apologies," as Colin caught me by the arm. This human body was so clumsy and awkward compared to my own. At this rate, if I didn't get used to it, Colin was going to have to carry me everywhere.

After Colin closed the barricade behind us, we came to a pause beside the rest of the team members.

Garbage was strewn across areas not covered with snow in the vacant lot. Graffiti was sprayed on the inside of the barricades and along both walls that ran the length of the lot, and at the back was a chain linked fence with another building beyond the fence.

"Where is it?" Mandisa spoke from beside me and I almost jumped out of my winter clothing at the sound of her voice. I didn't think I'd ever heard her actually speak before. "This portal you spoke of."

I started to unbutton my coat so that I would be able to reach into the pocket of the slacks I was wearing. "Despite the fact that this keystone is over twenty-two years old and was found in Otherworld, it should show us where the portal is. At least that's what Desmond and the Sentient Bryna believe."

It took me longer than normal to undo the buttons because I wasn't used to having long, manicured fingernails like Candace did.

The moment I moved aside my coat I sucked in my breath. Freezing cold instantly stabbed me like hundreds of icicles wherever I wasn't covered. My arm was shaking I drew out the keystone and held it up on the palm of my gloved hand.

Nothing happened, the portal didn't appear. It should have. I knew that from Bryna's now confused thoughts.

"You might need to take off your glove," Colin said with an apologetic look.

I groaned. What if my fingers fell off from the cold? I told myself to stop being a baby and held the stone in my left hand while Colin helped me pull the glove off my right hand. My fingers burned from the cold the moment the glove was removed.

A sensation like an electrical shock jolted me as I clasped the stone in my bare hand.

Air in the space between the two buildings grew dark and I held my breath. The darkness grew deeper and deeper yet until a moving mass of gray fog appeared before us. The gray cloud-like fog swirled like water going down a drain.

My heart pounded, my mouth dry, the coldness in my body almost forgotten as I stared at what must be the portal. My first thought was, Would we have to step through that?

Bryna's essence told me no at the same time the gray began to fade and a hole opened in the air in front of us.

Through the hole was a world with lavender-streaked skies, a world of sunshine and beauty. Its warmth began to defrost my chilled body.

But the sight of it, along with the overly sweet smell of flowers coming through the opening, made my stomach churn.

Through that opening into another world, I knew that it was the same world, the exact place, where my brother had gone to when he disappeared from Otherworld.

Twenty-two years ago.

THIRTY-FOUR

Friday, December 31
Noon

Fear gripped my chest as we stared through the opening. It was like I was reliving the same emotions that I had when I was a youngling and saw my brother being taken through the portal.

For the first time I gave serious thought to the possibility that my brother could still be alive. I hadn't wanted to build up any kind of hope, but here I was.

Then the image of him came to me, through Bryna's essence. I saw my brother. I saw Tristan. And I was seeing him from her memories.

"He's alive," I whispered and Colin looked at me. "His body is a Host and his essence is in a stone, but he's alive."

"Who's alive?" Colin asked.

The desire to run through the portal and find Tristan was so great that I started to run toward the portal. If I was in Drow form and Colin wasn't a Dragon, he never would have caught me in time. But in Candace's body I was slow, not to mention encumbered by the heavy winter clothing.

"Stop." Colin grabbed my arm and pulled me around to face him. "You simply cannot charge through the portal without thought."

"My brother's alive." My Host was breathing hard. "Tristan's body and his essence are still alive."

Colin frowned. "You can tell me what you are talking

about after we get to where it's safe. We need to get through this portal before it closes."

"Right. You're right." I glanced around me at my team members in their various forms then looked through the portal. I pointed. "That rock outcropping. We'll gather in the shaded area and then we'll decide where to go from there."

My team members—those I could see—acknowledged me with quick nods.

As if I might bolt through the entrance, Colin took me by my arm and led me to the opening. We paused one moment and then stepped through.

A gooey, gelatinous feeling overcame me, like I was sliding through mucus. Instinctively I held my breath, as if I might suck in some of what I felt coating my body.

Going through the portal was like walking against a current, through a river of goo, and into the wind.

My chest began to hurt with the need to breathe. If it weren't for Bryna's essence inside of me, I might have panicked. Thanks to her I knew we'd make it within steps.

Even as that knowledge came to me, Colin and I burst from the portal into warm sunshine. I no longer felt like I was covered in goo. I stared around me, surprise and fear mingling inside me.

A utopia. No wonder Desmond had talked about his home world with such sadness in his eyes. He had to miss this amazing place that was sharp and clear, even to the imperfect human eyes of the Host body I was in.

Lush green grass covered rolling hills between purple-hued mountains. I knew then what majestic really was. Huge trees and brilliantly colorful flowers sprung up in places throughout the landscape making the gorgeous scenery look like a patchwork quilt I'd seen in Olivia's apartment.

In the distance was a huge manor that sprawled at least an acre wide, its pink stone walls sparkling in the sunlight. Large trees lined the front of the manor, offering shade to its many balconies and along its paths. I couldn't see all of that detail but I could visualize it from Bryna's memories.

If it wasn't for Colin, I might have continued to stare in

wonder at everything around me. Even coming from the Otherworld of all Otherworlds, I hadn't been prepared for such beauty. The lavender streaks in the sky were especially lovely.

Then I remembered that this was the world Tristan had disappeared to and the sick feeling of his loss replaced the wonder.

My brother was truly alive? Was Angel somewhere around here? Would I be able to find all of their stones with their essences? I wished my Host mind had more details about him, but she knew enough that I had an idea where to start my search. It would be a matter of the right time to do it.

Colin dragged me toward the outcropping, out of sight of the manor, and I saw that my team members were waiting for me. The heat in my Host body's cheeks surprised me as I realized I had to be blushing from my continued failure to pay attention to what our task was, and for my lack of focus. I wondered if that had anything to do with the Host I was in, or Bryna, a distractibility that was uncommon for me.

Regardless, that had to change and it had to change now.

I covered up my embarrassment by concentrating on putting the stone back into the pocket of my slacks, then focused on getting out of my coat. I'd started to sweat under its weight. Colin took the coat from me and stashed it in a small cove of the rock outcropping. I unwrapped the muffler from around my face and tossed it onto the coat.

After I pulled off my gloves, I handed them to Colin. I tugged off the wool cap, which he also took to add to the pile of discarded winter clothing. Static crackled in my hair. I shook my head, then flattened the strands with my palms.

When I was finished, I cleared my throat and looked at my team members. All of them were assembled around me now. Joshua, Meryl, and Ice in their human forms, and Mandisa and Penrod were now visible. Meryl sat on a boulder while Joshua knelt on the grass. Ice stood with his feet apart, his arms crossed over his chest, and Mandisa had one hand on her hip. Penrod reclined on the ground, his back up against a boulder.

"Knowledge from the Sentient that inhabited this body before me indicates that we need to go toward that manor." Even though we couldn't see it from behind the rock outcropping, I gestured toward the pink manor. "That's where the Sorcerer Amory is."

They focused on me as I continued. "According to Desmond, there's absolutely nothing we can do to Amory here in Doran. He's too powerful for us to take out or even capture, so this is entirely a recon mission. We must find out what his plans are."

"Does the Sentient you're sharing that body with tell you anything about his plans?" Meryl asked from her perch on the stone.

"Bryna knows that something big, really big is in the works," I said. "But she doesn't know what that might be. Amory had alluded to his plans before she left, but she hasn't been in on anything since that time. I'm going to have to find Amory or figure out another way to get this information."

I pointed to the team members as I gave them direction. "I want Shifters together on one team, and those who will go in glamour on the other team."

They nodded as I continued, "Meryl, you're with Joshua and Ice. Mandisa, you'll be working with Colin and Penrod. As teams you'll find out everything you can. In the meantime I will—"

"No damn way." Ice's voice cut through the air. "You're not going alone, Nyx."

"Ice is correct," Colin said and everyone else nodded, frowns of disapproval on their faces.

"I'm going as Amory's niece," I said with protest in my tone. "I know what to do and say. I'm the one who'll be fine."

"What if he insists on sealing your Host, Nyx?" Colin spoke in a low, deliberate tone. "If that happens, it will not be easy for you to transfer back. You may not be able to if something happens to Desmond."

"Are you so easily forgetting what the Vampires did to you?" Joshua said.

"This is different." I shook my head. "I'll be fine—"

"No." Everyone on my team said the word at the same time. It was loud enough that I winced, afraid someone in this world might be nearby.

"Okay." I held up my hands. "You're right."

"I'll go with Nyx." Colin met the gazes of Mandisa and Penrod. "The two of you will work well together in glamour."

Mandisa glanced at Penrod, disdain on her features before she glanced back at me. She said nothing.

Penrod looked like he'd swallowed something rotten.

"Remember, we are here on reconnaissance. I am to gather information. You are to see and observe what you can and to protect each other, and if it comes to it, rescue each other," I said.

"Shifters," I continued, "you'll take the grounds, Mandisa and Penrod, you'll go around to the back." I glanced at Colin. "Colin and I are going in."

"Let's do it," Meryl said right before she shifted into an oriole and flew above our heads. She circled once before heading in the direction of the manor. At the same time Ice joined her as a pure white falcon and Joshua sped across the ground as a shadow.

Penrod had already vanished. Sprites are pretty much impossible even for paranorms to spot when they're in glamour. Colin and Mandisa disappeared. Because I was in a human body I couldn't see them. I hoped the Sorcerer wouldn't be able to catch sight of any one of them.

Once everyone but Colin and I were off and running, I turned and headed around the outcropping, toward the manor.

The human body I was in was fortunately in good shape for a norm. It was a bit of a hike to the manor and the sunshine was warm as we traveled over the rolling hills.

My Host's heart pounded harder and harder the closer we got to the manor and my throat was dry. I don't know if I really felt Colin's presence or I just knew he would be at my side. We'd been silent during our trek and I knew he was concerned about me.

On the way I'd thought about stopping the Sorcerer and finding out how we could do exactly that. My thoughts continually returned to my friends and my brother and my hope that I could help them all.

We finally reached the manor. An arched gate was in front of the entrance and a low wall of the same sparkling pink stone stretched out and around the circumference of the place that seemed almost palatial but not quite.

Guards stood to either side of the gate. The twins reminded me of Roman gladiators in their simple tunics and sandals. They both looked at me with questions in their eyes. Guards of the manor were used to Sentients returning in new Hosts, so they didn't seem particularly alarmed.

"Good day, Pet. Theo." I gave them each a nod as the action and their names came easily to me. "Do you know where my uncle is?"

"Bryna?" Theo said in surprise. "Is that you?"

I frowned. "Who else calls the Sorcerer 'uncle'?"

"Of course." Theo lowered his head in a deep nod. "My apologies."

Pet said, "His lordship sent Una and Tieve to search for you."

The scowl came just as easily as Bryna reacted. "Idiots. They left me to die."

Pet gave a slight bow. "I will locate Lord Amory for you."

I waved him off. "I'll find him myself. Likely he's in the gardens."

"Your new Host is an excellent choice," Theo said, openly admiring Candace's body.

"If you serve me well," I said in Candace's sultry voice, "I might give you the opportunity to get to know the new Bryna better."

I touched Pet's arm and he looked down at my hand. I lightly dug in my manicured nails before I gave them each a sensual look that made both men stare at me with hunger in their eyes.

Bryna had always enjoyed men, but because of the frailty of her former body she had been forced to abstain. Now that she was in a fit, strong, and beautiful Host, she wanted these two males—at the same time.

I had to mentally shake Bryna off. *Down, girl.*

"That would certainly be a pleasure." Theo's voice was husky as I walked closer. Both guards bowed again as they let me pass.

"Was that necessary?" Colin's voice was close to my ear and I startled. He sounded almost jealous.

"Shush," I said under my breath. "It's how Bryna's mind works. I'm simply being her. If I didn't, it might be suspicious."

The manor doors were open, letting in the sunshine along with the smell of flowers and the twitter of birds. As we walked further in, the recesses were cool, shadowy, and quiet. I caught the scent of exotic spices.

I stood for a moment inside the huge open area that had multiple doors leading from it and a staircase that spiraled up one side. I let my human eyes adjust to the dimness as I looked around.

Even though Bryna felt at home in this place, I needed to get a feel for it and I needed to stay on guard. I didn't have my keen Drow senses to rely on in case someone was coming, my glamour to hide me, or my fighting skills if I needed them.

Colin touched my shoulder and I nodded at the opposite side of the large area we were in. We crossed the huge marble floor then entered a short hallway. At the end of the hallway was an arched doorway. Much cooler air flowed over me from the direction of the arch. Along with it came scents that were familiar. Maybe not to Candace, but to me and Bryna.

It smelled of old rock and earth and mineral-filled water, smells I was used to from my home belowground in Otherworld.

When we reached the room, we walked over the threshold. My lips parted in surprise. Steps led down into a huge cavern filled with hundreds of thousands of stones with hundreds of candles lit among them.

Due to the imprint of Bryna's essence, I shouldn't have been surprised at the immensity of the cavern, but for some reason I was. Seeing it for myself as opposed to her memories was like the difference between a dream and reality.

"Amory calls this the Room of Life." My heart sank as I walked down the steps into the cavern. "How will we ever find Angel, Olivia, and Lawan here?" Or Tristan. What about my brother?

An overwhelming feeling of helplessness made my human body feel even weaker and more impotent than it already was. I glanced behind me and saw that Colin had dropped his glamour. His blond hair shown in the flickering light of the candles.

"For that matter," I added, "what about the Paranorm Council members and anyone else we know? Bryna has no idea. How will we find them?"

Colin rested his hand on my shoulder and warmth from his palm caused a small shiver to run through me. "We'll figure it out, Nyx," he said in his deep, compelling voice.

"One way or another." I responded with a firm nod, trying to add conviction to my tone.

Colin let his hand slide away from my shoulder as we walked through rows of stones and stones and more stones. I missed the warmth of his touch and had the entirely irrational desire for him to hold me.

My focus needed to shift completely to the job at hand. Why was I having such strange thoughts now? It must have been the Host body or Bryna making me feel that way.

Throughout the room the candles were too many to count. Their flames danced and bobbed and caused the stones to glitter like Christmas lights woven through tree branches in New York City.

I paused and started to pick up a stone before I snatched my hand back. "Don't touch," I said. "Bryna doesn't think anything would happen, but she doesn't know for sure."

We both stared at the stone that I'd almost picked up. A well-built man who could have been an athlete was staring out at us. I wondered how long he'd been in the stone. Who he was. How he'd gotten there.

I tore my gaze away from the image of the man and Colin

and I kept walking and looking. Some of the stones looked dark, empty.

"If the stone doesn't have a face in it, that means the Host body died." My voice echoed in the cavern. I felt a twist in my belly at the thought that maybe that had happened to one of my friends or Tristan, and Bryna just didn't know about it.

My search through the room for stones with the essences of people I cared about grew more and more frantic. "Where are they?" I whispered to Colin. "How are we ever going to find anyone we know here?"

"We will be able to return and locate all of them." Colin's tone was so positive, so confident that I paused to look up at him. Determination was etched on his strong features.

The sense of urgency I felt only increased as I went up one aisle of stones and down another. My hip brushed a stand and the stones on it rocked. One of them threatened to roll off and I caught my breath.

As the stone came to a rest in an indentation of the granite stand, my breath left me in a rush. The face inside the stone was of a young woman with long blond hair and wide brown eyes, like she was perpetually surprised. I'd almost killed her with my carelessness in this Host body. Yes, Candace wasn't graceful like the Elves, but that only meant I needed to be more careful.

It made my heart twist to see someone so young trapped like that. Unless we found her Host body, she would be inside the stone forever.

The prickling sensation behind my Host's eyes was familiar, but then the sensation of something on my face made me pause. I touched my cheek. It was damp. In surprise I drew my hand away and looked at my fingertips. They glistened with moisture in the candlelight.

"A tear." I looked up at Colin in shock. "I have tears."

"You're crying." He reached up and brushed wetness across my opposite cheek with his thumb with concern in his eyes. "Are you all right?"

I gave a slow nod and touched my face again. "Dark Elves don't have tear ducts. We can't cry."

"I think you can cry, Nyx." Colin pushed hair behind my ear. "You simply cry without tears."

"It's not the same." I wiped the moisture from beneath my eyes. "It feels almost freeing to be able to cry with tears."

Colin gave me a gentle smile, then surprised me by kissing my forehead. He let his lips linger for a moment before he drew away. "Come." He took my hand. "We should hurry if we are going to find your friends."

Warmth from his hand spread throughout me and I still felt the imprint of his lips on my forehead. A tickle grew in my belly, a feeling of awareness of him not only as a friend, but as an entirely desirable male.

Keeping Adam out of my mind wasn't easy at all. Just finding Colin attractive made me think about Adam.

I needed focus and I needed it now.

"I wish I had my Drow senses to search for them." I released Colin's hand. "And my command of the elements."

"My Dragon senses will help." Colin ran his gaze over the enormous cavern. "I've met Olivia, Lawan, and Angel, which will make it feasible."

"Let's split up," I said and we started searching in earnest for my friends.

I wondered how impossible it might be to find my brother among the countless stones around us without my senses or magic on my side. I doubted Colin could find Tristan since they'd never met.

We must have been searching for over an hour when Colin caught my attention with a wave. "I think I found your partner."

"Olivia?" I rushed toward Colin then had to slow down because my clumsy human Host body nearly knocked a couple of stones off their perches.

When I reached Colin, who was in a crouch, I knelt before the stone he was studying.

"You found Olivia." My heart pounded and I stared at my friend whose face looked out from the stone. Not surprisingly, she looked pissed. For some reason that made me smile a little. As if that meant she was all right and that she'd be okay.

I dug in my pocket and pulled out one of the cloths Desmond had given me. I almost touched the stone, then remembered I was supposed to trap it in the cloth without touching it. I managed to do it and gripped it tight in my hand, so afraid to drop it that the fear was almost immobilizing.

"Thank you." I tucked the stone into my pocket and then reached up and kissed Colin on the cheek. "Thank you for finding her."

His skin was warm against my lips and I drew in the smoky sandalwood scent of him. My face went hot when I realized what I'd just done and I backed away. Colin was smiling and I turned away, hoping my Host's face wasn't too red.

We continued searching. And searching. And searching. Having found Olivia made me feel a little lighter in spirit, but really not much. We may have located her stone, but it was a long road to get her essence back into her own body, and to solve this whole Zombie mess.

At least an hour later, Colin said, "Here is Angel." His voice had made my heart jump and I turned to see him beside a stand of several stones. I hurried to him and saw that it included one with Angel in it and her distinctive corkscrew curls around her face.

A huge measure of relief poured through me as I handed Colin a cloth. "Two. You found two."

He eased the cloth over Angel's stone, then wrapped the stone safely inside it. He slipped it into his pocket. I took Olivia's out of my own pocket and handed it to him. "It's too dangerous for Amory to catch his niece with stones belonging to Earth Otherworlders," I said. He took it and put hers away, as well.

With more hope than I'd had before, I turned to continue looking.

Colin grabbed my upper arm and jerked me to a stop.

"My Dragon senses tell me someone is coming," he said as I brought my gaze around to look at him.

"It's the Sorcerer Amory," Colin added before he slipped into a glamour and faded away.

THIRTY-FIVE

Friday, December 31
Afternoon

My heart pounded harder. Blood rushed in my ears. I whirled to face the doorway.

I drew from Bryna's essence and straightened in my Host body. I pulled back my shoulders, forced a smile, and prayed that he couldn't tell that Colin and I had taken Olivia's and Angel's stones.

"Uncle Amory," I said the moment the big male walked through the archway, and I started toward him, making my way down the rows and rows of stones. My body grew hot as I hoped he had no way of sensing that two stones had been removed.

Then I realized I'd just spoken in the French-sounding language without even thinking about it. What came naturally to Bryna must come naturally to me.

It was interesting, feeling like I did in Bryna's world. I didn't have to try and be her, it just came to me, as though it was who I was. As Nyx I could control it, but it came naturally, like someone almost acting in character. An actor becomes the character and in a scene doesn't just become himself. He knows he can control it. This was similar. Only I didn't have to try to act. It just happened. Although I controlled Bryna, I could come out of character at any time.

The Sorcerer hadn't looked surprised to see a stranger in his Room of Life. He came to a stop, clearly waiting for me.

"Bryna," he said as if he'd already known who I was before calling him uncle.

Had the guards told him? Or had he *known* in some magical way?

Amory's power was so palpable that even my human Host body recognized his magical strength. Bryna's essence backed up that awareness, telling me that the Sorcerer's power went beyond what most beings could imagine.

However, I was used to the Great Guardian, so I could imagine a lot.

When I reached him, the Sorcerer engulfed me in a strong embrace. His arms felt like steel bands around me and I winced from the pain he caused my Host body's scrapes and bruises when he squeezed.

"Bryna," Amory said. "I am most grateful to have you back with me." His voice was a low growl as he added, "Una and Tieve almost paid with their lives when they gave me the news that you had been injured and taken to an infirmary."

"It is good to be back," I said as my stomach twisted, knowing that his powerful Host could physically crush mine. I hoped Amory wouldn't sense me inside of Candace's mind and body. The fact that Colin was near in his Dragon glamour made me feel slightly more at ease. Only slightly because I knew Colin was no match for the Sorcerer magically.

Amory was so tall his roughly woven tunic scratched the side of my face. At least it was the side not scraped up from Bryna's tumble onto the asphalt when she was hit.

Bryna's essence relayed how strange it still was to see him this way when she was used to a frail, brittle-looking old man. Her essence also told me that despite her close relationship with her uncle, his power and his bursts of anger sometimes frightened her. She would never show that he scared her, but the fact was he did.

Amory kissed my cheek and I tried not to shudder because the monster was touching me. I tilted my head and gave his jaw a light kiss like Bryna always did. My stomach churned the moment my lips touched his face.

The Sorcerer drew away. "I am so pleased to see you,

niece." He smiled, his straight, perfect teeth white against his dark complexion, and Bryna recalled how yellowed and crooked his teeth had been in his old body. She much preferred this Host body he was now in.

I, on the other hand, wasn't so sure about his new Host. He was so incredibly physically strong that he could easily crush this human Host that I was in. He wouldn't even need magic to hurt me.

All I had was Bryna's knowledge and my own wits to get me through this. Which I was seriously beginning to doubt after my lack of focus so far today.

"Did Una and Tieve come back with you?" Amory asked as he patted my shoulders then released me.

I shook my head. "I haven't seen them."

The Sorcerer frowned. "They did not recover you from the Earth Otherworld? Then how did you escape?"

He could have looked into my mind but Bryna's essence told me that he respected his niece enough to not do that. At least most of the time.

"It was uneventful. When I recovered, I found an opportune time to escape." I'd already rehearsed this part. "This Host's clothing was in the room and I changed into it then slipped away when no one was looking," I said. "Then I went to the portal as fast as I could."

Amory's callused fingers were warm as he touched the side of my face. A frown crossed his strong features. "You were injured."

I nodded. "This Host body is bruised and scraped, but I am well."

"Una and Tieve are at fault for this." Amory's words were harsh, angry.

My natural inclination to protect almost overrode Bryna's much less caring essence. "Tieve almost lost my stone." I brushed my hand over my pocket, hoping Amory didn't sense the keystone, too. "I almost died to save it."

"What were you doing in the Room of Life, Bryna?" the Sorcerer asked in a soft, firm tone that had an edge of warning to it. And suspicion?

Even without magic I thought I felt Colin stiffen beside me while still in his Dragon's glamour.

"After my near-death experience in the Earth Otherworld," I said, carefully drawing upon Bryna's essence, "I felt the need to be among life. I thought of the Room of Life and how you find solace in it, and came here to renew myself before locating you."

"Your Host must be sealed soon." Amory met my gaze and a sick feeling dropped to my toes. "It is dangerous to be amongst occupied stones when you have not been sealed. You know this, Bryna."

The thumping of my heart and the perspiration breaking out along my skin was going to give me away if it didn't slow down. This was happening too fast. I couldn't let him seal me into this Host and it was too soon to leave. It created too much risk to transfer back later.

I took a huge inward sigh of relief when Amory added, "However, it must wait until after the meeting with my Inner Circle. I am pleased you shall make it this time. I have much to tell you all that is of great importance."

"Of course, Uncle Amory." I gave a low bow of my head. "Not only are you my favorite uncle, but I am ever at your service."

The Sorcerer put his hand on my shoulder and started to guide me out of the enormous cavern. He paused to look down at me. "It is good to see you before you return to the Earth Otherworld, Bryna, to serve in your new Host's position."

"It is good to be home," I replied before he led me up the stairs and over the threshold, back into the manor. "As much of a home as we could call Doran after twenty years," I added and when Amory nodded in knew I'd said the right thing.

Bryna's confidence in herself made it easier to hide my unease at being in the Sorcerer's company. Knowing Colin was nearby helped immeasurably.

We walked across the great hall, rounded a corner, and headed down another hallway. Everything was familiar thanks to Bryna.

When we entered the Inner Circle chamber we went down several steps. The sheer size of the enormous round room amazed me despite having Bryna's knowledge of it. The chamber was at least the size of a basketball court.

Eleven faces stared back at me from a round table. I offered a haughty expression. It was expected in keeping with Bryna's attitude and her position as Amory's niece and confidante as well as an advisor.

Like we'd seen in the detention center, all of the Kerran Sentients who had not taken Host bodies had long, delicate fingers, small ears, and petite noses.

Present was the obnoxious Jalen in his new Host body that Bryna had seen only once on the day she'd departed. Also in their new Hosts were Fala, LeeLa, and Xella.

Most of the other advisors were still in their old Host bodies but preparing for their trip to the Earth Otherworld to secure their new ones.

Not if I could help it.

"Bryna is back in our Inner Circle." Amory presented me to the group with a genuine smile. "Her new Host is Candace Moreno, and she is the CEO of a brokerage house in the Earth Otherworld's Manhattan."

The advisors each gave me a nod. Bryna knew she wasn't popular among the advisors. The real Bryna didn't care if she was accepted by any one of them, or not.

I took one of the two empty chairs that were side-by-side at the circular table. Bryna always sat beside Amory at the meetings. All of the advisors seated themselves, including me, when Amory made a slight gesture with his hands.

The wooden chair was hard and I winced from the press of it against the back of my bruised thigh.

Amory's voice boomed throughout the room. "All of the Hosts brought over after the mass takeover at the theater have been sealed and returned to the Earth Otherworld."

My stomach flipped and my throat and mouth felt dry. *Angel.* Angel must have been sealed. Had her Host body returned with the others?

The Sorcerer gave a sardonic nod to Jalen. "This was

accomplished thanks in great part to Advisor Jalen who worked tirelessly until the very last of our people were sealed into their new Hosts."

Jalen scowled and I hid a smile that Bryna would have given. She despised Jalen and it was obvious that whatever it was he'd had to do hadn't been enjoyable by any means.

One thing was true—Bryna loved her uncle even though she feared him, and she didn't like how Jalen normally spoke to him.

Jalen's Host's face grew red with anger and it was easy to see that he wanted to say something. For once the big ass kept his mouth shut. At least that was Bryna's opinion of the scowling male—an ass.

I turned my attention to Amory as he said, "As we have planned, and you are just now hearing, Bryna, we will be able to take as many as half a million Hosts in one night."

The statement slammed me with the force of a tsunami that made my head swim and my mind whirl.

As many as half a million Hosts? In one night?

Shock continued to course through me in a way that made my skin cold, my scalp prickling as if being jabbed by thousands of needles at once. How could Amory expect to accomplish stealing such an incredible number of Host bodies?

The advisors around me applauded, all except Jalen and me.

Amory looked at me and I forced a brilliant Bryna smile and joined in the applause.

"Where will you accomplish such a feat?" I asked.

"New York City," the Sorcerer said.

My mind raced. When would that many people be gathered in one place at one time in the city in the near future?

Then it hit me so hard that it was like any remaining heat in my body rushed out of me in an ice cold wave.

"New Year's Eve, Times Square," I said as horror started to roll through me. "Tomorrow."

"Your Host mind knows well," Amory said. "You are correct." Then he smiled. "Although you are forgetting that time is different here. It is already New Year's Eve Day in the Earth Otherworld."

Panic nearly had me jumping up from my chair. "Over half a million people in one place. One time. In just hours."

"With five hundred thousand of our people in place early," Amory said as he nodded, "we will crowd out any amount of people over that number. Reporters will report unprecedented numbers. Before they know anything, we will have taken a half-million Hosts."

Shock almost made me forget where I was and who I was with—the Sorcerer and a roomful of his advisors. Then I felt Colin's warm palms on my shoulders as he gave them a squeeze meant to ground me. To remind me of where I was and what I was supposed to be doing.

I didn't look up, knowing Colin was still in glamour, then felt his warm breath in my ear. "We will get back in time to warn Rodán and the other Trackers," he murmured. "First we need to find out all that we can. A few more moments of knowledge will save more lives."

To let him know I'd heard and that I agreed with him, I gave the barest of nods.

A glow lit up Amory's end of the room and I turned my attention toward it, barely able to keep to my seat. Colin continued to rest his palms on my shoulders, reassuring me of his presence and that I could make it through this.

My skin itched with the desire to jump up and do whatever it took to stop the Sorcerer now. But I had no power of any kind here, including being able to slip out of the room unnoticed or use my elements to protect myself or my team members if any one of us was discovered.

I didn't like the helpless feeling coursing through the Host body I was trapped in. Didn't like it at all.

A glow emanated from the Sorcerer's hands and I watched as an image of Times Square floated up, almost like a projector casting an image onto the white wall.

"This is where we shall take many Hosts at once." Amory smiled, a cold, chilling smile. "Once we have secured such a large number, it will become easier and easier to accomplish our task of controlling this Earth Otherworld."

"What is your plan?" I asked. "I hate to have you repeat only for me, but I am excited to hear this fantastic news."

Xella shot me a look telling me she was obviously perturbed that Amory had to retrace the steps of the plan that everyone knew but me. She wasn't a pretty female—at least her Host wasn't—and the way her lips were twisted into a smile it made her look almost evil. From Bryna's familiarity with the female I knew she was exactly that. Evil.

"When it grows darker in the city of New York, we shall start transferring the rest of the stones," Amory said.

"The rest?" I couldn't help myself. "You have already sent some there?"

A pleased expression crossed Amory's features. "We transferred close to half a million stones last night."

My stomach dropped and I could almost feel my face whiten. I drew on Bryna's confidence and her feelings to recover from my own reaction.

"This is amazing, Lord Amory," I said and let Bryna's smile shine through. "How did you accomplish such a task?"

The Sorcerer gave me a hard look. A suspicious look. I had to force myself to meet his dark eyes. "How do you think, Bryna?"

"Your incredible abilities and power, of course." I tried not to rush the words out. Instead I spoke in the easy, careless way of Bryna. "Forgive me for asking."

Amory turned back to the image and began gesturing to it and explaining that the stones would be given out by his people as mementos of the evening. The moment a Sentient passed a stone to a human, the Sentient would take control of the Host and leave its Shell—a Zombie—behind. He said that the Zombies would be released for the first time en masse.

Inwardly I shuddered.

"I have been keeping a rein on the Shells until now," Amory said. "But as of this exchange, I shall leave them to wreak havoc among those we have not chosen to use as Hosts. Those not on our lists."

"How will the Shells know the difference between future Hosts and those we wish to dispose of?" Xella asked.

Amory looked at Xella, then for some reason, me. "I have programmed all Sentients with this knowledge that will remain with their Shells once they are in their new Host bodies," he said. "Just as the Shells do not destroy one of our own, they will not touch future selected Hosts."

The thought kept pounding at my head.

The Zombies would be free to terrorize the city.

I gripped the arms of my chair so tight my hands ached as I absorbed Amory's words. The pressure of Colin's grip on my shoulders increased and tension radiated from him.

The enormity of it was almost too much to comprehend.

How could we keep such a large-scale takeover of human lives from happening?

And if we didn't, how could a mere two dozen Trackers stop a half-million Zombies from terrorizing our city?

THIRTY-SIX

Friday, December 31
Afternoon

"Lord Amory," a male voice said from the entrance of the enormous chamber. "You said to interrupt when we found the creature. It was in the gardens."

Amory glanced toward the entryway. At the top of the steps was one of the guards I had met on my way into the manor.

The male held up a squirrel by the tail.

"Angel." Her name was out of my mouth before I could stop myself.

"Oh, shit," came Joshua's whisper from the shadows to my right, startling me on top of everything else. Without my Drow senses, I hadn't even known he was there in shadow form.

The Sorcerer whirled to face me, shock then rage on his features.

"I saw that paranorm while in the Earth Otherworld." I rushed to cover up my mistake even though I knew it was too late. "Her name was Angel. She shifts into a squirrel. Like that one."

I realized too late that I'd just made two more huge mistakes. Mistake number two—Bryna would never have hurried to explain anything. She would have maintained her haughty attitude and would have said the information casually.

Not like an idiot, like I just had.

And mistake three, probably the worst of all, I'd just spoken in English.

I'd operated undercover plenty of times and I'd never done anything so incredibly stupid. The only reason I could come up with was that I literally wasn't in my right mind. The shock of seeing Angel had thrown me out of character.

"Who are you?" the Sorcerer bellowed as he pointed his finger at me. "Where is my niece?"

I pushed my chair back and dropped to my knees on the floor.

Vibrant, sizzling orange ropes of magic lashed out.

I ducked under the huge circular table.

The ropes wrapped around the chair where I had been. Wood charred and smoldered where the ropes touched the chair.

My heart thundered. I smelled burnt hair. Two locks fell from my head onto the floor beneath the table. I'd barely missed having my head fried.

Then I realized he was only going to hurt me. If he killed me, he might lose his niece in the process.

"Who. Are. You?" The room reverberated with the power in the Sorcerer's shout.

I scrambled beneath the round table. The feet and legs of all of his advisors surrounded me.

Adrenaline pumped through my body. What good could the extra burst of energy do me as a human? Nothing more than amp up the fear that was causing my whole body to shake.

"Get out of here!" Amory bellowed and his advisors started pushing their chairs away.

At the same time I heard a roar that made even the floor shudder.

A Dragon. Colin.

The scream of a jaguar about to attack—Ice.

The shrill call of a bird—Meryl.

Battle cries from Joshua and Mandisa.

A shout from Penrod.

My team was here. And I was cowering under a table.

Feet around the table moved. The advisors were in a mad rush to flee.

Something furry bolted toward me.

I started to dodge it, then realized it was Angel's squirrel Host body.

I lunged for the squirrel and caught her to my chest.

The Sentient inside Angela's Host body fought and struggled, scratching me through my clothing and across my face.

"Stop it!" I managed to get her in a chokehold under my arm, but without actually choking her.

If I could get Angel's stone from Colin, maybe it would work in reverse if somehow I got the squirrel to touch it and then Angel would be back in her own body.

Sounds of shouts and confusion echoed through the Inner Circle chamber.

Blasts of magic made the chamber light up as if a lightning storm was inside instead of out. A flare, then dark, a flare, then dark.

"Kill them all, except the Bryna Host!" I heard the Sorcerer yell as pounding footsteps came from the direction of the entryway. Bryna's Host told me it was Amory's guard come to fight. "Capture her but don't kill her—*now*!"

Shouts, yells, roars, screams—

Complete and utter chaos.

The squirrel struggled as I crawled toward the big Dragon feet I saw behind the now upturned chair where I'd been sitting.

I scooted closer and just as I reached Colin, the squirrel bit my finger.

"Ouch," I cried out and the squirrel dove out of my hold. "Colin!" I shouted as I dove for her and caught her by her bushy tail. "I need Angel's stone!"

Colin ducked his massive Dragon head beneath the table and he blinked at me with his big burnished gold eyes. In a bright flash of light and a whirl of golden sparkles, he shrank down in size to his human form and crouched.

He dug the cloth covered stone out of his pocket and tossed it to me.

At virtually the same instant he morphed into a Dragon again.

With one hand holding the squirrel's tail, I reached up to catch the airborne stone with my free hand.

The cloth fell away. The stone landed in my open palm.

An explosion of colored lights in my mind. I felt like I was bathed in purple, orange, green, yellow, blue, red.

Sights and sounds twisted and whirled. Images flashed through my mind too fast for me to grasp. A whirlwind of color, light, and sound.

Everything grew suddenly very large around me. Gigantic.

I was shrinking.

And my butt hurt like hell.

I twisted—

And found Candace Moreno's Host holding my tail.

My tail?

Oh, crap.

We stared at each other for one moment. The stone lay on the floor between us.

The Host had her mouth open wide. My little squirrel jaw had dropped.

Angel's body must not have been sealed, just like Candace's hadn't been.

If I was in Angel's Host body, then who was in Candace's?

I squeaked out—in squirrel—"Angel?"

At the same time Candace's Host said, "Nyx?"

Someone grabbed Angel-Candace by her feet and dragged her from me.

She shouted and let go of my tail.

I scampered after her. Had to help her. Had to help Angel.

How was I going to do that as a squirrel?

Even as I thought that, I sprawled on the floor. My body elongated, stretched out. Everything started getting smaller again. Long blond corkscrew curls bounced around my face and I felt myself suddenly in a petite, perky, compact human body.

I'd just shifted into Angel.

"Angel!" I shouted. I started to crawl from beneath the table when I spotted the stone Angel had been in. I snatched up the cloth and wrapped it around the stone, which now had a mousy-looking woman staring out from it. Aela was her name, according to the remnants of her essence in Angel's Host body.

I shoved the stone into the pocket of the jeans I was wearing and crawled out from beneath the table.

Two guards were dragging Angel-Candace away.

"Help save Nyx!" came Joshua's shout.

Ice as a jaguar launched himself into the air and over the table.

I thought he was coming to help me then realized he was going after Angel-Candace, thinking it was me.

Knowledge came to me from Angel's essence—of the power and strength she had as a Doppler and as a Tracker.

Ice went for one of Angel's abductors and I dove for the other.

I slammed my shoe into the back of his knee. It buckled. As the guard came down I grabbed his head, turned it. Rammed my knee into his nose.

He screamed as blood spewed from it. I stomped on his wrist and ground it against the floor.

The guard screamed again and sagged.

It gave me just the right angle. I was operating on pure Angel-Nyx-drive.

I clasped his skull in my hands. Braced my knee. Then twisted his head and snapped his neck. I glanced at Ice who'd taken equally good care of the other guard.

Ice shifted into his human form and we dragged Angel-Candace up the stairs of the huge chamber and out into the hallway.

"Damn," she said and held her arm to her chest. It was broken, twisted into an odd angle. "A human? How'd I end up in a freaking human body?" She pointed back toward the chamber, which was illuminated with more flashes of light. "Go. Just go!"

Ice transformed into a white mouse and darted through the entryway.

Despite Angel's essence I was afraid to intentionally shift into a squirrel because I didn't want to get stuck in that form. I needed to fight in human form anyway.

I hurried to the entryway and peeked inside to see the battle going on.

Dead males and females, wearing the same uniform as the twins who had been at the front gate, sprawled across the floor of the chamber.

My heart dropped to my toes when I saw an oriole lying completely still on the floor between the Dragon and the Sorcerer.

Meryl. Was she still alive?

Amory whipped ropes of orange magic out at the Dragon who blasted them away with fire every time one of them neared him. Walls were scored with tracks of fire from Colin.

Mandisa was in glamour and I guessed that Penrod was close by, both trying to edge their way toward the Sorcerer. He wasn't looking toward Mandisa, as if he didn't know she was there, but Angel's senses told me Amory was not only aware of Mandisa but of Penrod, too.

The Sorcerer was entirely aware that they were there and letting them close in on him.

Ice as a white mouse was scrambling over rocks and debris toward Amory.

"It's a trap!" I shouted, my mind racing as I tried to come up with a plan. "He knows you're there!"

The Sorcerer flung out his arm toward me. An orange rope snapped in the air.

I reached up and grabbed the magic rope before it could wrap itself around me. I jerked it away from the Sorcerer.

My hand burned with fire, the pain shooting through my arm. I smelled sizzling flesh and I almost dropped the rope from the strength of the pain. Angel's hand would heal when she shifted but right now it hurt like hell.

Amory looked at me in shock as I snapped the rope in the

air. Angel was an expert with a whip, her choice in weapons, and my choice to fight with now.

The magical rope sizzled and crackled as I whipped it back at the Sorcerer. He had to fend off Colin's fire and my whip, and he knew the others were closing in on him.

As I snapped the whip at Amory, it hit something hard, solid, just inches from the Sorcerer's face. An orange shimmer in the air told me that he'd just thrown up a shield between himself and all of the Trackers.

"He's shielded," I shouted. Desmond had said it was impossible for any of the Trackers to truly defeat the Sorcerer on our own. I didn't know for sure if that was true, but I did know we needed to recoup and make our escape before more of Amory's guards showed up. "Get out of here. Now!" I screamed over the noise.

But everyone kept their places and continued to advance on the Sorcerer.

No one recognized me. Angel's Host body had been taken over by a Sentient, and for all they knew it was the Sentient trying to trick them.

"It's me, Nyx." I called out over Colin's roar and the sound of thunder in the chamber. "Somehow I got transferred into Angel's body. You have to believe me. We've must get out of here before Amory's guards come."

My team members were too professional to lessen their concentration on their task. They were listening, but also aware that it could be a trick, a trap.

"Colin. When you gave me Angel's stone I touched it by accident." I held onto the magic whip, ready to snap it at the Sorcerer if he dropped his shield. "And Angel is now in Candace's body."

"It really is Nyx." Colin had shifted back into human form before shouting out the words. "Listen to her and fall back. Get to the portal."

Penrod appeared beside the oriole. The Sprite put Meryl into a pocket of his baggy pants before cloaking himself in a glamour again and disappearing from my sight.

Ice transformed from a mouse into a white falcon and circled the room.

Mandisa nocked a poison arrow in her bow as she backed away from Amory.

Joshua slipped back into shadow form.

Colin vanished behind a glamour.

Everyone fled the chamber.

I dropped the magical rope that I'd used as a whip and with Angel's innate ability, I shifted into a squirrel and scampered back up the steps.

Outside the chamber I heard more of Amory's guard on their way to assist the Sorcerer.

Colin reappeared and scooped Angel-Candace into his arms. "To the portal," he shouted, then disappeared again, both he and Angel now invisible.

We all bolted for the front entrance of the manor. The guard charged directly toward us, but couldn't see Colin, Mandisa, and Penrod in glamour, or Joshua in shadow form. And clearly they didn't know that Ice flying overhead as a falcon, and me as a squirrel darting between their feet, were part of the invaders that they were supposed to stop.

As we ran outside, Amory's bellows echoed through the land with the power of thunder followed by the crack of lightning.

The Sorcerer's voice grew louder behind us. "To the portal!" he shouted and more lighting sizzled in the air. "You cannot see them, but they are there. Get to it before they can escape. I will close the portal when I am close enough. They will be unable to get through."

Rain started to pound on the land, nearly flattening me with the strength of it when the first bucketsful came down.

I shook it off, soaked through my fur to my skin, and fled. I was the only one who would be visible on the ground. I traveled over the rolling hills through patches of flowers and where the grass was taller, and skittered up trees and bounded from tree to tree through the branches.

The Sorcerer's presence was strong behind us and I knew

with his magic and the power of his Host body he could get close enough to the portal to close it.

The run was long and hard, but we made it before the guard or Amory.

A little breath of relief came to me when I spotted the portal and saw Mandisa stepping through it along with a shadow passing by her and the falcon sailing overhead. I assumed Penrod and Colin were there, too, even though I couldn't see them.

Just as I came within ten yards of the entrance, the portal opening grew dark. It swirled like a funnel cloud, its center starting to close.

No, I thought and scampered faster. But it was closing too fast.

The falcon flew back through the opening and came straight for me.

Ice swooped down with a falcon's amazing speed and grabbed my squirrel body in his talons.

He shot back through the portal just as the Sorcerer's shout was cut off with the final thunder of the portal closing.

THIRTY-SEVEN

Ice dropped me and I tumbled head over tail onto the snowy city lot where we'd first gone through the portal.

Snow coated my fur as I rolled to my feet. Through the natural ability that Angel was born with, I shifted from a squirrel into her human form. And ended up on my hands and knees in the freezing white stuff.

I pushed myself to my feet. Around me everyone was in their human forms, no one hidden behind a glamour. Angel-Candace stood with her broken arm held to her chest. Her face had new scrapes from where the Sentient that had been in her body had scratched me in her squirrel form before we changed bodies.

Talk about confusing.

Colin had grabbed the cold weather clothing we had left behind and was carefully cloaking the shivering female with it. Between being hit by a car and then beaten up by Amory's guards, Candace's Host body looked like hell.

Then I realized everyone was looking at Penrod. In his big hands he cradled the still oriole.

"The bird woman is dead." Penrod sounded sad as he raised his hands so that we could see the body.

My breath caught and I brought my hand to my belly. The pain of the loss of a fellow Tracker was acute, sharp, like a blade to the gut.

"Meryl." Angel stepped forward and with her Host's good hand touched a strip of charred feathers along the bird's side. Her voice shook a little. "What happened?"

I knew it before Joshua said, "She was caught in one of the Sorcerer's ropes."

"We are going to destroy that bastard." Ice's tone was filled with anger and hatred.

Everyone on our team gave a solemn nod of agreement. The only exception was Mandisa who remained still and quiet as always. Yet I thought I saw an even darker fierceness in her black gaze.

As horrible as the situation was, a lot more lives were going to be lost if I didn't take control and get us moving.

"The Sorcerer plans to make a mass exchange of essences tonight," I said and everyone turned their attention to me.

"What?" Angel said. "How?"

I explained everything that I had overheard and each member of my team grew more and more somber. Because I wasn't in my own Drow body, I couldn't tell what time of day it was.

"It's late in the afternoon already," Colin said, surprising me with an answer to my unspoken question. "We need to get to the others. Figure this out."

"Late afternoon?" I pushed the blond corkscrew curls out of my eyes as I looked at the sky. My heart started thumping. "No way." I glanced back at Colin. "Are you sure?"

He nodded. "We don't have a lot of time."

"Let's get moving, and fast." I nodded toward the Candace Host. "Angel and I will go to Desmond to get our own bodies back and get them sealed. Joshua, I'd like you to go with us to make sure Angel makes it there okay in her human Host.

"Ice." I turned my attention to him. "Please fly Meryl to the infirmary and they will make necessary arrangements there." He studied me with his ice-blue eyes. He said nothing but I saw the acknowledgment in his gaze.

"Colin," I said. "I'd appreciate it if you'd get Olivia's Host body out of containment and bring her to Desmond's as fast as possible. You can cloak her in a glamour to get her out."

Colin gave a nod of agreement. I added for the others' benefit, "We have Olivia's stone."

I looked at Mandisa and Penrod. "Rodán said the rendezvous point is the Mandarin. Head there and wait until everyone else arrives. I'll call Rodán now and let him know what's happening so I'm sure he'll be ready for you with the others."

Without anything further, everyone left to take care of their assignments. Ice was the first to leave, having shifted into a falcon before taking Meryl's oriole body in his talons and flying away.

With Angel in a human Host, we needed to take a taxi. Joshua hailed one within a couple of moments.

In the meantime I called Rodán and filled him in on the details. "I'll make sure everyone is ready," he said. "Get to the Mandarin as soon as you can."

We made the short distance to Greenwich Village in minutes. Joshua paid the cab driver as Angel and I headed into the apartment building. In moments Joshua was with us and he carefully scooped Angel into his arms and carried her to the elevators.

Desmond opened the door to his apartment just as I was about to knock. He looked haggard and disheveled. "You're lucky you got here," he said to the Candace Host. "I'm ready to kill you."

"You mean me," I said and looked at the wreck of his apartment. "We got switched. I'm Nyx and Angel is now in Candace's body. Where's mine?"

The Sorcerer looked confused for a moment. "Your body is the reason why I'm about to lose my mind." He gestured toward a closed door. "In my bedroom."

I frowned and opened the door. On a bed in the center of the room my Zombie body was strapped down. Loud groans came from behind the gag as it fought to break free of the many ropes binding it. And it looked like it was succeeding.

"It's been like this since you left." Desmond dragged me all the way into the bedroom. "I've been close to knocking you—your body—out." He held out his hand and looked from me to Angel. "What happened with you two? Where are the stones?"

"In your pockets, Angel." I looked to my struggling body as I spoke and saw that it was starting to break free of the restraints. "You'd better hurry."

Joshua helped Angel get the stones out as she gritted her teeth against the pain of her broken arm.

I explained to Desmond what had happened as I straddled my own body—which was a completely bizarre experience— and used Angel's body's strength to help pin me down. To pin my body down. Even I was getting confused.

"This makes things more of a challenge," Desmond said as he rumpled his hair with his hand. It was obvious he hadn't had a pleasant time taking care of my Zombie body.

He took the cloth-wrapped stones and set them on a nightstand beside the bed. My body was tossing me from side to side while muffled groans came out from behind the gag. It was still daylight so my body didn't have full Drow strength. As a Zombie I guessed it didn't know how to use the elements. For that I was sure everyone was thankful.

Desmond looked at the stones on the nightstand. The images of Candace and Bryna were in one and the mousy Aela in the other. "How in the bloody hell am I supposed to do this?" Desmond said.

Angel and I looked at each other.

Uh-oh.

"We have to hurry," I said and launched into a quick summary of what had happened in the Doran Otherworld and what was going to happen here in the Earth Otherworld if we didn't stop it.

"Just do whatever you have to do to get us back in the bodies we belong in," I said when I finished.

Desmond picked up the stone with Candace in it and handed it to Angel. "We'll start with you."

She took the stone and immediately her body started to twist and jerk and her eyes rolled back in her head. In one moment I saw Angel's determined personality had been in

Candace's eyes. In the next moment confusion followed by fear was in the female's gaze. Candace was back in her own body.

Candace started to scream. Joshua pinned the female to his body. Desmond touched her forehead and she slumped, unconscious.

I looked at the stone. Now Angel and Bryna were staring out from it.

"Hope this works," Desmond said as he tossed it to me.

I caught it by reflex and cried, "You hope?"

Then I felt nothing at all. Saw nothing. I just *was*.

Was nothing.

Nothing.

Light flashed in glittering array of colors and suddenly I was spinning.

Images spun in my mind. Memories. Memories that I was familiar with.

My memories.

I gasped and tried to suck in my breath but my mouth was stuffed with some fabric and my head was wrapped in duct tape securing it. I opened my eyes and saw Desmond and Angel looking over me.

"Is it her?" Angel said.

Desmond frowned. "I don't know."

I nodded frantically. "It's me," I tried to say but it came out, "Mmph mmph."

Desmond touched the gag. I felt a warm sizzle of magic and it all fell away from my mouth.

With a groan I drew in a deep breath. "I never, ever want to do that again."

I felt instantly comfortable being back in my own body. As a matter of fact it felt wonderful. I had an urge to get my hands on my weapons and battle someone, something. My leather fighting suit felt snug, familiar against my skin. I was ready for battle.

A knock came at the door, startling me. Joshua left the bedroom to answer it.

Desmond made a motion with his finger and all of the bonds strapping me down fell away. I gave another sigh of relief as I sat up in bed.

I'd never been so glad to be me than I was at that moment. I had never appreciated the strength and magic in my body as much as I did then.

Joshua came back into the bedroom followed by Colin, who was carrying Olivia's unconscious form over his shoulder. The bed dipped as Colin lay Olivia beside where I was now kneeling on the mattress.

"Is she all right?" My heart beat faster as I looked at my friend's unconscious form.

"She's fine," Colin said. "The Sentient who took over Olivia's Host body gave a bit of a fight on the way so I found a way to quiet her."

Colin shoved his hand out of his pocket and brought out the two remaining stones. The keystone along with the stone he'd found in the Sorcerer's Room of Life that had Olivia's essence in it.

Desmond moved toward the nightstand where the stones containing Bryna's and Aela's essences were. He unwrapped the two and the blank keystone rocked to a standstill when he set it down beside the others.

Then he was holding Olivia's stone on the cloth in his palm. Without even realizing I was doing it, I held my breath as he took Olivia's limp hand and let the stone roll into her palm.

Sparks flew. A rainbow of light flashed between Olivia and the stone.

Her eyes flew open and she sat bolt upright in bed.

Olivia's gaze swept over everyone in the room. Her dark eyes stopped on me. "What the hell is going on?"

"Olivia?" I said.

"Who else would I be?" She tugged her shirt down as she spoke. "The Avon lady?"

"What's Avon?" Desmond said.

"Let me see the stone," I said.

"What stone—" Olivia frowned, raised her hand and

opened her fingers. On her palm was a stone. A blond woman's image was inside it.

"It's you." I gave a huge sigh of relief then flung my arms around Olivia's neck. "Damn, it's good to have you back."

"How did I get here?" Olivia asked.

"You've been trapped in a stone for days, Olivia," I said. "Your body was a Host. There's no time for details now."

A scowl crossed Olivia's face. "No way. Someone else had my body?" She twisted around and looked at herself. "What did they do to it? Was I a freaking Zombie?" She looked at me and put her hands on her hips. "What happened? Makes me want to take a long hot shower. Several showers."

"Olivia, read my lips. Not now." I think she got my point, even though she scowled.

My skin started to tingle and I drew away from Olivia. "It's almost sunset," I said. "We don't have much time."

First things first. I headed into the bathroom, closed the door behind me, and shifted.

When I returned, Desmond handed me my weapons belt that he'd put away before I left for Doran. The belt felt good around my hips, the weight of my Dragon-claw daggers and buckler comfortable and reassuring.

I called Rodán as we prepared to leave and filled him in as fast as I could. He let me know what room he and the other Trackers were in at the Mandarin Hotel.

Before we left I raised my hands. "Hold on a sec. You all need to look more presentable before going into the Mandarin."

"We do not have the time to each take a shower," Desmond said with exasperation.

"Just watch," Olivia and Angel said at the same time.

With my hands still raised, I said, "*Avanna*."

The Elvin spell cleaned everyone down to the last speck of mud and repaired the small tears some of the group had in their clothing.

My blood was heated and I felt like we were moving much too slow as we headed outside into the darkness.

The ball would be dropping in seven hours. That didn't give us much time to do what we had to in order to stop Amory.

THIRTY-EIGHT

Friday, December 31
Night

Three cabs were waiting that Colin had called for while I was in the bathroom. Plumes of white exhaust, tinged with red from the cabs' taillights, rose in the frigid air.

Joshua took one of the cabs with the unconscious Candace to drop her off at the human part of Columbia University Medical Center. Joshua would meet us at the hotel as soon as Candace was safe at the hospital.

Colin, Olivia, Desmond, and Angel, along with me in glamour, split up between the two other taxis.

When the taxis pulled up to the curb, we practically ran up to the Mandarin Hotel's entrance. Since Dark Elves would likely cause a stir in the hotel I remained in glamour. Still, I half expected the hotel's staff to stop us. Despite the cleansing spell, Olivia and Desmond looked scruffy.

Fortunately the staff was busy with other hotel patrons and we managed to get by. It was New Year's Eve after all.

Just when I thought we were home free, at the elevators we were met by a uniformed human. "I need to see your keycards before you can get onto the elevator," the male said. "Only registered guests are allowed on the upper levels."

Desmond walked up to the man, stared him in the eyes, and smiled. "Have a pleasant New Year's Eve."

"And you." The male bowed and gestured for us to pass.

"How did you do that?" Angel asked, and Desmond shrugged.

"Now there's a useful skill," I said as we caught an open elevator and headed up to an executive suite where the rest of the Trackers were gathered.

Tracey opened the door to a roomful of watchful, tense Trackers and Rodán. The Trackers clearly relaxed when they knew it was us for sure. Rodán looked calm and knowing as always.

Ice, Mandisa, and Penrod had all made it there.

It was a somber bunch and it was easy to tell that Meryl's death was affecting everyone, as well as the fact Lawan was still missing.

Angel and Olivia were welcomed back and our group expressed relief that the pair was okay.

Rodán interrupted. "Nyx has much to tell you all and we have little time."

The group quieted and I gave a brief outline of everything that had happened from the time we'd all met at Colin's apartment in Queens to our escape from Amory's manor in the Doran Otherworld.

After I finished relaying the news, I said, "Desmond has a lot to say regarding the Sorcerer Amory and how we are going to stop this from happening."

Desmond stepped forward. "We can't stop the Sentients or Amory from crossing over nor do we want to."

"What the hell do you mean, we can't and don't want to stop the Sorcerer?" Olivia said among more rumbles of disapproval.

Desmond held up his hands. "I didn't say Amory couldn't be stopped. I said we can't stop the Sentients or him from crossing over."

"What is this bullshit?" Ice said.

"Half a million Sentients, and half a million stones," Desmond said. "Think about that. The number is almost unfathomable."

"Then we need to notify the authorities," Tracey said. "They need to clear out Times Square."

"Claim there's a terrorist bomb," Fere said.

"And stay out of the streets so that we're not trampled to death like everyone else?" Ice said with sarcasm in his voice. "Yeah, that's the ticket."

"It would create pandemonium that would be deadly," I said with a nod, my mind whirling.

"With the kind of crowd that will be in Times Square," Robert said, "it will be like shooting fish in a bucket for the Sorcerer."

Desmond said, "The only way Amory can be defeated is to do it on our turf. We must draw him in where he can be taken on in this world."

Olivia moved her hand in a motion for Desmond to hurry on with it. "Get to the part where we defeat the Sorcerer."

"*We* don't," Desmond said. "I do." He held up his hands, indicating we should hold off commenting further. "Amory is far too powerful for any of you to combat. He has not only his own immense power, but mine as well."

At that the room went silent. I felt the raw edge of panic start to set my nerves on a high thrum.

"I explained to you once before that Amory took my magic on Doran and left me powerless there," Desmond said. "But what he doesn't know is that I have my magic here.

"With Amory having his own magic as well as mine, I'm not as powerful as he is." Desmond lowered his hands. "But he thinks I am powerless."

"You're saying he's more powerful than you," Kelly said. "So what is it that you think you can do?"

"What we have is the element of surprise." Desmond began to pace in front of the other Trackers in the suite. He looked nervous yet at the same time almost excited. "His guard will be down. Mine will not. He will be too supremely confident that no one can touch him.

"We have hope." Desmond sounded almost like he was talking to himself. "It is my intense desire to see him destroyed. That makes up for any power that I do not possess. Sometimes it is not the strongest, but the most determined who wins a battle."

Kelly made a scoffing noise. "And you're going to beat this guy by desire?"

"Yes." Desmond stopped pacing, his attention fully on us. "Vengeance is a strong motive. Fear or protecting those you care about is another. I have both."

Desmond looked around the room and met each Tracker's gaze. "You have heard of norms doing superhuman things like lifting a car off of someone injured. It is similar with my power. The vengeance I feel for those I lost in Doran is an intensity I have never felt for anything."

He continued, "And the desire to protect those here in the Earth Otherworld that I care about knows no end. I care about every person in this world."

"How much of a chance does that give us?" Nadia asked. "In practical terms."

Desmond sighed and my stomach sank at the sound of his voice, a lessening of his enthusiasm. "It is hard to say. I have never done this before . . . Maybe less than twenty-five percent. But it's our only chance."

"Twenty-five percent?" Olivia said with incredulity on her features and in her voice. "That's it?"

"I don't know of any other way." Desmond slipped his hand into his pocket and drew out a cloth-covered stone. When he unwrapped it, and let the stone rest on the cloth in his palm, I recognized it as the keystone.

"I will create a concentration of power and will transfer Amory's essence into *this* stone," Desmond said. "When I do, all that he has done can be reversed. If I fail, I will be forever locked in the stone myself, and his plan will not be stopped. I know of no way then to defeat him."

"That's it?" Kelly said. "You don't really think you can win and if you don't succeed we are toast?"

Desmond looked solemn. "I *will* do all I can to defeat him. But yes, in your terms, you are toast."

Everyone was quiet with the exception of Ice who muttered, "Twenty-five percent."

Rodán came forward, his gaze serious, intent. "The mind is a powerful thing . . . most of it is untapped by not only norms but paranorms as well. My hope is that will be the difference here tonight with all of us. It appears it is all we have on our side."

"Don't forget all of the insurmountable odds that we have overcome," I said.

"Yes," Rodán said. "Do not forget that. And that you are Night Trackers. The best of the best of all paranorms."

"We will break up into teams to search the city for the portals and the Sorcerer Amory," Desmond said.

Joshua shifted where he was standing with his shoulder hitched against a wall. "Portals? There's more than the one we went through?"

Desmond nodded as he wrapped the stone in the cloth and then stuffed the whole thing into his pocket. "The keystone showed me where they are."

"Great," Angel shook her head. "Like one portal isn't bad enough."

"The one we knew of," Desmond said, "and four other portals."

"Five," Nadia said.

Desmond gave out the locations for the five portals—Riverside Park, Battery Park, Hudson Yards, Waterside Plaza, and the portal we'd gone through at the homeless shelter on Thirty-second Street.

We were down to twenty-four Trackers without Meryl. Rodán assigned teams of four per portal.

My team consisted of myself, Colin, Penrod, Fere. We would stay with Desmond on high alert in Times Square in case Amory got past one of the five portals.

If Amory was tracked down at one of the portals, we would go straight to it. The four of us were the fastest Trackers outside of Ice and Joshua, and we all could perform glamours. Colin had the ability to transport other beings with him, so he'd be able to get Desmond anywhere he needed to go.

"How do you know the Sorcerer is not already here?" Nadia asked.

"When Amory walks through one of the portals," Desmond said, "I will know it. I will feel his magic signature. Right now I feel nothing. I know he is not here."

Desmond held his hands a foot apart. Green light crackled from between his hands and a holographic image of Amory floated in the middle of the room.

Surprise made me blink. "You've never seen him in that body."

"The keystone showed me his new appearance." Desmond twirled his finger and the image of Amory rotated so that we saw him from all sides. "For those of you who have not seen him, study and remember the face. Your job is not to capture Amory but to follow him and report his location."

Rodán looked grave as he gave a slow nod. "Each team will be assigned to a portal and to communicate with the others when you see him. Follow him without being seen and report his position or movement until we can get Desmond and the stone in place for the fight."

I went through the team assignments, then everyone left with their professional game faces on and attitudes in check.

Rodán joined my team. We headed downstairs, all of us in glamour with the exception of Desmond.

It was dark outside the hotel, already after nine PM, yet the New Year's Eve night was brilliantly lit, more than any other time of the year.

Millions of holiday lights were strung through trees, along the streets, around storefront windows. Glittering angels, snowflakes, stars, and glowing orbs and snowmen brightened the night.

This could all be gone if we didn't stop the Sorcerer Amory.

I was glad to have my weapons with me and my elements were at the ready. They stirred inside me, the power of earth, air, water, and fire ready to aid me.

Fere, as a Tuatha D'Danann Fae warrior, was able to fly in glamour to Times Square where he would take his place on one of the buildings.

Colin would transport himself and Desmond to the Square, keeping them both in glamour until Colin had Desmond safely within the barricades. Then Colin would shift into his Dragon form and find a high perch, like Fere, and watch for Amory from the advantage of height.

Rodán, Penrod, and I would both patrol the Square in glamour and stay close to Desmond who was prepared to take on Amory.

I ran to Times Square and made my way through crowds. In glamour I slipped past hundreds of people holding stones and a sick feeling twisted my stomach.

Amory had done something to the stones. Something that made them look like they belonged in the streets and in the hands of the New Year's Eve revelers.

The stones glowed.

Eerie, neon glows like glow sticks. The crowd held them over their heads and swayed to music pouring from the massive loudspeakers. Thousands and thousands of glowing stones were being waved in time to the music.

Thousands and thousands.

Every other person held the glowing stones.

My stomach twisted and adrenaline pumped through me. We had to stop this. We had to stop Amory from stealing these peoples' essences and turning their bodies into Hosts for his Sentients.

When I reached him, I held onto Desmond's arm to keep him in glamour as we were jostled by media and other people who were allowed inside the strip of barricades that led to the countdown stage.

I looked around us at the dazzling lights and the colorful indescribable brilliance of the square. We weren't looking to see the sights. We were looking for Amory. And I didn't know how we were going to find him in time to stop him.

My senses felt almost overwhelmed by the press of hundreds of thousands of people around the barricades and the bustling energy of so many souls anticipating the drop of the ball down the flagpole atop the building. My ears rang with the sounds of countless voices and the smells of so many bodies packed together was almost too much.

Everything was so intense, the noise at such an extreme level that if I didn't have such excellent hearing, I might not have heard my phone when it finally rang thirty minutes from midnight.

Desmond shuddered and said, "He's here," before I had a chance to answer the phone.

"We've got him," Angel said when I answered. "Battery Park." She sounded breathless. "I don't think he knows we're watching him."

I looked at my team. "We'll be right there."

"We won't let him out of our sights," Angel said and disconnected.

"Battery Park," I said just as I saw Rodán on his phone and frowning.

"Joshua called," Rodán said. "The Sorcerer just arrived through the portal at Waterside Plaza."

"What?" I said and the five of us looked at each other.

The phone rang again. I felt frantic as I looked at the caller identification screen. "Olivia," I said as I rushed to answer.

"Hudson Yards," she said. "Hurry."

Ice called. Then Nadia called for Mandisa who never talked. Both reported Amory having come through the portal they were watching.

"What is going on?" My heart beat faster. "How can this be?"

"Decoys." Desmond looked grim. "Our only hope is to figure out which one of the five is the real Amory . . . in time to stop him."

THIRTY-NINE

Friday, December 31
Minutes from midnight

Time was ticking past.

The more time that passed, the more frantic I felt to find the Sorcerer.

Imagine by John Lennon began pouring from enormous speakers everywhere and chills rolled through me as thousands of voices joined in on the lyrics.

I looked up at a giant clock on a countdown screen and my heart started thrumming. "Little more than three minutes until the ball drops."

"Amory will feed off the energy of so many souls gathered together in one place." Desmond's eyes appeared intense, focused, as he searched the square with his gaze. He looked nothing like the harried, distracted artist I'd met just days ago.

"Where is Amory? We are running out of time. What if we fail? What if he escapes back to the Otherworld?" My thoughts swirled as the panic I'd started to feel earlier only grew more intense with every word Lennon sang. Every word that brought us closer and closer to the ball dropping.

"Imagine all the people living life in peace . . ."

Peace. There would be no peace if we didn't stop the Sorcerer.

Screams jolted me.

I cut my gaze to the direction from which I'd heard the sounds of raw terror and pain.

There were too many people. I couldn't get a good look—but then I saw colored lights starting to flash in the night.

My eyes burned white-hot with my fury. It was already happening.

Lennon's words of peace continued and I held on to them as if they might make a difference in what happened tonight.

We'd hoped to take on Amory before he made it here and that hadn't happened. We had to take him here.

He had to be close. The exchange of essences was already happening and Zombies were already being left to rip apart anyone who wasn't a Sentient now inhabiting a Host body. If we didn't stop the Sorcerer, half a million Zombies would tear the city apart.

Trackers started appearing around us, bringing in Amory look alikes. One group. Two. Three. Four. Four different Amorys.

Where was the fifth?

"And the world will live as one . . ."

I looked toward the countdown stage as the last line of "Imagine" trailed off.

The former president and his wife pressed the button to drop the enormous Waterford crystal ball from the top of Times Square One.

Three huge screens below the ball started showing the one minute countdown. The loud sound of a ticking clock filled the air as the countdown began.

59, 58, 57 . . .

And then I saw him.

I saw Amory.

The Sorcerer was on the stage, striding toward the center.

45, 44, 43 . . .

"There!" I shouted and started running in that direction, dragging Desmond with me as I pushed our way through the reporters and other people crowding the inside of the barricade.

30, 29, 28 . . .

A blast of orange light from the Sorcerer.

Everyone was blown from the stage.

I didn't have time to think about them and whether or not they were still alive.

21, 20, 19 . . .

Amory stood at the center of the stage and spread his arms wide.

Desmond, Colin, and I reached the base of the stage, to Amory's right.

Power crackled between Amory's hands like bursts of static electricity as the oblivious crowd started the final countdown aloud.

10, 9, 8 . . .

Desmond made it onto the stage.

Green sparks dripped from his fingertips.

Amory spotted Desmond.

Shock crossed Amory's features.

The surprised expression on Amory's face was replaced by an obvious realization that Desmond couldn't be a threat. After all, he'd taken Desmond's powers.

7, 6, 5 . . .

I glanced at the crowd. Thousands and thousands of glowing stones being held up even as some exchange of essences was starting to happen. The rest of the changes were imminent. The exchange was inevitable.

If we didn't capture and contain Amory in a stone, he was on his way to a mass overthrow of our city.

Amory held open his arms again.

4, 3, 2—

Desmond shot an immense burst of power at Amory.

"HAPPY NEW YEAR!"

The sound of thousands of voices pounded the air.

Fireworks exploded and exploded from the top of Times Square One.

Amory stumbled back from the power of Desmond's magic, his concentration on his spell broken.

He whirled, fury on his face.

"Auld Lang Syne" echoed throughout the square. Voices of those who hadn't a clue what was happening joined in on the traditional New Year's song.

Desmond's gaze was focused, intent, as he tossed the keystone on the stage between him and Amory.

Both fury and arrogance were in Amory's eyes.

Instead of coming to a stop between the Sorcerers, the stone rolled to the edge of the stage.

The stone tumbled off.

The stone had fallen off the stage!

Adrenaline pumped through me. I started toward the stone.

Something grabbed me. Something strong. Holding me back.

I drew one of my Dragon-clawed daggers and whirled. The Zombie went for my throat. I ran my blade through its chest.

That was only enough to cause it to stumble back. I jerked my weapon out from its chest. No time to finish it off.

I realized the entire stage was surrounded by Zombies. Two more Zombies walked in front of me. I dropped and rolled between them and was back on my feet and diving for the stone.

A second before I would have grabbed the stone I realized my mistake.

No protective cloth.

I looked at the stage and saw the cloth lying between Amory and Desmond.

"Start spreading the news . . ." Frank Sinatra's original rendition of *New York, New York* carried over the confused chaos of the mass of people.

A battle raged between the Sorcerers. The green glow of Desmond's magic stretched out, meeting the brilliant orange light of Amory's power at the middle of the stage.

Something grabbed my shoulder.

I reached for the hand, twisted my body, then flipped the Zombie over so that it flew away from me and slammed into a barricade.

Even through the countdown I heard more terrified screams.

It was happening. Happening too fast.

If we didn't stop Amory he would seal the new Hosts. Something that I didn't think could be undone in a mass way.

Desmond was the only one we knew who could save us and he had to live to do that.

Sinatra continued to sing.

I focused my air element on the cloth and swept it through the air, straight to my hand.

Another Zombie was in my face and I gutted it.

I went for the stone yet again.

Pain burst in my left shoulder and I screamed.

I was pinned up against the stage.

The cloth fluttered away from my grasp.

My gaze riveted on the Zombie that had just impaled me with a slender metal pipe.

Stars sparked behind my eyes as I reached up with my good hand and drove my dagger into the Zombie's brain.

Tears would have been flooding my face if I could cry. The pole was too long for me to pull out myself and I couldn't move.

"Help!" I shouted, forcing my words on the air so that another Tracker could hear.

Colin appeared beside me.

His mouth was set in a harsh line. He grabbed the pole. "You could bleed to death if I take this out."

"I'm Drow." I gave a loud grown. "I'll heal. Just do it."

He took a firm grip on the pole and jerked it from my arm.

I screamed again. It hurt so badly that I could feel myself starting to black out from the pain.

Blood flowed down my bare arm, flooding over my suit.

"I'm fine." I stumbled away from Colin. "Have to get the keystone."

The bursts of green and orange light filled the air like a pyrotechnics show.

People in the crowd who hadn't been changed into Hosts obviously thought it was part of the show from their laughter and shouts of appreciation. They continued to sing along with Sinatra.

But more panicked sounds, more shrieks of terror, were starting to fill the air.

Blood pounded at my temples.

I had to hurry.

The Sentients were taking over Host bodies. Amory's mere presence was allowing the change to begin.

I held my arm to my chest, gritting my teeth, and almost passed out again when my knees hit the ground.

With my good hand I reached for the cloth and clenched it in my fist.

My head was yanked back and I cried out.

A Zombie had a tight grip on my hair.

Colin came up from behind the Zombie and beheaded it with his sword.

Screams came from all around as those close realized this was no show.

At once the Zombie released my hair and I dropped onto my one hand, the cloth still in my fist.

I shifted my body so that I was balanced on my knees and snatched the stone up in the cloth.

Blood continued to pour down my arm from the wound and I felt lightheaded. I could bleed to death if I wasn't careful.

Stumbling, I somehow managed to get to my feet.

I tossed the stone onto the stage.

It rolled between the two Sorcerers.

Desmond's multicolored bursts of magic like small lighting, laser-like charges appeared out of his fingers and struck Amory.

Amory looked stunned as a multicolored sparkling liquid gel form of him began to be pulled slowly from his body. The gel was attached to him and was being stretched out toward the keystone.

Desmond's power must have been drawing his essence out.

A supernatural tug of war.

It was happening so fast Amory had a look of horror on his face.

"No!" he bellowed when he saw the stone. His image shot back into himself.

Suddenly out of Amory's liquefied form his magic flew out, full of sparks and multicolored laser lights, and the same amoeba and plasma appearance of Desmond's multi-colored magic.

Amory's magic came at Desmond's in such a powerful blast it lit up Desmond's entire body. I saw Desmond's form start to be pulled out of him—just like Amory's had.

I held my free hand to my shoulder, pressing against the wound, trying to stop the flow of blood as I nearly held my breath. I could do nothing but watch this supernatural tug of war. A tug of war that held the earth in the balance.

Sinatra sang on, as if there and oblivious to what was happening.

Desmond thrust back at Amory with an even brighter glow.

The battle between them looked evenly matched, their magic meeting at the middle, over the keystone.

But then Amory took control.

In the bright flare of light, Desmond appeared to grow pale. His features slackened as he weakened under Amory's assault.

Desmond's liquefied image moved from his body again, only more fully, and began stretching out toward the center of the stage, where the stone was.

It broke free and the floating blob form continued to move toward the stone.

I released pressure on my shoulder.

I grabbed my buckler from the center of my weapons belt.

Raised it and flung it at Amory.

The buckler bounced off a shield protecting Amory and landed on the stage instead of returning to me.

A shield. The Sorcerer had shielded himself.

My hopes sank.

I glanced at Desmond who was struggling against the pull of Amory's magic.

Then renewed determination strengthened Desmond's features. His image began to retract back into himself.

Amory gave a cry of rage and I saw a renewed glow coming from him.

Desmond's image wavered.

Something needed to happen. Desmond couldn't do this himself no matter what he'd thought. He was losing the battle.

We were losing the battle.

Waves of agony made me weak.

Still I hurried, running on the asphalt beside the stage.

I ran to the left of the stage, until I was behind Amory.

Every jostle of someone from the now screaming crowd made me come close to passing out.

I held back a shout of pain when I used my air element to raise me to the level of the stage.

On my knees and one hand I scooted onto the stage.

I looked at Amory's backside as I rested on my haunches.

My vision swam as I watched the powerful ripple of muscles beneath his tunic as he fought. I noticed the shine of lights on his bald head.

I reached across my body and drew my remaining dagger. Slowly I got to my feet and started toward the Sorcerer.

"Nyx!" Colin's shout morphed into a roar as an enormous Dragon rose beside the stage.

The Dragon breathed fire and smoke at Amory. It rolled over his shield, showing that the Sorcerer was completely encompassed.

There was nothing I could do.

Maybe it was the pain that had made me forget that the Sorcerer was shielded. Or maybe it was something inside me that didn't want to admit that I couldn't do something.

I stood behind Amory feeling impotent as I cradled my arm to my chest.

The stage trembled from the power of the magic battle raging.

A battle that looked like it wasn't going well for Desmond. Not the way his face had paled again.

My grip on my elements felt weaker and I didn't know how much longer I could stand.

I looked at Amory's feet. The stage he was standing on.

And wondered why I hadn't thought of it sooner. If I

could catch Amory off guard, maybe that would be what Desmond needed.

Dizzy from loss of blood, I braced myself with my feet shoulder-width apart. I raised my good arm as I called to my earth element.

I imagined the earth cracking open as everything began to shake and rock. Then I called to my water element, drawing water from the closest main.

Water, earth, and asphalt exploded through the stage where the Sorcerer was standing just feet from me.

The stage bucked and I fell to my knees.

Amory shouted in surprise as he lost his footing.

He started falling through the gaping hole in the stage.

The orange glow of his magic wavered. Amory had lost concentration.

Desmond's power strengthened.

The thick green glow of Desmond's magic reached Amory and encompassed him in a bubble.

Amory cried out as the magic caught him and held him above the rent in the stage, keeping him from falling into the hole I'd created.

Desmond's power pinned Amory's arms to his sides.

Laser-like illumination shot from him, striking and lighting up Amory.

And then Amory began slipping from himself.

I watched, transfixed at the image of Amory being pulled again from his body straight toward the stone.

"No, no, noooooooo!" He gave a painful, agonized cry.

Amory's entire body shuddered and trembled.

"*Yes.*" The word came from Desmond with the sound of vengeance and determination behind it.

The image of Amory reached the stone.

And then it was sucked down, whirling, like water down a drain into the stone.

"*New York, New York . . . New York . . .*"

Sinatra's powerful ending strain sailed through Times Square as the Sorcerer vanished.

FORTY

Saturday, January 1

A cool evening breeze blew my hair over my shoulders on New Year's Day when I reentered the Doran Otherworld with Colin.

"Everything that happened last night—or early this morning—seems almost impossible to believe now that it's over," I said as we walked through the grass toward Amory's manor.

Colin nodded. "Like the night lasted forever, but then was over before we knew it."

The moment Amory had been sucked into the keystone, all of his magic of the night had been undone.

Essences that had been stolen that night returned to their Hosts and the Sentients returned to their original bodies. That left no Zombies.

"Casualties were over two thousand beings." My heart hurt when I said the words.

"Considering all of the Zombies created from the exchange we could consider ourselves lucky that it wasn't more," Colin said.

"Every life matters." I looked up at the thousands of brilliant stars overhead. "They were lives lost and I hate that. It can't be undone."

"I know, Nyx," Colin said quietly. "I feel the same way, but it was small compared to what it could have been."

The media had reported it as a terrorist activity. Theories

abounded right and left from the media and the public. That was consistent with how the media and the public responded to every unexplained tragedy that we'd faced since I'd become a Night Tracker.

As far as the fight between Amory and Desmond on stage, in front of a billion people on camera, everyone thought it was a part of the night's festivities. Just an elaborate show. The authorities were not commenting, but with all the deaths being reported someone would be answering more questions. Tough questions.

Tough answers, though. What else could be said? An evil Sorcerer and his Sentients had been coming to the Earth Otherworld to steal their bodies, their lives, and to ultimately take over the world. Good it wasn't for me to figure out.

Colin studied me as we walked. "How's your shoulder?"

I rotated my arm, flinching at the memory of the Zombie impaling me with the metal pole and pinning me to the stage. It was only a memory, not real pain. When I'd shifted into human form I'd partially healed. Tonight when I returned to Drow, it had completely healed.

"It's fine." I let my shoulders relax as we went up another rise. "After the last shift, good as new."

Lights from the manor grew closer as we walked. "Did Desmond say how long it will take to match up essences?" Colin asked.

"Desmond believes he recovered what he's calling 'the source stone,'" I said.

Colin raised his eyebrows in interest.

"I don't know anything more," I said, "except that Desmond thinks it will help him do the exchanges en masse."

"Where did Desmond get this 'source stone'?" Colin asked.

"He found the stone on Amory's Zombie right after he defeated him. Desmond wanted to study it further before doing a mass transfer." Colin and I were almost to the manor now. "If that hadn't been found Desmond wasn't sure he'd be successful in saving most of those who'd been taken."

Colin shook his head. "The whole thing is hard to grasp."

"Yeah, it sure is," I said. "If Desmond fails we'll have hundreds working around the clock to do all that can be done. He's pretty confident it'll work, though. I lean toward trusting Desmond."

Colin reached for my hand and held it in his. "What do you think Desmond has done with the stone containing Amory's essence?"

His touch, the easy manner he'd taken my hand startled me, yet at the same time felt comfortable. I wasn't sure if it felt completely right or it was just my head fighting with my heart.

With all that had happened, it seemed like forever since Adam had broken up with me. Yet . . . my heart felt like it was bleeding and I wondered when it wouldn't feel like that anymore.

I let Colin continue to hold my hand, though, part of at least an easy friendship between us.

"Desmond just said he'd make sure the Sorcerer will never be able to hurt anyone again," I said.

Colin gripped my hand tighter. "Let's hope he's right."

When we reached Amory's manor, we headed through it until we reached the cavernous Room of Life. Colin released my hand when I tugged at it.

Desmond stood just inside the entrance when we walked in. He shook Colin's hand and gave me a quick hug and kiss on the cheek that surprised me.

I glanced over Desmond's shoulder. "All of the stones are still here. Haven't there been any transfers?"

"To take the stones and find their host body would have taken years," Desmond said. "Some would never have been found. Fate has given us a great big smile. I am completing mass transfers now." Desmond appeared worn out, his wild hair looking like he had a serious case of bed head.

"How are you doing this?" Colin asked.

"With the knowledge and power I obtained from Amory when I locked him in the stone, as well as with the source stone." Desmond rubbed his hand over his head. "I did not expect to take on Amory's mind when the transfer occurred. I would not have chosen to take the evil I took on."

Desmond's words send a chill creeping over me. "You took on Amory's evil?"

He shook his head. "I kept the important details I needed from him, and his power to combine with mine, then swept all of the evil away. It would have been crazy for me to keep it. It was beyond belief, the evil that had been within him," Desmond said.

Tingles of relief caused me to relax and I flexed my fingers. I hadn't realized I'd moved my hand to my weapons belt at the mere mention of Desmond retaining Amory's evil.

"From Amory's mind, I learned of something that he had found and was experimenting with," Desmond said. "A 'source stone.' He was going to experiment in exchanging essences in mass with it, but decided since the stones were in place here that he wouldn't take the risk."

"How is it used?" Colin asked.

"It takes a special magic and concentration to draw power from the source stone." Desmond looked over his shoulder at the many stones in the room and returned his gaze to Colin and me. "My power combined with Amory's power, along with the knowledge I gained from his study of the stone's magic, has provided us with what we need to reverse all the essences. I know I can do this."

"How are you going to do that?" I asked.

"I'll take the essences from stones here and perform the spell," he said, "and transfer the essences in the stones into this source stone."

Desmond pulled a stone from his jeans pocket and held it up. The stone was larger and not plain-looking like the others. This one was as black as lava rock and as big as one of Colin's big fists.

"Amazing," I said.

Desmond leaned against a bare pillar that had once held stones containing essences. "I'll return with the source stone to the Earth Otherworld and I'll complete the transfer. The essences will go out from this stone and find their bodies once I complete the spell."

"What about the Zombies?" I asked.

"They died within hours of Amory's containment," Desmond said. "Somehow Amory's power had kept them alive. Without his power to maintain them, they quickly expired and literally vaporized to nothing. No trace can be found by anyone."

I gave a slight smile. "One less question for the norms in the Earth Otherworld."

Colin shifted his stance and crossed his arms over his chest. "What about the essences from Amory's world? What will become of them? Will they be trapped in the stone forever? Many of them are innocent, are they not?"

"There is a world I know of from Amory's mind that he wanted to choose," Desmond said. "It was uninhabited. Amory's lust for power and to conquer was great, though. He chose Earth over this other world because of the challenge to take over the infrastructure."

"What does that have to do with those beings who are innocent?" I asked.

"This source stone is so powerful that it can restore those essences which are alive with a replica of their original healthy body in that world." Desmond's words surprised me into widening my eyes. "I will release them to that world and be done," he continued. "It is up to them to make their way from that point."

With that Desmond raised his hand, the source stone on his palm.

Brilliant colors and sparks flew from the stone. Loud crackling noises and thin, lighted laser-type trails soared from stones throughout the room into the source stone. It was almost blinding in its beauty of dazzling bright colors.

Desmond smiled after the last spark vanished. "That's it. Now to take it to the Earth Otherworld."

I stood there dumfounded. "Desmond, we owe our world to you. Thank you."

"Don't thank me." Desmond shrugged with genuine modesty. "Just about anyone would do what I did if it came down to it. There was no choice."

"What about Amory?" Colin asked.

"No Otherworld will ever have to worry about the Sorcerer Amory again." Desmond pushed his hand through his long wavy brown hair. He looked younger then, like the weight of worlds was off his shoulders.

"What did you do with him?" Colin said. "Where is his stone?"

"Someplace he can't be saved, someplace where he can't save himself," Desmond said. "In an Otherworld that is much like what is known as the Cretaceous period in the Earth Otherworld."

"Dinosaurs?" I said with surprise. "You sent him to live with *dinosaurs*?"

"Not a norm or paranorm in sight." Desmond gave me and Colin a tired smile. "If he makes it out of that stone in some way, he isn't going to be able to hurt anyone ever again."

I held out my hand and he took it. I smiled. "I hope you'll stay in New York City. You're pretty handy to have around."

"The city is my home now." Desmond squeezed my fingers. "I will see you."

I kissed him on the cheek. "Thank you."

Colin shook Desmond's hand and thanked him, too.

"There's someone you'll want to see." Desmond indicated with a nod of his head for me to look over his shoulder.

"Tristan?" I nearly held my breath as I saw the Drow male who looked so much like my brother. With his dark blue skin and blue hair, he stood out among beings of other skin tones.

"Considering he was the only remaining Drow male in this world, his Host was easy to match up with his essence." Desmond released my hands. "Just remember that to him no time has passed since he was trapped in the stone. He won't know you."

I nodded, barely hearing Desmond as I stared at my brother. Desmond squeezed my hand again. I gave him one more look, telling him with my gaze how much I appreciated everything he had done for us.

Then I left him and Colin to walk toward Tristan. I came to a complete stop when I reached him and met his gaze.

He cocked his head in a familiar way that made my heart ache. "You are a Drow female." Tristan looked me up and down with surprise in his gaze. "You are dressed much like a warrior." His black eyes met mine. "I know of no female Drow warriors. Why do I feel like I know you?"

His voice was so much my brother's that I had to hold myself back from running to him and throwing my arms around his neck.

"You do know me." I walked up to him and took his hands in mine. His skin was dark blue against my pale amethyst. He was tall like our father and I tilted my head to look up at him. "It's been a very long time."

He glanced at our joined hands and back at me. "My soul knows you," he said. "But it does not make sense."

I smiled. "I was five the last time I saw you." The memory of his being taken caused me to swallow. "You made me hide in the bushes the day you disappeared."

"Nyx?" Shock filled his gaze. "It is not possible. My sister is only five."

"Your essence was put into a stone, Tristan. Like these others that you see here," I said, "time froze for you. It didn't freeze for me."

Tristan's blue hair was a shade darker than mine and it brushed his shoulders when he shook his head. "It is as I was told earlier, but I cannot believe it." He caressed my collar that I'd worn since birth. "You wear this. Only my sister could and it bears your name as well as your station. How—how old are you now, little sister?"

"Twenty-seven." I smiled as more surprise registered on his features. "We could be twins now."

My brother enveloped me in a hug, squeezing me so tightly that I gasped for air. "To know that I did not see you grow is a great sadness in my heart." He drew away and I sucked in a deep breath. "But at least I am free now to get to know the sister that I always loved."

"I missed you so much, Tristan." My eyes would have filled with tears if they could have. "I thought you were gone forever. We all did."

"How are Father and your mother?" Tristan's hand seemed to shake as he pushed hair from my face.

"Very well," I said, my voice catching a little. "They'll be shocked and ecstatic to see you." I just couldn't get over seeing him. Right there. With me. "You are back from the dead, Tristan."

I shook my head, still having a hard time grasping it. "You're here, you are really here. This is the happiest day of my life."

Tristan hugged me tight. "It's so good to see you, little sister."

"Father has missed you so much that he could barely talk about losing you." I paused. "Nor could I, and for that I'm sorry. I just missed you more than I could bear."

Tristan hugged me again, squeezing me tight. I didn't mind. His scent was so familiar that it brought back waves of memories from when I was just a little girl. All of the things he did for me and with me. I'd loved him so much.

When I pulled away I smiled up at him. "Let's go see Father and Mother."

FORTY-ONE

Sunday, January 2

"Suuuure you missed me." I set down Kali's crystal dish of Fancy Feast on the floor of my kitchen and looked at the blue Persian. "No need to pretend."

Kali raised her head and stepped with a cat's grace that easily rivaled that of the Elves. She took her first delicate bite before giving me a look that said, "I don't like being watched while I eat," then looked away from me to take another small bite.

"Dahlia always takes good care of you when I'm gone." I turned and headed out of the kitchen. "There's no reason you should be mad at me."

I reached my bedroom door and sighed when I looked at the destruction Kali had left in her wake. The pretty panties I'd just bought were in shreds on the floor, scattered from one end of the room to another like black, hot pink, red and green confetti.

I quit trying to figure that cat out a long time ago. How did Kali get into a lingerie drawer three feet up? Had to be a paranorm cat—it just didn't shift I guess until I left. Maybe that was it. Surprisingly, the panties I'd picked out with Colin weren't among the destroyed.

Probably because she liked him. Maybe I'd have Colin do all of my panty shopping.

I smiled then turned as I heard a knock on the door. My first though was *Adam*, but it wasn't his familiar knock.

To be on the safe side, I sent feelers of my air elemental magic out, allowing it to slide beneath and around any gaps in the door's molding.

"Colin," I said to myself with some surprise.

I opened the door and gave Colin a smile as I gestured for him to come in.

He looked as sexy and hot as he had the first time I'd seen him on stage at the Pit. His long golden hair rested around his shoulders and his burnished gold eyes looked at me in a way he'd never looked at me before.

The twist in my belly sent shards of desire through me. "You aren't using your Dragon charm on me, are you?" I said without thinking as the door closed behind him.

He stopped in the middle of the room and his gaze held mine. "That's just you wanting me," he said and my face grew hot. "The same way I want you."

My fair skin had to be full-on red. "I—"

Colin came close to me and he cupped my face in his hands. They were strong, callused hands that sent an erotic thrill throughout me. His scent, his presence, everything about him was enough to make my head spin as though I was drunk on him.

"I don't think—" I started, but then he brought his mouth down on mine.

And kissed me.

A kiss that set my whole body on fire.

It was urgent, demanding. Nothing soft or hesitant about it. His was a kiss of ownership.

That thought made me break away. I tried to catch my breath as I looked up at him. His gold eyes looked almost bronze as he let his hands slide down to my upper arms then held onto me.

"What—what was that all about?" I said between breaths.

His smile was confident and sexy. "I've been waiting for this to be over," he said. "And waiting for time to be alone with you."

"You can't just do that." I wasn't sure what I was saying, except that a man having ownership over me was not in my list of reasonable expectations in a relationship. "What's gotten into you?"

"You've gotten into me." Colin drew me up against him. It was a side I hadn't seen. He'd been everything from friendly to flirtatious to someone who'd worked hard with me side-by-side. "From the time I first saw you watching me on stage, I knew you were the one."

My face grew impossibly hotter.

Colin looped his arm around my waist and pinned me to him. "You and I are destined for one another, Nyx."

I shook my head. "You are acting absolutely nuts."

My breasts were smashed against his chest as he gave me an incredibly carnal smile. "I think not."

Then he kissed my remaining words of protest away until I couldn't remember what I'd been protesting.

He tasted warm and masculine. The hard press of his body against mine made me groan into his mouth.

A knocking at the back of my mind told me I wasn't ready for this. It was too soon.

Why was it too soon?

But it kept knocking at my brain.

Then I realized I heard real knocking.

This time, familiar knocking.

I came back to myself and pushed Colin away.

This time I was breathing a lot harder and my heart was beating like crazy.

I cut my gaze to the door and heard the familiar knock again. "Adam," I said, my voice hoarse.

When I looked back at Colin he gave me a gentle smile before bringing me to him and kissing my forehead. "I understand," he said. "You need to work things out in your head. I'll give you time." His mouth quirked. "But not much."

What was there to say? My recently ex-boyfriend kept knocking at the door, and another male had just given me a kiss worthy of his Dragon reputation.

Still, I knew he hadn't used his Dragon charm on me. It had been the real thing.

"I'll save you some embarrassment and questions." He smoothed my hair. "You talk to him. I'll see you later." He said in a gently teasing tone. "Just remember what I said about not having eaten human males in a while."

And then he was gone.

I knew he'd been teasing, but at the same time I knew he was serious about me. And him. The two of us.

For a moment I stared at the spot he'd been standing in, wondering if he'd just used a transference to leave my apartment, or was hanging around in glamour.

"If you're still here," I said as I walked to the door, "you'd better leave. I need to talk with Adam alone."

No answer and I didn't expect one. I couldn't sense his presence in my apartment and I was sure he was gone. I knew he'd respect me and my privacy. Even if he had gone from friend to wannabe lover in sixty seconds flat.

My belly flip-flopped for another reason as I opened the door.

Adam looked so good with his tousled brown hair, his warm brown eyes, and the stubble on his jaws.

"Hey, Nyx." The tenor of his voice sent a shiver through me, but then the look in his eyes made me pause.

"Do you want to come in?" I didn't move out of the doorway, just waited for his response.

He shook his head. "I just wanted to talk with you for a moment."

I tried not to show any outward sign that his mere presence was affecting me. I wanted to be in his arms. Wanted to feel his embrace. Wanted to feel like everything was okay and nothing had changed.

"I won't be working as a liaison to the paranorm anymore." He paused, and a prickling sensation traveled over me. "I've been promoted and am moving to another precinct."

"Congratulations." My voice wavered a little. "Guess I won't be seeing you around."

Adam shoved his hands into the pockets of his bomber jacket. "I've been thinking about it over and over again. I'm sorry, but I just don't see now how it could work between us."

I met his gaze. In his eyes I could tell he was hurting as much as I was, but he was right. How could it have worked? Maybe if I were a Doppler or Shifter and had a normal human appearance any time I wanted. But I'm Drow, and it just doesn't work that way for me.

"You're right." I tilted my chin a little. "Meeting your family proved that our worlds are too different."

"I'm going to miss you, Nyx." He looked down at his shoes before returning his gaze to me. "I already do."

"Me, too." The words came back in a whisper that I had to force out.

Adam took a step toward me and in the next moment I was in his arms with him just holding me. I would miss his coffee-and-leather scent, would miss his smile and his laugh. Would miss everything about him.

He released me and took a step back. "I'll always love you, Nyx."

Those words almost sent me over the edge. At that moment I was glad I didn't have tears, because I wouldn't have wanted to cry in front of him.

I met his eyes. "I love you, Adam."

He studied me for a long moment before he said, "I'll see you around."

I nodded. "Yeah. See you."

I shut the door behind Adam, then placed my forehead against the smooth wood and closed my eyes. I could hear his footsteps growing fainter as he walked away.

I took a deep breath, pulled my cell phone out of my pocket, and dialed Nadia's phone number. While the phone rang, I wandered into my room and saw the blank space where the picture of Adam and me in Belize had been sitting on my nightstand. I had put it in a drawer earlier, unable to look at it without feeling heart-wrenching pain.

Nadia answered, her "Hello" sounding like a word in a song.

"You up for a sappy movie and some popcorn?" I asked my friend who was *always* up for a sappy movie. If I wanted action-adventure, I would have called Olivia.

It was obvious Nadia heard something in my voice. "I'll bring over *Casablanca*. You start up the popcorn maker."

"Deal," I said before disconnecting the call.

I straightened my shoulders and headed into the kitchen, straight for the pantry and the popcorn.

FOR CHEYENNE'S READERS

Be sure to go to CheyenneMcCray.com to sign up for her PRIVATE book announcement list and get FREE EXCLUSIVE Cheyenne McCray goodies. Please feel free to e-mail her at chey@cheyennemccray.com. She would love to hear from you.

"Another Tracker is missing." Rodán set his wine glass on
the white tablecloth of our table for two in the exclusive
paranorm hot spot, Some Other Place. "Kennedy appears to
be gone."

The hum and buzz of the restaurant and bar filled the
pause as I digested Rodán's statement. Another Tracker?

A busboy stopped by our table and cleared our dinner
dishes after asking if we were finished. I waited until he was
gone before I responded to Rodán.

"Kennedy, from Seattle?" I frowned as I spoke. "Any
idea what happened to him?"

Rodán slowly shook his head. "The Proctor Directorate's
investigation teams have found nothing."

"That makes how many?" I asked.

"One Proctor along with eight Trackers." Rodán's handsome Elvin features remained amazingly impassive, his
crystal-green eyes betraying no emotion as he spoke.

"What does the GG have to say about it?" I asked.

Rodán looked thoughtful. "The Great Guardian has other
matters that concern her at this time."

"More important than the disappearance of paranorms
who are important to the safety of this world?" The GG drove
me crazy in the ways she chose to "help."

"It is not for us to decide where her attention is best suited,
Nyx." Rodán was gentle yet firm in his statement.

"I'm having a hard time believing what's happening." I
shook my head and my cobalt blue hair tickled my shoulders,

which happened to be bared by my strapless Versace minidress. "There's something very wrong going on." A brilliant understatement.

Rodán gave a deep nod. "Exceptionally so," he said, making me wonder for a moment if he meant my understatement.

I shuddered at my next thought. "Unless Zombies are back."

"We are well and rid of Zombies, Nyx." Just hearing Rodán say "Zombies" made me shudder again. It had been a few months since we'd faced the threat, but it seemed like it had only been days ago.

"Desmond thinks we're rid of them permanently." The silk of my dress slid across my thighs in a soft caress as I crossed my legs at my knees. My light amethyst skin contrasted with the black material of my dress. "I do have faith in him."

"As do I." Rodán took another sip of his chardonnay and I watched the play of muscles in his arm, beneath his golden skin. "Which is why I planned to speak of Desmond with you."

I cocked my head. "What about him did you want to talk with me about?"

"The Great Guardian and I have spoken." Rodán leaned forward, his forearms resting on the tablecloth. "I intend to offer the Sorcerer a position as a Night Tracker."

Surprise made me blink. First of all, Rodán never told me about his choices for Night Tracker candidates. Secondly . . . *Desmond?*

"Desmond has qualities that would benefit our team," I said. "He isn't the sword-and-dagger type, though."

A slight smile curved Rodán's lips. "Indeed he is not. He has other talents that would serve him well."

I smiled, too. "I'm not being negative, Rodán. The thought just caught me off-guard. I actually think Desmond would make a terrific addition. Providing you can convince him to join the Trackers."

"That may be a challenge." Rodán gave a nod of acknowledgment, his long white-blond hair shimmering beneath the low lighting, his movement revealing the points of his ears. "Desmond has been a loner, but after seeing what he and the Trackers did together to strike down his enemy, Amory, I know the difference he can make with us."

"Ah." I sipped my chardonnay before setting the glass back down. "I wondered why you were telling me about a candidate. You never have before."

"That will potentially change, Nyx." Rodán's expression grew more serious. "I want you to take a larger leadership role."

I stilled and set my wine glass down. "More than being in charge of special teams?"

"Yes." Rodán studied me. "You have proven yourself to be an effective leader. You are respected by others and you have a charisma about you which is not learned. You were born with it. You will still primarily track, but you will be involved in more strategy development, training processes, and team assignments."

Surprise kept me from speaking as he continued.

"I am not considering you full-time in another position by any means," Rodán said as he studied me. "However, having more responsibility in the over operations will make better use of your skills."

When I finally found my ability to speak, I said, "I had no idea you thought of me this way."

Rodán's gaze was focused, intent, like he was evaluating even my response. "As a Night Tracker you have already provided balanced leadership, and your judgment is sound.

"I am thinking of one behavior, however, that must change," Rodán said. "This has nothing to do with my feelings for you outside of being your Proctor."

"Okay." My words were slow and deliberate as I spoke. After what had happened during the Zombie op I was wary of what he might say. "What in your opinion do I need to work on in relation to the soundness of my judgment?"

"The only caution I have, you have heard before," Rodán said. "You are an exceptional Tracker. However, at times you have had no regard for your own personal safety. You need to think through what is best overall, before you jump into certain situations.

"For example," he continued, "too often you have charged forward without waiting for backup. It has almost cost you your life on more than one occasion. An effective leader needs to remain alive, or he or she cannot be effective. Do you agree?"

I wanted in some way to fire back that I'd done what I'd had to. As a Drow princess, I was raised around warriors and I had trained as a warrior myself. Dark Elves don't sit back and watch—they act. But I knew Rodán was right.

With an inward sigh, I brought my fingers to the collar I'd worn to favor my father. When I considered the last operations, I had to admit Rodán was right. I'd put myself into some pretty bad situations, including getting injected by a deadly virus. Dark Elves are aggressive fighters, but they still lay battle plans and work as a team.

To a point, my restraint during the last case may have had more to do with my team than me. They had been adamant that I not charge in on my own without them, as I had during previous ops. The members of my team had been right, and I'd known it.

"Yes," I said, "that's fair. It's not easy for me, though. It's my nature to give it everything I have, despite the dangers, but I understand what you're saying."

"Consider what I have to say." Rodán wore a serious expression. "I believe you, above all others, have the skills necessary to lead the entire team. Under my guidance, of course. I don't have all the details worked out, but I wanted you to know what I was thinking for your future."

Wow. I took a deep breath. "It means a lot that you have so much confidence in me and my abilities."

"You have earned it." Rodán steepled his hands on the tabletop. "Time and time again, on operations you have been assigned to, you have proven to be an exceptional leader. I only have the one concern."

"I think I understand." I clasped my hands in my lap.

"But I'm not management material. You *know* me—I can't sit back and watch."

"I would never expect you to do so." Rodán smiled again. "That is not the Nyx Ciar that I know." I felt perplexed at his words but he continued. "I am only asking for a little restraint on your behalf."

"Can I think about it?" I brushed my palm over my belly, absently smoothing the silk of my dress. "I need a chance to let this digest. Not only that, but I do have my PI agency to consider. I'm not sure adding extra responsibility as a Tracker will help me in my day job as a PI."

"Of course." Rodán raised his glass and sipped his wine. I watched the movement of his throat as he swallowed, observed his fluid grace as he set his wine glass on the table.

"It is my intention to groom Colin to take a leadership role," he said. "I would like him to start leading a special ops team."

Warmth spread through me at the sound of Colin's name. Yet that warmth was followed by the feeling of confusion that had plagued me ever since my break-up with Adam, and Colin's insistent pursuit of me.

Now was not the time to think of either of the two males. Detective Adam Boyd was no longer in my life, and Colin, a Dragon paranorm, wanted me to take things a step further with him.

It was times like this, being comfortable with my Drow appearance in this paranorm restaurant, and not worrying about how I looked at night, that made me realize it could never have worked with Adam. I couldn't look like I did right this moment and be out with him. However, I didn't have those same reservations with Colin, as far as dating another paranorm went.

At this moment there were more pressing things to consider, though, than my love life.

"Is Desmond the only new Tracker who you and the GG are considering?" I asked.

"I believe Tristan would make an excellent Night Tracker also," he said. "The Guardian agrees."

"My brother?" I thought about him as a Tracker candidate. Tristan had been locked in a stone for twenty-two years, but to him it had been as if no time had passed. He'd returned, not recognizing me since I was no longer the five-year-old younger sister I'd been when he disappeared. He was now in Otherworld visiting with our parents.

"I hope he can be convinced," I finally said. "Though he was an artist before he was taken, never a warrior, I think he could be a tremendous Tracker."

"Tristan has always been a warrior," Rodán said. "A warrior with an artist's skills. It is time to use all of his abilities. As a Tracker he could add much to the team with some training.

"We'll let him out in the field with you for a couple of days to give him an idea of what a Tracker's night is like," Rodán said. "Then we'll send him to the training program in Chicago. Once he's fully trained, we'll team him up with an experienced Tracker in New York City."

"Rodán!" The pair of voices exclaiming his name came from a pair of blonde Nymphs who stopped at our table. They looked like excited, giggly airheads as they bounced up and down on their toes. I recognized them—they were backup singers for Festival, a new paranorm rock band that I'd seen for the first time last weekend.

"Trixie." Rodán nodded to Nymph One. "Bubbles," he said to Nymph Two.

Trixie and Bubbles. I had to bite my tongue to keep from laughing. It might not have been the first time I'd heard their stage names, but it still got me. By the looks of the pair of airheads, I wondered if those *were* stage names, or their real names.

I settled back in my chair to watch. This should be good.

"We haven't seen you for a while." A small pout was on Trixie's lips. "Bubbles and I were just saying how much—" the Nymph glanced at me then back at Rodán—"we have missed you."

I didn't think that was exactly the sentiment she'd wanted to express.

Then Bubbles said, "After we perform at the Pit next, are you going to invite us back to your chambers?"

Uh-huh. That statement confirmed what I'd been thinking.

I toyed with the stem of my crystal wine glass as Rodán gave them a sensuous smile. He couldn't help it. He could simply have been trying to be polite, but no matter, his expression would still have the power to set a female on fire.

"I will talk with you beautiful ladies at another time." Rodán said it in a way that was appealing rather than off-putting. "At this moment I am enjoying Nyx's company."

"Can't wait!" Trixie said with a giant explanation point in her voice. "We'll see you soon."

Bubbles nodded with enthusiasm, her blonde curls bouncing. "We'll be ready!"

I bet they would.

Rodán gave a slight inclination of his head. "Have a good evening, ladies."

The bubbling airheads slipped into the bar crowd, but I could still hear their giggles. I wanted to roll my eyes but I smiled at Rodán instead. "Your adoring public."

Rodán leaned back, holding his wine glass. He looked at me for a long time without saying anything.

I tilted my head. "Are you all right?"

"You know that for you I would give up everything," he said quietly.

My cheeks burned a little at the intimacy of his expression and his words. "We both know you couldn't, Rodán." I continued, even though he looked like he wanted to say something. "It's how you're wired. You're a sexual, sensual being and I get that," I said. "You would never be happy with one person."

"With you . . ." He looked thoughtful as he paused. "With you, everything is different. You make me want to be with you alone."

I was surprised. I had never heard Rodán say this before in quite this way.

"Then why weren't you?" I said, more out of curiosity than anything else. "You continued to see others while you and I slept together. If I made you feel different, then why didn't you stop inviting others to your bed?"

During the time I was with him, I'd never considered Rodán enjoying sexual pleasures with others as abnormal. He'd invited me to join in on the experiences, but I'd always refused. It wasn't my thing.

"One female would never satisfy you. Oh, maybe for a time, but I refer to a lifetime," I went on before he could respond. "I could never share the man I decide to be with. It just wouldn't happen."

His green eyes were dark with something I couldn't identify. "For you I would give it all up."

Warmth filled me as I studied the beautiful male sitting across the table. Rodán was truly like no other. Not a soul on this Earth Otherworld, or any Otherworld for that matter, could fully compare to my Proctor, former lover, and friend who was dear to me in more ways than I could count. What I felt for Rodán was different than my feelings for any man.

"You know that I love you," I said quietly. "But I've always known that you have desires, you have lust for others. And I realized, in the end, I couldn't change that. I simply am thankful for our deep friendship now."

Rodán opened his mouth to speak, but I pushed back my chair and got to my feet.

Rodán's eyes raised and his brow wrinkled. As he stood, his slight smile and a slow shake of his head indicated his understanding.

"I'm late getting to work and my boss is real hardcase," I said as I gave him a teasing look.

"Your employer told you to take the night off," Rodán said with an equally teasing expression. "Perhaps you should listen to him."

"I don't think listening is one of my strengths." I moved toward Rodán and tilted my head to kiss his cheek. "I'll consider your offer on the leadership position," I added as I drew away. "Not the girlfriend spot."

Rodán took my hands and kissed my cheek in return. "You would be the one, Nyx."

At the same moment, three females came toward us from the direction of the bar. They were dressed in next to nothing. When they reached us, two of them took one of Rodán's arms as one of them said to me, "You must learn to share."

Rodán met my gaze and I raised my hands, amusement rising in me. "See? Have fun."

He smiled at me, then at the females who had swooped down to take him away. "One moment please," he said to them. "I will join you shortly."

"You'd better," one of the females said with a coy look on her delicate features. "Or we'll hunt you down."